Happ

love!

THE BLUE
AFTERNOON

THE BLUE AFTERNOON

A NOVEL

WILLIAM BOYD

ALFRED A. KNOPF

New York *1995*

THIS IS A BORZOI BOOK

PUBLISHED BY ALFRED A. KNOPF, INC.

Library of Congress Cataloging-in-Publication Data

Boyd, William.
The blue afternoon / by William Boyd.—1st ed.
p.   cm.
ISBN 0-679-43295-7
1. Man-woman relationships—Philippines—Manila—Fiction. 2. Physicians—Philippines—Manila—Fiction. 3. Fathers and daughters—
Fiction. 4. Manila (Philippines)—Fiction. I. Title.
PR6052.09192B58   1995
823'.914—dc20   94-26091
                    CIP

Manufactured in the United States of America
First American Edition

For Susan

He brushed away the thunder, then the clouds,
Then the colossal illusion of heaven. Yet still
The sky was blue. He wanted imperceptible air.
He wanted to see. He wanted the eye to see
And not be touched by blue . . .

. . . Had he been better able to suppose:
He might sit on a sofa on a balcony
Above the Mediterranean, emerald
Becoming emeralds. He might watch the palms
Flap green ears in the heat. He might observe
A yellow wine and follow a steamer's track
And say, "The thing I hum appears to be
The rhythm of this celestial pantomime."

—WALLACE STEVENS,
"Landscape with Boat"

PROLOGUE

I REMEMBER that afternoon, not long into our travels, sitting on deck in the mild mid-Atlantic sun on a slightly smirched and foggy day, the sky a pale washed-out blue above the smokestacks, that I asked my father what it felt like to pick up a knife and make an incision into living human flesh. He thought seriously for a while before replying.

"It depends on where you cut," he said. "Sometimes it's like a knife through clay or modeling wax. Some days it's like cutting into a cold blancmange or . . . or cold raw chicken."

He pondered a while longer and then reached inside his coat pocket and drew out a scalpel. He removed the small leather sleeve that protected the blade and offered the slim knife to me.

"Take this. See for yourself."

I took the scalpel from him, small as a pen but much heavier than I had imagined. He looked down at the remains of our lunch on the table: an edge of cheese with a thick yellow rind, a bowl of fruit, four apples and a green melon, some bread rolls.

"Close your eyes," he said. "I'll get something for you, an exact simulacrum."

I closed my eyes and gripped the scalpel firmly between my thumb and first two fingers. I felt his hand on mine, the gentle pressure of his dry rough fingers, and then he lifted my hand up and I felt him guiding it forward until the poised blade came to rest on a surface, firm but somehow yielding.

"Make a cut," he said. "A small cut. Press down."

I pressed. Whatever I cut into yielded easily and I moved the blade down an inch or so, or so it seemed, smoothly, with no fuss.

"Keep your eyes closed . . . What did it feel like?"

I thought for a second or two before replying. I wanted this to be right, to be exact, scientific.

"It felt like . . . Like cold butter, you know, from an icebox. Or a sirloin, like cutting through a tender sirloin."

"See?" he said. "There's nothing mysterious, nothing to be alarmed about."

I opened my eyes and saw his square face smiling at me, almost in triumph, as if he had been vindicated in some argument. He was holding out his bare left forearm, the sleeve of his coat and shirt pushed back to the crook of his elbow. On the bulge of muscle, three inches above his wrist, a thin two-inch gash oozed bright blisters of blood.

"There," he said. "It's easy. A beautiful incision. Not a waver, with even pressure, and with your eyes closed too."

The expression on his face changed at this moment, to a form of sadness mingled with pride.

"You know," he said, "you would have made a great surgeon."

LOS ANGELES,

1936

ONE

I TURNED OFF Sunset Boulevard and drove up Micheltoreno to the site. The day was cloudy and an erratic and
nervy wind rattled the leaves of the palmettos that the contrac-
tor had planted along the roadside. As I pulled into the curb at
number 2265 I saw the old man. It was the first time I had really noticed him, but in doing so now I immediately, for some
reason, remembered I had seen him loitering around the site
before. When he spotted me staring at him he looked first at
his hands and then, most oddly, with some awkwardness, at the
soles of his shoes, as if he had stepped in dog dirt or on a ball
of chewed gum, and then, finding nothing, he turned and
walked briskly away.

I thought little of it, he looked scruffy and unsure of himself, perhaps someone searching for work. Perhaps, also, he
didn't realize that I was the architect—it happened all the
time. I forgot about it as I slipped off my shoes and pulled on
a pair of galoshes. The house was built on an incline and last
week's rain had left the exposed earth and clay around the
house moist and slidey.

This small almost-finished house on its steep plot was my
future, and whatever future frustrations it held for me every
time I saw it, I still experienced a small frisson of . . . of what?
Of love, I suppose, or something akin to that emotion. I had
dreamed that house, had designed it, was overseeing the build-

ing of it, and nailed to the fence post was the ocular proof of this fact—my shingle. Kay Fischer, architect. The small blue sign was only slightly marred by the blunt erasure of my ex-partner's name—no more Eric Meyersen—a simple stripe of black paint obscuring his identity. I wished I could obliterate as easily the memories of our association: Meyersen and Fischer, five years of lies and duplicity, of cheating and bad faith. The only consolation was that I knew that one day he would get what he deserved.

I stepped across the threshold into the shadowy hall. From upstairs came the noise of hammering and sawing and the en-thusiastic tenor of Larry Rugola, the foreman, singing "If You Was the Only Girl in the World." I walked slowly through the downstairs rooms. The house was small, its size dictated pre-cisely by the shape of the site, and of two stories: the second floor consisting of two bedrooms, a bathroom and a wide porch—which I rather fancifully called the "wind landing"— and the first of a large living room with dining room, kitchen and patio garden. The roadside façade presented a series of cream stucco curtain walls, flat rectangles of painted cement arranged to reveal gaps—of glass, of space—or to overlap slightly, giving a sense of the house's volumes receding. The strict geometry of this composition was highlighted, and coun-terposed, by the two pine trees that I had left growing at the road edge. The juxtaposition of sinuous knotted pine trunk and flat sun-washed cement with clear hard shadows worked exceptionally well. The valley façade was pure International Style: sheer walls of glass with hard horizontals and odd verti-cal stucco panels. The gap formed by the wind landing looked as if an entire segment of the building had been removed, as if by a giant hand, but the integrity of its space remained, formed by the big oak beams of the trellis.

Inside, it was all simplicity. Low ceilings, teak cabinets, clos-ets and paneling, walls either of glass looking out to the view or of smooth buff stucco. The floors were a pale buttery oak, and where I thought a softer texture would complement the severe planes I had had laid a rough-weave, taupe carpet. All this took on a life in my mind's eye, of course, as I stood among the stacks of lumber and blond curls of wood shavings and discarded tools, walls unpainted, wiring dangling from would-be sockets. We were still a short way from perfection.

"Ah, Mrs. Fischer." Larry clattered down the stairs, a ball peen hammer spinning in one hand like a hoodlum's six-gun. "We never got that paneling. Lumberyard said . . ." He grinned at me shyly, knowingly. "They said, ah, they can't take an order that size without there being a cash deposit."

"But we have a credit account there, for God's sake."

"That's what I said. But the guy says it's Meyersen and Fischer, the account. He don't have no Kay Fischer."

I swiveled around and walked to the plate glass of the window wall and looked out at the view. Silver Lake was the fancy name given to the area bordering an artificial reservoir cut between two ranges of hills, north of downtown and east of Hollywood. Narrow metaled roads swerved and looped around the contours through the pepper trees and the oaks. Micheltoreno was one of the longest, starting on Sunset and rising and falling, weaving and winding all the way up to the reservoir. At the top, views were to be had both east and west, but here the steep sides furnished a panorama of the sprawling city below which, in certain cases, could stretch all the way to the ocean, its fish-scale glitter a lucent line of shimmer on the horizon. I concentrated hard on what I could see, noting the burnished glare off the roofs of the traffic moving up and down Sunset; a small man hanging out a big Mexican blanket on a line; a woman in a cobalt two-piece sunbathing on a tar paper roof. I rested the palps of my fingertips on the warm glass and felt the tiny sonic vibrations of the city shiver through the transparency. The girl on the tar paper roof smoothed what looked like oleomargarine on her midriff. When I was calm again I reassured Larry that I would go down to the lumberyard and sort everything out myself.

"Oh, yeah. That old geezer was here again looking for you. Least I figured it was you."

"What do you mean? What old geezer?"

"He was just here. He asked if your name was, ah, let me get this right . . . Carriscant—I think. Yeah. Miss Carriscant."

"Carriscant?"

"I said he must be mistaken. There was a Mrs. Fischer, but no Miss Whatever. Always had been Fischer too. Far as I was—" He paused and peered at my taut frowning face with, for Larry, some genuine concern.

"I hope I didn't—I mean—"

"No. Strange, I just . . . No, fine. Absolutely no problem."

TWO

M Y NAME is Kay Fischer. My name is Kay Fischer and at the time of this story I was thirty-two years of age, divorced and by profession an architect. I was five feet six inches tall (I still am) with dull brown hair and bright brown eyes. I had a pretty round face and a keen intellect. And, as with most people who know themselves to be cleverer than the vast majority of their fellow human beings whom they encounter as they go through life, my intelligence inclined me to be a little cruel, sometimes. In those days I smoked too much and I drank and I ate too much as well, because, I suppose, because at the time I was more often sad than happy, and as a result my once neat figure had become plump and haunchy. But I didn't care, really. I didn't care.

I drove back from the lumberyard, where, after enjoying years of trouble-free credit facilities, I had to pay two hundred dollars down in order to open another account. Clerks who had dealt with me since I began to practice now sorrowfully quoted rules and regulations and referred me to the young manager in his glassed-in office. "You don't understand," I said to this blinking, gray person. "Meyersen is the bankrupt one, or at least he will be when I'm through with him." Bravado made my voice boom. "Rules is rules," the manager said, skillfully avoiding my eye, and in the end I meekly paid.

At my home, a small apartment in a newish apartment court

off Laurel Avenue in West Hollywood called, shamelessly, the Escorial Apartments in tribute to its Spanish colonial roots, I brewed myself a pot of coffee, potent and viscous, and brooded again on betrayal and Eric Meyersen. The Taylor House in Pasadena, the shopping mart in Burbank . . . Three years of work, my work, now belonged to Meyersen and his glossy new firm. In a sudden, squally rage I called my lawyer, George Fugal, but his answering service said he was out of town for the weekend. Still, the coffee tasted just fine, scalding and aromatic, and I smoked three Picayunes one after another just to keep my dander up and paced vengefully about my neat room.

There was not much I had been able to do with the sturdy functionality of the Escorial. I had reduced my furniture needs to a minimum and had had the whorled featured plasterwork of the interior walls smoothed flat and painted white. Two Breuer leather and chrome armchairs faced each other across a glass coffee table which was set upon a blue and yellow Gertrud Arndt rug. The only other furniture in the room was my drawing table. There were no pictures on the walls, either, and I kept my books in my bedroom. The result was as spare and soothing as could be achieved in a Los Angeles bungalow court, I maintained. My watchword had been borrowed from Hannes Meyer: necessities, not luxuries.

The Escorial Apartments were knocked down in 1963 by a realtor and three ugly new houses were built in its place. When I lived there the choicer apartments—mine not included—surrounded a small aquamarine swimming pool. If I leaned out of the corner of my kitchen window (which I did as I rinsed the coffeepot) I could make out a bright triangle at the shallow end. The afternoon sun lit the tiled roofs and the tangerine stucco of the apartment walls and sent jostling rigmaroles of light from the water shuddering along the glass fascias of the balconies. I heard the splash of water and the delighted laugh of a girl—deep in her throat—and I felt a powerful urge to swim, to immerse myself in that overchlorinated blue, and wash Meyersen and the small humiliations of the lumberyard away. In my bedroom I selected a swimsuit and stepped out of my dress, but then caught sight of my thighs and buttocks in the square of mirror on the dressing table and decided instead to do some work. The larger humiliations of disrobing in front of the residents of the Escorial were an unignorable disincentive.

So I sat at my drawing board, adjusted the lamp and unrolled the interior elevations of 2265 Micheltoreno. My credo as an architect was the simplest I could devise: what space did I require, or my client require, and how was it to be confined. The great liberation bestowed by the new materials of the twentieth century had reemphasized the architect's priorities: the space enclosed became more important than what enclosed the space. Others have put it more eloquently than I, but for me stucco sheathing, glass bricks and reinforced concrete, Bakelite and chrome, plywood and aluminum were blessings insofar as they served the space they were to contain. My second criterion was simplicity. The task was to design the space and employ the minimum to construct it. The house on Micheltoreno had been conceived, if you like, as an assemblage of blocks of air. Some of these blocks were to be found between stucco walls, some were bounded transparently by sheets of glass, some by beams and wood battens and balcony outriggers and some by the organic shapes of the trees that I had ordered left when the site was first cleared.

My current dilemma was that I needed a closet in the main bedroom but to build one in would mean diminishing the square footage of the bedroom. Not too grievous, in the scale of the world's problems, you might think, but if I did so the bedroom would no longer possess exactly the same square footage as the wide balcony porch onto which it gave—the space I had designed, and the harmony I wanted, would be compromised. I toyed with the dimensions awhile and made a few sketches before a solution presented itself. Build in the closet and then echo it on the porch by placing two wooden struts as off-center "supports" to the shade trellis. Their function would be notional but the symmetry would be maintained, the wind landing would remain a spatial replica of its neighboring room. So much, so perfect. Now I began to worry what a bed would do to my empty blocks of air . . .

The concierge called up from reception.

"There's a gentleman here to see you, Mrs. Fischer."

I checked my watch: Philip Brockway (my ex-husband) was early. I knew he wanted to borrow money. I had accused him of this when he telephoned and he denied it with such vehemence that I knew I was right. He merely wanted to see me, he said, and added some lame tosh about "old times."

All the same, I strolled along the walkway toward reception thinking not too unkindly of Philip—he was so pretty, with his pretty handsome weak face, his small girl's nose and his thick tawny hair. I would play with him awhile, make him take me out for a cocktail, before I gave in and paid him to leave me alone once more.

I pushed through the swing doors into the lobby and saw the man from the site, the man who had asked for Miss Carriscant. He was old, gray-haired, but broad-shouldered and stocky, dressed in black as he had been at the house. He clutched his homburg in front of him like a steering wheel and took three paces toward me, staring at me intensely, as if searching for some sign of recognition. His own manifest apprehension put me at some ease.

"What do you want?" I said. "Why are you—"

"Miss Carriscant?"

"No. No, I am not Miss Carriscant."

He reached out and touched my bare arm fleetingly, as if to reassure himself. His fingers felt dry, abrasive, heavily calloused.

"Peter?" I called the concierge. "This gentleman is leaving."

"You are Kay Carriscant."

"I am Kay Fischer, Mr.—"

"All right, all right. You were once Kay Carriscant. You were born on the ninth of January 1904 in the afternoon. You see, I—"

"Would you please leave me alone. This nonsense is beginning—"

"My name is Carriscant. Salvador Carriscant. Do you know who I am?"

"Of course not."

The pungent denial in my voice, its plain tetchiness, caused the look in his eye to change. A shadow of sadness crossed his gaze and a deep hurt was revealed there for an instant. For some reason this mellowed me and I felt sorry for him and his hopeless quest for his Miss Carriscant.

"What do you want?" I said, with more kindness in my voice. "Who are you?"

His face seemed to tighten, drawn down as if there were a pain in his gut. He closed his eyes a second and pursed his lips. He sighed.

"I am your father," he said.

THREE

PHILIP ACCEPTED the five ten-dollar bills I gave him as casually as if they were cigarettes. Trying not to smile, he folded them into a calfskin wallet.

"Thanks, Kay. I owe you."

"You surely do. Two hundred and counting."

"Ho hum. It's only money."

"Only *my* money." I laughed all the same. Philip was being sweet tonight, as only he knew how, and I was enjoying it. We sat in a piano bar called Mo-Jo's. It was downtown, on Broadway and Third, a joint Philip knew, where his credit was good. It was a curious place, a unique blend of Polynesian idyll and Nantucket fishing village. In the lobby you parted a bead curtain and crossed a log bridge over a moving stream to be confronted by a dark room with a bar decorated with signal flags and cork floats with barmen who wore striped matelot jerseys and red neckerchiefs. Lush groves of potted palms screened intimate booths made from packing cases and driftwood. Carved backlit native gargoyles served as sconces and cast a hazy crimson-orange light on a bamboo-framed, wall-sized mural of a square-rigged clipper running before an icy, eye-watering wind. It represented the antithesis of everything I believed in, architecturally, and it made me laugh. Philip and I would fantasize about the Mo-Jo's brief to his interior designer: "Sorta Moby Dick meets Paul Gauguin, ya know?" "Kinda hot and steamy but cool and unpretentious at the same time."

"Nathaniel Hawthorne's wet dream." On every table was a gilt electric bell push designed to summon one of the browned-up cocktail waitresses—halterneck tops over grass skirts, flowers behind ear—who sulked in the gloom behind the bar bickering with the matelots. As Philip reached over to press the button he allowed his knuckles to graze my breasts.

"You look different, Kay. So . . . you know, bigger. I like it. You, ah, you carry it well."

"That's meant to be a compliment?"

"OK. Try this: Can I come home with you tonight?"

"Won't Little Miss Peroxide object?"

"That's not fair. It's over, long gone. You know that."

"No."

"Please—"

"No, Philip. No." That particular tone of weariness crept into my voice, memories of ancient arguments, and he knew that he should not ask anymore.

He stood up. "I've got to go to the john. I'll have the same again."

I watched him stroll easily through the tables, light-footed. His tall thin body swayed past waitresses and drinkers as he led with his left shoulder and then with his right, as if he were dancing. Like a Scottish dance, figure of eight . . . Why did I think of a Scottish dance? I smiled as I recalled Philip's pale body, almost hairless, and his slim ankles, the Achilles tendon stretched and exposed, like a catwalk model's. He used to make love to me proficiently but selfishly, his head buried in the angle of my neck and shoulder, never looking up, never seeing my face, never looking me in the eyes, until he was finished.

I ordered us both another drink and thought about the man, Salvador Carriscant, who said he was my father.

When Carriscant had made his bizarre claim I told him at once that my father was dead, but it gave him no pause at all, he merely gripped my forearm more fiercely and said, softly, insistently, "Your father is here now, before you, alive and breathing. I know I have done you wrong but now I need your forgiveness. Your forgiveness and your help."

I called again for Peter and wrenched my arm free of Carriscant's grip.

Peter came quickly up behind him and clutched his elbows, pulling them together. "OK, brother, outside."

"Release me," Carriscant said, his voice suddenly uneven with anger. "Do not lay your hands on me, I warn you."

Some rare quality of emphasis in his voice made Peter comply. Carriscant backed away toward the wrought iron gates of the Escorial's entrance, still holding me with his persistent, pleading gaze.

"We just need to talk, Kay," he said. "Then everything will become clear." He pronounced the last word "cleah," in the English manner, and for the first time I registered that his voice had an accent: English, in a way, but unlocatably so, with the slightly formal perfection of the complete bilingual. "Please, Kay, it's all I ask." His jaw muscles clenched and his square face seemed to redden, as if the effort of suppressing what he had to declare to me was bursting within him. Then he turned and left, striding off—surprisingly jauntily for an old man—down the concrete path and across the street.

Philip and our fresh drinks arrived simultaneously. Philip dipped and slid himself along the banquette until his thigh was brushing mine.

"I've got a lunch party at the beach tomorrow. Lisa Van Baker's house. Want to come with me?"

"Can't, I'm afraid."

"But there'll be movie stars," he said, hands spread, eyebrows raised, mock-horrified at my indifference.

"I hate movie stars."

"OK, what's the alternative attraction?"

"Home cooking."

FOUR

I WATCHED my mother slice peeled, cored apples into a tin colander. The sharp worn knife blade slid easily beneath the pale yellow flesh as she cut slim disks with a crunching noise, like cautious footsteps on icy snow. She was meticulous in her slicing, each disk a precise thickness, her concentration fixed exactly on her task. She was a small woman, shy and modest. She wore her hair always in the same way, as long as I could remember, combed back from her face and held in a vertical roll from crown to nape. Her features were ordinary and unexceptional: it was only when she put her spectacles on that her face acquired some personality.

She lived with my stepfather, Rudolf Fischer, in a small house in Long Beach. It was an old fading canary yellow clapboard bungalow with a shingled hip roof, and there was a newer addition of a two-car garage which took up most of what had been a patchy lawn. A cypress hedge separated it from a house of identical design painted flamingo pink. This was where I had grown up but it was not where I was born. My birthplace had been in the former German colony in New Guinea. It always seemed to me one of my life's crueler oppositions: born in New Guinea, raised in Long Beach. I possessed no memory at all of my real father. Rudolf—Pappi, as we called him, my mother included—had always been there in my life, with his big ruddy face, his fuzzy, balding pate, the curious wen on his face, half an inch below the right side of his mouth, hard and shiny like a sucked boiled sweet stuck there. "Like Oliver Cromwell," he used to say, "I come wart and all." He was a big-boned friendly man whose easy geniality hid a weak character. My neat, timid mother was the real center of force in our household, something that Pappi's large shambling loud presence seemed to belie. Only the family really knew the truth.

Pappi was an American, second generation, son of Westphalian immigrants who, in a conscious act of assimilation, had ceased speaking German as soon as they could string some English sentences together and ensured that their children had grown up monoglottally American. My mother had stopped talking German when she married him, she said, claiming that she even dreamed in English now. But I still heard her singing to herself, favorite songs, "An die ferne Geliebte" and "Es war, als hatt' der Himmel," when her guard dropped.

I looked over my shoulder into the parlor. Pappi sat in an easy chair listening to the radio, his mouth open, ready to laugh. My mother carefully spooned the apple disks into a shallow pie base.

"Tell me about Father," I said.

"Pappi? Oh, his leg is still sore. I told him—"

"No. I mean *my* father."

She ran her hands under the faucet, thinking, then glanced at me, one of her keen, sharp looks, watchful. It was at moments like these—when I surprised her—that I saw her toughness and knew where I derived my own.

"Hugh"—she said his name quietly, like a sigh, as if testing it, a strange fruit, an exotic dessert. "What's there to say? It's been so long now."

Hugh Paget, my father, an Englishman, a missionary and teacher, who met and married my mother Annaliese Leys, a schoolteacher, in German New Guinea in 1903. In 1904 I was born, and two months later Hugh Paget was dead, burned to ashes in a fire. Two years later we were taken under the capacious wing of Rudolf Fischer, widower, merchant and coir and hemp importer from Los Angeles, USA. Seventeen percent of the doormats in Southern California were made from coir supplied by Fischer Coir, was the company's proud boast. Rudolf and Annaliese were married in 1907 and settled in Long Beach.

"What about his parents, relatives?" I said casually, searching in my pockets for my cigarette pack.

"His folks were dead when I met him. There was a sister, Meredith, in Coventry. Or maybe Ipswich. They moved a lot. We would correspond, but I lost touch." She smiled. "It's like that. You work hard at first to keep a memory alive. It's hard, everybody's life goes on in different directions. After a while . . ."

"Have you still got her letters?"

"I doubt it. Why all this interest?"

"I . . . I just got curious. You know, you get to thinking."

"Sure. I think about him too." She looked sad, bringing to mind this stranger, my father.

I lit my cigarette. "Can I see the photograph?"

"Of course. When?"

"Now."

HUGH PAGET STOOD in front of a square corrugated iron building with a palm-thatched roof with wooden cross-shaped finials at either end. He wore a drill cotton coat and trousers tucked into canvas mosquito boots and at his throat was the white band of his dog collar. I could see a slim tall man with blurry features that I knew not even a magnifying glass could force into anything resembling an individual face. A breeze had lifted a lock of hair off his forehead and the photograph had fixed this one dishevelment in time, for all time. It seemed—specious thoughts, I knew—a clue of sorts, a gesture, a hint as to his nature. Boyishness, enthusiasm, an awkward gaucherie . . . I tried to paste some sort of personality onto this nugatory image with my usual lack of success.

Fair hair. Fair hair. Mine was dark.

"You must have had wedding photos."

"I told you, we lost everything in the fire. This was in the chapel, I was lucky."

I left it at that, for the time being. I knew she would go on talking quite contentedly, but soon she would begin to wonder what had prompted all these questions and would start asking some of her own. And then what would I say? In fact I could not really explain my own newfound curiosity about my father. Why was I acting on one strange man's allegations, and ones so evidently preposterous? Who was Salvador Carriscant and why had he singled me out for this filial identification? Los Angeles was full of crazy people, but what unsettled me about Carriscant was that he did not seem particularly unbalanced. And what could he possibly know about Hugh Paget? And why should he appear now, over thirty years after my father's death, insinuating that the man was an impostor? . . . The whole idea was ridiculous, I said to myself, and I was about to tell my mother about this odd fellow I had encountered when my stepsister Bruna arrived at the front door with her two children, Amy and Greta, and interrupted me. Pappi's histrionic cries of love and adoration filled the small house.

My mother slid the pie into the oven and wiped her hands carefully on her apron.

"When was I born?" I asked. "I mean, what time of day?"

"Oh, about four-thirty in the afternoon. Why?"

"I was just wondering. Just curious."

"I like that suit, Kay," she said, smiling faintly at me. "You look smart. Very efficient."

So the matter was closed, anyway. I thanked her, complimented her in return on the brooch she was wearing, and we walked into the living room.

FIVE

I SAW the corner of the envelope peeking from beneath the front door of my apartment when I inserted the key in the lock. I stooped, slid it out and put it in my pocket. Inside, I placed it on my drawing board and went to pour myself a small Scotch. I knew it was from Carriscant even though it was not addressed.

I sensed, immediately, that I was at some kind of watershed, now. You know that feeling, when you can almost see the two or several directions your life might take ahead of you, a moment when you know that the next choice you are about to make is going to be crucial and possibly final, that there is no going back, and that nothing will ever be the same again? I could tear the letter up, unopened, ignore the man in future and call the police if he continued to pester me. Or I could open the letter, read what it had to say and thereby allow myself to be drawn in ever further to his curious world and his strange obsession about me and our relationship.

I opened the letter:

My dear Kay,

I know you must be wondering if you are dealing with a lunatic. Believe me, you are not. I am as sane as you are. We must talk properly without fear of interruption. I shall not bother you further but will let you know that I am staying at 105 Olive Street for the next ten days only. Please do communicate with me, there is so much to say.

Dr. Salvador Carriscant

I had made my choice.

SIX

I EMERGED from the Third Street Tunnel and drove down Hill Street, swinging back up Fifth and up onto Olive Street high on Bunker Hill. From up here I could see the tower of the new city hall, tall and white, shining in the crossbeams of its searchlights. Between the ancient houses and over vacant lots I caught glimpses of the glowing electric arrow of Wilshire Boulevard thrusting west its sixteen miles toward the ocean and the last cinnamon stripes of the setting sun.

105 Olive was an old Queen Anne mansion, probably built in the 1880s. It was nicely asymmetrical and not as overdecorated as some I had seen. It had a roof of fish-scaled shingle and a big domed turret with a bent lightning conductor. Its veranda circled three-quarters of the house and its elaborate carved porch frieze was badly broken, looking like the tattered edge of a paper doily. A dusty pepper tree with a tire swing stood on the patch of beaten earth that had once been a lawn. The old mansion was now doing humble duty as a boardinghouse for transient workers. A handwritten cardboard sign in the window said ROOMS $1. A few men sat and smoked on its front steps, small brown men in cheap but clean clothes. I assumed they were Japanese.

I pulled over to the curb and settled down to wait—for what? I wasn't exactly sure, but I felt that I needed to turn the tables momentarily, to observe Carriscant himself, covertly, as he had observed me, before we embarked on this momentous and earnestly entreated communication.

Carriscant appeared at the front door about forty minutes later. He was wearing a tight blue over-jacket, with a naval cut, and had his homburg on. I left the car and followed him to the funicular railway that led down from the heights of Bunker Hill to Hill Street below. I felt relatively inconspicuous, almost masculine, in fact: I wore slacks and a trench coat and had a beret pulled down low on my brow.

Carriscant entered the little cream-colored car and moved up to the front, where he took his seat. I waited until it was about to depart and slipped in at the last moment and stood at the door. There was a small jolt and the car began to move down the gradient toward the busy streets below. It was a clear night, so clear I could see the lights of Huntington Park and Montebello and, over to the south, the glow of big orange flares burning at the Dominguez oil fields at Compton.

I followed Carriscant as he crossed Hill and walked over to Main Street. The sidewalks here were busy: on either side of the street were movie theaters, burlesque joints and dime museums, penny arcades and shooting galleries. There were many Mexicans among the passersby and groups of sailors up from the naval yards at San Pedro. Carriscant paused at a second-hand bookstall and browsed awhile through the boxes set out in front of the store. I turned to face the window of a steak house and concentrated my attention on a display of plank steaks, unnaturally red against the bed of crushed ice upon which they were fanned out, like fat rubber playing cards. Eventually Carriscant moved on and turned into an all-night lunchroom, blazingly lit, and sat himself down at a rear table. I strolled to and fro past the window a couple of times and watched him place his order. I noticed he did not remove his hat from his head, and as I turned to begin my third discreet trajectory I decided at once that any further delay would be foolish. I pushed open the glass door and went in to join him.

He did not seem at all surprised to see me, which made me irritated for a moment and made me regret my impulsiveness. He rose halfway from his seat and tipped his hat in a formulaic gesture of politeness. The act seemed to remind him he had the thing on his head and he removed it carefully, setting it down on the empty seat beside him, then he brushed his hair flat with the palms of his hands in two slow stroking movements. He looked fatigued, much older suddenly, and the bright lights of the lunchroom cast sharp shadows across his face, making the prominent lines deep, like gashes. I took the seat opposite him.

"I would offer you some food—" he began.

"No, no. I came to see you. Your letter . . . You said you needed help."

"I do, indeed I do." He smiled at me. "Did you follow me here?"

"Yes."

He chuckled. "Dear Kay."

I ignored this. "Are you in trouble?"

"Trouble?" He appeared to think about the word, as if pondering its semantics. "Not exactly, but I do need help. I am a total stranger, you see. Total."

A waiter brought him his food, a large plate of dark pasty stew with mashed potatoes and what looked like squash. He ostentatiously searched for the meat and then cut the few cartilaginous strips deliberately into small cubes before beginning to eat.

"More meat on a wren's shin," he muttered angrily. "This is disgraceful food," he said. "There's no excuse, in this country of all places. I would have cooked myself but there are no facilities at the lodging house."

"Do you like to cook?" I knew I was making conversation, gauche conversation, and disliked myself for it, but I felt strangely awkward with him, as if in responding to his invitation I had somehow lost the advantage of our encounters. He, by contrast, appeared very relaxed and smiled patiently at me.

"I am a cook. I love cooking."

"What do you mean? It's your job?"

"Yes. At least it has been for the last fifteen years."

"On your letter you signed yourself 'Dr.' "

"I was a doctor first, then a cook."

HE ATE his meal with surprising speed, as if someone was likely to snatch his plate away, with a concentration and energy that was almost alarming. After he had finished he said he was tired and did not wish to talk further. We walked back toward the funicular—the "Angel flight"—that would take us back up to Bunker Hill. He was silent but I noticed he was looking about him at the city almost fearfully, awestruck by its scale and busyness, its din and brightness. His skin under the diffused electric light of the street took on marked olive tones, to the extent that he might have passed for a Mexican or Latino, and I thought again of this gift of patrimony he had brought me and how preposterous it was. My own skin was pale and insipid beside his. Shared dark hair and brown eyes made a flimsy case in a paternity suit.

At the door of his lodging house we made an appointment to meet the next day. The little men sat on the steps up to the front door where we had left them an hour since: they stared at me curiously, with no malice or hostility.

"Why are there so many Japanese here?" I asked him quietly.

He turned and spoke to the men on the steps in a language I did not recognize. They all laughed, with genuine hilarity, it seemed.

"Japanese?" he said reproachfully. "These men are Filipinos."

SEVEN

I SAT with Salvador Carriscant on the slatted wooden bench of a red car that rolled and rattled as we crossed over Pico Boulevard at Sawtelle and headed out westward through the bean fields toward Santa Monica. Here and there the boulevard was being widened and long stretches of the small one-story shops had been flattened to take the new roadway. Soon everyone would be able to drive to the beach.

The trolley car stopped at the Ocean Avenue depot and Carriscant and I wandered down to Ocean Park. Once again I noticed that the press of people, the noise and the vivid colors of the sunshades seemed both to attract and disarm him. We stood at the Japanese gambling galleries watching men and women gambling for merchandise rather than money, and strolled past the beach clubs and the many piers, the loop-the-loop and the ride-the-clouds attractions, the air jangling with the shouts of children and the fretful buzz of the speedboats carrying anglers from the shore to the fishing barges—old mastless schooners and wooden-hulled clippers—anchored a hundred yards or so out in the ocean. Only the Monkey Farm seemed to upset him. The crowd around the cages was six deep and when we managed to push through to see what the lure was I saw the expression on his face change at once from curiosity to disgust when he contemplated the melancholy chimpanzees and the neurotic mangy gibbons in their close-barred pens. He took hold of my elbow and steered me away.

"What's wrong?" I asked.

"Those monkeys in the cages, I don't like it . . . They remind me of someone." He changed the subject. "Let's eat," he said. "I want to eat fish."

We went to one of the new apartment hotels, the Sovereign, which had a public dining room. Carriscant ordered broiled Spanish mackerel, which he ate with his usual concentration. "This is fresh," he said grudgingly, "the best food I've tasted in America."

The success of the menu dispelled the anger caused by the Monkey Farm and I sensed he was beginning to enjoy himself.

"I could never get enough fish," he said, "for all those years, even though we were not far from the coast. We sold all the fish we caught."

I did not press him, or ask him what "those years" were. There would be time enough later for interrogation, and besides, I thought he would tell me everything in his own good time, if he felt like it. I realized that this jaunt to the sea was just a means for him and me to become further acquainted— very much the father reestablishing his relationship with his long-lost daughter—and my silence, my reticence, encouraged this mood and that would please him, I knew.

And then I wondered why I should want to please him, why I was encouraging this—what?—this friendship. He knew my date of birth, but what did that prove? He knew what time of day I was born, but that could have been an inspired guess, a lucky shot . . . But there was a quality of confidence about his dealings with me that seemed different, indicated a fundamental certainty of purpose that I felt no trickster or flimflam man could simulate. It was not striven for, did not seek to impress. He appeared relaxed in my company—as if my company were all that he wanted—and that in turn relaxed me.

He looked up now from his meal and gave me a quick,

strong smile, his broad face creasing momentarily. Perhaps, I thought, perhaps because Rudolf Fischer was so manifestly *not* my father, and Hugh Paget possessed all the substantiality of myth, I was seizing too firmly on this new candidate, all attractive flesh-and-blood, all very much here and now? It was a form of temptation, I knew, a kind of seduction, and, I realized as I contemplated this sturdy, handsome old man, it was one I was not as well equipped to resist as I had thought.

When I asked him if he wanted a dessert he said he would prefer to eat another fish. He ordered a poached steak of yellowtail tuna which he consumed slowly and with much intense savoring of its flavors as I ate ice cream and smoked a cigarette. After his second fish he ordered a cognac, the cheapest in the house. He discreetly picked his teeth with a quill tip (he carried a small packet of them with him) and then seemed to rinse his mouth with the brandy. I started to chatter—most uncharacteristically—to cover my mild embarrassment as this dental toilette, this sluicing, went on. He listened politely as I told him about Santa Monica, Venice and the Malibu as I had known them over the years, but all the while I was aware of him sipping brandy and then, more disturbingly, I could hear the foamy susurrus in his mouth as he swilled and flushed the liquid between his teeth.

". . . and the Roosevelt Highway didn't exist," I was saying. "I mean, now you can take it all the way up the coast to Oxnard, but I remember I came down here with Pappi once—I must have been about twelve—"

"Twelve?"

"Yes, I—"

He frowned. "That would be about 1916?"

"Thereabouts. Twelve or thirteen, I guess. Pappi had this client—it was J. W. Considine, in fact—who had a house at the Malibu and we had to catch a boat out there from the Santa Monica Pier. It was real cut off in those—"

"Kay—"

I stopped talking at once. I realized he had not been listening to me.

"—If I was looking for a man in California," he said, "how would I set about finding him?"

"It depends . . . Do you know his name?"

"He's called Paton Bobby. All I know is he lives in California. He used to, anyway."

I stubbed out my cigarette. "Paton Bobby. Have you got any more information?"

"He's a little bit older than me. And I think he was a policeman."

"That might help. Anything else?"

"That's it."

I looked at him. I knew that our business, whatever it would turn out to be, was beginning now, irrevocably.

"May I know why you want to find him?"

He smiled a faint, dreamy smile. His mood had changed ever since I had mentioned my childhood trip to the Malibu, my age and the date. It had sent him back through time, perhaps to that place where he could never get enough fish, and his thoughts had stayed there.

"I'm sorry, my dear, what did you say?"

"Why do you need to find this Paton Bobby?"

He sighed, looked down at his empty plate, turned his fork so that its tines pointed downward, and returned his gaze to mine.

"I suppose you could say," he said, his eyes innocently wide, his expression bland, "that I'm looking for a killer."

EIGHT

P HILIP WROTE OUT the check with evident but ridiculously disproportionate pride and handed it over with a
courtly flourish.

"Pay to the order of Mrs. Kay Fischer, two hundred dollars," he said through his grin.

"So you got a job," I said.

"And a bank account. I've got six weeks' work with MGM.
I'm the third writer on *Hell Hath No Fury*."

"Sounds fulfilling."

"Sounds like money."

We were sitting in my office on Hollywood Boulevard.
From my office window I could see the top three stories of the
Guaranty Building and the dusty fronds of a palm tree. I
rented three rooms above a clothing wholesaler—Tex-Style
Imports Co.—who specialized in blue jeans, dungarees and
work boots that were sold to the petrochemical industry. The
room that faced the boulevard was my office; beyond that was
a small corridor that led to a windowless cube which was the
drawing room where my solitary assistant, Ivan Feinberg,
worked. Off the corridor was the reception area with a view of
the parking lot. Mary Duveen, my secretary, had her desk
here, squeezed between two banks of filing cabinets. It was all
a bit shabby, a little make-do, especially compared to what I
had become accustomed to at Meyersen and Fischer, but since

the great schism and the lawsuit I had been obliged to econo-
mize. I had heard from one of my former colleagues that
Meyersen had moved into my old office. Perhaps that was
what he had been after all the time? . . .

I took Philip's check and folded it away in my pocket-
book. He had had his hair cut and was wearing a new sports
coat, cotton, a greenish plaid, and wide mushroom-colored
trousers. His short hair, I thought, made him look even
younger, a superannuated college kid, and for a moment I
felt a brief squirm of self-pity as I reflected on our short marriage and what I had lost when I kicked him out. I kept the
appellation "Mrs.," not because it impressed my clients but
because it made them relax, but joined it up with my maiden
name. The conjunction seemed to me to reflect ideally my
social and personal status. But Philip was offended and hurt:
I was having my cake and eating it, he said truculently. But
isn't that what life's all about, I replied, the goal we're all
chasing? A brief squirm of self-pity, but one that disappeared
soon enough.

"Movies," I said breezily. "Going to get your name on this
one?"

"There's a chance."

I laughed. "And pigs may fly one day, they tell me." I stood
up. "I'll walk down with you, I've got to get some lunch."

As we descended the two floors to the street I asked Philip
if he knew any way of tracking down a man called Paton
Bobby, who was in his sixties and might have been a
policeman.

"Tried the phone book? Who's Paton Bobby?"

"A friend of mine needs to find him. I thought you might
know how."

He shrugged. "You could hire a P.I., I guess . . . Or maybe
I could ask the head of security at the studio—" He grinned.
"Did you hear that? 'At the studio'—I'm a natural, success

simply cannot continue to elude me. This guy used to be a cop, he might have some idea."

We sauntered down the sidewalk toward a street vendor. The sun was hot on the crown of my head and I undid the top button on my blouse. It was a fine day with a baby blue sky up above and a few perfect dawdling clouds. A fresh breeze moved through the fronds of the new palm trees, still only half the height of the streetlamps. They made a sound of nail scissors snipping or of matches tipped onto a glass table. I put on my sunglasses as the sun bounced off the white walls of the buildings across the street. Too much Streamline Moderne for my taste these days. Curved walls, curved glass, mirrored panels set here and there, stringcourses picked out in red and black to emphasize the horizontals, canopies swooping around corners or ducking into forecourts whenever possible ... What was going on here? It was all vitiated anyway by the garish lettering, shouting signs in primary colors hanging off buildings or else set on cantilevered wooden hoardings on the flat roofs. GOOD CHOW! HAM 'N' EGGS, CAMERAS, GIFTS, PARKING. We passed through a tangy waft of fried onion as we walked by HARROLD'S CHARCOAL BROILED STEAKS and made for the street vendor with his refulgent silver chariot. I ordered a super chili dog with mustard and extra onions.

Philip touched my arm. "Listen, you're not in any kind of trouble, are you, hon?" He was sincere, and it was a kind thought. I realized I was still very fond of him.

"Of course I'm not," I reassured him. "It's some old fellow I know, needs to track this party down."

Philip looked at me shrewdly, not wholly convinced, as I paid for and received my food. I could see him wondering how many "old fellows" I might know and why I might want to help them locate a missing person.

"Stop looking at me like that. You don't have to do anything if you don't want to."

"No, no, I'll see what I can do."

I could wait no longer. I bit avidly into my chili dog, my nostrils suddenly filled with pungent heat. With a finger I helped a stray ribbon of onion into my mouth. I chewed.

Philip looked at me. "I was going to ask you to dinner to-night, but now that I've seen your lunch I guess you won't be hungry."

"Ha-ha. Call me later, you may get lucky."

WHEN I RETURNED to my office George Fugal was there waiting for me, a wide smile on his narrow face. George was a tall thin forty-year-old with a restless, jumpy demeanor that sat oddly with a professional manner that could only be described as the last word in pedantry. He had thinning brown hair, big watery eyes and a weak chin that always had a bluey, unshaven look to it. If I had not known he was a lawyer I would have placed him as a minor criminal on parole, or a debtor on the run from the IRS. George never stopped looking around whatever room he was in, or over his shoulder; in restaurants he insisted on sitting with his back to the door, the better to twist around in his seat.

"So what's the good news?" I asked him.

"We got a buyer for the house. I'm sure. A"—he checked his notebook—"a Mrs. Luard Turner. Pleasant lady. I just showed her around."

"I'm going to finish it first. I hope she realizes that," I said with some ungrateful belligerence. All at once I felt oddly sad. Someone was going to buy my house. Someone else was going to live in my carefully constructed volumes of air.

"She knows that, she knows that. But she loves the place. 'Classy,' she said. 'Grade A class,' she said. Her very words, Kay, her very words."

He chattered on, excited and pleased for me, his gaze leaping from me to Mary to the office door to the trash can. We needed the sale to make the profit to permit Kay Fischer to survive and move on to bigger and greater things. But I was still feeling my loss keenly.

"We've done it, Kay," George Fugal said. "You're there."

I smiled at him. Somehow I did not believe it was ever that easy.

NINE

IN ARCHITECTURE, as in art, the more you reduce, the more exacting your standards must be. The more you strip down and eliminate, the greater the pressure, the import, on what remains. If a room is only to have one door and one window, then those two openings must conform *exactly* to the volume of space contained between the four walls, the floor and the ceiling.

My aesthetic mentor, my inspiration, in all this was the German architect Oscar Kranewitter (1891–1929). He was a friend of Gropius and like him was heavily influenced by the austere ideologies of Johannes Itten. Kranewitter was one of the first members of the German Werkbund and taught occasionally at the Bauhaus between 1923 and 1925 (he departed, never to return, after a savage row—it came to blows—with Hannes Meyer). There is no doubt that had it not been for his tragically early death (in an automobile accident) Kranewitter would be regarded as one of the foremost German architects and leaders of the International Style. Because of his demanding temperament and the strictures he imposed on himself and his clients he built very little and his published work is confined to a few articles in obscure reviews such as *Metall* and *Neue Europäische Graphik*. And it was in these densely argued pieces that he introduced the concept of *Armut* into modern architecture—or "Poverty." But the sense with which Kranewitter charges and loads this abstract noun is complex: for him the meaning of the word loses any negative or pejorative import and its implication is transformed into something more akin to "Purity." The abstruse theorizing behind *Armut* was given a physical dimension in Kranewitter's masterwork, the Lothar House (1924–1929) in Ober Traubling near Regensburg. It was here during the painstaking five years of construction that Kranewitter's obsessiveness and fanatical attention to detail took on legendary proportions as his conception of *Armut* took on plastic form. When the house was all but completed he had the entire ceiling of the dining room torn down and rebuilt four centimeters higher. He designed all the furniture (teak, chrome and leather were the only materials used) and there were no carpets or curtains. The floors were made of a dark polished flint. The color of the walls was white on the first floor and primrose yellow on the second (yellow is a "lighter" color than white, according to Kranewitter, and therefore suitable for rooms above ground level). All the door furniture was forged aluminum and unpainted, as were the massive and specially designed central heating radiators. The rooms were lit with naked light bulbs. It was destroyed by a stray stick of bombs during a raid on Regensburg in World War II.

The more I studied Kranewitter, the more I came to admire the dedication of the man and the ruthless consistency of his ideas. Rigor, clarity and precision seemed to me attributes that were both admirable and practical. Kranewitter's *Armut* is not something miserable and deprived: it has a liberating, purgative quality to it. The more the twentieth century advances and the more crassly complicated our lives become and the more the hectoring injunctions of the commercial world intrude—EAT! BUY! PLAY! SPEND! ENJOY!—and come to dominate our every waking moment, so do the calm and emptiness, the clean, unimpeded, untrammeled nature of the world Kranewitter tried to create, grow ever more appealing.

These were ambitions that I tried to realize and incorporate in my own work and they are manifestly embodied in the two completed buildings I designed—the Taylor House in Pasadena, and the Burbank Shopping Mart. Everything extraneous is stripped away. The interiors are ruthlessly plain, the only lines are vertical or horizontal. Even in such a temple of self-indulgence as a shopping mart—the American antithesis of *Armut*—Kranewitter's ascetic philosophy is evident. And it works.

It worked so well it cost me my job. The success of the Burbank Mart meant that Meyersen and Fischer were approached by Ohman's Retail Group to design their new store and restaurant complex on Wilshire Boulevard. I did the initial drawings and plans, and had a scale model constructed. Shortly before the final contracts were signed, Eric Meyersen called me into his office and informed me that I was fired. When I asked him why, he said equably, "No real reason, honey. I just don't want to see your face around here anymore, I guess." Meyersen had, to put it simply, got what he needed from me—a body of work, a small but growing reputation, a style. Now, with the Ohman deal secure, he figured he could go it alone. Fugal looked at the document of partnership I had signed so avidly five years previously and duly unearthed the subclauses that granted Meyersen this unilateral power. I told him to sue the bastard in any case. Writs were served as the Ohman's Building contract was signed by Eric Meyersen Architects Inc. The Taylor House and the Burbank Mart records were similarly altered. My only course of action was to go out on my own and show the world who really was responsible for these buildings. 2265 Micheltoreno would be the first nail in Meyersen's coffin.

P HILIP WAS RENTING a small clapboard cottage in
Venice, one street back from the boardwalk and the
ocean. I walked up the two steps to its sun-blistered porch,
tucked the flask under one arm, set down my grocery bag on
an old cane rocker and rapped loudly on the frame of the fly-
screened door. From inside I heard a couple of plaintive
coughs and then Philip appeared in a creased and grubby robe,
his hair lank and greasy. He had shaved recently, but it had
made little difference, his eyes were dark, his face slumped and
pasty-looking.

"Hello, sunshine," I said. "Momma's here."

He had made up his bed—a Navaho blanket and three
pillows—on a winded davenport in the living room. From next
door the sound of his neighbor's radio, playing "American
Dreamer," was thinly audible. By the time I had poured the
soup into a bowl and brought it through to him he was back
on the couch under the blanket, his knees drawn up, his face
set in an expression of stoical suffering.

"Potato soup and pastries, right? I got you pecan pie, lemon
cheese cake and four assorted Danish."

"Bless you." He took the soup from me and started to slurp
it up eagerly, like a starving peasant. "I haven't eaten for forty-
eight hours."

I had seen the empty quart of bourbon in the kitchenette.

"What's wrong?"

"I got fired. After four fucking *days*, they fired me."

"Well, it was a crappy movie—"

"It was work, Kay. Four-hundred-dollars-a-week work." His voice was sulky and heavy with self-pity. I sat and watched him finish his soup, whereupon he immediately started on the cheesecake. He took too large a mouthful and swallowed painfully. He coughed crumbs onto the davenport.

"Take it easy," I said. "No one's going to snatch it away. You want a coffee?"

"I think I got a tumor in my throat. Could you take a look?"

He gaped at me. I held his handsome, damaged face between my palms and tilted it so that the light from the window fell on his gullet. I saw nothing but pink pulsing gorge and a certain amount of lemon cheesecake, but I knew Philip in these moods, he needed something to hold on to.

"I don't see much . . . Maybe it's a little red."

"Jesus . . . What about my eyes? Any yellow tinge?"

"Red's your color today, I'm afraid. Why yellow?"

"I get these pains in my back. I worry my liver is shot—cirrhosis or something. Maybe a cancer."

"I'd lay off the bourbon." I stood up. "I'll fix you a coffee."

I walked back through to the kitchenette and put a pan of water on the stove to heat while I looked for some coffee grounds. I heard Philip's doleful footsteps shuffle up behind me and then felt his arms go around my waist. He nuzzled at the back of my neck, little pecking kisses.

"Kay-kay, can I come and stay over a few days? I hate it like this on my own."

"No, Philip, you know it won't—"

"I just can't cope. I just—"

"—have to stop drinking. So you got fired. It's not the end of the world. This town's full of crappy movies looking for writers. And full of fired writers looking for crappy movies."

"It was a good job, Kay. The best." He stepped away from me and thrust his fists deep into his robe pockets. "Six, eight weeks, I'd have been set up." He pulled a crumpled slip of paper out of one pocket and looked at it strangely. "Jeez, I forgot, this is for you." He handed it over. "They found your—whatchacallim—Paton Bobby. McGuire at the studio . . . The fucking studio."

I smoothed out the sheet of paper and read what was written there: "Sheriff Paton Bobby, Los Feliz Ranch, White Lakes, Santa Fe."

"Santa Fe?"

Philip said: "He wasn't even in California. Just as well you told me he was a cop. We'd never have found him."

I turned and looked out of the kitchen window. I could see a stunted, abused cypress, its top three feet broken off and hanging there, and beyond that a chain-link fence which marked the boundary of a spur track of the Electric Railway. So Paton Bobby was a sheriff in Santa Fe, New Mexico. What could Dr. Salvador Carriscant want with him?

"Any chance of that coffee?" Philip said. "My throat's killing me."

I MET Carriscant at the rail station in Pasadena early in the morning. He had asked me to come with him to Santa Fe and, for some reason, and much to my astonishment, I agreed at once, without any reflection or any regrets.

He had asked and I had said yes, and it was only later that this had struck me as presumptuous on his part and paradoxical on mine. But he had fired my imagination, and his easy assumption about the bond that existed between us was one I was ceasing to be on guard against or question. But I steered my reasoning away from this particular motivation to another that was more acceptable, if quixotic. This was an adventure, I told myself, an intriguing quest, and one that I would regret not seeing through at least a little further along the way. We could make the return journey in two days and I was curious about Carriscant and this Paton Bobby—and besides, I had never been to New Mexico.

The waiting room at Pasadena was clean and redolent of carbolic, the first commuters were arriving and the newsstands were still plump with unsold newspapers and magazines. Carriscant was standing at our prearranged rendezvous at the entrance to the coffee shop looking apprehensive and lost. The smile on his face when he saw me was genuine. He held up two tickets as I approached.

"I bought your ticket," he said. "There is no need to reimburse me."

"Don't worry," I said. "I haven't changed my mind."

"I'm very grateful that you're accompanying me," he said as we made our way toward the platform for the Santa Fe Express. "You might find this hard to believe, but the last time I took a train was from Glasgow to Liverpool in 1897."

PATON BOBBY'S RANCH turned out to be south of Santa Fe, a few miles outside White Lakes on a grassy butte with the Sangre de Cristo mountains dark and solid in the background. We hired a taxi for the day (a modest twenty dollars) and set out from our hotel near the railroad station after breakfast. I asked Carriscant if he had taken the precaution of cabling ahead to warn Bobby of our arrival. He said he had decided against the idea.

"But what if he's not there?" I said, irritated.

"Oh, I made sure he was there. I just didn't want him to know that I was coming." Carriscant's English accent had the effect of making him at times sound insufferably smug, and this was one of those times.

"Who is Paton Bobby?" I said. "How do you know him?"

"We met a long time ago. We were quite close friends, for a while."

I did not press him further; I did not want to give him the satisfaction of practicing his maddening obliquity on me anymore. As far as this quest was concerned, Carriscant was very reluctant to tell me anything. Facts about his aims and his past were eked out sparingly, and usually when unsolicited. From time to time a nugget of information would be placed in front of you like an *amuse-gueule*, the better to whet your appetite, but if you sought for information he withdrew. I was not sure whether he was playing some complex, teasing game with me or whether he was simply guileless—an old man whose memory was occasionally stimulated—or whether he was one of the most sophisticated liars I had ever met. What prompted the reference to the train journey from Glasgow to Liverpool in 1897, for example? Was it just his insecurity, his vulnerability manifesting itself, or was it a piece designed to fit some larger puzzle? I had given up trying to extract information for the time being: I too could play at being indifferent and opaque with the best of them.

We turned off the Albuquerque–Las Vegas road and followed the signs for Clines Corners and Encino. In White Lakes we were directed up a white dirt road running along the edge of a wide sagebrush mesa. We hit a line of split-rail fencing and soon saw the gateway and the sign RANCHO LOS FELIZ burnt deep in the wooden lintel.

"What's that? 'Ranch of the Happy Ones'?" Carriscant said. "Funny how the Spanish saves it from vulgarity." The smile on his face died. "I would never have imagined Paton Bobby in a place like . . ." He trailed off. All of a sudden he seemed a worried man.

However vulgar its name, the ranch had a well-run, neat and tidy air to it. Big boulders set at the entrance were freshly whitewashed, the twin-rutted track up to the ranch house was weed-free, its central stripe of grass clipped short, like the

verges. On either side horses grazed in well-irrigated mead-
ows. Prosperity and order seemed to breathe from the alfalfa
grass and the manzanita trees.

I looked again at Carriscant. He sat rigid now, tense, his
teeth chewing vaguely on his bottom lip. His eyes seemed lost,
distant, barely aware of his surroundings. It was as if he had
never decided to come on this trip of his own volition, but was
being led here somehow, like a prisoner to a scaffold, or a con-
script to a battlefield, passive, powerless to change whatever
would ensue. I felt sorry for him, and oddly protective, aware
suddenly of his strange helplessness in this big country, and
was glad that I had come with him.

Dogs set up a barking as we drew up in front of the ranch
house, a new building, with stone gables and a long shady
porch with bright borders of flowers along its façade. I told a
Mexican ranch hand that we were here to see Mr. Bobby and
we were directed to the front door, where a maid duly showed
us into a small parlor. Presently, a woman, not much older
than me, joined us and introduced herself as Estelle Bobby. I
had her placed as the daughter, but it soon became apparent
she was a new wife. She was shy and pretty with slightly bulging blue eyes and fair hair. If Bobby was in his late sixties he
had a thirty-year start on his wife, it was clear.

I introduced myself and Carriscant, who was by now so to-
tally subdued that I felt like his chaperone. When I said his
name it seemed to mean nothing to her.

Estelle Bobby directed us to chairs as if she had learned her
manners from a correspondence course.

"My husband will be back within the hour," she said. "He's
out riding. May I pertain what your visit is concerning?"

I turned to Carriscant.

"I, ah, I'm an old friend of your husband's," he muttered
gracelessly. "I haven't seen him in over thirty years ..."

"We were in Santa Fe on business," I improvised. "Mr.

Carriscant thought it would be worth calling in on the off chance."

"Certainly, of course, you're more than welcome," Mrs. Bobby said, and went off to fetch us some coffee while we waited.

Two cups later, with Mrs. Bobby busying herself elsewhere in the house, we heard the sound of a horse's hooves and saw a neat buggy with a high-stepping bay between the shafts enter the yard and move out of sight behind the back of the house. I glimpsed a large stout man at the reins, quite bald and with a big wide mustache. We heard a rear door open and the sound of voices conversing. I turned to Carriscant. He was pale, his mouth slack.

"I feel sick, Kay," he said hoarsely. "I think I'm going to vomit."

He extended his hand shakily and, without thinking, I took hold of it and squeezed.

"Come on, drink some coffee, you'll be fine."

"I think we should leave. Now." Panic lit his eyes.

"Don't be ridiculous. We've come all this way. What's he done to you, this man?"

Carriscant shook his head wordlessly. To give him some time I rose to my feet and went through to the hall, closing the parlor door behind me. Paton Bobby was emerging from the kitchen. Under his perfectly smooth, shiny pate he had a square, seamed face, with kind eyes, and a wide, neatly trimmed gray mustache that effectively bisected his face from ear to ear. He was broad-shouldered and carried his big belly easily, almost proudly. Some men seem to suit being fat and Paton Bobby was one of them, comfortable, attractive even, in his solid obesity.

He shook my hand and I introduced myself and apologized for arriving unannounced.

He looked at me. "My wife says this gentleman is an old

friend of mine. I have no old friends called Tarrant." He had a slow easy voice, with a harder rumble somewhere at the back of his throat. I saw a leather cigar holder, like a Pan's pipe, jutting from the breast pocket of his jacket.

"No," I said carefully, flashing a smile at Mrs. Bobby. "Not Tarrant. Carriscant. Dr. Salvador Carriscant."

The genial curiosity on Paton Bobby's face vanished instantly, transformed completely into an expression of astonishment that would have done justice to a cartoon character. His brows arched, his eyes wide, his open mouth forming a soundless "What?" He began to blink rapidly.

"Salvador Carriscant?" he repeated. "Are you out of your mind?"

"No, Paton, she's not."

We turned to see Carriscant, framed square in the parlor doorway, composed, clear-eyed. Paton Bobby took half a step back, as if to focus better, still frowning, staring.

"My God Jesus Christ," he said softly, almost fearfully, his voice ragged with emotion. "Salvador."

And at just that moment I felt a flush of anger rise through me. I was so ignorant, had been so willfully kept in that state that to witness now the profound shock of this reunion, to see plainly its melodramatic impact made me feel used and exploited. Carriscant vigorously, two-fistedly shaking Bobby's hand, the two of them manfully loud in their mutual exclamations of astonishment . . . This was the craven fellow who moments ago was threatening to vomit, who needed his hand reassuringly squeezed. I stood there watching them and resented, with special force, the way this man had insinuated himself so deeply into my life already. And with such *ease* . . . What did I owe him? What hold had he over me? What responsibilities were due? None, was the quick and simple answer, and I resolved to have nothing further to do with him and his bizarre private schemes.

"What's going on?" I said, a little too abruptly. "What is there between you two?"

Bobby turned, surprised. "Didn't he tell you? My God, Salvador was—"

"Later, Kay, please," Carriscant interrupted courteously. "If you don't mind. I have to talk to Paton first."

"Fine. I'll be in the car. Let me know when you're ready to leave."

I sat in the car for ten minutes, maddened and cross at myself, until the stickiness of the hot leather under my thighs drove me outside again. I paced around smoking a cigarette, watched with only the mildest curiosity by the taxi driver, an old taciturn hacker called Arthur Clough, who had large uneven yellow teeth and a persistent sniff. From where I was standing I could see the top of Paton Bobby's head, which seemed to do nothing but nod all the time. I asked Arthur if he knew of Bobby.

"Sure," he said. "I think he used to be sheriff of Los Alamos—and didn't he run for mayor of Santa Fe once? After he came out of the Army or something. I seen his face in the paper a while back."

He accepted one of my cigarettes and smoked it fastidiously, like a Victorian dandy, held palm upward between thumb and forefinger.

Carriscant and Paton Bobby came to the front door about an hour later. From my position, although I could not swear to it, it seemed as if Bobby had been weeping, but the idea seemed so incongruous as to be almost incredible. But his posture was stooped, that canted-back, spread-legged confidence seemed absent now, and I distinctly heard him say as they made their farewells: "...I hope you can forgive me, Salvador."

"Of course," Carriscant said, with what sounded like genuine feeling. "I never blamed you, Paton. Never. You were doing your job, and"—he paused—"and it was a difficult time."

Carriscant climbed into the car beside me, stiff-faced, upset. He sat back in his seat and closed his eyes.

"Poor Paton," he said.

"What's happening?" I said, full of angry curiosity. "You can't keep this from me anymore."

"Oh, Kay, Kay, give me a moment."

The car pulled away from the house. Paton Bobby had not lingered on the porch. Carriscant looked at me and managed a smile of sorts.

"I'm sorry, Kay . . . It's not fair, Kay, I know, but this was crucial, essential for me, my dear Kay, if you could only—"

"Stop saying my goddamn name!"

My vehemence seemed to shake him out of his patronizing complacency, his sense of triumph. For some sort of victory had ensued in that house, long overdue, I suspected, and he was savoring it. In the event, he stopped talking and reached inside his coat and drew out a small leather wallet, which he opened. Inside it was the folded page of an illustrated magazine. I glimpsed an advertisement for a beer I did not recognize and some phrases in Spanish, or so I thought. Without further explanation Carriscant handed me the sheet and I spread it open on my knees. On the page there were six photographs with captions beneath them. The language was Portuguese, I now saw, and the pictures appeared to be of routine society occasions or news events. My eye caught a wedding, an arm-waving top-hatted politician making a speech, an elaborate villa damaged by fire. Carriscant's finger indicated the bottom right-hand photograph. A man in tennis whites was being presented with an enormous silver trophy by a flamboyant young woman in a cloche hat and many strings of pearls. I noticed the date at the bottom of the page: May 25, 1927. I glanced at the caption, trying to translate it. A charity tennis match . . . Jean-Claude Riverain the winner—I remembered the famous tennis player, and looked curiously at him now in his loose dusty flannels, a damp comma of hair pasted to his high tanned forehead—and Miss Carmencita Barrera, the celebrated motion picture actress, all winking sequins and lace, her face as white as pipe clay . . .

"The actress?" I said.

"No, the woman two along from her."

I peered closer. An elegant woman, in her fifties, perhaps, still attractive, applauding, a faint ambiguous smile on her face. The focus was sharp, I could make out the paisley motif on her dress but I could not judge whether her smile was one of polite boredom or polite enthusiasm. Between her and the actress was an elderly man with white hair in a dark suit; on her other side a naval officer of some exalted rank; the other figures were blurred. No one else apart from the actress and the tennis star was identified.

Carriscant took the page away from me and folded it carefully, slipping it back into its wallet.

"That is her," he said simply and with curious authority. "I was never sure, never *really* sure, that's why I needed to find Paton. He was the only one who could confirm it."

"Confirm what?"

"That she was—that she is—who I thought she was."

"And he did?"

"Without hesitation. Without a moment's hesitation." He let a slow shuddering breath pass from him. "And now I know. You can't imagine what it's like, after thirty-three years."

"Dr. Carriscant, you have to tell me what you're talking about. There's no point if I don't—"

He held up a hand to stop me and then breathed in and out, a dozen deep breaths as if to invigorate himself, as if he had been asleep for a long time. It was most irritating.

"All this time," he began, "I thought she might be dead,

you see. Thought I'd never know what happened. But then I found this picture, by some . . . some miraculous, some devious twist of fate. And now I know she's alive."

"But the picture's almost ten years old."

"But she's alive. She looks—" Tears bulged at his lids, his voice thickened. "I know she is waiting for me." He said this with adamantine confidence, and then turned to me.

"We'll go and find her."

"*We?* What're you talking about?"

"You and me, Kay—dear Kay. We will go to Lisbon and find her."

ELEVEN

*I*T IS hard to find a small cemetery in Los Angeles. And I
was set on my son being buried somewhere small and private, a place where there would be few passersby, where there
would be fewer incurious glances than in some multiacre ne-
cropolis or the vast landscaped death park that is the norm.

I found an old, partially rebuilt mission at the north end of
the San Fernando Valley where, by dint of a hefty donation to
the restoration fund, I was provided with a plot in one corner,
shaded by a grove of eucalyptus trees. I go there from time to
time, about once a month, trying not to make a ritual out of
my visits, in good moods and bad, but inevitably the place has
forged its associations (I have no real memory of him, after all)
and now it is the rattle of dry leaves, the tomcat smell of eucalyptus, even the filigreed shadow of sun through branches
that conspire to remind me of my dead son.

I spent some time on the headstone also: what does one in-
scribe when a life has only spanned sixteen days? "Whom the
gods love . . ."? "Vanity of vanities, saith the Preacher . . . all is
vanity"? In the end I chose white marble, very simple, and had
the name and the date inlaid in bronze. COLEMAN BROCKWAY,
10 APRIL 1930—26 APRIL 1930. Over the years since his death
the verdigris on the bronze lettering has run and stained the
marble beneath, like green tears. Green tears for my blue baby.
Coleman Brockway came into the world with a stacked deck
against him from day one—he had a hole in his heart.

TWELVE

M RS. LUARD TURNER WORE a white fox wrap with her aquamarine suit even though the day was hot and the sky above was a changeless blue. She was heavily made-up too, like an actress, I thought, with a thick base of panstick and powder over skin that was beginning to show signs of slippage and slackening. I closed the door of the big closet in the bedroom.

"You'll notice the house has many closets," I said, "and that many of them are twice as large as is normal."

"What? Why, yes, I did think—"

"The idea, you see, is that there should be no clutter. Everything can be stowed away." I smiled at her. I was starting to hector, I knew, a habit I fall into when I suspect someone is not really paying attention. "I can't stop people owning possessions, but I can encourage them to keep them out of sight."

"Oh, sure." She smiled back, uncertainly. "I, ah, like to be tidy too."

"Everything in this house has been thought through, Mrs. Turner. Every proportion is precise. Wherever possible I have built the furniture in—like the kitchen, like that unit of drawers and shelves in the living room—because you simply cannot, in a house of this style, of this, if I may say so, ethos—"

"I'm sorry? Eeth what?"

"—You can't just put in ordinary furniture, your average sofa, armchairs, et cetera."

"I can't?"

"Where you need new furniture I would ask you—actually, I would beg you—to go to specialist furniture makers. Order items that will suit the house, you'll never regret it. I can give you half a dozen names of—"

"Mrs. Fischer is very proud of her house," George Fugal interrupted with a nervous laugh.

"Oh, sure," Mrs. Turner said, looking around. "Ah, is the bathroom functioning?"

I showed her where it was.

"It's a done deal," George said. "She's crazy about the place."

"Could have fooled me. Is she all right? She seems sort of distant, not in touch. Is there—"

"Kay, I have ten percent in escrow. She's not fooling around." He looked nervously over his shoulder and lowered his voice. "Will I be able to hear the noise of the flush? I mean here, in this room?"

"Probably. Why?"

"Could we go downstairs? It makes me uncomfortable, you know, when she comes out—I hate that moment."

George and I descended the stairs noisily, our feet clattering on the bare boards, so Mrs. Turner could flush the toilet without fear of embarrassment.

"I think you could have made these stairs wider."

"George, I don't advise you on points of law."

Mrs. Luard Turner duly appeared and was duly satisfied. She forgot to ask but I still gave her a list of names of cabinet-makers who could provide her with dining room tables and easy chairs that would not destroy the clean lines of my perfect rooms. It was agreed that the contracts would be signed in Fugal's offices the next day at 10:00 a.m.

· · ·

I DROVE west on Sunset and turned up Normandie onto Hollywood. Carriscant was pacing up and down outside the front door of my building. It was five days now since our trip to Santa Fe and I had not seen him in the meantime, all my efforts having been concentrated on ensuring that the house was ready for sale. The by now increasingly familiar aggregate of emotions coagulated inside me as I pulled up at the curb and I saw him hurry over—a tacky mass of surprise, curiosity, fractiousness and fatigue. The trip to Santa Fe had proved too sustained and rich a diet of Salvador Carriscant. For the moment smaller doses were what was required.

Carriscant followed me into my office, close on my heels, as if he were expecting me to make a run for it; I could sense his impatience and his excitement brewing in the air around us, but I refused to be cajoled or hurried, taking my time checking my messages with Mary and spending five minutes with Ivan looking over the preliminary drawings that he had made on a new site we had found in Silver Lake, a few streets north of Micheltoreno.

Eventually I allowed Carriscant to take a seat in my office while I made a call to Fugal to confirm that all was proceeding normally with the Luard deal—everything was in order. I recradled the phone.

"Look, you can't stay long," I said. "These are my office hours. If you knew how busy—"

"Kay, I understand. No one understands better than me. I simply thought you would like to be the first to know."

"What?"

"What I've discovered about the photograph." He removed the soft wallet from his coat pocket. "It's amazing what information you can mine from a well-equipped public library."

"Fire away."

Carriscant told me he had discovered more about the tennis match that the photograph featured. It had been part of a series of charity events taking place over three days—bicycle races, boxing bouts, a raffle with cash prizes—cosponsored by the U.S. legation, the Portuguese Red Cross and an Anglo-Portuguese charity welfare group called the Knights of 1147, commemorating the year, Carriscant informed me with an annoying pedagogical air, when English crusaders helped capture Lisbon from the Moors. The festival had occurred between the twentieth and twenty-third of May to celebrate the Knights' golden jubilee and the visit of the U.S. Navy's light cruiser *Olympia* and a British destroyer flotilla to Lisbon. The tennis match had been the highlight of the three days' entertainments, an exhibition game between Riverain and Carlos Pellicet. "Riverain won 6–2, 6–4," Carriscant informed me. "Apparently it was a closer match than the score suggests." What was interesting, he went on, was that the cup had been named after the wife of the U.S. envoy—the Lillian Ailshie Cup.

"And what was even more interesting," Carriscant said, leaning forward, placing both hands on my desk, "is that the envoy's wife did not present the trophy."

I assumed Carriscant would inform me why this was "even more interesting" in his own good time.

"I know," I said dutifully, "that actress—what's her name—did."

"Exactly. Q.E.D."

"I don't follow."

"The envoy's wife couldn't have been there."

"Possibly. So what?"

"So that means the other people on the dais were more than likely U.S. legation staff."

Finally I began to see the meandering line his reasoning was taking. "So," I said, slowly, "no ambassador's wife for the presentation of her own trophy—"

"Call in a cinema actress. But someone has to be there from the legation."

"Why not the Red Cross or the Knights of diddly-squat?"

"Because this was the USA's event." He removed his precious photograph from its wallet and spread it out on my blotter. The actress, the white-haired man in the dark suit, Carriscant's lady with her enigmatic smile, the naval officer.

"The guest of honor," Carriscant said, his forefinger on Carmencita Barrera (the nail was rimmed with dirt, I noticed), it jumped the next two faces down the line, "the naval officer," it moved back for the white-haired man, "the envoy and"—he paused—"the envoy's guest, or the naval officer's wife."

I could see that this last appellation affected him. "It sounds plausible," I said, "but you can't know for sure." I turned the magazine page around to face him. "All these people are on the gorgeous Carmencita's left. The really important people could be on the right."

"No, absolutely not. Press photographers always make sure the dignitaries are in the shot."

I could see he was in no mood to quibble. He was convinced with all the unreasoning certainty of a zealot, and he was not going to be shifted.

"So, you're saying—" I began.

"I'm saying that this woman"—there was now a distinct tremble in his voice, an emotional vibrato—"this woman was the friend or wife of a U.S. embassy official in Lisbon in 1927." He reclined in his chair, his face set in the curious clenched half-grimace of someone fighting to hold tears back. He folded his arms tightly across his chest, embracing himself.

"This is where the trail starts," he said, his voice husky with triumph. "This is where it must begin."

"Well, good luck to you."

He looked at me blankly for an instant, as if I had suddenly spoken in a foreign language.

"No, Kay, *we* begin. Us, you and me. I can't go without you."

"I told you the last time, I'm not going anywhere. I have a

house to design. I have a life to live here, for God's sake."

"It would only be for six weeks, two months."

I laughed: more a gasp of incredulity than a laugh, actually.

"Dr. Carriscant, this is your . . . your obsession, not mine. I barely know you. I can't simply—"

"I can't afford to go to Lisbon," he said petulantly, accusingly, as if it were my fault. "I have no money."

"Neither of us has money."

"You've just sold your house."

"Yes, *my* house. To build another one. We work on a shoe-string here, look around you."

He lowered his head to stare at his hands, which were held in his lap, half-clenched fists. His shoulders hunched and sub-sided a few times, as if he were relieving an ache, and when he looked up at me again shameless tears were flowing from his eyes.

"Kay, I'm asking you as my daughter—"

"Stop that, right now—"

"—as your father. Come with me, help me."

"You are not my father," I shouted at him. "Hugh Paget was my father. How dare you—"

"No, I am, I am, Kay!" he shouted back. "I am!"

The fervent confidence with which he made this claim si-lenced and unsettled me. I realized that in my association with Salvador Carriscant, the hours I had spent in his company, our two-day trip to Santa Fe, I had tacitly set aside my doubts and had complacently—perhaps voluntarily—allowed the assump-tion he had made to lie there between us, like a gift proffered, but not yet accepted. Nor yet rejected. Now was the time for that act to occur.

"If you are my father," I said reasonably, under control, "then who is my mother?"

"Why, your mother, of course. Annaliese."

"She is alive and well and living in Long Beach, California, if you want to go visit."

He looked sad and shook his head, wordlessly, then sniffed and wiped the drying tears from his cheeks. Not for the first time I asked myself if he was an innocent fool or simply a very bad actor.

"She would never see me," he said. "She would never acknowledge me."

"Why not?"

"Because of what I did to her."

"How long were you married?"

"Two years."

I stopped myself from asking any more questions even though dozens of fresh ones were lining up, clamoring in my head. What was the date of the marriage? How old was I when it ended? ... The problem was that all my questions presupposed the veracity of his version of events—and I saw that this was how Salvador Carriscant drew you in, enmeshed and enmired you. I was not going to play his dangerous games any longer.

"I'm sorry, Dr. Carriscant," I said abruptly. "I can't help you on this, no."

He stared at me balefully, sullenly, his eyes full of a new dislike and resentment. And then, all at once, the mood passed and his face brightened. He exhaled and let his shoulders slump and smiled weakly.

"Oh, well," he said almost lightheartedly, "what can I do? I hope you won't object if I try to change your mind—from time to time."

"You can try," I said, "but it won't work."

THIRTEEN

P HILIP'S THIGH was still warm against mine. Too warm. I moved farther away from him, very slowly, shifting myself along the mattress until I felt the moistness on my flank begin to cool. No portion of my body touched his, none of the calorific glow emanating from him warmed me. If it had not been for the surprisingly loud sound of his breathing, I might have been alone in my bed. I spread my fingers and the tips touched a damp patch on the mattress—his semen, I supposed, and immediately my mind turned to the banal routines of housekeeping, of needing now to change my sheets even though they had been on the bed barely a day . . .

It had been a mistake to invite him to stay a night with me. We had made love, which of course was what I had wanted, a sudden and simple need for effective sex of some prolonged duration—so I could experience its visceral uncomplicated joys with none of its complicated personal preambles and aftermath. Philip was the only person who could furnish me with that, and he had, with, for him, an extra dimension of delight (it had been over a year since the last time), but he had fallen asleep, literally a minute after it was over, it seemed, his head heavy in the hollow between my shoulder and my breast, his legs against mine, a palm flat on my thigh. It had taken me ten minutes of small patient maneuverings to free myself from the various contacts with his body, and I lay now, still and untouched in my small area of coolness, wishing he was home and trying not to feel cross with myself.

I met Philip in 1928 on the campus at UCLA where I was taking evening extension classes in German. Philip was studying German too, with a vaguely conceived view of going to work in Germany, in the film business there. I was keen to better understand and translate some of Kranewitter's *Metall* articles, whereas Philip only sought a basic conversational fluency. It had been one of his many passing fads; it lasted three weeks in this case, but the enthusiasm survived long enough for us to note each other, find each other attractive and contrive oh so casually to meet.

We dined, we dated. I was much slimmer in those days and, I'm sure, much jollier company. Without much ado we began an affair. Some weeks later, when Philip was between apartments, he came to sleep over at my little house in Westwood Village and discreetly stayed on. We married soon after that, in the spring of 1929. Coleman was born a year later—blue and damned—and when he died all happiness left us. We divorced in Mexico that summer and it took us an awkward year to become friends again. I knew that Philip was still attracted to me, but I had changed and could now see the conspicuous weaknesses in him, however much he amused me. It was a long time before I relented and we slept together. Tonight had been the fourth time. These occasions were becoming progressively less enjoyable.

I slipped out of bed but managed still to tug the sheet away from him. He did not move. In the shadowed screened dusk of the room I could clearly see his long thin penis curved over the swell of his thigh and the thin slug-trail gleam of his semen running from its tip onto my clean but crumpled sheets. I covered him and walked through to the bathroom, closing the door behind me before I switched on the light. I was startled—a regular occurrence, this—at the pale solid size of the woman reflected in the mirror, the soft wide breasts, the firm belly creased below the navel . . . My mental image of myself remained trapped in 1926, the year I graduated from MIT, "Master in Architecture," licensed to sign "Architect and Engineer" after my name, never aging, slim and enthusiastic with my big-lashed, hopeful gaze. The hefty, haunchy reality always caught me unawares at moments like these. I switched the light off again, sat down and did my business in the dark, thinking suddenly, for no particular reason, of lanky, blurry Hugh Paget, my English father, and this dark maddening stranger who so brusquely wanted to frog-march him out of my life and memories. Dr. Salvador Carriscant, small and broad-shouldered, intense and emotional, absurdly quick to tears for an adult male, arrogant and impatient, strident in the pursuit of his own bizarre interests . . . Annoyingly, I was beginning to feel I had known him for years.

FOURTEEN

M Y MOTHER AND I ate lunch at the Spanish Kitchen, the one on Beverly Boulevard. There was nothing out of the ordinary in our meeting like this: we would lunch together every two months or so, often at her prompting. I am sure she was curious about me, about my life, but she was far too polite ever to ask direct questions. But often I sensed her scrutinizing me, as if minute changes in my physical appearance—a different shade of lipstick, a new blouse, a wave in my hair—would provide her with clues as to who I was seeing, whether I was content or not, how life in general was going. They were amiable encounters, these, as we were fond of each other and, more important, we respected each other, and in addition my mother seemed altogether more spirited and self-possessed away from Rudolf's booming geniality. We passed our two hours together with no sense of strain or forced good manners. She liked spicy peppery food—which Rudolf could not stomach and which she never cooked at home—so we tended to eat in Spanish or Mexican restaurants where she would consume *menudo* or *chiles verdes rellenos* with evident pleasure. Not for the first time I wondered where she had acquired this taste—in the East perhaps? Along with me, a legacy of her short marriage to Hugh Paget?

Toward the end of our meal I asked her casually if she would do me a favor, nothing special, but one that might involve her sitting with me in the car for an hour or two. I was deliberately vague and unspecific.

"Well, sure," she said. "Is it something to do with your lawsuit?"

"Yes and no," I half lied. I had told her all about Meyersen and his devious ways over lunch, trying not to let too triumphant a note enter my voice. George Fugal had telephoned me at eleven-thirty that morning to say that the Luard contract had been signed and the sale had gone through. Kay Fischer Inc. had made an operating profit of $21,058 on its first property deal and deeds were being drawn up for the next development on the new Silver Lake site we had found, a two-acre plot that, at a pinch, could take two houses or a bungalow court. I already felt my animus against Meyersen beginning to subside, diminishing, distancing itself in history.

We drove back down Beverly toward downtown and the tall white tower of the city hall. On Olive I parked the car obliquely across the road from Carriscant's lodging house and my mother and I each smoked a Picayune as we settled down to wait.

After about thirty-five minutes I saw Carriscant walking down Olive on our side of the road from the direction of the funicular. He was wearing a fawn raincoat I had not seen before and carried a brown paper parcel under his arm. I let him draw nearer and, as he was about to cross the road, I said to my mother in as idle a voice as possible: "That man crossing the road ... Have you ever seen him before?"

My eyes never left her face.

She peered at him.

Carriscant paused at the lodging house's front steps, which had its usual complement of lounging Filipinos, and obligingly removed his hat while he chatted with them.

"No," she said slowly, "I don't think so. He looks a bit like that old actor fellow, you know the one."

I saw nothing, not a tremor, not a blink, not a tautening anywhere. She turned to meet my gaze.

"Who is he?" she said.

"I think he might be a private detective, hired by Meyersen. I wondered if he had come by you, maybe, snooping around, asking questions . . ."

"No, definitely not." She smiled. "Is that it? Can you drop me off at Bullock's?"

FIFTEEN

I STAND INSIDE 2265 Micheltoreno. It is built now, done, finished to all intents and purposes. The afternoon sun shines obliquely through the plate glass of the west wall, casting a sharply defined shadow on the smooth ocher stucco. I sense the house's space gather about me, its stacked and assembled volumes of air boxed and confined by their particular materials. The simple trellis on the yard, the planes of the walls of glass and abutting walls of stucco, the roof garden defined by its two oak beams, the way the corridor slides into the courtyard volume that in turn slips down the stairs to the gravel terrace below the western façade. Calmness and order. Absence of clutter, a cool world of clean edges, exact angles, and all designed by me. For a moment, as I stand here in the empty room, a peace descends on me. I think this is as close to happiness as I can manage these days.

MY MOTHER'S LIE was good. In fact its skillfulness was nothing short of brilliant. What tremendous shock she concealed, what massive turbulence of emotion she hid beneath a surface of total calm and placidity. Her only mistake was to forget about natural curiosity. When your daughter informs you that a business rival may have hired a private detective to spy on her, you do not immediately ask to be dropped off at a department store.

Salvador Carriscant's wild and incredible assertion was now taking on the lineaments of incontrovertible fact. With a strange mixture of reluctance and relief, of puzzlement and pleasure, I had to admit that what I had half suspected all along was now looking like a biographical certainty: Salvador Carriscant was my father.

SIXTEEN

*L*ARRY RUGOLA, freshly but crudely shaved, the blood still gleaming on a bad razor nick below his ear, collected me from my apartment at 7:00 a.m. and we drove up to the new site at Silver Lake. The plot was another steep one (I could not afford flat ground yet) and had a distant view of the reservoir. A short new concrete spur road had been laid to open up this flank of the hill and at its foot was a chain-link fence with a padlocked gate. There were lurid realtors' plac-ards tied to the fence advertising the lots for sale, declaiming LAKE VIEW! in excited letters. It was true: in the clear morning light I could just see a stripe of gray water between the live oaks and the pepper trees.

Larry unlocked the gate and we paced about the two acres with the plans and a measuring tape. I turned and looked back up at the roadway: you would be able to step right off it onto the roof of any single-story bungalow, such was the incline.

I called to Larry, who was pacing solemnly about count-ing his big strides: "We could cantilever out, instead of cutting in."

"It don't come cheap."

"Say, what about duplex? Duplex apartments, a row of three, maybe four?"

Larry wandered toward me, winding in his tape measure.

"It's a thought," he said. "That way you could go with the gradient."

"Living rooms on top, bedrooms below. Step it down and you've got a deck on top of the bedroom roof."

"With a lake view, even."

We set about measuring again with renewed fervor. The plot was an odd fan shape, splaying out at the foot of the hill. We pushed our way through the sage and wild laurel bushes to the bottom of the slope, where the ground dropped away into a vegetation-choked arroyo. The plots on either side were still vacant, but through a line of trees on the left came the echoey sound of hammering.

"You'll get a lot of extra ground in front," Larry said.

"So we landscape it, charge a premium."

"Sounds good to me."

We relocked the gate and drove up the spur to Ivanhoe.

"Our street got a name yet? How about Lakeview?" Larry said.

"Lago Vista's better. The 'Lago Vista site.' I like it." I tapped Larry's shoulder. "Turn right here, Larry, let's go to Micheltoreno, I want to see the old house."

We weaved west until we hit Angus and then turned south on Micheltoreno. I felt a pleasant shifting in my gut, an old unfamiliar sensation—happiness, excitement. The naming of the street, saying "the old house": it spoke of progress, the development of a body of work, an avenue of bright tomorrows.

We came over a rise on Micheltoreno and there was number 2265. A thin crane stood above it and hanging from its arm was a flat section of roof being guided up and away by a gang of men in green overalls. A green bulldozer was backing away from the completely flattened porch area, snorting diesel fumes, and other men were collecting the solid timber spars from what remained of the roof trellis in the sheltered yard.

Two dump trucks were parked at the curb and on their sides was written JOHN DEXTER DEMO-LITION.

"Holy shit!" Larry Rugola said, stopping the car, his eyes wide and uncomprehending. "Holy fuckin' shit."

We ran toward the house, where a man in green overalls tried to stop us from approaching as the roof section was swung over our heads toward the truck. From inside the house came the groaning rip of chain saws and the tearing, nail-popping sound of jimmies being enthusiastically employed. From the opening where the front door had been, two men emerged carrying the bath and behind them followed three men in business suits and aluminum hard hats, handkerchiefs held to their noses against the dust. One man removed his helmet and a hank of thin blond hair was caught by a breeze.

"Ah, Mrs. Fischer," Eric Meyersen said. "Always premature. I wanted you to see the vacant lot. I was going to call. I hope you took a photographic record."

The crane swung around to collect another roof panel.

"Where's Mrs. Luard?" I said, staring at him, trying not to look around me.

"I think she's up for a part at Metro," Meyersen said. "Talented lady. Charges a modest fee."

Then I stepped forward to take a swing at him, claw the pale eyes out of that smiling face, but Larry Rugola caught me by the elbow.

"Come on, Mrs. Fischer. Leave the bastard."

We walked quickly toward the car.

"Don't worry," Meyersen shouted after me. "We're going to build another house here. Very similar design, in fact. Different architect, that's all."

We drove away down Micheltoreno. Larry was laboriously and vehemently calling Meyersen every obscenity he could summon to mind. His dogged cursing was obscured by a muted roaring in my ears, my boiling blood, I supposed, a foaming red surf, heating my arteries, scalding my internal organs with its furious rage. The noise dimmed eventually, or was drowned by the traffic, as we turned west on Sunset and headed thoughtlessly on out, aiming somewhere for the distant sunlit ocean.

SEVENTEEN

CARRISCANT TURNED AWAY from the window. Through its oval I could see the studded silver wing and the engine nacelle and half the blurred disk of the propellor hauling us through this thin high air. We were flying Transcontinental and Western's "Sky Chief" service to New York. Somewhere below us was Montana. We had eighteen hours to go.

"It's quite extraordinary," Carriscant said, palms patting the armrests of his seat, then gesturing up the aisle at the other passengers and the neat stewardess pouring out cups of coffee. "Here we are, sitting in an armchair being served a beverage ... To think we can do all this, in such a short time, up in the air like this. Unbelievable. I feel I've been given a mighty dunt on the head and woken up in a different world. Rip van Winkle isn't in it."

" 'Dunt'? What's a dunt?"

He chuckled. He was in a fine mood, clearly. "It's a Scottish word. Means a 'blow,' a 'hit.' My father used it."

I sensed one of my rare opportunities approaching: he seemed as if he might be receptive to a few questions.

"Your father was Scottish?"

"Yes. From a place called Dundee. His name was Archibald Carriscant."

"Is Carriscant a Scottish name, then?"

"It's the name of a small village in Angus. There's a River Carriscant, too, tributary of the Tweed."

"So you're Scottish by origin," I said slowly, taking all this in. Angus. Tweed.

He looked at me carefully, not fooled by my ingenuousness, stroking the cleft in his chin with his middle finger, pondering whether to answer me. I wondered for my part whether he might be thinking up some intriguing falsehood, to lead me on a little further.

"I'm half Scottish, actually," he said. "And a quarter Spanish and a quarter Filipino."

I hid my intense surprise at this news. "Ah. Hence the Salvador."

"Exactly. Do you think you could ask the young lady if I could have some coffee?"

FROM ONE POINT of view it had been among the easiest decisions of my life—he was my father and he had asked me; from another the most unconsidered and spontaneous. But Eric Meyersen and his wanton, brutal destruction of my house had been a powerful propellant. When George Fugal told me I could do nothing, that Meyersen was completely within his legal rights, I knew that I had to leave the city for a while, escape the shame, leave behind the focus of my anger and bitterness. I needed time, above all.

So, when Salvador Carriscant came calling again with his now alluring proposition of a trip to Europe he found me teary and weak and easily persuaded. He put his arms around me, patted me on the back and muttered consoling words in my ear. "There, there, Kay . . . Don't worry, all this will pass." I held him close and blurted out my woes, told him about Meyersen's betrayal and my impotence. "Come with me, Kay," he said. "Just the two of us, you and me. Take some time off, think things through, then come back and put the world to rights again." For once this was what I wanted to hear and for once I wanted someone else to steer the course of my life for a while. I was tired of standing up for myself . . . You must know that feeling when you long for someone else to take responsibility. So my father did just that and asked me to come away with him. And I was glad to go. What else could I have done?

I put all plans for the Lago Vista apartments to one side, told Larry Rugola I was taking a vacation—he understood— and spent some of the profits from the sale of 2265 to embark on this "quest." We were sailing from New York to Lisbon two days hence on the SS *Herzog*, of the Hamburg-American line, courtesy of Eric Meyersen. I tried to draw some satisfaction from this but failed. In the days since the house had been destroyed my spirits had never been lower. Carriscant, contrarily, was positively rejuvenated by the news of our journey, almost intolerably jaunty and good-humored. I was determined, however, that he would not keep me in the dark any further, that I would not be pacified by dribs and drabs of information delivered when the whim took him. As I was doing what he had asked of me I insisted that the partnership had to be honored. Candor was to be the watchword of our association and before we left I made one sole and unmovable proviso: he had to tell me everything, what all this was about, who this diplomat's wife was and what mystery was about to be unveiled in Lisbon, should we find her there. I reminded him now of his obligation.

"Oh, I'll tell you," he said. "It's quite a story. By the time we reach Lisbon you'll know everything I do."

"Right," I said. "Let's start with the family tree."

EIGHTEEN

*T*HIS IS WHAT he told me. (I am summarizing his rambling, wistful account.) His father's name was Archibald—Archibald Muir Carriscant—an engineer, one of that worldwide diaspora of Scots professionals and in his early forties when he first arrived in the Philippines—(then a colony of Spain)—in 1863, sent by his Hong Kong firm of Melhuish & Cobb to supervise the rebuilding of the southern breakwater that formed the entrance to Manila's docks on the Pasig River. When that task was over he was transferred to the construction of the narrow-gauge steam railway that linked the quaysides with the warehouses and storage sheds behind the customhouse. Melhuish & Cobb won the contract for the construction of the Manila-Dagupan Railway from the English syndicate that was financing it and the rest of Archibald Carriscant's working life was spent traveling up and down the hundred miles of country that lay between Manila Bay and the Lingayen Gulf planning culverts and embankments, cuttings and bridges. A tall, pale, shy man, bald since his early twenties, Archibald Carriscant had resigned himself, with few regrets, to a life of permanent bachelorhood. But during a time when he was positioning the goods sidings at Tarlac he was befriended by a local *mestizo* landowner, Don Carlos Ocampo. In the month he stayed at Don Carlos's summer estate near Tarlac he was most surprised to discover that his timid, almost imperceptible wooing of Don Carlos's eldest daughter, Juliana, proved successful. A year later they married and moved into a large house Don Carlos provided for them in Intramuros, the old walled city in the heart of urban Manila. In 1870 Archibald Carriscant was appointed area manager for Melhuish & Cobb's operations in Luzon and a son, Salvador, was born to Juliana. Salvador, an only child, intelligent and lively, was educated at the Municipal School for Boys and went on to study medicine at the University of Santo Tomás. In 1893, at his ailing father's request, he left for Europe to complete his medical studies and take a degree in surgery at the medical school of the University of Glasgow. Archibald Carriscant died while his son was away in Scotland. Salvador Carriscant returned to set up practice in Manila in 1897.

"And shortly after, I met your mother," Carriscant said.

"In Manila?" All these revelations were confusing me.

"Of course. Where did you think?"

"It doesn't matter." We were strolling back to our hotel from a chophouse on Forty-first Street.

"And then the war started," Carriscant said with a shrug.

"What war?"

"The war between the USA and the Philippines."

I decided that was enough questions for this evening.

IN THE MORNING, after I had visited the Portuguese consulate to have a visa stamped in my passport (Carriscant, being British, did not require one), I visited a bookshop to try and discover more about this American-Filipino conflict but could find nothing. However, in a small volume entitled *A Pocket History of the United States of America, 1492–1930* I came across the following paragraph and copied it down.

One consequence of the Spanish-American War was that the Philippine Islands were liberated from the yoke of imperial power when Commodore George Dewey destroyed the Spanish fleet in Manila Bay on May 1, 1898. Filipino rebels, led by Emilio Aguinaldo, who had been in revolt against their Hispanic masters for several years, saw the Spanish-American War as an opportunity to declare their independence and form a Philippine republic. When they discovered that the United States proposed merely to substitute its rule for Spain's, the *insurrectos*, as they were known, promptly attacked their former liberators on February 4, 1899 and laid siege to Manila. The subsequent war lasted three years and was only concluded on the capture of the rebel leader, Aguinaldo, in 1902. This war, one of the most prolonged and deadly in the annals of empire, exerted a high toll. Some 230,000 men, women and children perished, of which 4,234 were brave American soldiers, and the cost to the nation's fisc was an enormous six hundred million dollars.

Archibald and Juliana Carriscant and their son Salvador . . . Commodore George Dewey and the battle of Manila Bay . . . The capture of Emilio Aguinaldo . . . Six hundred million dollars of American taxpayers' money spent on a forgotten and bloody colonial adventure half a world away . . . What did all this have to do with me? I wondered how it could possibly explain my journey to Lisbon with a man who claimed to be my father in search of a woman whose face I knew from a torn-out page in a 1927 pictorial magazine.

WE HAD a rare and gratifyingly tranquil voyage on the S.S. *Herzog*. The Atlantic swell remained glassy and docile as we cruised eastward through mild hazy sunshine, the fraying rope of smoke from our two tall stacks trailing behind us as if reluctant to be dispersed on the gentle oceanic breezes.

During our ten-day journey Carriscant was as good as his word—he told me everything, and answered every interrogation I put to him without demur, however embarrassing my inquiry or however damaging it might prove to the portrayal of his character and motives. As you will see, his candor was impressive. I kept copious notes of everything he told me and wherever possible attempted to catch him out on corroboratory details. In the relaying of his story I have allowed myself some of the license of a writer of fiction, have embellished it with information I obtained later and with facts gleaned from my own researches. But in the end this is Salvador Carriscant's story and I have had to trust the teller, but what follows is, I believe, as close to the truth as anyone could come.

MANILA,

1902

TONGUE

A CCORDING TO his best recollection, on the day of the first killing Dr. Salvador Carriscant—the most celebrated surgeon in the Philippines—suffering from a mild headache, left his house and decided, as was his occasional habit, to walk to work. Nobody of any importance or self-regard, with even the slightest modicum of self-esteem, walked in Manila in those days, but Dr. Carriscant relished the short stroll from his fine house on the Calle de la Victoria to the San Jerónimo Hospital, not only for the pleasant sensation of libertarian fellow feeling it provoked in him but also because the interlude allowed him to calm down, to forget the irritations and frustrations of his home life and clear his mind for the exhilarating but complicated business of the day's work waiting for him in the surgical wards.

The San Jerónimo Hospital in Manila was a comparatively recent building, having been completed in 1878 and renovated again nearly twenty years later, when the electric light was installed. It was to some extent modeled, so Carriscant had been informed by an elderly member of the hospital's board of governors, on the Palazzo Salimbeni in Siena, and certainly the street-front façade bore some resemblance to a crude quattrocento building, made of well-cut adobe brick, with a simple hipped roof of terra-cotta tiles, much overgrown with ferns, moss and other greenery. There was a very high arched gateway with heavy wooden doors and a row of small square windows set in the walls above, bestowing a solid and uncompromising character, as if the place might have to be defended in times of insurrection or be called on to do duty as a prison. Inside, however, was a wide paved courtyard with arched cloisters on three sides and set behind that was a mature walled garden and arboretum crisscrossed by graveled paths. Various consulting rooms for physicians, administrative offices and the dispensary led off the cloistered arcades, but the operating theaters, and there were two of them, were each contained in two stubby projecting wings, east and west, on either side of the garden, almost as if they had been added as an afterthought. Dr. Carriscant's theater was in the east wing. The medical director of the San Jerónimo Hospital, Dr. Isidro Cruz, practiced his art in the western projection.

The design of the San Jerónimo was simple and, as long as the number of patients did not grow too rapidly, as they did when the cholera and smallpox epidemics erupted, was quite effective. Patients first visited the physicians on the ground floor, who then, where necessary, referred them to the surgeons. Postoperative care took place in the wards that occupied the floor above. The one disadvantage of the place was that there were no laboratories or dissecting rooms and the morgue was a little on the small side. Consequently any anatomical or experimental work had to be carried out at the San Lázaro Hospital or in private premises. The reputation of the San Jerónimo had been high, almost from its inception, owing to the celebrated dexterity of Dr. Cruz (who on one day in 1882 had performed over three dozen amputations), but it had been augmented in recent years as a result of Salvador Carriscant's return from Scotland in 1897 and his introduction of Listerism and the latest surgical methods and the remarkable success rate these innovations had produced. The hospital board had increased his basic salary four times and had awarded him the honorific title of surgeon-in-chief, a move that Dr. Cruz had vehemently and publicly protested and which had set the seal on and, as it were, formalized the doctors' personal animosity toward each other. In public the two men maintained an air of courteous but professional reserve, but everyone knew that Dr. Cruz detested Dr. Carriscant and everything he stood for medically. The feelings were reciprocal: to Cruz, Carriscant was an obsessed faddist and heedless experimenter; to Carriscant, Cruz was an antediluvian sawbones cum sinister circus performer, and so on.

Dr. Salvador Carriscant passed through the wide arched gateway, acknowledging the respectful salute of the porter on duty. His headache was easing, he was happy to note, and he was looking forward to the first operation of the day, the extirpation of a large tumor from an adolescent boy's tongue. He was planning to make a new form of incision, one that would allow him to sew up the wound rather than sear it, as was normal, in a way that should allow the lad to speak, after a fashion, once he had healed. Such extirpations were Dr. Cruz's stock-in-trade, it took him a matter of seconds, he boasted, like lancing a boil, but Manila was full of mumbling semimutes with needlessly stumpy tongues as a consequence of Cruz's heavy-handed speediness. If that day's operation proved a success it would further undermine Cruz's unwarranted eminence: the medical director of the San Jerónimo Hospital would have even less work to do.

Carriscant crossed the courtyard toward his consulting rooms, noting that the waiting room was already full and there were half a dozen people sitting on a wooden form outside. He glanced over at Cruz's equivalent suite of rooms and saw that the main door was closed and the shutters unopened. Cruz's patients had declined steadily in the years since Carriscant had arrived, and now it was either ignorance or agonized desperation that led anyone to demand a consultation with the old surgeon. He was a dying breed, was Cruz, Carriscant reflected, a historical curiosity, an emblem of the bad old days of the profession, but he was good with the knife, Carriscant had to admit, and his eye was impeccably sure. He was fast, Cruz— damned fast. The war had seen a surge in demand for his expertise—he had carried out hundreds of amputations—but since it had ended, business had slackened again, and now the old man spent much of his time on his large ranch at Flores and in the personal laboratories which he had had constructed there and where he kept his hand in by operating on monkeys and dogs. Carriscant never forgot the first and almost the last operation he had performed with Cruz. Cruz had watched him washing his hands prior to entering the theater. "You prefer to wash your hands before the operation I see, Dr. Carriscant," Cruz had commented acidly. "I prefer to wash mine after- ward." On his rounds of the wards too his brutal frankness was legendary: "That's one of the worst cancers I've seen," he would tell some suffering soul cowering in his bed. Or, "The leg will have to go, off at the hip too, let's not take any chances." Or, "Conditions such as yours, my dear fellow, are inevitably fatal. I doubt you'll be seeing the outside of this hos- pital again."

Dr. Carriscant was greeted by his secretary, Señora Diaz, a small, homely, efficient woman with an unfortunate profusion of facial hair, and glanced through the day's schedule she had prepared for him. The boy with the tumor was already here and prepared. He had time briefly to visit the patients in his ward before he started work.

"Is Dr. Quiroga here?" Carriscant asked.

"Yes. He went to the dispensary."

Pantaleon Quiroga was his anesthetist and his best friend. He was a young man, in his late twenties, a Filipino—an *ilustrado*, as the educated classes were known—from southern Luzon who had been educated in Manila and who had studied medicine in Madrid and later Berlin. Like Carriscant, he had become enthused with the latest developments in surgical practice and had returned to Manila determined to provide his people with the benefits of medical science. He was not a natural surgeon, however—he lacked the mysterious "touch," that gift one possessed and that could not be acquired—and it was Carriscant who had persuaded him to concentrate on anesthesia. Working as a team at the San Jerónimo, the two of them had developed an understanding that was unique in Filipino medicine. Because of his training Quiroga could also assist at the more complicated operations if required—it was like having four hands, Carriscant said—and his skill with the chloroform bottle was the equal of any more exalted anesthetist in Baltimore or Paris, Carriscant maintained.

There was a soft rap at the door and Pantaleon Quiroga came in. He was already wearing his white surgical gown and carried his skullcap in his hand. He was a painfully thin young man and tall, unusually so for a Filipino, a good head higher than Carriscant, with a neat mustache and melancholy eyes. He was unmarried and lived alone (his parents were deceased) outside Intramuros in Santa Cruz, whence he traveled each day by horse team. Carriscant often found himself wondering what Pantaleon did with his considerable salary and the supplementary fees that were charged on his behalf. He supposed that much of it went back to the family in Luzon—the uncles and aunts, the grandmother, the endless cousins—certainly Pantaleon lived very frugally as a result.

They shook hands warmly, as they did at the beginning of each working day.

"The dough is in the oven," Pantaleon said. "Ready to bake."

"Have I time to do my rounds?"

"I think the poor fellow will have a fit. The sooner the better, you know."

"Let's go, then." He glanced at Señora Diaz's list on his desk: two amputations—a hand, then a leg at the knee—a strangulated hernia and a vaginal fistula. He could do the amputations before luncheon; the hernia and the fistula would take up the afternoon. He followed Pantaleon's tall frame down the corridor to the preparation room, noticing that the young man's hair was thinning rapidly at the crown. He tried to imagine Pantaleon bald and for some reason the notion filled him with a sharp and sudden sadness. He needed something more in his life, did Pantaleon, something beyond his work at San Jerónimo—a love affair, a fiancée, a wife, a family . . .

Carriscant removed his coat, put on a freshly laundered white gown, changed his shoes and washed his hands with a powerful carbolic soap before going into the operating theater. Here the smell of disinfectant made his eyes tingle as he greeted his nurses, Nurse Santos and Nurse Arrieta, and glanced around the room. The wooden floor was scrubbed to a pale gray; every surface was clean, gleaming and moist. A faint hum emanated from the big electric arc light mounted above the operating table and there was a tinny rattle of instruments vibrating in the steam sterilizers set on tin tables to one side. He took a discreet deep breath: already he could feel that delicious weakening sensation spreading upward from the soles of his feet, a loosening, a slackening in his bowels, the hairs pricking on the nape of his neck.

The patient was a young Chinese boy, fourteen years old, son of a wealthy merchant from Cavite. He leaned back against the steeply angled table, angled so his tongue could better fall forward, the tumor clearly visible, the size of a small apple, forcing his lips apart, making him look imbecilic. There was sweat on his forehead and his eyes flicked toward Carriscant and then flicked away again.

Carriscant uttered some token words of reassurance and

turned to his instruments as Pantaleon fitted the gauze mask over the boy's mouth and nose.

"I see the bridge is down at Jacinto," Pantaleon said.

"I had terrible trouble getting in this morning," Nurse Arrieta said, handing Carriscant a scalpel. "Terrible."

"You should take a *barca* to work. Have you got that clamp?"

"I can't see Nurse Santos in a *barca*," Pantaleon said. "She doesn't want to drown before she gets married."

"Dr. Quiroga, do you mind!" Nurse Santos was portly. There was a lot of banter in the theater about her size. Everyone laughed. The Chinese boy looked at their grinning mouths and shaking shoulders.

"Don't fit the mouth wedge before Pantaleon knocks him out," Carriscant said. "Do your stuff, Doctor."

Still chuckling, Pantaleon began to drip chloroform from the calibrated glass drop bottle onto the gauze mask, holding it upright from time to time to check the reading. When the boy lost consciousness the two nurses held his head forward and forced his jaws apart. Carriscant fitted a clamp just behind the tumor, turned it tight and drew the tongue as far out of the mouth as possible. Nurse Santos took the handle from him, pulling on the tongue firmly. Pantaleon touched the boy's eye to check the lid reflex. He opened the eye with thumb and forefinger: the size of the pupil would tell him to what extent the nervous system was depressed. He nodded his approval.

Carriscant felt his breathing slow and his brain clear as he paused for a moment before exchanging his scalpel for a smaller one with a long fine blade. After all these years, all these operations, the feeling never altered: his senses felt fresh, newly minted, acutely aware; his consciousness seemed suddenly highly attuned, not simply in an extra appreciation of the physicality of the objects in the room—the spangling glare of chrome, the perfect fan of the boy's eyelashes resting against his lower lid, the frayed cuff of Pantaleon's right sleeve—but also in a preternatural understanding of the other human beings present at this moment. He sensed the unrelenting melancholy in Pantaleon's soul as if it had been his own; he felt the weight and softness of Nurse Santos's breasts pressing against the starched blue cotton of the smock she was wearing; he shared in the weariness of Nurse Arrieta, who had been up throughout the night tending to her fractious and incontinent father-in-law ... All these emotions, all these sensations were present to him, gifted to him, flowed into his all-encompassing and receptive mind and were logged and acknowledged. I know you all, his silent gaze said to them, I know your suffering humanity, your anxieties, your needs, your itches, your callouses, your aching backs, your tiredness ... I know. I *understand*. I understand everything.

He raised the scalpel, felt its small weight, his eye caught the gleam of its thin beveled blade. Nurse Santos, unbidden, moved an enamel bowl beneath the boy's chin. With three careful swift strokes Carriscant cut through the fungiform papillae to the muscle tissue beneath, slicing back at an angle of forty-five degrees toward the throat. Blood welled from the partially severed tongue. Nurse Arrieta applied a swab. He lifted the clamp, revealing the underside, and he cut again, making a lateral fork in the tongue so that a longer lower flap was formed. The tumor fell dully into the bowl. Nurse Arrieta handed him the needle and gut. Antiseptic fluid was poured over the wound and he sewed the two short flaps of the tongue together.

He turned away, his brow dry, his throat parched, the fingers of his right hand slick with the brightness of the boy's blood. He moved to a sink at the side of the room and ran water over his bloodied fingers. There were fat spots of blood on his tunic too, he noted. He removed the gown slowly and dropped it in the wicker basket by the door thinking, suddenly, of Cruz and how he still persisted in operating in a black frock coat, its reveres and front encrusted with dried pus and blood like some obscene blazon honoring his trade.

A rare and untypical nausea made his gorge rise. The tongue was such a curious part of the body, a flickering pulsing muscle with its two senses—taste and touch—a kind of amphibian organ planted in the throat like an anemone anchored to its rock, unsure whether it should be inside or outside the body. When he cut, it seemed to flinch—

He stopped himself: why was he thinking like this? He felt his keening headache return and with it the memory of its cause, the brief intense argument he had had with Annaliese that morning. "Work, work, work," she had cried at him as he dressed for work. "Why get married, why bother having me in your life? . . ." "Why indeed," he had shouted back, "if this is meant to be wedded bliss." Stupid, purblind woman.

The porters wheeled away the still comatose Chinese boy and he and Pantaleon moved next door to change back into their clothes.

"What do you think?" Pantaleon asked. "It seemed to go well."

"We'll see how it heals. At least he's got some tongue left."

"Cruz will go mad if it works," Pantaleon smiled. "Madder."

"If it works we photograph the next one. Write it up."

"The Carriscant glossectomy."

Señora Diaz interrupted their self-satisfied chuckles to tell them that someone from the governor's office was looking for Dr. Cruz. Carriscant shrugged on his coat, straightened his necktie and walked up the corridor to his office, rubbing his hands together vigorously—the carbolic in the soap dried the skin and caused flaking at the knuckles. He opened his office door and a man in military uniform—khaki, leather-belted—rose to his feet from the chair in front of the desk and saluted.

He was portly, running to fat, and his uniform was tight across his belly. He had a high forehead and thinning hair, and a neatly trimmed wide mustache that effectively divided his face in two.

"Dr. Carriscant, thank you for seeing me," he said. "I'm Paton Bobby, chief of constabulary."

(It was after he had described this operation that I asked him what it felt like to cut into living human flesh and the incident with the scalpel took place. He wiped away the smear of blood on his forearm with a napkin, then smiled at my distressed face. "It's nothing," he said, "the tiniest scratch." He then told me about an old surgeon he had known who routinely tested the blade of a scalpel prior to an operation on the palp of his left thumb. "It's not a dagger or a machete," he said, taking the scalpel from me and resheathing it in its leather sleeve. "Think of it as a precision instrument, something that parts tissue rather than cuts it.")

THE FIRST BODY

D<small>R. CARRISCANT STOOD</small> beside Paton Bobby in the rice field looking down at the naked half-submerged body of what had been an eighteen-year-old Kansas militiaman.

"That is no fucking gugu," Bobby said, a frown pulling his eyebrows together and cabling his forehead. "In fact that is just about the whitest man I've ever seen."

There was a peculiar bluish, icy tone to the body's general pallor, it was true. The fat on the buttocks seemed to shine through the skin like ice cream wrapped in parchment, Carriscant thought, quite pleased with his simile.

"That's because we're standing in a solution of his blood," Carriscant pointed out. The body lay in the center of a dark brown stain, still spreading, stirred by the sloshing of the men's boots. Carriscant leaned over: there was a pestilential buzzing of insects and the solitary eye that was above the surface of the water was dark with flies feeding on its jelly.

"Has anybody moved it?"

"The farmer who found him turned him over. Got a look," Bobby said. "That's how we knew we needed a doctor."

"What about Dr. Wieland?" Dr. Wieland was acting medical superintendent to the U.S. Governor. Carriscant had met him several times, a genial, superannuated alcoholic whose medical knowledge was about as far advanced as Cruz's.

(93)

"Dr. Wieland is . . . unwell today," Bobby said, half concealing a smile. "He suggested we consult Dr. Cruz." He shrugged. "He wasn't there. But we are very happy with you. No disrespect."

"None taken, Mr. Bobby, none taken . . . May I look?"

Carriscant turned the body over gently with the toe of his boot; it rolled easily, buoyant on the brown water. The flies rose up with an irate hum. He fanned them away from his face.

There was a long inverted L-shaped wound carved into the torso, and laced like a football. The long cut extended from the breastbone to the genitalia. The short arm of the wound ran at right angles across the left side of the chest, two inches below the nipple. The wound had been effectively and tightly sewn together with string. The flies resettled and began to investigate.

"It's quite neat."

"You can see why we thought a surgeon should look at it."

"Who is he?"

"We think he's Private Ephraim Ward. Absent without leave for three days. I'll get one of his unit over to identify him. May we use your morgue?"

Carriscant was somewhat surprised at this request. "Well, yes, I suppose so, but isn't this a government matter?"

"Sure as shit it is, Doc. But it's also a Paton Bobby matter. This fellow didn't prick his finger with a sewing needle." Bobby grinned, after a fashion: only his mouth moved beneath the wide mustache, his eyes stayed watchful, alert. "I get to say where this stiff goes."

They waded back to the roadway. A few young American soldiers stood by the carriages that had brought them to the paddy field. They slouched in their loose baggy uniforms, the blue shirts over the khaki trousers dark with sweat. Sullen and nervous, they held their Krags needlessly at the ready, as if in-

surgents were about to spring from the roadside ditch. Bobby
ordered them to collect the body and offered Carriscant a
small cigar from a pewter tin. Carriscant declined, stamped the
mud off his boots and looked around him: the paddy field was
near Paco, a village a mile or so southeast of Manila. Everywhere were the remains of old trenches and earthworks overgrown with grass and straggly *milim* bushes. This had been the
American front line when the rebels attacked in 1899.
Carriscant remembered the day well, standing on his *azotea* in
the city, with a cup of tea in his hand, listening to the mum-
bled boom of artillery, feeling the air shiver, setting the dust
motes dancing to the distant percussion, the teaspoon rattling
on the porcelain.

He turned to Bobby, who was blowing on the end of his cigar, puffing it orange.

"You do know where we are . . ."

"Yes," Bobby said. "I just wonder if it's significant."

PRIVATE EPHRAIM WARD LAY supine on the marble-
topped examination table in the San Jerónimo morgue, free of
flies at last, the blaze from the lamps above him enhancing his
remarkable bloodless lucency. Carriscant had told Bobby that
he was not prepared, nor really qualified, to perform an au-
topsy. Bobby demurred politely, arguing that Carriscant was
probably the most qualified person in the Philippine archipel-
ago to do just that, but in any event he would be more than
happy with an expert's investigation of the wound and perhaps
some hazarded interpretation of what exactly had occurred.

Carriscant inspected the sutures. Sailmaker's twine, he
would guess, and sewn with a sailmaker's needle. Or a leather-
worker's needle. Manila was full of people who could do a job
such as this: anyone who had ever made a jute sack could have
stitched up Ephraim Ward's belly. Carriscant began to snip his

way up the length of the incision, turning left at the breast-bone. Here he saw, as the lips of the wound yielded beneath his shears, a great clotting of blood. He fitted a pair of retractors and held the wound open, cleaning and scraping away the black muddy residue of the clot. He saw very soon that the heart had been torn, badly gashed.

He opened wide the wound at the abdomen, revealing the vermiculate coils of the intestines and the other internal organs, strangely reduced, washed by their long immersion in the paddy field, isolated somewhat in the stomach cavity like mean portions of food in a too large bowl. He completed a swift check: everything appeared to be there, if not exactly in order. So, Private Ward had been stabbed in the heart, between the sixth and seventh rib and the entry wound had been temporarily disguised by this subsequent mutilation. It made no sense to him at all.

Bobby called round later that afternoon to hear his conclusions. Carriscant sat behind his desk as he relayed them, while Bobby paced to and fro, smoking another small ill-lit cheroot, occasionally setting a big haunch down on the desk corner and letting the freed boot swing as he listened.

"You're not Spanish, are you?" Bobby said suddenly.

"No. Well, my mother is half Spanish, my father was British."

"So, you have British nationality."

"Yes . . . Why do you ask?"

"It makes it easier, when I report to the governor. Especially if we're going to work together."

Carriscant did not respond to this, though he was curious about what manner of collaboration Bobby was talking about, but as collaboration was being mooted he decided to enter into the spirit of the arrangement.

"There was one thing," Carriscant began, slowly. "It was impossible to be sure, but I had the impression that the organs in

the gut—the intestines, liver, kidneys, stomach—had been . . . I
don't know, had been displaced or manipulated."

"I don't follow."

"Have you ever opened a dead body?"

"I came here from the Boxer rebellion," Bobby said. "I've
seen a lot of dead and mangled men."

"Not the same thing. When you open the abdominal lining
and reveal the organs below, you wouldn't believe how"—
Carriscant stopped and searched for a word—"how neatly it all
fits together. How astonishing the design, how compact." He
stood up and clapped his hands on his chest, his side, his belly,
pushing his fingers into his stomach. "They call it a 'trunk'
and the word is apt. Everything is packed in, held. It can move
but it's secure. Everything in its place, working. And the jobs
being done . . . I won't go on, but there was something about
Ward's organs, even though the blood and the fluids were
gone. It didn't look—"

"Someone been poking around, that sort of thing?"

"Possibly."

"Where does that get us?"

"You're the sleuth. I'm just a surgeon."

Bobby had to leave to make his report to the governor. His
own hunch, he told Carriscant, was that Ward had been killed
by a man in his own unit, a fight had gotten out of hand, a
blow had been struck. Filipino insurgents often mutilated their
victims, he said, the guilty party in this case probably wanted
it to seem as if a rebel had done the deed.

"They don't usually mutilate in that fashion," Carriscant
said.

"Sure," Bobby said. "Then *you* go and cut your buddy's
pecker off and stick it in his mouth. Kinda hard. Simpler to
make some, you know, L-shape or something."

"Why sew it up, then?"

"I don't *know*, Carriscant, I don't know," Bobby said, a rasp of irritation in his voice. "Yet . . . I'll try and find out, but we got so many crackers in this army I don't count on being successful."

"Crackers?"

"Southern boys. They all seem to be from Mississippi, or Texas or Kansas. Patriots all. Stick together."

Carriscant smiled. He could see the quality of robust intelligence behind Bobby's vulgar confidence, sense the energies that stirred beneath the corpulent ease.

"I got to go see Governor Taft. Been a big help, Carriscant."

CARRISCANT SHOWED Pantaleon the body in the morgue. They had postponed their fistula operation designated for that afternoon.

"An American?" Pantaleon said dispassionately, walking around to the head. He took hold of it and moved it to and fro, as if to obtain a better angle on the man's slack features. "At least they can't make any reprisals, now."

"They think another American did it." Carriscant told him about Bobby's theory, but Pantaleon seemed uninterested. The dead American soldier seemed to have preoccupied him and he began to tell Carriscant a rambling story he had heard from an uncle about a company of American soldiers who had been pursuing General Elpidio in Batangas. One of the soldiers had fallen into a pit, the base of which had been lined with bamboo spears. In retribution every inhabitant of the nearest two villages—men, women and children—had been shot and their bodies burned.

"I think about two hundred people paid with their lives for that one man's life . . ." He shrugged. "It seems very unfair. I mean—"

"I would rather you didn't talk about it," Carriscant said abruptly. He stood very still, stiffly, like someone who has just put his back out and is terrified to move.

Pantaleon was upset and very apologetic. "I'm so sorry, Salvador," he said. "I forgot. I'm very sorry, please forgive me."

Carriscant recovered himself. "It's been a strange day," he said. "Normally, I'm fine. I think the American—" He stopped talking and managed a kind of smile. "Pantaleon," he said, "could I come home with you? Just for an hour or so. I don't feel ready for work, and—"

"Of course," Pantaleon said, hiding his surprise. "In any case I've been meaning to ask you back for a while now. I've got something I want you to see."

THE *NIPA* BARN

D R. SALVADOR CARRISCANT and Dr. Pantaleon
Quiroga boarded a horse tram at the Plaza Magallanes,
crossed the Pasig at the Bridge of Spain and made their way
toward the suburb of Santa Cruz. The tram was crowded with
indio workers returning from their jobs in the city and Carriscant was conscious of their candid stares as they tried to divine what these two *kastilas* in their suits and ties were doing
on this poor man's mode of transport.

The two men left the tram at Calle Azcarraga and walked to
Pantaleon's house, a two-story adobe and lumber building on
a relatively smart street. Pantaleon occupied half the rooms,
sharing the rest with an American couple, teachers, who were
setting up the reformed educational program at the local
school. They paused only long enough to collect a key and
then set off down a dirt lane through kitchen gardens and out
onto an area of waste ground on the north bank of an *estero*,
one of the Pasig's many meandering arms. Ahead of them was
a line of trees that marked another wormy loop in the river's
progress and over to the left Carriscant could make out the
galvanized iron roofs of Sampaloc. He had not realized Pantaleon lived quite so close to Sampaloc; he filed that piece of information away in his mind.

The afternoon sun was obscured by a layer of hazy clouds
and the heat was going out of the day, and from time to time
the breeze from the south carried the rich yeasty smell from

the San Miguel brewery. Pantaleon was striding out with genuine enthusiasm and Carriscant had to stretch his legs to keep up with him.

They pushed through a gap in a plumbago hedge, and beyond that, on the edge of an elongated meadow of blond grass, he saw a recently built *nipa* barn, unusually broad, its bamboo walls still green and its palm-leaf thatch only partially faded.

"What's this?" Carriscant said.

"It's mine," Pantaleon said. "I had it built. I own this land here." He gestured at the blond meadow stretching in front of them.

Pantaleon unlocked the padlock on the barn doors and swung them open. Carriscant peered into the gloom and saw what he took to be a curious assemblage of wood and wires that was raised from the earth floor on numerous wooden trestles. It looked, at first glance, as if Pantaleon was constructing a giant hollow cross, laid out horizontally, but as his eyes became accustomed to the murky light he began to make out other details that were less easy to explain: various wheels, levers with wires attached to them and what looked like two large bicycle saddles set in tandem. Carriscant wandered around the construction, touching the tightly strung wires, plucking at them with his fingers. It made no sense at all.

"You made this?" he asked Pantaleon.

"Local carpenters. To my specifications."

"A kind of dwelling? A prefabricated shelter?"

Pantaleon laughed, high-pitched, delightedly.

"No, no, no," he said. "You couldn't be more wrong. It's"—he paused for effect—"it's a heavier-than-air flying machine."

CARRISCANT WAS late returning home. After the visit to the *nipa* barn he and Pantaleon had gone to the café opposite the Zorilla Theater in Santa Cruz and drunk a few glasses of

American beer—Schlitz—and Pantaleon had tried to explain the concepts behind the flying machine he was building. Carriscant had been cheered by his friend's excitement and realized he now had the answers to the question he had posed earlier in the day regarding the expenditure of the Quiroga salary. He had taken a *carromato* back to Intramuros and had reached his home long after dark. The wide front door was opened for him by Danil, his cook's wife, whom he asked to bring him some coffee. He passed on through the ground-floor area of the house where, as well as providing room for his servants, his two carriages were stored and his ponies stabled. The taste of beer was still sour in his mouth and he felt a slight tension in his shoulders as he walked up the steps from the interior courtyard to the living quarters on the first floor. Oil lamps burned in the public rooms, their orange glow reflected in the glossy polish of the hardwood floors. At the rear of the house, overlooking the walled garden, was a wide stone patio—the *azotea*—and he could see Annaliese sitting there reading by the fuzzy light of an Aladdin lamp. The night was cool and breezy and from the garden came the guttural croaking of frogs and the monotone *brrrr* of cicadas.

Annaliese looked around as he crossed the living room, the oval disks of her spectacles flashing white for an instant as they caught the light. He kissed her lightly on the forehead and sat down on a rattan chair opposite her, apologizing for his lateness. He explained about the discovery of the murdered American and how his day had been disrupted.

She looked at him evenly, as if he were a witness and she a lawyer assessing the veracity of his evidence.

"Do you want to eat?" she said eventually. "There's some pork left." Her German accent was mild: Carriscant remembered how he had been attracted to it once, how it had seemed exotic and strange, how it had excited him at certain moments.

"No, thanks. I had some beers with Pantaleon. You won't believe what he's—"

"I thought you said this murder business had detained you."

"Well, it did. But then Pantaleon asked me to see this contraption he's building. A flying machine—can you believe it?"

"He's such a child, Pantaleon."

"Don't be ridiculous."

This was the disagreement they had been waiting for, and they had a short and vicious argument about whether it was childish to build a flying machine or inspirational. The barely covert venom in their exchange seemed, paradoxically, to reduce the tension in the air. The animosities had been freed, loosed momentarily; as with a lanced abscess the flow of purulence relieves the pain for a while.

Carriscant's coffee was served and he sipped it slowly, studying his wife's face over the rim of his cup, watching her read. She wore small oval spectacles which had the effect of aging her somewhat, especially as her hair was pulled tight around her head, tucked behind her ears. She had never looked beautiful, he considered, but neither could she be described as plain. There was no feature of her face that could be listed as objectionable, but there was nothing particularly attractive, either. He asked himself, as he often did in the aftermath of one of their arguments, what on earth had made him want to marry her.

Annaliese Leys was the youngest daughter of a German tobacco wholesaler, Gerhardt Leys, who with his brother, Udo, had a small but thriving business in Manila exporting cigars to Europe. Carriscant had met Annaliese at an open-air concert on the Luneta, shortly after his return from his medical studies in Scotland in 1897. She had seemed to him petite and lively and intelligent, and—more relevantly—she reminded him acutely of a girl he had met and silently yearned for in Edinburgh one summer, where he had spent a damp and lonely vacation wandering the wide beaches at Musselburgh and trying vainly to master the secrets of the game of golf. He and Annaliese had been married within a year, but shortly after that her mother died and her father, whose health had been affected by the tragedy, sold up and returned with the rest of his family to Bremen. It was then that their marriage began to run into difficulties, perhaps because she was on her own for the first time in her life, perhaps because she was grieving, but there had been, Carriscant reckoned, a perceptible hardening in her personality from that date on. The warmth began to ebb from her.

They had made no private acknowledgment of this distancing, and to the outside world all was well. Annaliese worked part-time for the bishop of Manila, assisting with the accounts of the cathedral school (she had a good head for figures) and generally participating in diocesal matters where it was felt an enthusiastic member of the laity would be more use. The Americans arrived in 1898, but as the war with the Filipino insurgents began and then continued and as it became apparent that their life in Manila was on the verge of irreversible change, so too did they finally admit that it was time to drop the pretense and privately confirm that the happy marriage of Salvador and Annaliese Carriscant had become a convenient sham. They had wealth and reputation, they were prominent and respected figures in the foreign community in Manila, which was rapidly enlarging as the process of American colonization remorselessly consolidated itself—Annaliese was even on cordial terms with the governor's wife—but whatever affection, whatever love that had existed between them, was gone.

The prime indication of this state of affairs was that for over a year now, there had been no sexual relations between them. It had begun most curiously with Annaliese asking him what operations he had performed at the hospital that day. If he had done any amputations she refused to let him share her bed. This animus, directed more at his profession than at his person, had grown. Some evenings she would taunt him cruelly: "How many legs did you cut off today?" Usually he ignored her, until one night, goaded too far, he had replied, "Two, actually, plus an arm and an eyeball," and she had fled weeping from the room. She complained also of the smell off his clothes, a sweet stench that clung to him, which he claimed he could not detect, but which he knew was the smell of putrefaction, of pus. All this dismayed him: he felt impotent and clueless. What was he meant to do, find a new job? Troubled by this bizarre collapse of his marriage and exhausted from his work at the San Jerónimo, he had taken to sleeping on the divan in his study, a temporary arrangement, he had told himself, to avoid disturbing her when he came in late, but it was a circumstance that had inevitably become permanent.

He looked at his wife now, objectively, a little sad, and tried to conjure up an image of her naked body, some detail or special character that he used to cherish—the wide-slung shape of her breasts, the fine downy hair on the areolae of her nipples, her surprisingly deep navel—that would stimulate the old feelings, cause old memories to flare up, like a hot coal breathed upon, but nothing stirred. His thoughts turned instead to a view and an idea he had had that afternoon as he stood in Pantaleon's meadow and looked over at the tin roofs of Sampaloc. Sampaloc and its notorious Gardenia Street, with its bright bars and brothels . . . What did they call the girls there? "Low-flying doves." It was not natural, this restraint, this forced celibacy. A man of his age masturbating on his divan in the dark like an adolescent. Perhaps a low-flying dove on Gardenia Street was what he required?

CHEZ DR. ISIDRO CRUZ

DR. CARRISCANT PACED slowly down the aisle between the beds in the postoperative ward. He had just
examined the Chinese boy and had discovered that although
the tongue appeared to be healing well, he was now running a
temperature, some three days now since the operation, which
was a little worrying. He looked up: Pantaleon was signaling to
him from the far end of the ward, trying not to attract the attention of the nurses.

Carriscant walked over. "Pantaleon, what's—"

"The body has gone."

"What body?"

"The American soldier. It was taken yesterday."

"By whom? Bobby?"

"No. I think it was taken by Dr. Cruz."

PAT ON BOBBY, with Salvador Carriscant by his side, drove
his carriage into the small village of Flores. It was midday and
the stall holders in the plaza had already packed away their
goods. Only a man selling salted fish seemed reluctant to
leave; sitting on a low stool, waving away the flies with a palm
frond whisk, he stared curiously at the *americanos* as their fine
carriage with its two glossy Abra ponies clattered by.

Carriscant directed Bobby to turn right at the adobe church

and they passed between two crumbling brick gateposts and drove up a potholed dirt track, lined with rozal bushes, toward Dr. Isidro Cruz's imposing house.

"I still can't understand the man," Bobby repeated. "How could he just go in there and take it? Who does he fucking think he is? The Lord Mayor of the Universe? I ask you."

"Typical Cruz. Remember, he's a *peninsularo*. He'll never change."

"What do you mean, '*peninsularo*'? He's a Spaniard, isn't he?"

Carriscant explained about the various class divisions that existed in the Philippines during the Spanish period. At the top of the tree were the settlers and officials who had been born in Spain, the *peninsulares*. They looked down on the *insulares*, Spaniards who had been born in the islands, whom they regarded as coarse and unrefined, rejects from Spanish society who could only find a niche in a distant colony. The *insulares* in turn disdained the *mestizos*, half-castes, Spaniards or Chinese who had intermarried with the locals. Everyone looked down on this last category, the *indios*, even those educated *indios*—the *ilustrados*—who had studied abroad. And the *indios* themselves? They made no distinction: everybody white was a *kastila*—a Castilian—and their enemy.

"Until you Americans came," Carriscant said cheerfully. "Now they have a new white man to dislike."

"So you're a *mestizo*?" Bobby asked.

"Yes, but not of the family, if you know what I mean. My father was British, my mother's people *insulares*. Very complicated. But Cruz is old school: he hates everybody, except perhaps Alfonso."

"Who's he?"

"The king of Spain."

Bobby was not impressed. He was a straightforward man, he told Carriscant, whose working maxim in life was "fair play."

"And I mean fair play for all. Not just for peninsulars or insulars or whatever the Sam Hill they're called. Fair play for one and all, that's my motto. But I don't mind playing unfair once in a while to bring it about."

Carriscant said he could understand the skewed logic of that position.

"This Cruz'd better not mess with me," Bobby said. "I lived for a year once off nothing but birds' eggs and rainwater. He'd be well advised to step real cautiously."

Cruz's house was a substantial stone building with a tiled roof, hairy with weeds, and a saffron lime wash on the walls which was flaking and dirty. Two big buri palms grew on either side of the wide balustraded staircase which ran up to the front door. Behind the house, screened by a grove of guava and balete trees, was a range of wooden outbuildings with steeply pitched roofs thatched with grass. Beyond the gardens were a few scrubby acres planted with beans and tobacco.

A manservant informed them that Dr. Cruz was in his workroom and they were led around the house to the buildings at the rear. There was a large bamboo pen containing half a dozen mangy-looking mongrel dogs, and in an iron cage hanging from the rafters of an empty stable, two sad-looking gibbons groomed each other listlessly. The manservant rapped on the door of the largest hut and stepped back apprehensively as, after a pause, it was hurled open.

Dr. Isidro Cruz was wearing a black alpaca suit with the cuffs unbuttoned and the sleeves rolled back to the elbows; his hands were dripping with blood and his waistcoat and jacket front were shiny with some other dark viscous fluid. He was a tall man, in his sixties, with a big powerful head, a gray pointed goatee and wiry hair brushed straight back from his brow. He started to swear venomously at his servant in Tagalog.

"Listen, you cunt of an ancient whore, don't you know—"

He saw Carriscant and beside him the solid uniformed figure of Bobby and halted abruptly. He gestured to his manservant to turn around and wiped his hands on his back.

"What do you want, Carriscant?" he said, changing to Spanish, his hauteur impeccable.

Carriscant introduced Bobby and explained who he was.

"We're looking for the body of Ephraim Ward," Bobby started.

"Tell him I don't speak English," Cruz said.

Carriscant knew that in fact Cruz spoke English passably well, but he agreed, in the interests of maintaining some decorum, to translate. He patiently repeated Bobby's statement and then added a comment of his own in a lower voice.

"You had no right moving that body."

"I had every right in the world," Cruz said confidently. "I am medical director, I would remind you, and on top of that I resent the tone of voice you employ."

"It was the chief of constabulary himself who asked for—"

"It was Dr. Wieland himself who asked me to do whatever I thought necessary to protect the evidence."

"Dr. Wieland has no authority in this case. Provost Marshall Bobby—"

"Where is it?" Bobby interrupted their argument impatiently.

Cruz looked at him, face blank.

"Where is it?" Carriscant translated with a sigh.

"Here. And quite safe."

After more terse exchanges Cruz agreed to let the two men into his laboratory. The room was lit with carbide lamps which cast an unnatural bleached glare. Long spiraled tapes of speckled flypaper dangled from the ceiling and there was a strong reek of putrefying meat in the air that made Carriscant's gorge rise. On a wide dissecting table were the spatchcocked bodies of two dogs. Bobby recoiled violently at the stench and lurched outside, where Carriscant heard him raking his throat and spitting. With a piteous shake of the head Cruz picked up a tin pump-action carbolic spray and vigorously wielded it until the smell of disinfectant overlay the more feculent odors, not quite concealing, but helping, like a pomade on a sweating laborer. Carriscant held a handkerchief to his nose and looked about him. On another table were two other dogs, one with its chest cavity open and rubber tubes running from it into the body of the other dog, which he could see was still shallowly breathing, its stretched rib cage rising and falling erratically. By the dog's head was a chloroform bottle and a wad of gauze.

"I kept these two dogs alive, on one heart, for five minutes," Cruz declared proudly. "In case you were wondering."

"Don't be absurd."

"Your tiresome skepticism doesn't affect me, Carriscant." He tapped a blood-smudged ledger. "It's all there, witnessed too."

"Witnessed by your servants, no doubt. Most reliable."

"Those two dogs were alive for five minutes!" Cruz shouted, his big face red, suddenly enraged.

"Physically impossible. Unless you're Jesus Christ!"

"I won't listen to your filthy blasphemy!"

"Gentlemen, gentlemen!" Bobby reentered, calming them. "Where is Ephraim Ward?"

Muttering to himself, Cruz led them through to a back room. Here in the center of the floor were two large wooden chests, eight feet long and four high. As Cruz lifted the lid of the first one, Carriscant saw that there was another chest inside, made of lead, the gap between the two stuffed tightly with straw. The second lid was raised and there lay Ephraim Ward's naked etiolated corpse, packed on ice like a side of beef. Carriscant frowned, and reached forward into the chest and scooped away some ice granules beside the shoulder.

A woman's face was revealed, gaunt and bloodless. An *india*.

"For Christ's sake," Bobby said, hoarsely. "How many more have you got in there?"

"Three and some organs. What's it got to do with you?" Cruz said, in Spanish, forgetting he was not meant to understand English.

"There is no room at the hospital morgue," Carriscant explained. "Most surgeons have to store cadavers in their own premises."

"But why?" Bobby said. "Why not bury them?"

"For the advancement of medical science," Carriscant said reasonably. "How else do you think we are able to do so much? To cure, to heal?"

"*Precisamente*," Cruz agreed, nodding his big head.

Carriscant watched Bobby's glance flit between the two of them; he could see he was troubled and unsettled.

"It's a common practice," Carriscant said gently, a little unhappy to find himself siding with Cruz, "and essential."

Cruz stepped away from them and pumped some gusts of carbolic spray into the atmosphere. Bobby gathered himself and had Carriscant explain to Cruz that Ephraim Ward's body was to be returned to the San Jerónimo morgue immediately. Cruz refused to do anything without the authority of Governor Taft. Bobby said he would provide him with that forthwith.

"That man is a monster," Bobby said passionately as they drove away from Cruz's house. "Those poor fucking dogs and monkeys. The bodies stacked up in the next room . . . It's not natural."

"Always remember," Carriscant said. "He is a *peninsularo*. They assume the world is organized for them. In *Filipinas* they decide what is normal. Or at least they used to for three hundred years. It's hard for them to adjust."

Bobby disagreed, but Carriscant was not really listening. He pursed his lips, frowning. He was thinking: those dogs . . . Two animals, one heart. What was the old fool trying to do?

(Carriscant frequently became agitated in his retelling of his story to me, leaving his chair and pacing around the deck, gesticulating, almost acting out the emotions he was reliving, his expressive face alternatively puzzled or irate, patient or sad.

We had established a routine by the third or fourth day out of New York. The afternoon, after our lunch [we ate surprisingly well on the *Herzog*], proved to be the most fertile time for his reminiscences. Before dinner, in my cabin, I would write down as much as I could remember and then the next morning go over it with him once again, expanding on the facts, asking questions, confirming details, making notes. The dossier grew quickly.)

THE *AERO-MÓVIL*

*P*ANTALEON SPREAD the plans flat on the ground in
front of the *nipa* barn and weighted the corners with
stones. Carriscant squatted down on his haunches in front of
them and made suitable noises of appreciation.

"The Aero-Mobile," he read. "Good name."

"I thought: you've got an automobile, what better description for a flying machine?"

"Sounds ideal."

Carriscant scrutinized the fine drawings. What he saw
looked like a cross between a cantilevered bridge and a stylized
bird. There were two wings, boxy with many struts and wires,
but the tail at the end was curved and semicircular, with flut-
ings, like the fanned tail of a dove. He found Pantaleon's
dream of powered heavier-than-air flight touching, a harmless
obsession, but he sensed his natural curiosity about the project
growing, despite his skepticism, and despite the fact that he
had only invited himself here on a pretext.

"It's a competition," Pantaleon said, explaining. "Two businessmen, an American and a Frenchman, have set up this
prize, the Amberway-Richault Prize. They've offered ten
thousand dollars for the first flying machine to lift itself off the
ground under its own power and fly for one hundred meters.
Under its own power, no ramps, pulleys, gradients. It must be
fully authenticated, of course."

"And you think this . . . this 'Aero-Mobile' can do it?"

"In principle, I'm sure," Pantaleon said, with quiet authority. "There are a few problems . . . The power plant is the major one, of course. But I'm on the right lines. The glider models have worked very satisfactorily." He smiled shyly, confessing. "It's what I've been up to this last year."

"Most impressive," Carriscant said. "Well, I really must be—"

"Fortunately for me,"—Pantaleon lowered his voice, even though they were quite alone in his meadow—"even though I hate to admit it, the arrival of the Americans has made everything so much easier. They're at the forefront, you see. Them and the French." He looked about him, a small expression of contempt on his face. "We were rotting out here," he said, "in every way. Nothing had really changed since the eighteenth century, when you think about it. Nothing."

"Yes. Yes, you're right," Carriscant said, suddenly caught up in some of Pantaleon's passion. "Look at us, at our own discipline. We had to leave, go abroad, to discover what astonishing progress was being made. Yet we still have to deal with old quacks like Cruz and Wieland."

"Can you imagine," Pantaleon said dreamily, not really listening, "if I, Pantaleon Quiroga, were the first man to achieve powered flight. Here, in the Philippines . . ."

"You know that Cruz has kept the American's heart and his liver," Carriscant said darkly. "Can you believe the arrogance? Bobby has protested again to Taft."

"The twentieth century . . . How incredible to be living now. Everything will change, Salvador, everything."

The two men fell silent, preoccupied with their own thoughts, as the evening light gathered around them in the blond wind-combed meadow, peachy and warm, and across the river came the sound of the Angelus tolling mournfully. Carriscant clapped his young friend on the shoulder.

"It's good to talk to you, Pantaleon," he said sincerely. "It's good for me, anyway. Gets my mind off . . . things." He gazed back at the meaningless mass of struts and wires in the *nipa* barn. "I'm mightily impressed with your machine, your Aero-Mobile. Let me know if I can help in any way."

"Actually, you might be able to, Salvador. Do you want to go for a beer?"

"Another time, my friend. I have to get back."

Carriscant left Pantaleon at his barn, as he said he was about to start affixing the fabric to the wings and intended to work into the night. He retraced his steps to Santa Cruz and picked up a *carromato* that took him the short distance to Sampaloc.

SAMPALOC WAS little better than a slum, one level up, perhaps, from the squalor that was Tondo, but all the same it presented to the eye a mean scatter of wooden shacks with galvanized iron roofs and unpaved narrow lanes noisome with filth and sewage. Calle Gardenia was its one mark of distinction, a short cobbled avenue of shops that had been converted into makeshift bars and cafés. These establishments still retained the canvas awnings of the old shop fronts, great skirts of material that projected out from the façade on a metal beam and then hung almost to the ground, designed to produce maximum shade. The effect was to curtain off the interior from the casual passerby, but one could see and hear, in the gaps between the shop fronts, the glow of colored lights, the sound of music and the laughter and noise of men's voices. This partial shrouding was more enticing, Carriscant found, than any overt display of license.

He sat in a small *bodegón* on the outskirts of Sampaloc reading a newspaper and drinking many cups of coffee until the gathering darkness outside necessitated the lighting of the oil lamps. Once he felt he could venture out with some hope of maintaining his anonymity he set off down Gardenia Street. It was busy with men, American soldiers and sailors, and the air was loud with English voices, a disorienting and unsettling experience for him. He realized that he had not heard so many English voices since he had boarded his ship at Liverpool for his trip home in 1897. As he wandered up and down the length of Gardenia Street he felt a sudden clutch of melancholy seize him as he contemplated his younger self all those years ago. He remembered his rapt astonishment as he walked the streets of Glasgow at the commencement of his medical studies. How he would take the horse tram from Gilmorehill, with the new university on its crest and the infirmary at its foot where he worked and studied, and travel into the center of town. All these people in their heavy dark clothes. He would walk about the thronged streets dazed with the noise of the traffic and the gabble and blather of English in his ears. Paving underfoot, every square yard, hard stone. The iron wheel rims of the trams and the cabs and the drays clattering and ringing. Writing everywhere, names and advertisements on every vertical surface, it seemed. In one shop a window filled with two hundred straw hats. It seemed to bring a presentiment of sun, of the tropics, to this solid square city, with its tall, ornate, soot-black buildings, muscly with commerce and civic pride.

How different from his home, Manila, the low green odorous city on its lazy steamy estuary, clustered around the vast, crumbling weed-shagged walls of Intramuros. A dome, a spire here and there, peering above the trees, and the plain of white tin and terra-cotta roofs. The heat, the damp, the crawling pace. Life moved at the speed of a *carabao* cart, people said, one mile per day. And now here in Sampaloc he heard those loud white voices again, different accents but with the same bustling swaggering confidence. Here too commerce held sway. He felt a brief pang of nostalgia for the life he had known before the Americans came. The late start to the day, the city stewed in humid lethargy, the siesta, then the polite curiosity, the discreet and civil flirtations of the *paseo* . . . But he shook the mood off as his more immediate needs reimposed themselves, and he decided to enter an establishment called the Thichupwah Ice Cream Parlor, one of the street's larger and more substantial buildings. On its second floor, above the awning, there was a crazy-looking wrought iron balcony and through the open windows in some of the rooms Carriscant could see the flitting shapes of what he took to be women moving to and fro.

He pushed past the canvas awning and opened the door onto a large noisy room, blurry with smoke, filled with American servicemen, most of them in uniform. Many games of cards were in progress and the unself-conscious shouts of bid and counterbid almost drowned the noise of the large phonograph in the corner, playing "My Kentucky Belle" for the few listless couples shuffling about the small wooden dance floor at the rear. Carriscant pushed and weaved his way through the tables to the bar where a large sign said AMERICAN BEER 40 CENTS MEX. He ordered a Schlitz and glanced carefully and, he hoped, casually around him. Behind the bar a white woman with a pinched face—a face never designed to be painted in the way it was—asked him if he wanted to dance. She spoke English with an unlocatable foreign accent. Polish, for all he knew, Corsican, Walloon.

"With you?" he asked, not thinking. One of her front teeth was badly chipped, and the armpits of her thin cotton dress were dark with sweat.

"Any of the girls. I cost extra." She smiled, showing a lot of gum, and gestured at the girls sitting on a bench by the dance floor waiting for partners. "Fifty cents for a dance. Two dollars, Mexican, for a 'dance' upstairs. The white girls cost five dollars." She smiled at him again. "I'm ten . . . You American?"

"Yes. Thank you." He could barely pronounce the words. He left the bar and made his way through the yelling gamblers toward the dance floor, beyond which, he saw, was a flight of stairs. Among the half-dozen women not dancing were three white girls, two thin, one plump, all with unnaturally colored hair. The plump girl was a pure white-blond, her hair piled untidily on top of her head, with a few uncoiling ringlets hanging down reminding him, unfortunately, of the flypaper in Dr. Cruz's laboratory. The other girls were *indias*, dressed in lurid versions of their traditional clothes: wide-sleeved abaca blouses and bright shawls around their waists over ankle-length calico *sayas*. They all waved fans against the fug and heat, causing the paste bracelets on their wrists to wink and gleam in the light and click in uneven rhythm to the plangent scratchy music. One of the girls wore her dark hair down, glossy and congealed with coconut oil. She was small with unusually full lips and heavy eyebrows which gave her an air of unlikely seriousness. Carriscant watched as she snapped her fan shut and reached behind and around her to scratch an itch on her shoulder blade. He walked around the dance floor toward her, having made his decision, his hand reaching in his pocket for money.

He spoke English. "Two dollars," he said gauchely, like an ignoramus, showing her the notes, "upstairs." In the moist heat of the room he could smell the coconut oil on her hair, sweet and spicy.

She took the money, folded it away somewhere gracefully, discreetly. "You come me," she said, "we room five." She set off immediately across the dance floor toward the stairway. A swaying couple cut directly across Carriscant's path and he had to pause and then negotiate their maladroit shuffle before he could follow his girl. His girl . . . "You come me, we room five." It was all so clear-cut, a matter of plain business dealing, no fuss, no pretensions. He was always struck by the simplicity of this exchange, its no-nonsense straightforwardness—money in return for the short loan of a body—on the few occasions he had resorted to it before. By the time he reached the foot of the stairs, however, the girl had already ascended. And coming down, adjusting his belt, was Dr. Saul Wieland.

"Well, if it isn't the esteemed Dr. Carriscant," Wieland said loudly, showing both rows of teeth in a yellow grin. "That your little chicken I just patted on the keester?" Wieland was drunk, as usual.

"What are you talking about?" Carriscant held himself stiffly, arms by his side.

Wieland had reached the foot of the stairs, and lounged on the banister. He was a small man, in his fifties, with loose folds of jowl, like wattles, overlapping his stiff collar. He had a shaggy untrimmed mustache and an odd loose pouting mouth with wet lips.

"I won't tell Mommy. Relax." He lolled forward and patted Carriscant's elbow.

Somehow Carriscant managed a contemptuous snuffle of a laugh. He reached forward and took hold of the handle of the door in front of him.

"I don't know what you're talking about," Carriscant said. "I'm here to attend my cook's mother. She has a hernia. Good evening to you."

With that he snapped down the handle and swung the door open, stepping through confidently and closing it behind him. He heard Wieland say, with grotesque sarcasm, at the closed door, "Oh, *so* sorry, I'm sure." Carriscant did not pause further, in case Wieland should try to come after him. He walked down the corridor, past an opening that led to a cramped dark kitchen, and then out a rear door that gave onto a long narrow high-walled yard. One side was lined with chicken coops and he could hear the soft clucking of the roosting hens and smell the nutty, brothy reek of their accumulated shit. He felt his way carefully to his left and squinnied through the gap in a shutter. He could see Wieland sitting at a table with three other white men in civilian clothes, one of whom was dealing out a pack of cards.

Carriscant had no desire to allow Wieland any further opportunities to glimpse him in the Ice Cream Parlor or to practice his scornful innuendo further and so he decided to wait until it was possible to leave unobserved. No one, it seemed, had spotted him enter the yard so he was probably safe there for an hour or so. He moved farther down into the darkness at the rear until he found a screened position against the wall. He pulled a section of old matting over and sat down upon it, snug in the angle the wall made with the solid wooden wheel of a *carabao* cart. He stretched his legs out and rubbed his face, laughing at himself a little halfheartedly: so much for his "low-flying dove"—she would be up there in her nest, wondering where her *americano* had gone. Fool, he said to himself, fool, fool, fool . . .

He woke up, his head canted against the rim of the wheel, the keening whine of a mosquito in his ear. He slapped it away and stood up shakily, stamping the circulation back into his legs. He could not believe he had slept like that . . . He moved to the light from the window and checked his pocket watch: 2:30 a.m. Music and chatter still emanated from the Ice Cream Parlor, and peering in through a gap in the shutters, he saw that the place was still crowded and, more irritating, that Wieland and his cronies were still engrossed in their gambling. This was absurd, he said to himself, now what was he supposed to do? To walk past Wieland at this time of the night would simply encourage more ribald speculation. He paced up and down the yard, thinking, disturbing the dozing poultry further. Wieland, at this rate, could be there until dawn. And Annaliese would have been in bed hours ago, he realized, no doubt further disgusted by his behavior. He walked down to the foot of the yard, set an old box against the foot of the wall and hauled himself up onto its crumbling top. In front of him was only darkness, but a shifting sighing darkness that suggested vegetation—no glimmer of light was to be seen. He hoped that his pale gray alpaca suit would not become too soiled and that the drop down would not be too steep. Tensing himself, he pushed off.

Mud.

Up to his knees, he stumbled, reached out to steady himself, and his hand went into the softness up to the elbow. He straightened, swayed and just held his balance. He took a couple of sucking, clinging steps, his hands held before him like a blind man. His fingers brushed leaves, thick, glossy, with a small serrated edge, and he stepped forward, out of the filth of the path and up onto blessedly firm and drier earth around the bole of the tree. Mango, he thought. He turned to look back at the glow of lights from the rear elevations of the Ice Cream Parlor and the establishments on either side of Gardenia Street. The path he had dropped into must run along the backyards of the houses at this end of the street, recipient, no doubt, of every kind of slop and detritus imaginable and unimaginable. He was not going to attempt to walk out of this particular spot until he could see where he was placing his feet. He lowered himself carefully onto a wide exposed root: there was nothing for it but to sit it out.

First light arrived just before six. It had been a brain-deadening wait: he had smoked all the cigarettes he had on him—seventeen—had planned his future career in the smallest detail and had sung and hummed every melody, it seemed, he had ever heard, and still the slothful night crawled on. But now it was dawn and the mud on his clothes was almost dry. He rubbed his jaw, feeling the roughness of stubble on his palm. Home, as quickly and discreetly as possible.

The tree he had waited under was a mango, it turned out,

part of a small grove that, once traversed, gave onto a prospect of misty cane and paddy fields and, beyond them, the low bluey mass of Manila's northern suburbs, blurred by the smoke of morning cooking fires a mile or so away. He set off, trudging down a path along the top of a dike, making for San Miguel and, he hoped, the first horse tram he could board.

It proved more complicated going than he had expected. The path had joined a dirt track, but he had taken a wrong turn, as he discovered when the track looped northward again, and had had to retrace his steps. Then he had to make a detour around a brackish meandering *estero* of the Pasig and pick his way southward once more along the squelching fringes of more paddy fields before he saw, in the middle distance, the glowing terra-cotta roof and white walls of the Malacañan Palace through some woods ahead—Governor Taft's official residence. Now he knew where he was. He consulted his pocket watch again: almost eight o'clock; with a bit of luck he would be home within half an hour.

He knew there was a ferry across the Pasig not far from the palace and so followed a path that led directly toward it, abandoning the one he had been following. Another mistake, as it turned out, when the path terminated at a semi-demolished bamboo barn. He hurried on, nevertheless, cutting across the middle of a mung bean plantation toward a thick grove of acacia trees. In his travels cross-country, he had acquired a busy swarm of persistent flies, attracted, though he hardly dared to speculate, by some noxious ingredient in the Sampaloc mud that still daubed his trousers. He swatted wildly at them, tried vainly to outsprint them and then, pausing, removed his jacket and twirled it like a demented bullfighter around his head and shoulders as he went on his way.

It was cooler among the acacia trees and the path was well trodden and the going easier. But as the sweat began to dry on his brow this relief proved to be temporary: he started to reflect on what had happened over the previous few hours and he began to generate a potent anger at himself. What could have persuaded him to go to Sampaloc, to a bordello? But then, having made his choice, why had he not been more worldly with Wieland, more of a man among men? What was so disgraceful, in that company especially, of admitting that one occasionally visited a prostitute? Really, he must have seemed absurdly, laughably prim, stalking off through that door like a virgin importuned by a leering cad. And look where his sudden attack of craven dignity had landed him: a mosquito-infested, shame-tormented, mud-encrusted, exhausting, cross-country—

He actually saw—actually *saw*—the arrow as it flew toward his unsuspecting face.

He had turned, alerted by a rip and flap of foliage, reflexively snapping his head to the right, and saw the missile fly at him. He could not remember if he had stopped or ducked or flinched, but he felt the child's breath of its passing on his cheek and then heard the *whungggg* of its impact in the acacia tree beside him. He turned. Head high. Its white fletch still vibrating.

He dropped to his hands and knees and scrabbled behind a bush, a little whimpering noise in his throat, waiting for other arrows to fly at him, waiting for his assailants to surge from the undergrowth, razor-edged *bolos* swinging sharp in the morning air.

Silence. No twig snap, no . . . Then he heard it, not far off. Laughter. Women laughing.

He pulled the embedded arrow out of the tree trunk and paced back along its trajectory, feeling the anger in him distort his face, drawing it down almost as if he were trying to make a snarling snouty point out of his features, to force his brows, nose, mouth, cheeks into a furious and threatening horn with which to gore his persecutors. The fear had gone, the terror was over: people were laughing at him, women were laughing.

He pushed brutally through a dense dark screen of *cogal*

bushes, scratching the backs of his hands, and found himself blinking in the brightness of a sunlit lawn. In front of him stood three round canted archery targets and beyond them stood half a dozen women, white women, in leg-of-mutton-sleeved blouses and long drill skirts, wearing straw hats against the sun, carrying bows, with quivers of arrows slung across their shoulders. One of them was actually fitting another arrow to her bow, drawing it back—

"STOP!" he screamed, emotion cracking his voice. "Stop now, you bitch of hell! God damn you!"

He strode out to confront them, brandishing the arrow.

"One inch more and this would have buried itself in my head," he shouted at them. "Less than an inch, you mindless idiots! Less than an inch and I would have been killed by your foolishness, your foolish stupid carelessness!"

They stared at him, big-eyed, ogling, mouths gaping, completely astonished. He felt his rage begin to vent from him, as if a plug had been pulled, and self-consciousness rush in to fill the void. He saw them now, clearly: these were respectable American women—good God—young women. What must he have looked like advancing out of the wood, covered in mud, unshaven, screaming his anger? Had he sworn? Oh God, he had a sudden terrible memory of using an oath, a foul oath.

"Who is the person responsible?" he carried on gamely, not wanting now to lose the advantage his outrage gave him. "Who is the person who fired this arrow?"

A woman stepped forward at once and he swiveled to confront her. A tall woman. Broad-shouldered. Pale strong freckled face. Some rare quality about that face, he thought, suddenly, throat tightening. Something he had never seen. Reddish brown hair held in a loose bun. The details came fast: she had a slightly hooked nose, he saw rapidly, with small arched nostrils, and he saw rapidly too how the leather strap of her quiver separated the soft roll of her bosom into two distinct breasts.

She faced him. Square, strong. Small pale lashed brown eyes. Odd, that combination. White skin, freckle-spattered but very white. You'd think blue eyes. But no, brown, like un-milked coffee, a fierce stare. Tiny blisters of perspiration in the well-defined groove of her top lip.

"I shot it," she said. A soft accent. *Shaht*. Southern, was it? "I'm very sorry, it was a complete accident. I'm just learning—"

His tongue sat inert in his dry throat.

"—and it just sort of kicked up when I fired it. It went way high into the trees. I'm so sorry."

"It's an outrage," he managed to say weakly. "I could have died. Apology. I demand apology. Your name."

"Look, I've already apologized several times. I'll apologize again: I'm sorry. No one was hurt. It was an accident."

"What is your name?" It came out almost as a shriek.

She looked at him.

She sighed. "My name has nothing to do with this, or with you," she said, her tone changing, becoming angrier, no-nonsense. "Whoever you are, you silly little self-important man, your behavior is most unreasonable, not to say offensive. Would you now please be on your way, as you are interrupting our lesson."

BAD BLOOD

*T*HE CHINESE BOY had died in the night, suddenly but not unexpectedly. Ever since his operation it had been obvious he was ailing: he was feverish, he had absolute constipation, his tongue—which had been healing admirably—began to ooze pus and blacken around the sutures. Listerism and asepsis had achieved marvels. Even here in Manila, in San Jerónimo, the recovery rate in his wards was five times better than in Cruz's, but when he saw these signs he knew his ability to intervene was over. It was rare to find peritonitis associated with erysipelas of the throat, but he had encountered it two or three times before. He assumed the streptococcus had reached the serous membrane through the blood somehow. Anyway, he had dosed the boy with opiates, tried to make him comfortable and stood uselessly by as the boy had died. He knew the worst when he had come into the ward and seen the boy lying on his back, his knees drawn up, his fluttering hands held above his head to increase the capacity of the thorax. His face was already gaunt, his eyes restless, his hands cold and damp. He began to vomit regularly and his abdominal wall grew rigid, boardlike. Meteorism became present, the abdomen tense and tympanitic on percussion. He complained not only of a burning pain in his gut but of a tormenting thirst. He was given a rectal injection of cold water. He drank a little iced milk and soda water; the tongue was painted with a solution of glycerine in an attempt to keep it moist. To no lasting avail. The boy's pulse grew rapid, hard and wiry. He began to hiccup violently, a most disturbing symptom that Carriscant knew marked a serious failure in prognosis. He developed the classic *face grippée*, pinched and sunken, the nasolabial crease very deep. His tongue became coated and foul and the vomited matter was highly offensive. Sordes were present on the teeth and lips. Carriscant watched the boy's piteous restlessness—there was no blessed coma in cases of peritonitis to ease the suffering—and watched as his limbs became cold and blue. In the act of dying there was a great gush of foul and brownish fluid from the mouth and rectum. Moments like these tormented Carriscant with a vision of the huge void of his ignorance and helplessness. His instruments were sterile, his operating theater clean and disinfected, his hands were scrubbed pink, he wore freshly laundered white gowns, and yet somehow, from somewhere, the dreaded streptococcus infected the boy's blood, corrupting it. From "somewhere" . . . That vague supposition alone was bad enough. An incision in the tongue had produced an infection of the serous membrane in the abdomen. He knew the intestines would be covered in an exudation of pus and fluid, a thick layer of lymph along the lines of contact between the various coils of the bowel. Once infected, the patient's body succumbed inevitably to the toxin of bad blood and a new impotency took over as you watched and waited for death. Bad blood . . . At times like these he understood his benighted precursors' vain obsession with leeches and bleeding.

He looked at the boy's naked body as it lay before him on the dissecting table in the mortuary while he prepared to examine its morbid anatomy. Slightly plump, with almost girlish breasts and a small scribble of pubic hair above the clenched genitals. He touched the cool, still yielding flesh, pressed down on the rib cage, allowed his hands to shape the contours of the youth's belly. He knew every component of that individual body, everything hidden behind that pliant but tough integument of skin. The inside of a man or woman was as familiar to him as the face of a friend or the layout of his sitting room, but it was a familiarity afforded only after death. The head, the chest, the spine, the heart . . . He did not dare advance across that threshold while the body lived. Here he was, a highly trained surgeon, the equal, he liked to think, of any in the entire civilized world, and yet to all intents and purposes he was trapped, pinioned by fear and the pathetic limits of his knowledge. He was like a man of vast wealth who has purchased a palace of immense and unparalleled splendor. He can wander on the grounds, circle the exterior, peer through the windows, admire the gilded furniture and the lavish textiles, the fabulous works of art and glittering chandeliers. It is all mine, he could think, and yet he was forever denied entry, on pain of death. On pain of death.

He turned the boy over. Of course, he thought scornfully, one is always allowed access to the bladder or rectum, and those other portals the body provided itself, where catheters and probes, pincers and scalpels, could reach. How many times had he patiently ground down a suffering man's gallstones, his thin instruments deep inside the bladder, sawing and grinding. He was renowned for the delicacy of his manipulation: of the dozens of operations he had performed on the bladder, only three had subsequently died of peritonitis. He knew at once when his touch had let him down. As the lithotrite was withdrawn, the catheter extracted from the penis, there was that small fatal signature of blood. Then the silent prayer: Oh Lord, let it only be a scratch on the bladder wall. Even the tiniest of punctures seemed to bring down the heaviest of sentences . . .

He rolled the boy over again and reached for his scalpel, about to pull back once more the curtains on the body's baffling fragile treasures. He had read recently of certain American doctors who were recommending the use of rubber gloves during operations—he could practically hear Cruz's incredulous scoffing. Even he, Salvador Carriscant, proud herald of all that was new in medicine, had some doubts about that course of action—what would happen to your "touch," the magic of the surgeon's gift? That unique combination, as he had heard it expressed, of a lacemaker's fingers and a seaman's grip? What was the point of honing a skill if you then willfully smothered it in rubber? It was like those Arab princesses hidden behind black veils. Why should a beautiful woman not bestow . . .

And he thought of the American woman again, of course. Hardly an hour seemed to go by these days without her coming, unbidden, to mind. Something about the quality of her gaze, the geometry of her face, her odd coloring, had acted upon him with fiercesome, uncompromising effectiveness. Never before, never before . . . Like an inert liquid galvanized into crazy effervescence by a strange catalyst. And here she was, in *his* city . . . He found himself wondering, futilely, how long she would stay. And for how long had she been here without his knowing? Weeks, months, a year? . . . This was what unmanned him: he felt that curious weakness come upon him again, flowing out from some new gland in the base of his spine, spreading through his body like a tree.

He set down his scalpel with a rattle and, bracing his arms, hung his head over the boy's pale ruined corpse. Jesus Christ, he said in unfamiliar prayer, heaven help me.

"Salvador, what's wrong?" Pantaleon stepped into the room, anxious, concerned to find him this way.

"I'm fine, fine," he said, straightening. "Just a little tired, I think. This can wait."

He turned. Pantaleon thrust his hands deep into his pockets.

"What is it?" Carriscant said.

"Can I have a discreet word?"

• • •

CARRISCANT HAD one of the hospital porters drive him down to the docks, where the quays on both banks of the Pasig were as clotted as ever with shipping—steamships, square and lateen-rigged schooners, junks and ferryboats, fat shallow-draught paddle steamers that could negotiate the silty reaches of the river upstream, and the great wallowing *cascos*, barge cum houseboat, homes for the river's transient population, moored four or five deep along the wharves. He was happy to be out of the hospital, quite content to do this favor for Pantaleon, as it gave him an opportunity both to compose himself and also scrutinize every European and American he saw in the passing carriages in the fervid hope of glimpsing that pale freckled face again and feeling the cool gaze of those candid brown eyes . . .

The carriage pulled up at the foot of a narrow lane, Calle Crespo in Quiapo, where it seemed every second shop was a tinsmith's and the air vibrated dully with the sound of hammers on galvanized iron. As he descended Carriscant saw a new illuminated advertisement across the junction: CONEY IS-LAND SHOOTING GALLERY—clearly the Americans were here to stay. At number 89, Crespo, he found the sign he was looking for: between SAM M. GOODFORTH, MARINE SURVEYOR and PABLO EULEGIO, HAT CLEANER was his destination—UDO LEYS, TOBACCO MERCHANT.

After Annaliese's father, Gerhardt Leys, and her sister had returned to Germany her uncle Udo had stayed on and had stoically watched the family fortunes remorselessly decline. Carriscant climbed the stairs and pushed open the office door. There was no secretary in the vestibule and in the office itself Udo was nowhere to be seen. The walls were lined with empty glass humidors and extravagant posters for Manila cigars. In the seventies and eighties the brothers had had the field more or less to themselves. Now there were eight cigar and cigarette factories in Manila alone: no one needed to buy from Udo Leys any longer, and he had been obliged to diversify, operating an opportunistic import/export business, waiting for a need to manifest itself and then racing desperately to supply it, whether it was bicycles or perfume, cattle feed or fancy goods. The last time Carriscant had seen him, Udo had told him in a conspiratorial whisper that he had seventy-five upright pianos in a warehouse in Tondo. "Think of all those new American schools," he said, his voice ripe with the allure of profit, "all those assembly rooms . . . Who will play the 'Stars and Stripes'? They'll be gone within a week." Carriscant smiled, remembering the old man's impregnable conviction, and wandered to the window. The noise here was infernal: in the courtyard below, ten men were making buckets.

He turned at the sound of a door opening and saw Udo emerge from a small cupboard at the rear of the office carrying a chamber pot, the buttons on his fly still undone. He looked unwell, a stout, compressed old man with a florid, noduled face and a small ungroomed bristling mustache that looked as if it were trying to grow in four directions simultaneously.

"Ah, Salvador, my boy, what a pleasant surprise," he said. "One second and I'm with you."

He limped to the window, opened it and flung the contents of the chamber pot over the bucket makers. The hammering never faltered.

Udo shrugged. "Those shit bastards are meant to stop at lunchtime, but who cares?" He spoke English with a marked German accent. Carriscant shook his extended left hand as the right still clutched the chamber pot; he was fond of the old man, but Annaliese liked to keep contact to a minimum. Udo set the pot on the desk and wiped some drops of moisture off his fingers onto the blotter. He opened a drawer and offered Carriscant a cigar, which he declined.

Udo waggled his plump fingers over the display, selected a cigar and rolled it sensuously under his veined and bulbous nose.

"La Flor de Isabela," he said, wistfully. "As good as the finest Havana. Have I ever told you that?"

"Emphatically," Carriscant said. "How are the pianos going?"

"Slowly. Did I tell you I was opening a laundry?"

They speculated awhile on the inevitable success of this venture before Carriscant told him why he had called. A friend, he said, had ordered a piece of industry machinery from France and he needed it shipped to Manila, but with discretion. This friend was concerned that as a Filipino he might not be permitted to import such a component.

"What is it?" Udo asked. "A howitzer?"

"An engine. It's . . . it's a special kind of engine. For a type of automobile."

"Is he building a motorcar? Very shrewd. I saw one the other day, down here at the docks. Astonishing. German, of course."

"Something like that. And he can't afford to pay the duty."

Udo assured him that the whole matter was very straightforward. It might cost a little extra, but he knew many agreeable ships' captains and many shipping firms who would be happy to oblige. If the engine could be conveyed to Hong Kong, then from that point forward the maximum discretion could be assured.

Udo limped to the top of the stairs to see Carriscant off.

"What's wrong, Udo?"

"Gout, or something. My leg's changing color. Turning blue."

"Come to the hospital, I'll have a look at it."

"You'll have it off, more likely." He looked at him dolefully. "No disrespect, Salvador, but I don't trust your lot."

He called down the stairs. "How's Annaliese?"

"Ah . . . Well. Very well."

"I'd love to see her again."

"Of course, Udo. Very soon. Thanks for your help."

PATON BOBBY'S OFFICE was on the second floor of the Ayuntamiento, Manila's town hall, a huge overdecorated coral and white building on the Plaza Mayor adjacent to the cathedral. Bobby sat behind his desk, out of uniform, wearing a light tweed suit and a bow tie. The effect was surprising: as if the burly law officer had turned into a university professor or music teacher. From his chair Carriscant could see one of the cathedral's domed towers with a seagull sitting preening itself on the top of the surmounting cross. Bobby was informing him of the series of unsatisfactory interviews he had undertaken with the men of Ephraim Ward's platoon: it seemed unlikely now, he reluctantly concluded, that Ward had been murdered by a fellow soldier.

The gull hunched itself into the air and soared off beyond the frame of the window.

"Somebody got him, though. He left his post and somebody fucking got him."

Carriscant shifted in his seat: Ephraim Ward's fate seemed remote from him now.

"He definitely wasn't shot, was he? Someone couldn't have gouged out a bullet? You thought he was stabbed, right?" Bobby scratched his skull through his thin hair with the end of a pencil.

"I'm sure. By the way, Cruz has still not returned the heart. The liver, but not the heart." Carriscant closed his eyes briefly and tried to set his tone of voice to neutral. "My wife," he began slowly, "my wife met an American woman at one of her church functions the other night, but she's completely forgotten her name. A young woman, late twenties, tall, freckled with fair hair. Apparently."

"Jesus, Carriscant, do you know how many American women there are out here now? Wives, nurses, missionaries, teachers . . . Must be hundreds."

"I told her. She wanted me to ask all the same . . ." He paused. "Perhaps she has a position of authority, some rank. She mentioned the Malacañan Palace. Some sporting club?"

Bobby thought. "Fair hair, you say. Quite a striking woman?"

"Yes. I mean, as far as I can gather."

"Now that you mention it, it sounds rather like Miss Caspar. What's her name? Unusual . . . Yeah, Miss Rudolfa Caspar. Rudolfa, that's it."

"Miss?"

"Headmistress of the Gerlinger School. The new one in Binondo."

"Thank you, I'll tell my wife."

The conversation returned once again to Ward's murder, Carriscant suggesting it could be any criminal from the Tondo slums, Bobby reluctant to concede it might be as random as that. They walked to the door and Bobby followed Carriscant onto the wide marble landing above the main staircase.

". . . But why dump him miles away?" Bobby was saying. "Why not leave him where he fell?"

A uniformed man walked by, stopped and turned. "Hello, Bobby," he said. "Any news?"

Bobby introduced him to Carriscant—a Colonel Sieverance. He had a pleasant, boyish face and a thin mustache, a little patchy. If that was the best-quality bristle your face could produce, Carriscant thought, then it would be better to go clean-shaven. Colonel Sieverance seemed remarkably young to hold such an elevated rank, and there was something familiar about him too, Carriscant thought . . . Perhaps they had met before, somewhere.

"Ward used to be in the colonel's battalion," Bobby explained. "Dr. Carriscant examined the body—he has been most helpful."

Sieverance smiled; he had an engaging, enthusiastic manner, not in the least warlike or military, Carriscant thought. "A doctor?" he said gladly. "Are you a physician, sir?"

"I'm a surgeon, I'm afraid."

"Damn. Why can't the U.S. Army hire a decent physician?" He grinned ruefully. "Thought you'd made my day. Nice to see you. So long, Bobby."

"He's on the governor's staff now," Bobby said, watching Sieverance stride off down a corridor. "Agreeable fellow."

A DIET OF BEEF TEA

*T*HE FISH ARE jumping," Pantaleon said. "Time to dig for worms."

Carriscant cut into the flesh of the loin. It was pulpy and edematous, which made him worried. The man on the operating table, a money changer from Binondo, had been one of Cruz's patients who had returned to the hospital after being discharged, complaining of pains in his abdomen and of a cloudiness in his urine. Carriscant cut through the integument and separated the muscles. He paused while the nurses swabbed and sponged.

"What did Cruz do with this fellow, Panta?" he asked.

Pantaleon checked his notes. "He thought it might be malaria, or else—you'll like this—'obstinate constipation.' "

"Good God."

"He applied a hot fomentation over iodide of potash. Look, you can see the remains of the blistering."

Carriscant felt disgusted. "You know, sometimes I feel we might as well be living in caves fighting dinosaurs. This man's dying of perinephritis and Cruz is smearing ointments on him to blister his skin."

"Don't forget the morphia given as a suppository."

"You're joking!"

"And a diet of beef tea."

Carriscant laughed loudly, joined by his theater nurses. You had to laugh, he supposed. If people knew what misplaced trust in their physicians subjected them to . . .

The incision was held apart by retractors and Carriscant looked at the exposed organ. What he could see of it was an unhealthy gray; there was a lot of fat and fibrous tissue obscuring much of the surface. He inserted his finger into the cavity, feeling between the kidney and the diaphragm. There was a spurt of pus, which spattered onto his sleeve. He smelled its farinaceous sweetness, noting that it was a brackish green in color. He had found the abscess, about the size of a tangerine, he guessed.

"How's the new project going?" he asked Pantaleon as he stitched the wall of the abscess cavity to the lip of the wound.

"Very well. I must say the standard of local carpentry is astonishing. They'll make anything."

"I know." Carriscant pulled away with his fingers loose sloughs of cellular tissue and shook them off into a bowl. "I remember having some marquetry replaced by a fellow who lived in Tondo. Just a little shack, really. This stuff had been done in Japan. When he'd finished you couldn't tell the difference."

"You should see the propellor blades—exquisite. How much longer? Pulse is a bit thready."

"Five minutes . . . Dressing forceps, Nurse."

Carriscant pulled away more of the adipose tissue. "Depend if there's a fistula, I suppose." He felt with his finger. "Don't think so."

"I hope to have all the panels done by next week."

"Really? Fast work . . . Lot of suppuration here."

He washed out the abscess cavity with a solution of carbolic acid and inserted a drainage tube. He had found out where the Gerlinger School was, where the American woman worked. Bad idea to wait there while the children were studying. Later in the day perhaps. He closed up the wound with some sutures. One of the nurses laid a large wadding of soaked cotton wool over the wound.

"That should do it," he said. "And I think a large and abundant enema might be called for."

Pantaleon chuckled. "Cruz would certainly approve."

"And some ergot of rye. Two doses for the next three days. Wheel him out."

He walked over to the sink to wash his hands. Stink of pus clung to him. How Annaliese hated that. Like being married to a fishmonger.

"What's up next?" he called to his nurse.

"Volvulus of the small intestine."

Busy day, he thought, busy day.

ON THE LUNETA

*T*HE GERLINGER SCHOOL WAS down a side street
off Escolta, a hundred yards or so from that prosperous
strip of elegant stores and the tinselly allure of the Chinese
fancy goods emporia. It was a former barracks of the *guardia
civil* and still had a somewhat institutional and cheerless aspect,
although some attempt had been made to pretty it up recently
by planting a border of zinnias along the foot of the façade.
The children were gone by the time Carriscant arrived at the
end of the afternoon.

An old woman swabbing down the stone flags in the entrance hall directed him to the teachers' common room, where
a trio of youthful nuns confirmed that Miss Caspar had gone
for the day.

"Is it urgent business?" one of them asked politely.

"Ah, no, Sister, it's . . ." He paused—how to express this?
"A personal matter."

Something of his anguish must have irradiated the familiar
phrase because the three nuns all glanced sympathetically at
each other and then one of them volunteered the information
that it was Miss Caspar's habit to take a walk on the Luneta
before she went home. Especially if the constabulary band was
playing.

• • •

THE LUNETA WAS a small park between the battlements of Intramuros and the seawall where traditionally the citizens of Manila gathered for the *paseo* at dusk. The custom had survived the arrival of the Americans and it was one of the few occasions during which foreigners, *mestizos* and native Filipinos encountered each other in some sort of relaxed and egalitarian social mix.

When Carriscant arrived at the modest esplanade around which most of the ostentatious parading and covert scrutiny took place, a few people were beginning to saunter away and the last Angelus could be heard tolling faintly from the old city. All the same there were over a hundred carriages still making their steady clockwise circuit around and around, beneath the now glimmering streetlights. He ordered his driver to stop and he proceeded on foot down the central paved area, with some difficulty through the dawdling crowds, toward the bandstand, from where the sound of a competently played Strauss waltz was carried to him on the sea breeze. He glanced about him rapidly as he went, scanning every white female face, completely confident that his eye would pick her out—rather in the way one's own name leaps out from any printed page—from the mass of people wandering to and fro, chatting, flirting, ogling, commenting on the burnished landaus and victorias and the lacy finery of the women they contained. There were many American soldiers present in their dress whites with their soft pinched hats, rich Chinese in vibrant silks, Englishmen in boating coats and solar topees, and here and there an old friar would shuffle past nervously, dreaming of the old days before the Revolution and the Americans' arrival. On his right was the wide placid bay, its waters dark now that the sun was dipping behind the Bataan headland, the darker shapes of the moored ships riding at anchor pricked out by colored lights.

He waited by the bandstand a few tense interminable minutes but could not see her. In spite of the cool of the evening, his fretful excited mood was making him perspire. He mopped his brow and dried his moist palms with his handkerchief before crossing the road to the seawall, where he stood for a while, eyes closed, telling himself to relax and fanning his glowing face with his panama. As he began to calm down a new mood of sober rationality began to infect him . . . What in God's good name did he think he was doing running about the Luneta like a lovelorn youth? He was Dr. Salvador Carriscant, surgeon-in-chief of the San Jerónimo Hospital, any number of people here would recognize him. He glanced tentatively left and right; it was just as well that dusk was advancing—beyond the streetlights' glow most people's faces were shadowed. And if the woman had been at the school, what would he have done? he rebuked himself further. He had had some story ready about wanting to enroll a mythical niece in the school, but the first elementary questions on her part would have exposed his visit for the evident sham it was. He felt a forceful disgust at his senseless impetuosity: it was not dignified. He settled his hat on his head and turned for home, thinking with rueful wisdom that dignity was the first quality to be abandoned when the heart took over the running of human affairs.

And then he saw her.

With two other women and, he saw a moment later, two male companions walking behind, two men in drill suits, all of them approaching the bandstand, upon which the band had now struck up an irritating oompah-pah Sousa march.

He crossed the roadway, darting between carriages, and began to follow the group, hanging back some way off to the side. She wore a small hat, which made her look more neat and formal than that day on the archery field, but he could see that her face was animated, she was enjoying herself, and for the first time he saw her smile.

They gathered around the bandstand and the music

changed again to a brassy but plaintive rendition of "Quando m'en vo' " from *La Bohème*. He moved to a position obliquely behind her, where her face was in quarter profile, and watched her clasp her hands to her throat in delight as she mouthed the words of the aria to herself, rejoicing in the music. His eyes dropped and he watched her haunches sway to and fro, pliantly twirling the folds of her long skirt this way and that as she shifted weight, almost dancing with herself, swaying to the poignant rhythms of the melody.

This was too much for him: this was too much for anyone in his position to bear. He felt a kind of hopeless swoon come over him, a lightness, as if his body had emptied, and he stood there, a husk, capable of being carried away by the lightest breeze.

Her two women companions stood a little way in front of her. One of the men at her side pointed out a girl selling candied sweets and nuts. She nodded and dispatched him to purchase some while the other man made the same request of the two women. Was one of these fellows her beau? he wondered. Or were these simply colleagues from the Gerlinger School? She stood now, alone for a few seconds, lost in the music. Three strides took him to her shoulder.

"Miss Caspar"—his voice was low, intimate—"excuse me . . ."

She did not respond, did not turn. He repeated her name, raising his voice somewhat. Nothing. He reached out and with trembling fingers touched the material of her air blue blouse.

She turned with a little shudder of surprise and he looked into that face once more.

"Miss Caspar, excuse me, I wanted to see you. I waited—"

"Who are you? I'm afraid I don't . . ." Her fingers brushed her forehead above her right eye as she focused on him. Her frown tightened.

"Good Lord, it's you. You're the mad fellow who rushed screaming out of—"

"Miss Caspar, I came to apologize. I wanted personally to—"

"Stop. Please. The matter is closed. No need."

There was a token smile and she began to turn away. On the periphery of his vision he was aware of her two men friends returning with their sweetmeats.

His voice became urgent: "Miss Caspar—"

"Listen, if you call me that once more, I'll—"

"Rudolfa, then," he said, bravely. "If I may, Rudolfa, I would like to explain—"

"What? What are you talking about? *Rudolfa?*" She stepped back abruptly. "Would you kindly leave me alone, or I'll call the police."

One of the men appeared suddenly at her elbow. He could sense all was not well and said to Carriscant aggressively: "What do you want?" He turned back to the woman. "Is everything all right, Delphine?"

Delphine . . .

"Excuse me," Carriscant said, somehow managing a small bow. "Forgive me, a case of mistaken identity."

He strode off up the esplanade, bumping into people as he went, heedless, face set in a haughty seigneurial grimace to mask his coruscating embarrassment, thinking only: "You damn fool, Paton Bobby, you damn stupid big American fool."

THE HOUSE AT SAN TEODORO

CARRISCANT WATCHED his mother shuffle onto the *azotea*, her arm held by a young girl, and then settle herself with some difficulty in her favorite chair. The cane blind on the east side was raised to allow the weak morning sunshine to warm her briefly. The house at San Teodoro (about a sixty-mile journey from Manila) was large and simple, two stories high and made up of big square rooms with highly polished wood floors. It had belonged to his mother's family for generations, and his father had always seemed a little out of sorts in it, a little lost, dwarfed by its massive generosity—what did one want with four public rooms on the ground floor?—and he never appeared truly comfortable within its walls. It was as if, as a foreign interloper, he were being haunted by the shades of the swaggering, complacent *mestizo* landowners who had run their fiefdom of San Teodoro for a hundred years, secure and unreflecting, until the *americanos* came. Who is this pale, sandy-haired engineer, these ancestral voices seemed to echo, what has this meek fellow from his distant rain-lashed country to do with this family, its heritage and its responsibilities?

And his father had felt it, Carriscant recognized now, as he supervised the laying out of the tea things, he was happier riding up and down his railway or in the syndicate offices in Manila. Whenever they came to stay at San Teodoro something in him seemed to shrivel and cower, until their carriage bore them away again, through the avenue of *nassa* trees that lined the driveway, and his father's spine seemed to straighten and his shoulders flex, and he was Archibald Carriscant, Dundonian, engineer, once again.

He poured out some corn coffee from the English teapot as his mother stared silently out at the clump of *madre de cacao* trees in the garden, just coming into bloom. He was used to his mother's silences, in fact he enjoyed the freedom of not having to make conversation, so he sat back in his chair and sipped the sour brew. Since his father had died she had become increasingly eccentric, not taciturn or withdrawn, exactly, but moody, in the sense that she allowed whatever mood she was in absolute sway over her demeanor. If she was merry, then she was delightful company; if she was depressed, then she was melancholia personified. She made no apologies for these swings, in fact she regarded her refusal to pretend as a positive virtue. Carriscant glanced at her: today was a little hard to evaluate. "Preoccupied" perhaps, or "thoughtful"— nothing too grim, anyway. Along with this new honesty she seemed to have cast off some of the pretensions of her *mestiza* sophistication, and as she had aged she appeared to have darkened too, as if her *india* blood were seeping to the surface of her skin, an old pigmentation reestablishing itself. She had rejected her Spanish and European wardrobe for more traditional clothes. Today she wore a simple broad-sleeved abaca blouse over a black velvet skirt and around her shoulders lay a *pañuelo* fringed with lace and heavily worked with delicate embroidery. A small ebony fan hung from her wrist and every minute or two she would snap it open and fan her face vigorously as a matter of reflex rather than need. Her face was sunken and seamed with wrinkles like a peach stone, but her brown moist eyes were alert and suspicious. She still ran the household at San Teodoro and had regular meetings with her farm managers. Once a quarter the tenant farmers would travel down from the estates in the north and present her with copies of the monthly accounts.

Carriscant sipped at his coffee and set it down: the stuff was vile, he thought, he only sipped at it to please her. No doubt her newfound taste for it was another move back to her forebears.

"You haven't asked me how I'm feeling," she said. "What's the point of having a doctor for a son if he has no curiosity about your state of health?"

"Because I can see you're fine. You look wonderful."

"I'm not fine. I've felt terrible since Flaviano was killed. Nothing's been the same."

Flaviano had been her majordomo; he had been killed in the war.

"Well, we've got peace now," he said. "Life will return to normal." How easy it was to express the sentiment: he almost believed it himself.

"We're all Americans now," she said. "That will be interesting. Not that I shall live to see it."

"Better this than what we were," he said halfheartedly.

She looked at him, full of scorn. "There were other options, you know," she said. "It wasn't a simple case of either-or."

"Realistically . . ."

"Do you know any of them? *Americanos?*"

"Plenty. Very friendly people."

"Don't forget I've seen how friendly they can be," she said, turning away to look out at the garden. She did not need reminding—and neither did he—of the day a company of the Third Wyoming Volunteers had visited San Teodoro.

"Look, I've got no quarrel with the Americans," he said. "From my point of view—with a few exceptions—they've done nothing but good. At least they're trying. We were rotting out here before. Backward, neglected. We were like some eighteenth-century province of Spain, all friars and hidalgos.

This is the twentieth century, Mother—" He stopped when he saw her face and changed the subject. "How's your hip?"

"Terrible. This last rainy season it was agony. Awful. I remember your father suffered from arthritis, I used to think he was making a ridiculous fuss. Now I know."

Carriscant thought about his father, how little he had known him. A fair, decent man, kind, not very demonstrative . . . All of a sudden he wished he were alive, wished he were here so he could ask his advice. He was surprised at the strength of this emotion. He missed him, and he felt the ache in his chest. And then he tried to dismiss the idea as absurd. Oh, Father, I've fallen out of love with my wife and am obsessed with an unknown American woman, what should I do?

"When you married Father," he asked his mother abruptly, "was your family opposed? Did they mind?"

"Why should they mind? We'd already intermarried. Anyway, my father knew I wanted to, and he wouldn't have stopped me."

"An enlightened man."

"An intelligent man." She wagged her fan at him. "*Le coeur a ses raisons que la raison ne connaît point.*" She looked sharply at him. "Who said that?"

"Ah . . . Voltaire?"

"Pascal, foolish boy. The great Pascal. When you're in that position there's nothing you can do. You might as well follow your heart. At least that way you might find some happiness." She looked at him shrewdly. "For a while, anyway."

Carriscant thought about this and gazed out over the garden. Some doves were wooing beneath the *madre de cacao* trees, pacing to and fro, wobbling featherballs of lust.

He stood up. "I should be going," he said, suddenly decided.

"Go on, go on. You've been here long enough. Go back to your darling *americanos.*"

Smiling, he bent and kissed her cheek. He rested his hands on her shoulders and felt the thin bones through the material. She held his face between her skewed and knuckly hands and kissed him on the brow.

"Goodbye, Mother. And thank you."

The thought came to him, as it always did on parting, that he was the product of the strangest union—the meeting of a timid Scottish engineer from Dundee and a combative provincial *mestiza* heiress from southern Luzon. No wonder he could not fathom his own personality sometimes.

"What do you mean, 'thank you'? Are you all right?" she asked. "There's nothing wrong, is there?"

"No, of course not."

"You're not going away again, are you? It was so long the last time. I'll be dead soon, you can go away anywhere then."

"No, no, I'm not going away. I'll be here."

"Well, be careful. And you can bring that wife of yours the next time, if you want. I won't be rude to her."

"I will, she'd like that."

He kissed her again and left her on the *azotea*. He waved back at the small figure as the carriage pulled out of the house's forecourt and bore him down the driveway toward San Teodoro, flashing in and out of the shade cast by the avenue of *nassa* trees. He felt his spine stiffen and his shoulders broaden as he contemplated what lay ahead, Archibald Carriscant's son, truly. There was a smell of molasses carried to him on the breeze.

DAWN ON THE PASIG

*F*RAIL COILS AND EDDIES of mist rose up from the turbid green-gray waters of the Pasig as the small flat-bottomed ferry nosed up to the jetty on the northern bank. Dr. Salvador Carriscant, wearing a frayed and worn dustcoat and a small peaked cap, was the only passenger at this hour. He stepped off the prow onto the wooden decking and pulled his collar up. He was dressed this way in an attempt to allay suspicion and to draw a minimum of attention to himself. It was still cool and fresh and the almost risen sun gave the air and dew-drenched landscape a pewtery, matte finish. He hurried past the curious glances of the few *indio* peasants, waiting with their sacks of vegetables, and disappeared down the path that led through a fringe of riverine trees toward the distant white walls of the Malacañan Palace.

This was his third crepuscular visit to the archery field, driven there by a vague and desperate plan of first seeing the American woman again and then perhaps following her back to her home or place of work. But it was the need to take action itself, primarily, actually to have something to do, that prompted these early rises. He felt that he could not make any more inquiries without drawing attention to himself, and he certainly could not, should he ever encounter her again in public, approach her and try to explain who he was and why he was there. He had to see her on his own, he realized, only then could he resolve the misunderstanding.

And he deliberately did not think beyond that moment, if it could be engineered, and what would happen subsequently; all his efforts would be directed simply to bringing it about, and after that, chance, destiny, fate would have to determine what happened next. He felt both foolish and exhilarated by these dawn excursions: he knew, from the vantage point of disinterested rationality, that all this creeping about in the bushes was preposterous and demeaning, and yet there was no denying that the sense of adventure, of what might be, was exciting and fulfilling in its own right. In the past few days he had lived more intensely, his waking hours had been more charged with anticipation, than he could remember in years. Perhaps this was a definition of obsession? The ability both to see the manifest error in a course of action and yet to pursue it fiercely just the same . . . Whatever it was, it fulfilled him; it allowed him to go about his business in the hospital, to lead a normal family life with some measure of control and equanimity, for he knew that in a day or so he would be sitting damply once again in the acacia wood near the palace, the sun warming the treetops, waiting for Delphine to appear.

Delphine.

He muttered the name to himself, tasting its two syllables, as the path entered the woods. Delphine. At least that ghastly encounter on the Luneta had procured her Christian name. The other day he had been on the point of asking Bobby if he knew an American woman called Delphine, but at the last moment an onset of caution had made him hold back. That question could only prompt others in return; better to keep his own counsel for the moment.

He left the path and made his way through the wood toward the screen of *cogal* bushes that marked the perimeter of the archery butts. He had found a position that gave him a good view of the field and of the track that led from the palace and San Miguel, up which carriages had to come. He settled himself down in his hiding place, his back against the seamed trunk of an acacia tree, and prepared to wait.

The grass field was fully sunlit and the first flies were beginning to buzz around his head when he heard the clopping of horses' hooves and the crunch of carriage wheels from the lane. Three carriages pulled up and about ten or a dozen ladies noisily descended, fussing around, fitting wrist guards, stringing bows and selecting arrows for their quivers. He saw almost at once that she was not there, and the frustration that this covert scrutiny had held at bay for the last forty-eight hours washed over him with full depressing force. He sat back wearily against the tree, rebuking himself all over again, the cries and laughter of these young American women at their sport carrying to him across the grass, and the soft padded thuds as the first loosed arrows struck home against the straw targets.

He called to mind her face, that first day he saw her; called to mind the way the quiver strap had defined her breasts—quite full and large, he thought now, larger and rounder than Annaliese's. And he found himself remembering too the way she had swung her hips to the music that evening on the Luneta . . . She was a tall woman, there was nothing gamine or petite about her, nothing girlish. And her skin was so strange, white as a milkfish . . . Her buttocks would be milk-pale too, he thought, and her thighs . . . He tried to imagine her naked, shutting his eyes against the dappled canopy above him, altering his position to allow his swelling erection a chance to shift freely beneath his trousers. A wand of sunlight beamed through a gap in the leaves above him and warmed his flank. Holding these images in his mind, embellishing them, he reached for his handkerchief with one hand while his other tremblingly undid the buttons on his fly. Delphine. Shucking off her quiver, her light fingers on her blouse buttons, her pale blue-veined bubs freed, swaying, her—

"Yay! *Pasaylua ako.*"

The old thin-chested man in a frayed knee-length *barò* stood about twenty feet away, staring in amazement at him through a gap in the trees, frozen in the attitude of picking up a fallen branch, a small bundle of firewood under his other arm.

Carriscant clawed himself to his feet, aghast, doubling over simultaneously, covering himself.

The old man smiled warmly at him, showing his few remaining betel-stained teeth, and said something in Tagalog, chuckling.

Carriscant thrashed his way through the undergrowth to the path. He heard the old man calling after him and somehow his delighted words penetrated the howling screeching mortification that reverberated in his head.

"It's only human, my son!" the old man was shouting after him in Tagalog. "Don't feel shame, it's only human!"

A NNALIESE WOKE him, shaking his shoulder gently, and calling his name. "Salvador . . . Salvador, there's a man here to see you."

Carriscant sat up abruptly, oddly embarrassed to find his wife in his study. She wore a woolen robe pulled tightly around her and her hair was uncombed and tousled. She let the mosquito net drop and stepped back uncertainly from the divan bed as if she too suddenly felt the shame of being confronted by their unorthodox sleeping arrangements.

"What man?" Carriscant said, peering at her through the gauzy muslin. "Pantaleon?"

"An American. He says it's very urgent."

Carriscant dressed quickly and went through to the living room. Paton Bobby stood in the middle of the carpet, dressed in uniform, wearing a full-length cloak. Nervous servants peered, big-eyed, from doorways.

"I'm sorry, Carriscant," Bobby said. "Wieland can't be found. There's been another killing."

JUST BEYOND Santa Mesa, a poor, mean hamlet two miles east of Manila, a stone bridge crossed the San Juan River. The carriage—Bobby driving, Carriscant beside him—rumbled across its cobblestones and stopped with a gentle lurch. It was three o'clock in the morning. Down below them, by the water's edge, Carriscant could see half a dozen American soldiers, some holding lanterns.

Carriscant slithered down the grassy bank behind Bobby, who was handed a hooded lantern by one of the soldiers. "It's under the bridge," Bobby said, swinging the beam in that direction. Carriscant followed its unwavering path cautiously, the ground damp and marshy beneath his feet, a reek of decay and human excrement filling his nostrils.

The body of the man had been propped against the stone supports of the bridge's first arch, almost as if it had sat down there for a rest and had fallen into a doze. It still had trousers and boots but there was no trace of the rest of the uniform. This time, cause of death was immediately apparent: a single blow from a *bolo* delivered to the top of the head, splitting it like a melon. The entire torso was soaked in treacly, dried blood, which had flowed from the head wound and, Carriscant saw, with a lurch of shock in his chest, as he crouched down to examine it, from a more torn and unstitched version of the inverted L-shaped wound that had disfigured Ephraim Ward's corpse. About two feet of intestine, ragged and frayed, had been dragged from the belly, probably by river rats. The right hand and forearm were missing, severed neatly at the elbow.

"Found at midnight," Bobby said, his voice reverberating beneath the vault of the bridge. "He was on furlough. Last seen last night at ten-thirty p.m. in a Sampaloc bar."

"Just over twenty-four hours . . . Sampaloc's only a mile or so from here. He's a soldier?"

"Corporal Maximilian Braun. German spelling."

"I can't examine him here. Let's get him back to the hospital."

There was the sound of wheels echoing on the roadway above their heads, and soon they were joined, to Carriscant's vague surprise, by the young colonel, Sieverance, who greeted them both with due solemnity.

"Christ's blood, what a stench there is down here! What do they dump in these rivers?" He leaned forward carefully, like a man peering over a parapet on a high building, and spat on the ground. He held his handkerchief to his nose as he talked. "Governor Taft wants a full report," Sieverance said, explaining his presence. He took off his hat and scratched his head vigorously, nervously. He was bleary-eyed, and the tuft of hair he left standing made him look absurdly young and vulnerable, Carriscant thought.

"I'm most grateful to you again, Dr. Carriscant," he said. "We did eventually locate Dr. Wieland, but he's incapable of conducting any sort of investigation. He couldn't even investigate the whereabouts of his boots when I tracked him down."

A stretcher was called for and Corporal Braun's body was carried carefully up the riverbank and loaded onto Bobby's carriage. A tarpaulin was thrown over it and Bobby and Carriscant, with Sieverance close behind, made their way back through the darkened, silent city to the San Jerónimo. Porters unloaded the body, placed it on a wooden gurney, and the three men followed its monotone rumble along gloomy corridors to the morgue. The door was locked; the porter's key did not fit, neither did Carriscant's. The sister on duty was summoned and she explained that Dr. Cruz had had the lock changed and the only key was in his care.

Carriscant managed to control his anger somehow and instructed the porters to take the body into his operating theater and strip and wash it. In the meantime he, Bobby and Sieverance drank a cup of hot tea laced with rum in his consulting rooms.

Bobby seemed moved and upset. "This is crazy," he kept repeating. "One, yes, you can explain. Some thug with a grievance decides to cut up his victim. Two, and it's a whole different thing. Major problem."

"Who did you say he was?" Sieverance asked.

"A Corporal Braun."

"Two soldiers. Got to be insurgents, surely?"

"Except the only insurgents left are three hundred miles away on another island being chased by thousands of American troops."

"I suppose so." Sieverance frowned. "Yes. Fair point."

"A major problem."

IN THE THEATER Braun's washed and naked body lay in a pool of brilliant light on the operating table. Both Sieverance and Bobby seemed more impressed by the gleaming chrome and general cleanliness of the room than anything else as they moved around investigating the equipment.

"This is quite an establishment, Doctor," Sieverance said. "No disrespect, I mean, I feel I could be in the U.S."

"Well, you'd have to be somewhere very special," Carriscant said. "Not all of this equipment is commonly available."

"I'm not surprised." Sieverance nodded. "When I think of Wieland's surgery—the filth, the primitiveness—"

"We got to talk about Wieland, Colonel," Bobby said. "Seriously."

Carriscant approached the body while they conversed briefly in low voices. Braun had been a stocky man, in his late thirties, with a sizable paunch. His chest and belly were covered in a thick growth of springy gray hair. Carriscant selected a thin probe from his tray of instruments and inserted it into the wide wound in the chest.

"The heart has gone," he said.

"What?" both men answered simultaneously and strode to the table.

"The heart—and the right hand, obviously. Removed competently but with no great skill."

Sieverance turned away, paling, his finger-backs to his lips. "That make any sense? Is there some sort of native cult out here? Sacrificial cult or something?"

"Not that I know of," Carriscant said.

"And what about this L-shape?" Bobby said. "Are the other organs there?"

Carriscant duly opened up the wound. There was some displacement of the intestines, as he had expected, but otherwise everything else seemed to be normal.

"And the last one was stitched up," he said, "but the heart was there. This time, the heart is removed and the wound left open. It makes no sense to me—I can't see any reason behind it."

"But it can't be a coincidence," Bobby said. "We know that it must be the same murderer. Or murderers."

"Where was he last seen?"

"He went out the back of a Sampaloc cathouse to take a leak. Nobody noticed he never came back in. Figured he was upstairs."

"What's in back of those places?" Sieverance asked.

Carriscant coughed and cleared his throat; they both looked at him expectantly, but he raised his spread palms in apology. Bobby shrugged.

"Some yards, a few shacks, vegetable plots, open country," he said. "Anyone can get in or out."

CARRISCANT AND BOBBY left Governor Taft's office in the Malacañan Palace and walked down the wide corridor in silence to the central stairway. Taft, a vast, genial man, sweating copiously in a white suit, had been suitably grateful for Carriscant's help and, in confidence, had asked him for his professional opinion of Dr. Wieland. "An incompetent and diehard quack," was Carriscant's candid verdict. On their leaving, Taft had asked for his compliments to be presented to Mrs. Carriscant, a request that had taken Carriscant somewhat by surprise until he remembered Annaliese's social connections with the governor's wife.

As they stood beneath the lofty porte cochere waiting for their carriages, Bobby said, "You know, Corporal Braun used to be in Sieverance's battalion as well."

"Odd. He didn't say anything."

"I guess 'Brown' *sounds* a common name. Can't tell how it was spelled. Didn't realize."

"Didn't recognize, either."

"I wouldn't recognize you with your head split to your bottom teeth," Bobby said with sardonic levity. "Got to shake him up some, though, when he finds out."

Carriscant thought. "You think it was someone who was in the unit? Some grudge?"

"That's one explanation." Bobby smoothed his wide mustache with his thumb and forefinger. "And here's another thing, your colleague, Dr. Quiroga—"

"What's he got to do with this?"

"One of his uncles is General Elpidio. Esteban Elpidio. The one who led us on such a merry dance in Tayabas this spring."

"What are you saying? You captured Elpidio."

"No, it was something you said about the organs in Ward's body. The disturbances. Now a heart's missing—'competently removed,' you said—maybe a professional's hand was—"

"Just stop now, Bobby. This is ridiculous. If you're going to start suspecting any Filipino related to an *insurrecto*, you're—"

"I'll suspect anyone I fucking want, Carriscant, anyone." Bobby looked at him fiercely, irritated by his tone, then his shoulders slumped and he smiled apologetically.

"Sorry, sorry . . ." Bobby said, laying a hand gently on his sleeve for a moment. "I don't know, my head's just spinning with this one. Spinning."

PITCH, YAW AND ROLL

Y OU HAVE no right, no right at all to address me this way," Carriscant said, trying to keep the tremble of fury out of his voice. There was an air of hostile self-assurance in the room, an unpleasant, potent complacency in the atmosphere. These two men, Carriscant thought—promising himself that he would remain absolutely calm no matter how he was provoked—these two men think they hold the balance of power, feel sure the dealt cards favor them. What did they know? he wondered. What could explain this smug and threatening confidence?

Dr. Isidro Cruz and Dr. Saul Wieland sat stiffly like magistrates in chairs in Cruz's office. Cruz had just come from an operation: there was an exclamation mark of bright blood on his stiff collar, like a brooch, and his clothes carried with him an odor of something frowsty and corrupt. Wieland, cold, blankfaced, scrutinized the cuticles on the nails of his right hand, then his left, affecting disinterest. Carriscant had refused a seat—he did not intend to linger—and stood in the middle of the silk rug in Cruz's office, a gloomy place with dark, polished floors and heavy, overelaborate furniture. Only the privileged knowledge that those few leather-bound books in the glass-fronted bookcases were medical texts would have alerted you to the fact that you were in the consulting rooms of a once eminent surgeon.

Carriscant began again, moderating his voice, trying to sound as reasonable as possible. "None of this is at my instigation. Chief Bobby has only called me out whenever Dr. Wieland has been, ah, unavailable."

"But you accepted the invitation to the governor's palace," Cruz said, unable to keep the note of sneering triumph out of his voice.

"Exactly," Wieland echoed.

"For heaven's sake, what else was I meant to do? The governor himself asked—"

"You should have come directly to me. As medical director of the San Jerónimo, it is *my* responsibility. You are on *my* staff. I speak for the board, for the institution."

"These killings have nothing to do with the hospital."

"The American corpses are being kept in my hospital and I am the last to know. It's intolerable!" He banged his fist down on the arm of his chair. "And what is more," he went on acidly, "Dr. Wieland, a close friend and colleague, has been officially reprimanded by Governor Taft as a result of testimony you provided."

Wieland rose to his feet, the studied neutrality all gone. His eyes were heavy with resentment and distaste. "I demand to know what you said to the governor."

"And I order you to tell him," Cruz added.

Carriscant felt his jaw muscles knot and his shoulders hunch. He deliberately waited a few seconds before replying, adding a drone of bureaucratic indifference to his voice now, the better to goad them. They had just handed him the advantage with their hectoring pomposity; they no longer unsettled him.

"That must remain a confidential matter between me and the governor. The governor requested that our discussion of Dr. Wieland's merits, or otherwise, be conducted under such conditions. I regret—"

This was too much for Wieland, clearly. He stepped toward him. "Listen to me, you nigger bastard—"

"What did you call me? I warn you, I—"

"You meddling half-breed nigger, you keep your nose out of—"

Carriscant's swinging fist caught Wieland too high, on the left ear, and it caused his knuckles to ring with pain, but the force was sufficient to send Wieland down and a moment later Carriscant was astride him, fingers around the plump and pleated throat, his thumbs searching for his windpipe. Cruz threw himself bodily at him, charging him with his shoulder like a man trying to break down a door, and sent him flying into his desk, his head connecting with one of the mighty turned legs. For a second or two all three men were sprawling on the floor, Manila's medical elite in professional dispute. Wieland was the first to his feet, coughing, massaging his throat, and helped Cruz up shakily. Carriscant, somewhat dazed, rubbed his face with his hands, both excited and shocked by the violence which had risen in him. He got to his feet slowly, his head was aching and his body was trembling.

"I'll get you, Carriscant!" Wieland shouted at him hoarsely. He spat on Cruz's polished floor. Twice. Two silver dollars.

Cruz seemed not to notice or care. "I'm reporting you to the board," he bellowed also. "You'll be dismissed!" His chest was heaving, his gray hair spikily awry.

Carriscant said nothing. With one hand held out, fingertips brushing the wall, he walked around the room to the door. There he paused and turned to face them.

"If you ever insult me again, Wieland," he said in a low, quavering voice, "I'll kill you."

"I heard that," Cruz yelled. "I am a witness to that threat!"

He turned to Cruz. "And as for you, I'm going to ask the board for your removal as medical director. You are a disgrace to the profession."

He left the room, heedless of their furious shouts.

• • •

"MY GOD," Pantaleon said, with an enthusiastic smile. "It's war."

"It had to happen sooner or later," Carriscant said. They were walking from Pantaleon's apartment toward the *nipa* barn. "But I have a feeling everything will go quiet." He smiled with some bitterness. "Cruz knows full well that you and I are the source of the hospital's real prosperity. And I have Bobby—even Taft—on my side. Cruz is washed up. Wieland's a fraud and a hopeless drunk. You and I could move to San Lázaro tomorrow—they'd take us with open arms." They pushed through the gap in the plumbago hedge. "No, I'm expecting something more underhand, something more insidiously worthy of the two of them."

He saw that the barn doors were open wide and that the sounds of delicate hammering came from within, small hammers on fine tacks.

"By the way," Carriscant went on, "you know that storeroom, just off the corridor to the theater? I've had it cleaned out."

"Really? Why?"

"It's our new morgue. I'm having some of Cruz's freezing boxes put in there. Big locks on the door, to make sure Braun stays safe. I'll see if I can get Ward back from the other place." He shrugged. "It should make a difference. Keep Cruz and Wieland out of our hair." He turned toward the barn. "What're you up to now?"

"Wait here," Pantaleon said. "I'll show you."

Carriscant waited while Pantaleon entered the barn and the sound of hammering ceased. He exhaled and closed his eyes, feeling his aches, feeling the tension in his limbs groan and tighten. At the moment his life was complicated enough, confused and disturbed enough, without violent animosity breaking out between him and Cruz, but the uneasy neutrality that had existed since the war had ended in July was bound to founder eventually. Perhaps it was better this way, he tried to tell himself, it would at least take his mind off this impossible, obsessive infatuation he had developed . . . Put Cruz out to pasture with his dogs and monkeys, run the hospital in his way, according to his principles and advanced scientific method, sweep out the dead wood—

"Salvador, look."

He opened his eyes. Pantaleon's flying machine was being wheeled out of the shed by a quartet of local carpenters. The thin tapered body rested on a carriage of four bicycle wheels, with a fifth, a smaller one, farther back to provide stability. The Aero-Mobile, as he remembered it was called, had two wings, one above the other, a dense network of slim bamboo struts and tensed wires between the two. Thrusting up from the rounded nose was a third, shorter wing held out and aloft by cradling wooden arms. At the rear was the horizontal semicircular tail, and he noticed that both this and the small panel wing at the front were attached to wire pulley devices that led back to simple wooden levers mounted above the four-wheel carriage. Most of the body and wings were covered with near transparent panels of silk. He reached out and touched the end of a wing: the material was hard and varnished; it reverberated beneath the tap of his fingernail like a drum.

"Extraordinary," he said, genuinely amazed. "And you're sure this thing will fly?"

"In theory. Far enough to win the prize, certainly."

It looked, to his eyes, very frail and very ugly. Like a giant botched model of a dragonfly, crudely conceived, as if by someone who had only had a dragonfly described to him, rather than seen it with his own eyes, and been told to construct a simulacrum from basket-weave, matchwood and paper. It looked front-heavy and impractical . . . And yet there was something touching and ethereal about its backhandedness, its very inelegance. Like certain insects, certain ephemera, which look as if they were never designed by God to fly and yet somehow take to the wing to everyone's surprise. Perhaps Pantaleon's machine would be the same.

"What's missing are the propellors, two of them," Pantaleon said, indicating a wooden mounting on the lower, leading wing. "Screw propellors, based on the marine model but larger. The power plant will be here in the nose, and we'll run chains out here to drive the propellors."

Carriscant wandered around to the rear of the machine. He really had to congratulate Pantaleon: this idealistic dedication, this single-minded pursuit of a dream, was rare in anyone, and now it produced a Pantaleon he hardly recognized. He felt sudden tears of emotion in his eyes and his gaze blurred with salty water. Tears of pride and admiration, tears of love for this lanky young friend of his.

Pantaleon was wiggling the large semicircular tail. It was mounted on a block that could turn, allowing the tail to rotate partially on its axis: one tip dropping two feet while the other rose, and vice versa.

". . . This is the crucial control," Pantaleon was saying. "It took me a year to develop, and long observation of gliding birds—hawks, buzzards. It's this ability to twist their tails"—he demonstrated with his spread fingers, waggling left and right—"that controls rolling in flight." He smiled at Carriscant. "Pitch, yaw and roll," he said. "That is what the Aero-Mobilist really has to conquer. Once we control these three devils, then the air will become our new domain . . ." He walked over to Carriscant and put his arm around his shoulders. "Please, Salvador, don't cry, there's no need."

Carriscant, wordless, moved, turned away and blew his nose into his handkerchief.

"I'm overwhelmed, Panta, overwhelmed." He embraced him. "After a day such as I've had you don't know what a tonic you are, my friend, what an inspiration."

. . .

CARRISCANT SUPERVISED the installation of the ice chests in the new morgue himself. They were in fact used for the refrigerated transportation of perishable food at sea, first developed in Australia, Udo Leys had told him when Carriscant had first described Cruz's arrangement. And it was Udo who had managed to procure these three secondhand examples for him, not quite as large as Cruz's but capacious enough to hold two bodies very comfortably. He had had the interior lining cavity restuffed with new straw and had had the stenciled sign on the side, OH CHUNG LU, MEAT & FISH IMPORTERS, painted over. Filled with ice, the chests (one containing Ward, whom he had rescued from the old morgue; one containing Braun) were pushed against three walls of the new morgue, while in the middle of the room was an enamel-topped examination table with three tin basins beneath. There was already a sink against the fourth wall and the wooden floorboards had been covered with a waterproof cork carpet on his instructions. The morgue would function perfectly until he could secure Cruz's dismissal. It also provided him, he realized, with an ideal place for his own dissections and investigations, should he require it. There was no longer any need to visit the anatomy laboratory at the San Lázaro Hospital: everything necessary was now under his own roof.

He was standing in the new morgue at six o'clock the next evening, indecisive, wondering whether he should return home, now that the day's work was done, or whether he should make one further tour of his wards, when a porter knocked on the door with an envelope marked "Urgent" and "Personal." He tore it open and read the large rapid scrawl.

Dear Carriscant,

I need your help with the utmost urgency on a delicate medical matter. I would be most grateful if you could call on me this evening at my house, 5 Lagarda Street in San Miguel, at your earliest convenience, anytime this evening. I count on your help and your confidentiality.

Yours faithfully,
Jepson Sieverance

Sieverance's house was one of five large newish villas built in the Antillean style not far from the Malacañan Palace, all occupied by members of the governor's staff, that formed a small compound called the Calle Lagarda. There was even a marine on guard at the entrance to the cul-de-sac, sitting idly in a sentry box. He waved Carriscant's victoria through with barely a glance.

Carriscant was shown up to the living room on the first floor, where Sieverance greeted him, clearly in a state of anxiety, his face drawn and somehow sucked in, as if he had lost weight dramatically in the last twenty-four hours. He shook Carriscant's hand overeagerly, almost abject in his gratitude.

"I can't thank you enough, Carriscant. I'm in your debt."

"It's nothing, really. What's the trouble? You don't look at all well, I must say."

"This way, please."

He led Carriscant out of the living room and down a corridor toward, Carriscant imagined, a bedroom where he could be examined in privacy. He paused at a door and knocked gently on it.

"Delphine?" he said. "May we come in?"

He knew at once, of course, immediately, with no doubts or second thoughts. He was vaguely aware of Sieverance opening the door, and of following him into the room. Oil lamps, turned down by a bedside. A gauzy tent of mosquito netting. The sway of the punkah fan on the ceiling, to and fro, to and fro . . .

He ordered his legs to carry him to the bedside as Sieverance gently folded back the netting. He held his face immobile, eyes still, as she turned from her doze to see who it was.

She was propped on several pillows, her dull chestnut hair spread, loose, a moist sheen of perspiration on her pale stressed face.

Sieverance said to her softly, "This is the doctor I was telling you about, my love. This is Dr. Carriscant."

She frowned, lifted an arm as if to block the glare from a lamp, and her eyes grew wide with incredulity.

"How do you do, Mrs. Sieverance," he managed somehow to say quickly. "I'm very sorry to find you unwell."

He felt his face hot; his skin itched.

"Dr. Carriscant? . . . Doctor?" She shook her head, trying to clear it.

"The doctor I told you about. The hospital, remember? Every latest style of equipment."

She closed her eyes and exhaled. He knew, suddenly, instinctively, that she would say nothing.

"Dr. Carriscant . . ." she repeated. "Thank you for coming."

He allowed himself a weak, twitching smile. He felt he was about to fall over. He felt the sweat roll from his armpits, his shirt sticking damply to his back. He reached out and pulled a chair to the bed. Not too close.

"What seems to be the trouble?"

She told him, prompted occasionally by Sieverance, that she had been suffering from pains in the abdomen for a week or so but she had thought nothing of it, suspecting a digestive problem. Then that afternoon she had been stricken by a severe attack of vomiting and the pain had reached intolerable levels. She felt feverish. A friend had called the doctor.

"She called Dr. Wieland," Sieverance interjected. "I was at work. Dr. Wieland was called." He glanced meaningfully at

Carriscant, apologetically. "He *is* our medical officer. It was the natural thing to do, unfortunately."

"What did he diagnose?"

"He didn't offer one. He prescribed a purgative and opium."

"I see. Have you taken them?" He turned his gaze back to her. Delphine. Even sickly and in pain, that face, her hair loose, makes me ... He smiled, all reassurance.

"Yes, of course," she said, a hint of irritation in her voice. "What else was I meant to do? The pain has gotten less, but the purgative ..." She winced. "But the fever is worse, and the pain is coming back, badly."

"Which is why I called you." Sieverance looked pleadingly at him.

"Strictly speaking, Mrs. Sieverance is Dr. Wieland's patient now. I can't really—"

"To hell with that," Sieverance said with untypical fierceness. "I'm not going to worry about the niceties of medical protocol. My wife is seriously ill. I don't care—"

"Jepson," she said wearily. "Don't worry. Dr. Carriscant will help."

She knew her power. Already we have a secret between us. A silent promise has passed between us, he thought.

"Where is the pain?" he asked.

"My stomach, low to the right side."

"Did Dr. Wieland examine you?"

"No."

He sighed. Unbelievable. "I have to," he said. "If you'll permit me. I'm sorry to sound like a textbook, but palpation is often our best diagnostic tool. May I?"

Sieverance looked at his wife for permission.

"Of course," she said. "Please do."

Carefully he folded the sheet back to her knees. She was wearing a white cotton nightdress with frilled bib-effect over the chest. A smell rose up from the bed briefly, her smell, a trace of perfume and powder, of fresh sweat and a sour, momentary reek of shit. He filled his nostrils before the punkah fan swished it away.

"Would you mind indicating . . ."

Her finger went to a point three inches to the left of her right hip. Very gently he rested the tips of his right hand's fingers on her body, feeling its softness through the cotton, feeling its heat, and pressed down.

"It's generally sore down there. I can't really say—"

"Tell me when there's a spasm."

He moved his hand farther to the left. Beneath the tip of his little finger he felt the prickle of her pudenda, a wiry yielding. He moved again a little lower. She gave a gasp of pain. Beneath his fingers he felt the stretched ripe capsule of the abscess, tuberous, rotten, ready to burst.

"May I smell your breath?" He moved his face, not capable of meeting her eyes, and she breathed upon him, brackish and foul. He took her temperature: 102 degrees.

"Dr. Wieland said I should take the purgatives every four hours."

"Of course he would. He has no idea what he's doing. May I have them, please?"

Sieverance handed him a dozen brown paper sachets from the drawer of a bedside cabinet and Carriscant put them in his pocket. He sat back in his chair, steepling his hands, pressing the fingers together to stop them from trembling.

"Mrs. Sieverance, you have what they call in America 'appendicitis.' "

"What's that?"

"There is a small vermiform appendage to part of your intestine called the 'blind gut.' Literally an 'appendix' to your gut, which has become inflamed and swollen. I imagine it is already perforated, which is causing the pain and vomiting. It has caused an abscess which will rupture, I should say, some-time in the next twenty-four hours." He paused. "What happens then is that the corrupt matter will be released into the abdominal cavity, the peritoneum. And once that occurs there is very little we can do."

"I'll die." She looked at him candidly.

"Yes."

WHEN THE TWO MEN returned to the living room Sieverance sat down in a chair and began to weep softly. Carriscant felt a huge awkwardness but managed to stand by him until he composed himself, squeezing his shoulder in what he hoped was a comforting way. He felt like weeping himself as he explained what the future held for her and what had to be done.

"There is no other course of action, Colonel Sieverance. She'll die, I've seen it happen countless times."

"But this operation, have you ever performed it?"

"It's rare. I've done it twice, but without success, unfortunately."

"Meaning what?"

"I was too late. The appendix had ruptured, sepsis was advanced, uncontrollable."

"Jesus Christ, you want to cut her open and you've never saved a patient with this operation?"

"Look, Wieland's ridiculous purgatives are just going to weaken her faster. You might as well cast a spell for all the good it'll do. She has to have the operation."

"I can't risk it."

"Ask her."

"She's in pain. How can she make a clear judgment?" His voice was shrill, girlish, demented with worry. He stood up and walked to the window and peered out into the night. "Wieland's due here in half an hour."

"Don't ask him, man. He knows nothing. Take her to the hospital, we'll operate tonight."

"I want to wait for Wieland. Then I'll decide."

DR. WIELAND DID NOT bother to conceal his huge displeasure, and neither did Dr. Cruz, whom Wieland had asked to accompany him, so he said, to confirm his diagnosis.

"Dr. Carriscant has absolutely no business here," Wieland said, anger distorting his voice. "Mrs. Sieverance is my patient."

"He has my authority," Sieverance insisted. "My wife is ill and I want the best for her."

Wieland had to accept this, which he did with manifest bad grace before pronouncing his diagnosis.

"We think, and Dr. Cruz agrees with me on this, that the gut is inflamed due to a lack of mobility. The colonel will encourage movement of the gut and at the same time the opium will control the pain. Within two or three weeks—"

"—she will be dead and buried," Carriscant said brutally. He saw Sieverance flinch.

Cruz rounded on him and spoke harshly and rapidly in Spanish. "How dare you contradict us. This is as clear a case of perityphilitis as I've ever seen. All this fashionable nonsense about the appendix is unforgivable in the current circumstances. I deplore your presence here and I order—"

"Gentlemen, please," Sieverance said. "Let me understand this: you completely oppose Dr. Carriscant's idea of surgery, and you wish to continue with the purgatives and the opium."

"And a broth four times a day," Cruz added in English. "With alcohol. For to strengthen."

"Colonel Sieverance, do not delay, I beg you," Carriscant said. "Your wife must be operated on at once."

"This is a colic which has inflamed the intestine!" Wieland

shouted at him. "To open the abdomen is tantamount to murder."

"The king of England had his appendix removed a matter of months ago," Carriscant retorted, keeping his voice calm. "It saved his life."

This seemed to silence them for a moment. Then Wieland said, without much confidence, "We are not talking about the same problem here, it's a false analogy." He turned to Sieverance. "The problem with someone like Dr. Carriscant is that he will operate without reflection. If you had indigestion, he would suggest removing your appendix. This is the so-called 'modern' approach, and Carriscant does not care—"

"Just one minute," Carriscant interrupted, approaching Wieland, who backed off. "Be very careful what you say, Wieland. If you slander me, I won't answer for—"

"For God's sake!" Sieverance was exasperated. "I'm going to talk with my wife. A moment, please." He left them alone in the room.

Cruz said malevolently, "You're finished, Carriscant. This is a gross violation of medical ethics."

"Sieverance called me in himself, you stupid old fool."

"Yes, you bastard," Wieland shouted at him, "only because of the filthy rumors you've been whispering in Taft's ear." He pointed a shaking forefinger at him. "What is it with people like you, Carriscant? You're knife-happy, can't wait to cut, cut, cut. Mrs. Sieverance isn't some corpse in a dissecting room!"

"Of course she's not." Carriscant caught himself just in time, his voice heavy with emotion. "She is on the verge of death. I can save her. You two idiots would just prolong her agony, draw it out for a day or two with your useless potions."

"You disgust me," Cruz said. "You're a worm, an insect, you dishonor the profession."

The three of them faced each other, silenced by their virulent animosity. Carriscant felt a vast weariness of spirit sweep through him. They could trade insults for hours, he realized; neither of them would yield an inch of ground. He turned his back on them and walked across the room. There was a small grand piano at the far end, with piles of sheet music stacked on the cover. This was her music, he knew intuitively, as he picked up some of the scores—Brahms, Mendelssohn, Mozart—and he raised the edge of a piano concerto to his nose, as if expecting it to be redolent of her somehow.

"Dr. Carriscant," Sieverance said, reentering the room, "my wife would like to see you."

Sieverance accompanied him back to the bedroom. Her face had a wracked, exhausted look to it. Her hair was damp around her brow and temples.

"I heard your voices raised," she said. "What's happening?"

"Dr. Wieland counsels against surgery," Sieverance said.

She looked at Carriscant directly. The dark eyes seemed bigger than ever. "What do you think?"

"I think . . ." The question unmanned him completely and he felt an upswelling of an emotion in him that he did not recognize. Her gaze held him to the exclusion of everything else. "I think Wieland is a fool and a charlatan and anyone who listened to him would be mad," he said. He wanted to reach forward and take her hand and press it to his lips. "You don't have much time," he said with controlled passion. "This operation is very straightforward. It's only when people delay that there is real danger." He hoped his eyes said everything his words could not: I will save you, I will make you well, trust me with your life, no one else will cherish it like I do.

She raised her hand weakly and seemed to offer it to him, as if she had heard his thoughts. Sieverance stepped forward and took it.

"I want to go with Dr. Carriscant," she said.

INTO THE BODY

THE MORPHINE HAD sedated her, her mouth was slack, her eyes half-closed, unfocused, seeing the world through the screen of her lashes. Pantaleon stood at her head with his mask and his chloroform drop bottle. Two theater nurses with their starched pinafores and frilled caps waited beside the grooved trays of gleaming instruments. Delphine Sieverance lay on the operating table, still in her nightgown, having been brought directly to the theater from her house. There was no time to lose; everything had been prepared with the utmost speed.

Pantaleon looked at him. "The wind is freshening. Time to weigh anchor."

Carriscant nodded and Pantaleon dripped chloroform onto the mask. She was unconscious within seconds. Carriscant reached for the hem of her nightgown and remembered. A crucial act of preparation . . .

He cleared his throat. "Would you please leave the room. Just for a moment or two. Everyone, please, Pantaleon."

The nurses and Pantaleon glanced at each other and left the room without further question. Carriscant closed his eyes and a slow shudder ran through his body. He gripped the nightdress hem and lifted it up, pulling it up her body until it bunched at her ribs. His eye went first to the dense golden ginger furze of her pubic hair and then took in the paleness of her torso, almost bleached in contrast to the stretched in-

flamed area of her lower belly, where the infection glowed lu-
ridly beneath her skin, the fateful roseate blush of incipient
peritonitis. He drew a great gulp of air into his lungs, turned
and went to search in a cupboard beneath the sink for the im-
plements he needed. He found them and stropped the razor
rapidly on the thick leather band hanging above the taps.

Over her body once more he quickly foamed up a lather on
the shaving soap with the brush and then, with short circular
sweeps, he worked the white spumy suds into the wiry curls of
her pubic hair. Reflexively he tested the edge of the blade on
his thumb before, with four or five firm passes, he shaved away
the hair on her mound. He wiped the remaining soap away
with a towel and, unable to resist, he placed his hand there a
moment, feeling it smooth and cool, until the heat of his palm
warmed the skin. He moved his hand inches to the left and,
palpating gently, felt the engorged shape of the abscess. He
made tiny marks on her skin with a chinagraph pencil to act as
a guide—his marks, he thought, my sign—and delineate the
area where he would cut. He laid white cloths over her belly
and thighs, leaving only the area to be operated on clear, and
called the others back in. They said nothing, made no reference to what might have happened in their absence, and took
up their positions again.

"Scalpel."

Carriscant felt the nurse press the slim weighted heel of the
knife into his open palm. His fingers closed around it and the
sudden terror that sluiced through him almost made him stag-
ger with alarm. In all his years as a surgeon, all the hundreds
of times he had stood poised with a knife above a living human
being, he had felt nothing but the elation of the job he was
about to do. This bowel-loosening anguish was shockingly unfamiliar. He felt a tremor in his hands as he laid them on her
taut flushed belly. What was happening to him? Where was
this awful fear, this uncertainty, coming from?

He forced the curved blade to indent the flesh, just above

Poupart's ligament on the right side, and forced himself to apply more pressure until it bit through the epidermis and the blood came. He drew the knife across, making a cut of about six inches, revealing the blood-flecked fatty tissue and then the nacreous surface of the peritoneum, like a soft red-veined yellow marble. Here was the moment: another cut and the abdominal cavity was exposed. He widened the opening and then reached down with his finger and pushed it into her body to find the appendix. He located it, now enlarged to a swollen suppurating abscess, and drew it gently out of the body. He inserted a rubber tube into the cavity it left, and drained the fluid out. The nurses swabbed and cleaned. He tied off the appendix from the cecum and cut it free. He closed the wound and stitched it, dressing the cut with iodoform gauze.

He stepped back and looked at the clock on the wall—only thirty-five minutes had passed. He felt exhausted, ruined. He washed his hands and moved through in a daze to the dressing room. He sat in a chair, elbows on his knees, head hanging, watching the sweat drops fall from his nose onto the hexagonal tiles beneath his feet. He heard Pantaleon come in and felt his reassuring squeeze on his shoulder.

"Very successful," Pantaleon said. "I think we had an hour or two to spare."

"I'd better see Sieverance."

He changed his clothes and went through to his consulting room where Sieverance was waiting and told him that the operation was over and seemed to have passed off well. To his alarm and embarrassment, Sieverance collapsed in his arms, in a kind of weeping swoon, and had to be revived with a small glass of brandy.

"It's all right," Carriscant said to him. "It's over. It went well. I'm sure she'll be fine."

Sieverance clung to him, fingers clutching his biceps, like a drowning man just hauled from the water.

"Bless you, Carriscant," he said. "Bless you, I'll never forget this."

Carriscant said something to him, something bland and consolatory, knowing that there was a double dose of truth in Sieverance's affirmation. He would never forget, that was for sure, as it was also for sure that he would never cease to regret, either.

A SIMPLE SURGEON

S ALVADOR CARRISCANT STARED at the interleaved
fingers of his hands, trying to pray, contemplating the
horizontal and vertical creases on his knuckles, each one
unique and different, like Chinese ideograms scored in the
loose flesh above the finger bones. Why should that be? he
wondered, idly. The first joint, say, of my left little finger
moves identically to the right joint, yet the creased flesh on the
left forms a distinct starburst effect, whereas on the right—

He raised his eyes to the nape of the man's neck bowed in
the pew in front of him. Collar too tight, small canopies of
flesh overlapping on either side. Hair growing right down the
neck too. No. Rather growing up, from his back. How far
down should the barber trim? Kindly remove your shirt, sir.
He looked back at his prayer-clasped hands: the skin between
the finger joints with their small neat patches of hair, almost
tended-looking, all growing in the same direction. Densest on
the ring finger, curiously, wonder if that's true of other men?
Liver spot on his hand-back. Or a big freckle, maybe?

He thought at once of the freckles on Delphine Sieverance's
forearm, upon and over which his eyes had rested and traveled
as he had taken her pulse the day before. Freckles at her throat
too, at the top of her chest and the tender indentations of the
collarbone. How far down did they go? he asked himself.
Would her breasts and shoulders be dappled with pigment, like

a trout, like some hen's eggs you see, a light shading? There were none on her belly, none on her—

He closed his eyes as the priest invited the congregation to join him in prayer. Carriscant moved his lips and felt a sound blurt from his chest, half moan of longing, half frustrated grunt of pain. Annaliese nudged him sharply with her elbow and he looked around at her, his eyes full of pious apology, and he tapped his chest and made a face as if he had indigestion.

"... *tibi Domine commendamus animam famuli tui, ut defunctum saeculo, tibi vivat...*"

"Amen," he managed to say.

The congregation gathered on the steps of the Santa Clara Church while they waited for their carriages to arrive. Annaliese chatted with acquaintances while Carriscant stood alone, hands behind his back, head down, the toe of his shoe tapping out a rhythm on the cracked marble steps. He exhaled and put on a smile for a Spanish family that he vaguely knew—a man helping his ancient, lace-shrouded mother-in-law down the shallow steps to the waiting victoria. Her face was white and dull, matte with face powder. How old? Somewhere in her eighties. What changes she had witnessed! If she looked to her right she could see the big Stars and Stripes flying over Fort Santiago; to her left the Plaza Mayor, now renamed Plaza McKinley in honor of the assassinated president. Sixty years ago, when she was a haughty young *peninsulara*, such notions, such transformations, would have seemed beyond the bounds of wildest fantasy. She was settled delicately in the little carriage now and some granddaughters climbed in beside her. She looked straight ahead, squid black eyes moist and unforgiving. How much more of this new century would she see? he wondered. Probably ready to go now, keen. It happens. The body tires, the mind senses its fatigue: ready to go.

He was still pondering this question as he and Annaliese sat side by side in their carriage as they were driven down Calle

Palacio toward their house. Annaliese was relating some article of gossip which he was barely registering. The carriage had to make a detour up Calle de Ando as the Americans were digging up a cobblestoned stretch of Palacio in order to macadamize the street. They turned left and as they crossed the Calle Real he suddenly told Constancio, the coachman, to stop.

"Where are you going?" Annaliese said in surprise as he opened the small door at his side.

"The hospital. As we're so close. It occurred to me that there's a patient I must see. I operated yesterday. I'm a little concerned."

"But it's Sunday," Annaliese protested, her eyes heavy with . . . With what? Disappointment? Suspicion?

"My dear, ill health doesn't take weekends off."

"Don't patronize—" She started again in a low raw voice, conscious of the broad back of Constancio, listening. "But you're never at home, never, nowadays. Why don't you move in, set up your bed there?"

"A most amusing suggestion, my dear, but really—"

"Salvador,"—her voice brooked no further argument—"it can wait till tomorrow. Nothing is so urgent."

"You don't understand. The new American hospital's providing stiff competition. All these contract surgeons they're bringing over. I'm only thinking of our future." The lie sounded feeble and inept; he felt he could taste it in his mouth, a sour, ashy thing. He backed away without a further word, waved and smiled and strode off up the Calle Real toward his hospital.

DELPHINE SIEVERANCE HAD MADE a slow but sure recovery from her operation. The first week had been the worst, with the agonizing fear of peritonitis on everyone's mind, but as time passed and she regained her strength it became clear that the operation had been a total success. She had been in the San Jerónimo now for almost two weeks, in a private room, and was now able to swing herself out of bed and take a few shuffling steps across the floor to the window. Carriscant saw her every day without fail, even if it was only for a matter of a few minutes, but rarely alone. Sieverance had employed an American nurse to sit with her at nights and he himself was often there. She had many visits from friends also, and the news of the operation, its danger and her steady recovery, had already brought Carriscant an increase in American patients. His renown had spread and he was busier than ever. But the important factor for him was her presence: she was *there*, close, under his roof. He could climb the stairs, knock on her door, take her temperature, consult her charts, order her dressing changed. He could be near her, he could be with her whenever he wished. But now it was the thought of her leaving that began to weigh on him. Sieverance had asked if she might be home for Christmas and Carriscant said that he was sure it would be possible. The very fact that she was beginning to walk again made it difficult for him to insist on her staying in the hospital any longer.

He climbed the stairs to her room and met a nurse at her door, leaving, carrying a tray with the remains of a meal on it. He knocked, and entered when she called. She sat up in bed, propped against pillows, her dull red hair down on her shoulders, an open book in her lap. Through the open window he could see over the huge overgrown city walls to a portion of the Botanical Garden, with its ill-tended, scrubby, dusty allées bordered by a turbid brown loop of the Pasig. Lunchtime smoke rose from the kitchens of Quiapo beyond. There was a haze this morning, he thought, humid, it might have been a day in June.

"Mrs. Sieverance, how are you?"

"Better than ever." She smiled at him. She was always pleased to see him, he knew. The man who had saved her life: she trusted him, her friend, her savior. "I sat in the chair to read. I got in and out of bed. Not a twinge."

"We'll have those stitches out soon."

"Can't wait."

"May I?" He laid a palm on her brow. These excuses to touch, how much longer did he have? Her brown confident eyes looked up at him. He reached for her wrist and proceeded to take her pulse. Her lips were slightly parted and he saw the pink tip of her tongue moisten her front teeth with saliva. Her hair was thick, dry, no shine, almost matte. Her nightgown was pale blue cotton. Her bed jacket was quilted in small puffy diamonds, badged with embroidered crimson crosses. He had to speak.

"Henry James," he said, pointing to the book. It was *The Portrait of a Lady*. "I prefer the topographical essays." He let go of her wrist.

"I met him once, you know," she said. "In Switzerland, in Geneva a few years ago. I was introduced by a friend of mine who knew him well. Constance Fenimore Woolson. She was an extraordinary person, wonderful. Do you know her novels?"

"No, I'm afraid not. Out here we fall behind."

"I'll lend you them."

"Thank you, I'd like that." The plan grew, flourished, in an instant. An exchange of reading matter. Annaliese was always reading novels, the house was full of them. "Were you and Colonel Sieverance traveling through Europe?"

"No, I wasn't with him. He'd—" She was about to go on, and say something a little uncomplimentary, he guessed, but she stopped herself. "We weren't married then. No, I was with a friend and her aunt." She smiled at him, a little mockingly, he thought. "Colonel Sieverance and I have only been married four years. We can do some things on our own, us women, you know. Some of us are even capable of buying a steamer ticket, taking a ship across the ocean and traveling in foreign lands."

"You mustn't make fun of me, Mrs. Sieverance," he said. "I'm only a simple surgeon."

Her shout of laughter both startled and thrilled him. It was a mock-indignant blare, unself-conscious and raucous. He heard it ring in his ears like a hosanna.

He grinned back happily at her. Like a loon. Like a jolly galoot.

She frowned suddenly. "You mustn't do that to me, Dr. Carriscant. I felt that." She reached her hand beneath the sheet to touch her side and twisted around to ease her position. Carriscant thought he detected, in the way her bed jacket moved, the roll of her breasts beneath her nightgown as she shifted from one hip to another. He felt an utter helplessness suffuse him, in the face of his feelings for this woman, a massive impotency.

"Simple surgeon, indeed," she said, wagging her finger at him. "I won't accept that for one minute. Not for one minute."

At that moment the nurse returned and he said he had to leave.

"That novelist you mentioned. What was her name?"

"Fenimore Woolson. I'll get my husband to bring the book."

"No," he said too quickly. "I mean, ah, no hurry. I'll have to come to your home occasionally once you've moved back. I can pick it up anytime."

He paused, suddenly fearful: this was the wrong note, exactly the wrong note upon which to leave. Too familiar, too full of assumptions. He had to think of something else and, as usually happens at moments of pressure, his brain came up with banalities.

"Is there anything you would like?" he said. "Anything special I can fetch for you? I don't know, I—"

"Well, there is, you know," she said. "I asked Jepson but he had no luck. I have this craving for sugared violets. Crystal-lized violets, you know? A complete craving. They're my fa-vorite thing. I brought pounds with me but I've finished them all. I sit here reading and want to dip my fingers into a bowl of sugared violets from time to time. I find my hand drifting out into midair. Do you think you could find them in Manila?" She looked at him slyly, teasing. "I'd be even more in your debt, Dr. Carriscant."

"I'll do my—" He cleared his throat, suddenly nervous, sud-denly moved. The air seemed lambent with potential, all at once. "I'll see what I can do." He managed a fast smile and then was gone.

TEA WITH PATON BOBBY

THE GOVERNMENT ICE PLANT was situated on the south bank of the Pasig, next to the Colgante suspension bridge. Carriscant watched three huge misty blocks of ice being winched out of the plant's store and lowered onto the creaking boards of a *carabao* wagon. The placid buffalos stood immobile in their traces, blinking away the fitful flies as loops of green cud dropped from their slowly working jaws.

As the third block was lowered onto the boards Carriscant repeated his instructions. "You have twenty minutes. We won't pay if even ten percent has melted." The *carabao* were enthusiastically flogged into action and the wagon slowly trundled off toward the Parian gate into the walled city.

He heard his name being called and turned to see who it was. Paton Bobby leaned out of a victoria and beckoned him over.

"I was looking for you at the hospital," he said. "They told me you were buying ice. Still keeping them fresh, huh?"

"Remarkably. If we change the top layer of ice, a foot or so, every three days, it seems to last very well. In fact the bottom of the case is solid impacted ice. Seems to melt and, as it trickles down, refreezes."

"Great. So we don't need to worry about the refrigeration plant."

There was a new refrigeration plant in San Miguel, recently

built beside the nurses' quarters. Carriscant had suggested that they use this facility as a place where the corpses could be stored indefinitely, but Wieland had officially turned the request down on the grounds of it being a health hazard. Now it made no difference: there was no sign of decomposition, the bodies were almost completely frozen.

"I must admit Cruz's trunks do their job well. And at least we know where they are, and who can get to them."

"Exactly." Bobby said. "It was a good idea. Smart."

"Any developments?"

"Maybe . . . You got half an hour? Can I offer you some tea or coffee? We can go to the American Club."

The American Club was on the Calle de San Augustin in Intramuros, not far from the hospital. It was an old rambling house with some of the interior walls on the first floor removed to create larger public rooms, notably a dining room and a spacious salon with punkah fans and rattan furniture and month-old copies of American newspapers. The windows had not been glazed, as was the usual American habit, and the old translucent *kapis* shells had been kept, producing a filtered soft light that left the corners of the room dark and shadowy. A Chinese waiter brought them American coffee and a plate of small sweetened rice cakes. The club was almost empty at this hour: Carriscant saw a naval officer sleeping in a corner on a steamer chair, a group of businessmen in white drill suits playing poker, the smoke from their cigars barely stirred by the slow sway of the punkah, and from a room at the rear of the house, overlooking the *azotea*, came the dull ivory click of cannoning billiard balls.

Bobby drank his coffee, ate three rice cakes and filled a small corncob pipe with tobacco from a soft leather pouch. The pipe had a tiny bowl, so small it seemed almost as if it were designed for an apprentice smoker. Bobby puffed it quickly alight and plumed smoke sideways from the corner of his mouth.

"You do grow great tobacco here, I will grant you that."

"Worth all the effort of colonization?"

"Oh, I don't know about these things. I just appreciate a good smoke."

They talked a bit about Taft, about the rumors that Roosevelt had offered him a post on the Supreme Court.

"Think he'll go?" Carriscant asked.

"He's a lawyer. Supreme Court judge has got to be the top of that particular tree."

They nattered on, Carriscant waiting patiently. He knew Bobby well enough by now to understand that this display of sociability was not disinterested. And soon enough Bobby leaned forward, elbows on his knees.

"Wieland says you were in Sampaloc. In a creep joint."

"Yes." This did not surprise him. Wieland was unlikely to keep that information to himself, especially now, but what was it to Bobby? "Wieland was drunk, by the way," Carriscant threw in for good measure. "Very."

"You go there often? Not that I care," he added quickly. "I whore myself from time to time."

"I was visiting my cook's mother. She was ill."

Bobby looked at him, his eyes expressionless. Giving me time to change my story, Carriscant thought. Old policeman's trick.

"A hernia." Why did he lie? It would be so easy to prove him wrong.

"Wieland never saw you leave. Reckons you spent the night there."

"What's all this about? Wieland wasn't capable of seeing anything. I left. I didn't see him either, come to that."

Bobby emptied his toy pipe with a couple of sharp raps on the rim of an ashtray.

"You never went back?"

"No."

Bobby made a face as if he had just heard baddish news. He

stood up, nodded at one of the card-playing businessmen and patted his uniform pockets absentmindedly, as if he had forgotten his wallet.

"I don't want to take up any more of your time, Dr. Carriscant, but I'd appreciate it if you'd make one more visit with me."

"I don't have all day," Carriscant said, rising to his feet. "Where are we going?"

THE POLICE STATION at the Parian gate was a building Carriscant had passed hundreds of times without it drawing anything but the most cursory glance from him. It was made of *bulik* adobe and its ground-floor windows were extravagantly barred, as if baroque cast-iron cages had been built around the window embrasures. Inside, it was surprisingly cool, the thick walls fending off the heat of the afternoon sun. Bobby led him down a corridor and swung open an iron-studded wooden door. There was a small desk in the middle of the room occupied by a Filipino constable, and against the opposite wall was a rickety wooden form. An old man was sitting on this, patiently smoking a cigarette. Carriscant recognized him at once.

"Do you know this man?" Bobby asked.

"No."

The old man began to jabber in Tagalog, pointing his cigarette directly at Carriscant, grinning and chuckling, exposing his few betel-stained teeth.

The constable translated. "He says he saw this man in the acacia woods between Sampaloc and Nactajan on the morning of that day. He lives in Nactajan. He was gathering firewood at dawn and he found this *americano* in the woods. This is the man."

Bobby turned to Carriscant, his face empty, neutral. "Is there any truth in this?"

"Of course not," Carriscant lied instantly, with composure, without fear, for some reason. "What's going on here, Bobby?"

"We have to follow everything up." He shrugged. "The only unusual thing, the only thing that was out of the ordinary around Sampaloc during the time Braun went missing was this 'American' that was seen at dawn. This old fellow here gave us a very accurate description. I have to say the more he went on, the more it sounded like you."

"I've never seen him before in my life."

"And there's a *barca* ferryman says he ferried a *kastila*. At least he spoke Spanish to him. At dawn that same day. But he can't give us any description. Seems all *kastilas* look the same to him . . . But somebody, some white man, was out around Sampaloc at that time. I want to find out who."

"You think this man might have killed Braun?"

"I don't know. I'm just investigating."

The old man started yammering again and everyone looked around. His face was held in a merry, creased grimace as he rocked to and fro, his fist pumping up and down in his lap, his other hand pointing the glowing end of his cigarette at Carriscant. The constable shouted angrily at him to stop.

"What's going on?" Bobby demanded, amazed.

The constable's embarrassment was clear. "He say this man"—he glanced at Carriscant—"he says he was holding him pecker. You know, with hand, he was playing—"

"Stop," Bobby said. "I heard enough. Get this disgusting old fool out of here."

BOBBY AND CARRISCANT STOOD in the afternoon sun on the police station's front steps, Carriscant assuring Bobby once again that he was fine, that he understood Bobby had his job to do and that he really *wanted* to walk back to the hospital.

"I can't tell you how sorry I am," Bobby repeated. "Sick old bastard." He was visibly sweating with embarrassment and discomfort, his thin hair stuck to his scalp in damp strands.

"You had to do your job. Honestly, I'd have done the same."

"He had you to a tee. Right down to that small scar thing on your eyebrow there . . . But I guess you're a pretty well-known man in Manila. Small town and all that. He could have seen you at the hospital, anything." He shook himself in exasperation. "Crazy old bastard. I mean, what a thing to say . . ." He grinned ruefully at Carriscant and Carriscant allowed himself a grin of collusion in return.

THE FOUR-CYLINDER
12 HP FLANQUIN

U DO LEYS HAD a bad cold, his eyes itched, his nose ran copiously and he had a dull pain in his chest from the dry, baying cough that erupted irregularly in his lungs. He sounded like some strange mythical animal in its rutting season, plaintively seeking a mate, half sea lion, half ape, he said, his amusement at this notion setting off another coughing bout. It subsided and he blew his nose, wiping his tufty mustache with considerable care.

"I may be an old man," he said, "but that's no excuse. There's nothing more disgusting than an old man's mustache when he's got a cold. My own father's, I remember . . ." He winced. "Full of dried snot. It quite put me off my food. You will tell me, Salvador, if I miss anything, please." He pushed his lumpy face forward for inspection, lifting his soft pulpy nose with a finger.

"Of course, Udo. There's not a trace."

"Is it far to go?" Pantaleon asked. Carriscant could sense the suppressed tremble of excitement in his friend's lean body. Like a gun dog, quivering with energy and anticipation.

"Ten minutes," Udo said. "They cleared customs this afternoon."

"And there were no problems?"

"I tell you, Dr. Quiroga, there is nobody like Nicanor Axel in the China Sea." Udo led them to the door. "When it comes to a discreet or delicate commission, Axel is the only man. He has worked wonders for me, wonders."

They descended from the office to the Calle Crespo, the street almost silent now that the tin shops were shut, but from the far end came the firecracker retorts from the shooting gallery and the sound of a barrel organ playing "In the Good Old Summer Time." They heaved Udo into Carriscant's victoria and squeezed in beside him. Constancio whacked the pony's rear and they clopped off in the direction of the docks, detouring Escolta's crowds and shoppers on Pantaleon's request (in case he was spotted, he said), going instead via the Plaza Calderón and swinging around through dark, malodorous lanes between warehouses to emerge at the quayside next to the fire station.

They descended and peered at the mass of shipping moored on the Pasig. Smoke rose from braziers on the sterns of the wallowing *cascos* and the glare of the electric light from the fire station and the customhouse made it difficult to see beyond the water's edge: nothing much more than a confusion of masts and rigging and here and there, farther out from the wharves, the solider, darker bulk of the interisland steamers and coasters.

"What about the way back?" Carriscant asked. "Will there be room?"

"Don't worry," Pantaleon said. "I'll take it straight home. I'll hire a *carromato*."

Constancio was dispatched in search of one and then the three men picked their way on sagging gangplanks across the banked houseboats toward where Axel's steamer was moored. Families sat around cooking fires preparing dinner, only the children curious about these three *americanos* in their white suits tramping through their homes.

"Why doesn't he put in at a jetty?" Carriscant asked.

"Nothing is meant to be easy or straightforward," Udo explained cryptically. "Your business with Axel has to be very important for you to make this effort."

Moored alongside the outlying *casco* was Nicanor Axel's ugly little steamer, the *General Blanco*. It was a wide, low-lying coaster with its tall single smokestack set aft and conspicuously raked. In front of the bridge superstructure were three holds with primitive-looking derricks above them. A foul smell, acid and corrupt, seemed to hang like a miasma about the craft. Carriscant felt his stomach turn, and he put his handkerchief to his nose as the three of them climbed the angled ladder to the deck, Udo's genial bellows of "Nicanor, Nicanor, where are you?" preceding them.

On deck Carriscant thought he had located the source of the smell. One of the holds was full of livestock, goats and kids, and the floor of the hold seemed to be lined with rotting vegetation, as far as he could tell from the light thrown by a hanging oil lantern.

"Goat shit," Pantaleon said. "Centuries old."

Udo explained that the crew fed off the livestock as they traveled about the islands and on the longer ocean crossings to Hong Kong and Japan. "You throw all your rubbish in there, the goats eat it, you eat the goats." He smiled, pausing to light a cigar. "Powerful smell, no? If I was a customs officer I wouldn't want to linger on this vessel, I tell you."

A man descended from the bridge house and advanced along the deck toward them, wiping his hands on a rag. He had a curious sidelong, diffident gait, Carriscant thought, as if some invisible accomplice were pushing him from behind, urging him forward against his will. Udo made the introductions. Nicanor Axel was a small, slight man with round shoulders, and dark swarthy skin that sat most oddly with his pale blue eyes and his fair, almost ash-blond hair. On closer inspection

Carriscant realized that it was grime that was responsible for the man's skin color: oil and dirt, grease and dust seemed to have worked their way through his pores and formed a subcutaneous layer beneath his epidermis, in the way that the ink from a tattooer's needle seems to shine *through* the skin rather than rest upon it. No amount of diligent scrubbing would ever return Nicanor Axel's cheeks to their ruddy Nordic glow—he was steeped and stained with dirt, impregnated with muck.

He was a taciturn, shifty fellow too, Carriscant thought, with a limp, fleeting handshake. He accepted Pantaleon's money grudgingly and counted through the notes twice, pedantically, before ordering two deckhands to board the *lorcha* that was towed behind the steamer, a semi-masted schooner hulk which, while it reduced the *General Blanco*'s speed through the water, allowed it to double its cargo capacity.

"I'm most grateful," Pantaleon said. "There were no problems?"

"No," Axel replied. "It was there in Hong Kong waiting."

The crewmen came toward them bearing a small wooden chest and set it down on the deck. On the side Carriscant read the stenciled letters: ETS. FLANQUIN. PARIS. With a chisel Axel prized off the lid, and there, secure in its wooden braces, was a small petrol engine, factory fresh, with a dull sheen of oil.

Pantaleon knelt before it, lightly resting his fingers on the cylinder casings. "The Flanquin, twelve horsepower," he said quietly, reverentially, his face entranced and wondering. The dream was one step nearer.

1903

CARRISCANT APPROACHED the Sieverance house on the Calle Lagarda in a state of some agitation and trepidation. Delphine Sieverance had returned to her home on December 22: the new year was now three days old and he had yet to see her. Christmas *chez* Carriscant had been tense but endurable, largely because he had spent most of his time at the hospital and Annaliese was preoccupied with her seasonal work with the bishop. Udo had come for dinner on Christmas Eve, had grown drunk and maudlin as the evening progressed, and ended up staying for three days. But at least his limping presence about the house dissipated the coolness that now existed between Carriscant and Annaliese. Nothing had been said openly, there had been no one moment, but somehow over that period a tacit understanding had been arrived at: there would be no more pretense that there was any affection between them anymore, and that was that. It was an inescapable fact, Carriscant knew, but its acknowledgment depressed him all the same, and he had deliberately arranged to see in the new year by constructing a new rectum for a Jesuit priest, returning home exhausted after a long and arduous operation to a dark and silent house.

He put on a smile now, as he climbed the stairs to the living room where Sieverance greeted him warmly, affably. He was out of uniform, wearing a seersucker suit with a thin blue stripe and a loose cerise bow tie which, for some reason, Carriscant found irritating and affected.

"How is Mrs. Sieverance?" he asked, once he had reassured the man about his own well-being.

"Excellent, improving daily, my dear fellow, thanks to you."

Carriscant accepted more compliments as he was led down the corridor to her bedroom. The American nurse, a plump young woman with a wide gap between her front teeth, opened the door to admit them. She had a busy, overefficient manner that verged on the insolent, Carriscant thought.

"You know Nurse Aslinger?" Sieverance asked.

"Indeed. Good morning, Miss Aslinger."

"Morning, Doctor, everything is ready for you."

He turned to the bed. She sat there patiently, smiling at him, a smile of such pleasure and such genuine warmth, he thought, that it made him want to weep.

"Ah, my favorite medical man. Dr. Carriscant, a happy new year to you."

He took her proffered hand and shook it briefly. "And to you, Mrs. Sieverance. A happy and healthy one."

"Not forgetting 'prosperous,'" Sieverance added with a silly laugh.

"Health and happiness will do fine for '03," Delphine said, and then continued, "I'm feeling very well, Doctor. I walk a little farther in the garden every day. I've even taken a short carriage ride."

"You'll be on the Luneta next," he said, "listening to the band. The police band is playing all next week." He approached the bed, avoiding her eye.

"Talking of the Luneta, you haven't seen anything of Miss Caspar recently, have you?" she asked. Her face was all smooth innocence.

He could not believe the temerity, the arrant mischief. "What? Ah, no, I don't think—"

"Who's that, my dear?" Sieverance asked.

"Miss Rudolfa Caspar," she said, her face deadpan, her eyes never leaving Carriscant. "A mutual acquaintance. She's an old friend of Dr. Carriscant, isn't that so, Doctor? A special friend."

"I think I should be—" Carriscant gestured vaguely toward the bed.

"Excuse me, I'll make myself scarce." Sieverance left.

Nurse Aslinger drew back the sheet over Delphine's lap. Carriscant saw that although her nightgown had been folded up to her waist, towels had been laid across her thighs and belly so that only the area of the dressing was exposed. Nurse Aslinger stood close by his elbow as he gently removed it. The six-inch scar was pink and vivid but it had knitted well. His mouth drying rapidly, he could just make out, beneath the towel's hem, the shadowed new growth of her pubic hair. Gently, with his fingertips, he touched the wound: a shininess, a hard smoothness, but no puckering or ridging.

"Beautiful scar," he said automatically, without thinking.

"Not the word I would choose," she said.

"It'll fade with time. In a year or two you'll hardly notice it."

Nurse Aslinger replaced the dressing while he routinely prohibited overexertion, sudden movements, horseback riding.

"Oh, I have something for you," she said, and reached into the drawer of the bedside table and held out a book for him. He took it: *East Angels* by Constance Fenimore Woolson. He opened the cover and saw her name written boldly in violet ink on the flyleaf: "For Delphine Blythe with affection, Fenimore." Another hand had added "Sieverance" after "Blythe."

"Delphine Blythe Sieverance," he said. "That has a fine ring to it. Thank you."

"You must tell me what you think."

There was a knock on the door and Sieverance reentered, his face alight, unusually full of invigoration.

"Mrs. Sieverance is making excellent progress," Carriscant said with jovial formality, like a doctor in a bad play, slipping the book into his coat pocket. "We are very pleased with her."

"Then this is the perfect occasion to express our gratitude."

"Really, there's no further need—" Carriscant began, but then stopped when he saw that Sieverance had closed his eyes and had raised his beaming face heavenward. He took his wife's hand and then, to Carriscant's profound alarm, his.

"Please join hands before the Lord," he said to Carriscant and Nurse Aslinger, who promptly slipped her hand into Carriscant's. "And please kneel with me."

Carriscant found himself being drawn down into a kneeling position at the foot of Delphine's bed. Sieverance's face was frowningly beatific, at once stern and devout, while Nurse Aslinger's head was piously bowed, revealing a nasty heat rash on her nape.

"O Lord above," Sieverance intoned in a low, intense voice, "grant us this day thy blessing and receive our thanks for thy blessed powers of healing visited upon our beloved Delphine."

"Amen," said Nurse Aslinger.

"And we thank thee, O Lord of hosts most high, for the dedication and skill thou hast bestowed on thy servant Salvador Carriscant. We thank thee, O Lord our God, for leading us into this man's care—"

Carriscant's ears closed as more gratitude was delivered up to the Almighty. He felt his cheeks and ears glow with a form of pure embarrassment he had not endured since he was a child. Nurse Aslinger's hand was hot and moist, Sieverance's was bony, its grip unnecessarily firm. He gazed at the needle-point rug (puce roses on an oatmeal background) on which he knelt and concentrated on the dull ache that was beginning to spread through his left knee joint. But something made him slowly raise his eyes: Delphine was looking directly at him and her lips moved as she mouthed one word—"Sorry." They were conspirators again, anew, and he felt himself begin the sudden headlong slide once more.

THE PRAYER OF THANKS lasted almost five minutes and after it was over Sieverance's exhilaration was almost insupportable. Carriscant made a brief farewell to Delphine and went through with Sieverance to the sitting room, where his host insisted he stay and have a glass of lemonade.

Carriscant took small rapid sips, keeping the glass to his mouth.

"As a military man, you know," Sieverance said, dabbing at his poor fair mustache with a knuckle, "we don't often give much thought to divine providence."

"I suppose not," Carriscant said aimlessly, not understanding where the conversation was headed. Not caring. *This lemonade is really not too bad.*

"It takes an occasion like this to make one realize just how fortunate one has been."

"I suppose so."

"I mean, what if, what if Delphine had fallen ill next week instead of before Christmas? Lord knows what would have happened." He shuddered, upset by this vision of a hypothetical future. "It doesn't bear thinking about."

"I'm afraid I don't follow."

"Didn't I tell you?"

"Ah, no."

"My regiment is being posted to Mindanao. Off to fight the wretched *moros*. We leave next week."

TWO PROPELLORS PUSHING

P ANTALEON QUIROGA CRANKED the handle on the front of the Flanquin and the engine fired into life. The Aero-Mobile shuddered and quivered, as if suddenly animate. The chain drives to the propellor mountings hummed and clattered on their sprocketed wheels. Carriscant and Pantaleon stepped back and looked on in a moment of amazement before Pantaleon beckoned Carriscant around the thrumming machine to where the spinning bosses of the pushing propellors (yet to be mounted) were fixed. Carriscant rested his hand gently on a panel of stretched and doped silk and felt the powerful vibrations travel up his arm. For the first time he sensed that Pantaleon's dream was not a deluded fantasy after all, the fellow might actually be on to something.

"Two propellors pushing," Pantaleon shouted, twirling his fingers in illustration. "But I'm a little concerned about the allowances I made for the fuel tank and the radiator. They were heavier than I thought."

"Is that bad?"

"We're getting close to the maximum weight, if my calculations are right. Very close."

Pantaleon walked forward and slung a long leg over the forward of the two bicycle saddles mounted above the four-wheeled carriage the machine rested on. He reached over and adjusted the throttle control on the engine and the noise slackened as the motor idled. He listened to it for a moment, his head cocked, and then switched it off.

Carriscant peered over his shoulder at the two wooden levers that were mounted in front of him and the pedal controls that were operated by his feet. Above his shoulders were two other levers sticking forward, like handles on a wheelbarrow, from the leading edge of the upper wing.

Pantaleon saw him looking and explained. "The whole front edge is hinged," he said, gripping the handles and demonstrating. True enough, he could move a front flap of wing up and down through an angle of forty-five degrees. "On leaving the ground it is pushed up to the full extent to provide maximum lift. Once we are in the air I can pull it down to reduce resistance, or up if we need to be more"—he searched for a word—"buoyant." Carriscant had a sudden perception of a vocabulary adapting itself, creating itself. Like medicine and surgery, new discoveries enriched the language—germ, appendix, bacillus, phagocyte, microorganism . . .

"I call it the 'air-catcher,'" he said. "I've applied for a patent. If it works, who knows? I might—"

"If it works? My dear Panta, you can't possibly take such a risk."

"On the gliding models it seems fine. But once we're up with a machine of this weight . . ." He turned and pointed to the second bicycle saddle behind him, with its own set of levers. "That's why I've reproduced the tail-warping mechanism here."

"You don't mean to tell me you're going to move seats in mid"—he was about to say "journey" but it seemed wrong—"while the machine is in the air? In its aerial trip?"

"No, no. My fellow flyer—my co-flyer, indeed—will be controlling the warping while I deal with the elevators"—he pointed to his foot controls—"and the air-catcher."

"I see. I suppose it makes sense." Carriscant frowned. He

had grown used to the Aero-Mobile by now, with its fragile, translucent ugliness, but these controls seemed unnecessarily complex. Surely there must be a simpler way? All these moving surfaces—warping, elevating, catching—all these levers, struts and wires. When you saw a bird fly it seemed . . . He stopped. Pantaleon was looking fixedly at him, his eyes wide, strange.

"What is it?" Carriscant said.

"I was wondering, Salvador, if you'd do me the honor."

"Of what?"

"Of joining me on this historic flight."

RAIN

*T*HE FIRST RAINS arrived early that year, but Dr. Salvador Carriscant, ever prudent, had been carrying his umbrella with him since the end of January and, as the first fat drops hit his head, he congratulated himself on his foresight. He folded away his small easel and sketch pad and closed his box of watercolors before retreating to the shelter of a nearby bamboo grove, where he was still afforded a clear view of the Calle Lagarda and of the entrance to the Sieverance home. The bamboo grove was on the other side of a small overgrown creek—the *estero* San Miguel—from the Calle Lagarda and its spacious villas. Conscious of the risks he had run on the last occasion he had indulged in espionage, he had gone to some lengths to make his presence here plausible should he be discovered. In his sketchbook were several indifferent and half-completed views of this undistinguished portion of Manila's suburbs. An expanse of marshland, some rice fields, a few palm trees and in the distance the neat dome and campanile of the San Sebastián Church and Convent. He had always vaguely planned to take up watercoloring as a hobby and respite from the relentless demands of the operating theater, and had seized on this pastime as the perfect way both to satisfy this urge and to "innocently" observe the Sieverance home. He had to admit, however, it was the proximity of the house and its occupant that distracted him and dominated his mind and not the soothing effect of his daubings.

Colonel Jepson Sieverance and his new regiment, the First Nebraska Volunteers, had embarked for Mindanao five days previously on the steamer *Brewster*, according to the gazette in the *Manila Times*, a fact that Paton Bobby had confirmed too. With the husband gone, Carriscant knew he had to see Delphine once more, but without the presence of Nurse Aslinger as chaperone. The nurse, he reasoned, must quit the house occasionally, but three days of patient watercoloring—two hours the first, four and a half the second—had seen no one but servants enter or leave the compound. He checked his pocket watch: he had been out for almost three hours again today, and now that the rain had started he wondered if it was worth lingering further. He looked up at the turbulent, livid sky. Rain in the Philippines is a full-blooded, uncompromising, natural phenomenon. The big drops noisily battered the material of his umbrella and he could feel the ground beneath his feet beginning to soften and deliquesce. Above his head the fine spiky fronds of the bamboo stands were thrashed and flung this way and that by a robust breeze. Some beetle droned by, searching for shelter, an angry noise in a black dot.

A faint clatter of hooves made him look sharply across the *estero* as, to his surprise, he saw the gate to the Sieverance compound open and a small *carromato* emerge containing, indubitably, the mackintoshed and ample figure of Nurse Aslinger. It trotted down the Calle Lagarda toward the Malacañan Palace and as it did so Carriscant, bent beneath his umbrella, hurried upstream to the Marquez Bridge and splashed his way down the dirt track that led back into San Miguel. He was at her front door in five minutes. Two minutes later he was pacing damply about her living room waiting for the maid to inform Mrs. Sieverance that Dr. Carriscant was here to visit her. In his hand he held her copy of *East Angels* by Constance Fenimore Woolson. As a dutiful and responsible borrower, he told himself, he was returning the book promptly to its owner.

She came slowly into the room, walking with two sticks to help carry some of her weight. She was wearing an apple green dress and her hair was up. Her wide smile of welcome was pronounced and irrefutable. His nervousness returned with perplexing force.

"Dr. Carriscant, what a surprise." She frowned suddenly. "I haven't forgotten, have I? We hadn't planned—"

"No, no. Ah . . . I was visiting my colleague, Dr. Quiroga. I took the opportunity of returning your book." He thrust it forward as if he had just learned the meaning of the phrase, realized it was going to be awkward for her to take it, what with her two sticks, and looked around foolishly for a table on which to set it down.

"Let's put it back in my library," she said, diplomatically easing his dilemma. "Have you seen my library, Dr. Carriscant? I shall need your help in any case."

He refused her offers of lemonade, tea and coffee and followed her into a small study which led off the living room. One entire wall was lined floor to ceiling with bookcases, and in front of a window that overlooked the rain-drenched rear garden was a small antique desk with a worn maroon leather top, cluttered with writing materials.

"I was writing to Jepson," she said, hastily clearing away pen and many leaves of paper.

"Long letter," Carriscant said. For heaven's sake, the man had not been away a week. My God, I'm jealous.

"Well, actually it's a play."

"A play? You're a writer? A playwright too."

"Not unless the aspiration itself permits the title. I've written journalism, some pieces for magazines, *Harper's*, *The Atlantic*. The play, well, it's a bit of a dream. But now that he's away I've got no excuse."

"What's it about?"

"It's about a woman—" She paused, and she looked disquieted. "It's about a woman who is married, but who feels that she's made a terrible . . ." She stopped again. "It's about the terrifying power of social institutions."

She seemed suddenly embarrassed by all these revelations and turned back to the view. "Lord, look at that rain! Is this it now?" she asked him. *"Le déluge est-il arrivé?"* Her French accent was fine, he thought, with an odd touch of pride. Intelligent, cultivated woman.

"I'm afraid so," Carriscant said, and embarked on a short disquisition about the rainy season in the Philippines, the enervating, moist heat, the typhoons, the constant downpour. "You can go up to the hills, of course, where it's not so humid, but most of us endure it. Look forward to October and the cool nights."

She reached for a small tin on her desk, opened it and held it out to him. Crystallized violets, dusted with fine sugar.

"The ones you gave me," she said. "I'm running out."

He declined her offer. "I'll get you some more," he said. "My source is very reliable." She took one of the violets and popped it in her mouth. He watched her suck on it briefly, her cheeks concave, her jaws moving as she worked to extract its sweetness.

"Perhaps I will have one, if I may," he said, his fingers taking a small mauve cluster from the re-proffered tin.

"I have a complete obsession for these sweets," she said. "I think it's because I like the idea that I'm eating a flower."

Carriscant felt he might pass out at any moment, the room seemed insufferably hot, the musty smell of the leather-bound volumes . . . He raised her novel in weakening, lethargic fingers.

"What should I do with this?"

"If you don't mind replacing it—Oh yes, what did you think of it? Didn't I tell you she was a fine writer?"

"Most enjoyable." He could not remember a word. He had read the book in a kind of daze, seeing the words, not understanding them.

"That episode where Esmerelda bests the despicable Captain Farley is quite wonderful. Such fine satire."

"I couldn't agree more. Absolutely." His enthusiasm, he hoped, he assumed, would conceal his total ignorance.

"Now that is the type of independent woman I admire," she said. "Don't you agree?"

"Mmm. Now where should I—"

She pointed at a high shelf, one from the top of the bookcase, at the dark oblong slot of a missing volume.

"The Woolsons are all up there, I'm afraid," she said. "You'll have to use the library steps."

She indicated a sturdy-looking oak chair, which seemed unimprovably chairlike, until a second glance showed that it possessed rather too many broad redundant struts and a brass captain's hook hanging uselessly from its side. "It unfolds into steps," she explained.

And sure enough it did, most ingeniously, Carriscant thought, as the chair, by a simple act of unfolding, turned itself beneath his hands into a flight of five wooden steps, locked in position by the now apt captain's hook.

"It's my favorite thing," she said. "I bought it in England on our honeymoon. A little town called Moreton-in-Marsh."

"Wondrously simple," he said. "And strong."

He climbed the five steps and slipped the book into its place beside the other Fenimore Woolsons. Everything alphabetical, he noted, dust-free. Fine orderly mind, I like that. He remembered his plan suddenly, and removed another Woolson, at random.

"May I borrow this? I've become a real admirer."

"Of course, with pleasure. We shall form an appreciation society, here in Manila. A club of two."

Is she flirting with me? he thought, at once uneasy on his high steps. A club of two, that speaks to my mind of a certain . . . *chaleur*. He backed nervously down the five steps and, as he did so, the brass captain's hook, only partially fitted into its eye, slipped the fraction of an inch necessary to make it tightly latched and secure. That tiny adjustment (they later analyzed)—just a nudge, a giving—was sufficient marginally to unbalance him in cautious backward descent. He swayed right and in compensation brought his right foot hard down on the final step. The crunch of its tendon joint breaking was like the snapping of a dry biscuit. He went over and back, arms grabbing at emptiness, and crashed to the floor with surprising noise, over which, however, he could hear her shriek of alarm. The breath was blasted from his body and his vision dimmed to a hazy tangerine-gray. His head began to toll with pain, audibly, he thought, from where it had bounced off the wooden floor. All he could think was: I have broken her most precious possession.

He opened his eyes to see her pale face hovering above his, her fingers scrabbling at his necktie, loosening it. He realized he must have passed out for a second or two and was overwhelmed by her solicitude. But the doctor in him was shocked to find her kneeling on the ground in her present condition.

"Are you all right?" she asked, all anxiety. "My God, what a fall it was. Spectacular!"

"Mrs. Sieverance, please." He struggled to sit upright, sucking in great mouthfuls of air. "Kneeling. You mustn't . . . I'm fine. Fine."

He felt woolly, stupid, his head both thick and light at the same moment. "I'm so sorry," he managed to go on. "Your library steps."

She was leaning forward now, taking her weight on her arms. He tried not to notice the way her breasts were forced to fall forward and push against her bodice as she turned on all fours to examine the library steps. He pushed himself over; he did not feel capable of standing just yet. Her fingers sifted crumbs of wood.

"Ant borings. It would have happened to the next person to

stand on it." She smiled at him. "It might even have been me. You've saved me again, Doctor."

That tone again. "You must let me repair it," he said quickly. "Dr. Quiroga knows the best carpenters."

"Oh, it's not important."

"But you said—"

"It's only a thing, after all. Someone owned it before me, someone will own it after. I'm only borrowing it, really. We all are. We all get too attached to possessions, to things. They cannot be possessed utterly, like food or wine. They are only on loan to us, these things we so cherish."

This little heartfelt speech silenced him.

"That's very true," he said dully. "But I'm still very sorry."

"Perhaps you could help me up."

Carriscant stood slowly, and offered his hands. She took them. She took them . . .

"I think you'll have to come behind me," she said. "The muscles in my stomach—"

"Perhaps we should call the maid?"

"Dr. Carriscant, please."

He stepped around behind her as she raised her arms to accommodate his hands, which he fitted into the warm hollow of her armpits. He felt the big muscle, pectoralis major, clench on his forefingers as he lifted her up, taking her full weight (no slip of a girl, this, he realized), and raised her from the floor. She stood and he quickly fetched her sticks.

"There," she said, a curious smile on her face. "What drama! The returning of a book, who would have thought it would lead to all this?"

He wanted then to declare his love, to seize her hand and tell her she was the most beautiful woman he had ever seen, that every gesture, every animated facet of her being irradiated him with longing. He wanted to press his lips to hers and taste the violets on her tongue.

His face was immobile. He blinked. A headache was starting. A shoulder muscle was in spasm.

"I'm so sorry about the steps," he repeated. "I insist on sending for them. Quiroga will know the right man."

"You've got dust on your coat," she said, and reached forward to slap his thigh with her fingers, lightly cuffing the dust away.

He felt indescribably puny, wholly unmanned. He had to leave.

She followed him to the top of the stairs as he made his farewells. Her smile was still ambiguous, a sense of power seemed to be emanating from her, he thought, of someone now perfectly in control. But how? Why? What had happened to bring this about? His clumsiness? His stunned, faltering behavior? He walked out into the rain, enjoying the drenching he was receiving, his hair soon slick, drops of water running down his hot face, not looking back. As he walked along the road to Quiapo, to the *bodegón* where Constancio was waiting with his carriage, the questions nagged at him again. As far as he could tell, he had behaved, before and after the fall, with absolute propriety, had been the very model of polite discretion. So why did she act as if she knew something he did not? The balance of this relationship had altered markedly, he thought, with a small thrill of foreboding: the weight had swung to favor her.

SCALPEL

*T*HE WOMAN'S BODY LAY face down in a small vigorous torrent, swollen by the rains, that ran into the Tatuban *estero*. The stream was some way to the north of the city, between the Dagupan railroad and the Santa Cruz racecourse. Carriscant looked around him: they were barely a mile from Intramuros and yet all around them was bushy scrub and marshy fields under low pewtery clouds. It was a depressing scene, drear. Drear was the perfect word, he thought. Or *drookit*, a good Scottish word, except that it had connotations of cold and here it was warm and steamy. The rain pattered steadily against his hat and yellow slicker. Bobby, beside him, held an umbrella above his head, and not far off half a dozen native constables stood by stoically, soaked through.

"This track here leads to Tondo," Bobby said, pointing, then swiveled round. "Go the other way and you get to the Chinese hospital."

"Is she Chinese?"

"*Mestiza*, I think. We can't identify her. Chances are she's from Tondo."

The woman was unshod and her clothes were mean and worn. Carriscant shrugged. "Tondo. It could take you months to find out who she was, if at all."

"We got to try," Bobby said tersely.

Carriscant frowned: Bobby was not in a good mood—understandable, perhaps, but he could not see why he had been summoned. "Is there anything I can do?" he asked.

Bobby signaled to the constables to move the body from the streambed and turned away and offered Carriscant a cigar which, for once, he accepted. They dithered and fussed over the lighting process, Carriscant taking three damp matches and Bobby two. Carriscant exhaled smoke, looking out over the drab scene. The cigar was cheap, tasted dry, of straw, hot on the back of his throat, an odd contrast as everything he saw spelled "cool": gray skies, muddy greens, rain, waterlogged ground. He felt he was breathing in tepid consommé. Under his shiny raincoat he felt completely damp, hot and damp.

Bobby blew on the end of his cigar and said, "I think it's the same fellow."

"What do you mean?"

"Same person killed her as killed Ward and Braun."

Bobby led him over to the four-wheeled wagon where the woman was now laid out. She was young, not much more than twenty-five, Carriscant guessed, her face covered in smallpox scars. She looked thin and malnourished and the right side of her muslin blouse was torn. As Bobby lifted her arm Carriscant saw, through the rip, the rough puckered slit of a knife wound between her fourth and fifth ribs.

"Stabbed in the heart," Bobby said. "And, like the others, found in or near water at the site of Filipino or American lines as they were on February 4, 1899."

"Who was up here?" Carriscant said, surprised.

"First Montana."

Carriscant was skeptical. "If she'd been a dead American soldier, I'd grant you your supposition. But she's a peasant, a sick peasant too, I'd wager, from a Tondo slum. And there's no L-shaped wound."

Bobby's hand went into his pocket and drew something out.

He showed it to Carriscant: it was a scalpel. Carriscant took it.

"We found it by the body, just on the bank there," Bobby said.

It was a Merck and Frankl scalpel, heavy-duty, with a strong two-inch-long beveled blade, Carriscant saw.

"It's what we call a straight, sharp-pointed bistoury. Not for precision work. It's a common make," Carriscant said, returning it.

"We figure the murderer was surprised. Otherwise I'm sure we'd have an L-shaped wound and a missing heart."

"But why a woman? Why a slum dweller?"

"I don't know."

"We . . ." Carriscant paused, not knowing quite how to express this. "We have these scalpels in the San Jerónimo."

"I know," Bobby said. "And in the San Lázaro and the First Reserve Hospital." He carefully put the scalpel back in his pocket. "Could you tell if one of these was missing?"

"Possibly."

"I'd appreciate it."

Carriscant looked back at the corpse. The soaked clothes were plastered to the small thin body. He could see that the belly was markedly distended. The mouth was slightly open, showing stained front teeth. His brain was working quickly, troubled and agitated.

"I think you'll find," he said to Bobby, "that this woman is pregnant. Four or five months." He pointed to the swell of her belly.

"Really? God . . ." The information seemed to have disturbed Bobby unduly. "That's awful."

"I'll confirm it at the hospital," Carriscant said. He made his farewells.

On the ride back to Manila he found his mind returning again and again to the same troubling conclusion. The scalpel found by the woman's body, he was sure, would be traced back to his operating theater at the San Jerónimo. He could not explain where this conviction came from. But it came to him with the numinous clarity of a revelation. Someone had stolen it and that someone, or some people, had placed it by the body for the sole purpose of implicating him in the murders.

THE BLUE AFTERNOON

W E ' V E   H A D terrible problems," Pantaleon said. His face looked drawn and his chin was dirty with stubble. "But I think we've solved them."

They were in the doorway of the *nipa* barn looking out at the rain falling steadily on the meadow. Behind them in the musty gloom stood the Aero-Mobile, almost complete, lacking only one propellor.

"Problems of torque," Pantaleon went on. "The propellors make the plane want to pull to the right and I've had to counterbalance one propellor with the other. Very complicated." He pinched the bridge of his nose. "And weight. I need extra fuel. It's put me back by several weeks, but we're almost there."

"Don't exhaust yourself, Panta," Carriscant said, laying a gentle palm on his friend's shoulder. "You can't hurry these things. One day, I'm sure, you'll take to the air."

"No, you don't understand," Pantaleon said excitedly. "I'm not alone. There are others."

"Other what?" Carriscant was beginning to grow concerned about him now, the mood was too sustainedly febrile and neurotic.

"Other flyers. You've got Santos-Dumont in France, Bosendorf in Germany, that fellow in America—what's his name?—with his manned gliders."

"But you're practically there." He turned and gestured at the machine. "Look at it. Amazing achievement."

"Chanute, that's him. But it's Santos-Dumont I'm most worried about. He's extremely rich. Money no object, you know."

"Panta—"

"And this!" He actually shook his fist at the rain. "It's not due to start for at least another two months. What's going on? Look at that field. It's a quagmire, practically underwater. That's why I bought this place. The ground is meant to be drained naturally. The farmer swore on his children's heads that would happen."

Carriscant peered up at the sky as Pantaleon ranted on about the farmer's duplicity. It was noon and the clouds seemed to be thinning. He could not be sure but he thought he could make out a bluey haze beyond the pale gray blanket.

"You need a road," he said without really thinking. "A metaled road, like the ones the Americans are building in Intramuros. Take any amount of rain—and smooth—then you could—" He stopped. Pantaleon was staring at him, his thumb and forefinger pinching his bottom lip. "What is it?"

"A road . . . Of course."

"Something firm, anyway. A beaten track, a—"

Pantaleon strode out into the downpour, heedless of the wet, measuring out the ground with his big strides. Carriscant sighed, erected his umbrella and followed him out into the field, tugging his collar away from his neck, the dampness making it chafe. He had actually found mold on a shirt in a closet that morning. A perfectly good white shirt with blue mold growing on it, mildewed like a cheese.

He caught up with Pantaleon at the end of the meadow. Through a fringe of guava trees was a paddy field and beyond that the swollen brown mass of the *estero*, dotted with more than its usual cargo of water cabbages, like vivid green footballs, no doubt. The Pasig had been full of them this morning, he had noticed as he crossed the Colgante bridge.

"I'll build my own," Pantaleon said fervently, holding his arms out straight in front of him, pointing back at the barn. "A base of crushed stones, bamboo poles set a meter apart, wooden planks nailed to the top of them."

"Panta, that's over a hundred yards. Think of the cost, man!"

"No, no. It's an excellent idea. Thank you, Salvador." He gripped his hand and shook it excitedly. "Thank you, bless you."

"My pleasure."

They squelched back toward the barn.

"Have you reconsidered, Salvador? You know how important it is to me."

"I told you, I can't possibly. I'd be terrified, I'm not like you. I'd be useless. Train some youngster. I'm too heavy, anyway."

"No, no, we can take the weight. It has to be you. I've calculated everything based on your weight."

"No, Panta, really—"

"Don't say no. Don't. Just think about it some more."

THE RAIN LET UP momentarily as Carriscant was driving back to Intramuros. The wind was coming from the east and he could see huge cloud continents building over the foothills of the distant mountains. Only a temporary respite, he thought, taking off his hat and mopping his face with a handkerchief, we'll really catch it this evening.

At the hospital, in his consulting rooms, he saw the inventory he had asked his senior theater nurse to prepare. Numerous items were missing from the stores, including one Merck and Frankl straight, sharp-pointed bistoury, as he had surmised. Who could say when it had gone, however? It could have been lost, it could have been stolen months ago, it could have been thrown out accidentally in a bundle of soiled swabs . . . So why did he suspect the hand of Drs. Cruz and Wieland? He started, as methodically as he could, to explore the ramifications of this supposition but stopped after two minutes, exhausted by its crowding implausibilities and inferences. In this kind of mood, he realized, anyone was capable of being turned into an enemy—Cruz, Wieland, even Bobby. Perhaps Bobby had planted the scalpel there, to unsettle him, to test him out in some way . . . But why? What did that imply? This way lay madness, he knew, and put the whole matter out of his mind. There was a long queue of patients outside his consulting room door.

LATER, his work over for the day, he stood at the rear window of his office looking out at a corner of the hospital's garden. The air was loud with the mumblings of distant thunder and tall plum-colored clouds were building high over the city. Yet to the west, over Manila Bay, the sky was clear and the sinking sun was shining brightly, filling the garden with a heavy creamy light, making the ancient tiled roofs of Intramuros glow, their vibrant terra-cotta temporarily renewed, set starkly against the boiling bruised mass of the thunderclouds. The first drops began to fall, silver like coins, through the garden's radiant light, and as the clouds hunched over the city, as if to smother this audacious sun, a brief blending of mauve thundercloud and late afternoon luminescence turned the air blue, it seemed to him, almost changing its nature from something invisible to something *there*, tangible, as if the blue light that filled the garden was a fine mist of droplets suspended in the atmosphere. Enchanted, rapt, not really thinking, Carriscant opened his window and stretched his hand out like a child trying to catch, trying to touch, this beautiful phenomenon.

His fingers closed on nothing. He saw instead the hundreds of shades of green in the leaves and bushes and grass; he smelled the ferrous, musty reek of the impending downpour; big gobbets of rain thwacked his outstretched palm and he heard the thunderclap break over San Juan del Monte as the afternoon turned blue before his spellbound eyes.

His reverie was interrupted by a small commotion of protesting voices in his anteroom. Señora Diaz's polite protests presaged her rap on the door, around which her plump, apologetic face appeared.

"There is a patient, Doctor, I'm so sorry. I said it was too late, but it's an emergency, I think."

"Show him in, Señora Diaz. And you may go. I'll be here till late."

He sat down behind his desk and with his fingernail idly drew joins between the inkblots on his blotter. The rain began to fall now in earnest, beating down, filling the gutters to overflowing, the sound of water plashing everywhere. That effect of the light in the garden, he thought, extraordinary. The atmosphere so charged with moisture, the white glare of the sun and the bluey grayness of the clouds seeming to fuse in the microscopic drops. Some sort of one-tone prism effect, he supposed, if that made sense, quite magical. Felt he could touch the air, scoop blue handfuls, almost.

He looked up and saw her. She had come into his room so quietly that for a crazy moment he thought she was a vision too, another sublime trick of the light. He gave a small cry of astonishment which he managed to turn into a cough, and rose abruptly to his feet.

"Mrs. Sieverance . . ."

She wore a straw boater, a navy blue cotton jacket over a pale gray ankle-length skirt. Her thick hair was gathered at her nape with a maroon velvet ribbon.

"I'm so sorry to be so late, Doctor. I wasn't feeling well."

Carriscant came around from behind his desk and pulled

out a chair for her to sit on. He noticed she was not using walking sticks any longer. He had not seen her for some days, but that still indicated rapid progress. She looked pale, her brow moist, and her breathing was swift and shallow.

"No sticks? You're overdoing it, I suspect."

"I feel so much stronger. Felt, I mean. But this afternoon I was writing and I began to feel faint, most odd."

"Nurse Aslinger, didn't she—"

"I gave her the day off. I felt so fine, you see."

He took her pulse. The way the electric sconce on the wall cast its light meant that, looking obliquely at her, he could see the fine down on her top lip. The finest peach bloom. Her fleece, her pelt. The tip of her tongue appeared to moisten her lower lip. An arc of light caught the lash-screened jelly of her eyeball. Some black stuff on her eyelashes. Face-powder dust in the wispy blond hair in front of her eyes.

"It is a bit fast, the pulse."

"I thought so. And my breathing. I can't seem to slow it. As if there's this tightness across my lungs."

"The wound? Any pain?"

"It's strange. A kind of tingling. A sort of . . . effervescence in that area, to the side."

"If you'd be so good as to get on the couch, I won't be a moment." He smiled at her and moved to the door.

"Where are you going?"

"To call for a nurse."

She laughed and shook her head, in amazement, he thought.

"Dr. Carriscant, really, you have cut me open and removed part of my body. I appreciate your sense of decorum, but it's not necessary." She removed her hat, set it down on the chair and went behind the screen to the examination couch.

"Could you help me? I don't like to swing my legs up."

He crouched quickly in front of her, dry-throated, his fingers on her ankles. Small black kid boots with low heels, a crisscross of laces wound through brass button hooks. He swung her legs up onto the couch. A faint creak of leather as she turned with him and they lay back.

"I'm very grateful, Doctor."

"No, no. You were right to come."

Her fingers unbuttoned the side of her skirt. Buttons on both sides. Gleam of buckles too.

"There are these small belt things."

"I have them." He unbuckled them at each side and folded down what was now the front flap of her skirt top. She undid the bottom of her jacket and pulled it wide. There was a cotton shift below, with a thin yellow chalk stripe. He could see beneath its hem a strip of her belly above the navel and the puckered top of her drawers, held tight by a cloth drawstring bow. She tugged the ends free and widened the waist to its full extent.

He was not thinking. His head was empty of everything but the rushing, finger-drumming noise of the rain. Scent of rose water from her, dusty, sweet. His eyes flicked to the window: the garden was darker, overshadowed, the lights in the room glowed brightly in the premature dusk.

"I just—" he began, his fingers on the loose waist of her drawers. He pulled down carefully, exposing first her navel and the pale plump swell of her belly, then the gentle jut of her pelvis. No farther.

"If you could just lift—"

"I'm worried it'll hurt, my muscles there are weak."

"Here."

He slid his hand beneath her, palm uppermost, into the small of her back. He took her weight and she arched carefully, her hands busy beneath her buttocks, freeing the rear flap of her skirt, pushing it down over the bulge of her haunches. His hand was hot on her spine.

Fingers on her drawer waist again as he pulled it lower to reveal the scar. It was looser than he had anticipated and his tug revealed a full inch of her pubis, the wiry golden hair grown back, almost.

He stiffened with shock at the sight, his chest suddenly full of air, his groin alive with stirrings, slackenings, as his penis thickened, pushing against his trousers. He pulled up the waistband a little, to cover it—so—tugging down the right side to reveal the scar. He kept his head bowed: he could not meet her eyes, in case she had seen that he had seen.

That bright shiny pink mark he had made on her. No inflammation. He ran his fingertips along the weal, the dots of the stitches faded to nothingness, practically. His hands on her again. He closed his eyes.

She said softly, "There is no one called Esmerelda."

"What?"

"In that novel, *East Angels*. No one called Esmerelda, no Captain Farley, no 'besting' of anyone in particular." She was looking at him with intolerable directness. He took his hands away from her belly.

"I don't understand," he said, realizing now what he had revealed of himself and his motives that day at her house.

"You never read that book. You lied about it to me, and yet you wanted to borrow another. Why?"

She propped herself on her elbows. Her voice was lazily quizzical as she stared at him. She was asking questions to which she already knew the answers.

"Because ..." His voice was low, confidential, almost a whisper. "Because I wanted to see you."

He leaned forward and as his lips touched hers he felt her arms go around his neck, drawing him down.

THE DOOR LOCKED, the lights off, they made love with great and tender solicitude and absolute minimum of movement for fear of tearing or damaging her healing wound. He slid off her skirt and drawers and then, with him helping her, she turned and knelt above his supine body on all fours as he prepared himself, unbuckling his belt and tearing open his fly, and she, inch by inch, with great care lowered herself onto him, easily. Her hair hung down, the ribbon loosened some-how, brushing his face, and once he slipped his hands up be-neath the cotton shift to hold her hanging breasts in his palms.

"It's not sore," she whispered, as she worked herself slightly to and fro.

He lay back, not moving, his hands on her thighs now as she gently moved up and down, tiny undulations.

He could not hold back for long and when the moment came the almost absolute stillness of their posture, the lack of bodily contact, of any heaving or straining, made it seem dreamlike, otherworldly, as if this extraordinary experience were happening while he lay buoyant in some tepid stream or was held in the wind-shifted topmost branches of some mighty tree.

Then she eased herself down and lay on him and only then did they kiss and touch, nuzzle and caress. He could think of nothing to say. Nothing. And so they lay still on his examina-tion couch, behind the screen in the unlit room, as the rain poured down and it grew dark outside.

THE GIRLS ON THE PONY

A FTER SHE LEFT he sat there in the gloom, numb with a helpless sense of joy, exhausted and stupidly happy. He closed his eyes and tried to bring to mind her smells and textures, the words they had said to each other, certain moments that he could hardly believe had happened. He found his memory maddeningly elusive. For a brief second he could reexperience the full softness of her breasts in his hands and then an image of the consulting room ceiling, its heavy lamp fixture, the sepia foxing of some damp stains, would push that aside, to be elbowed away in turn by the whisper of her voice in his ear—"I know, I know"—or the tickle of her thick hair on his face, the sight of her upper body twisting around rebuttoning her skirt, or her pale lovely face looming for a last kiss. What had their final words been? He could not recall. How had they arranged to meet again? Surely—surely—they had organized something? He was seized suddenly with an awful fear that this would be the first and last time they could come together in this way and, with a rush of bile, he cursed his marriage, and hers. He suddenly detested Manila with its provinciality, its small-mindedness, the impossibility of privacy among its resentful expatriates with their prurient curiosity, the ubiquity of servants, prying, whispering, the impossibility of ever being anonymous or alone.

In such a mood of frustration he left the hospital and

walked out through the blue dusk, down Calle Palacio and Fundación to the Real gate. He crossed the stagnant moat and headed for the Luneta, which he could see ahead of him, its ring of electric lights burning brightly in the encroaching night. Across the bay the Sierra de Mariveles hills were opaque and dark, a final stripe of citrus orange picking out their silhouette. Music carried to him from the bandstand as he approached the crowds and the dozens of carriages moving slowly around and around the grassy plots in the center of the oval.

As always the crowd was predominantly dressed in white, and at this hour—or was it something to do with his eyes? he wondered—the linen suits and muslin *camisas* seemed to glow in a stark, unearthly fashion in the gathering darkness. The music changed from a jaunty rendition of "The Yellow Rose of Texas" to a lilting waltz and again it seemed to him that the pace of the circling people and of the ponies drawing the carriages slowed to accommodate the new rhythms of the music. Men and women he knew greeted him as he moved aimlessly through the crowd and he raised a hand in brisk acknowledgment, keeping a vapid smile on his face and turning this way and that, changing course at each encounter to avoid having to speak further to them.

His mind was filled with wonderment still, reflecting on what had just occurred, thinking of Delphine and their delicate, tender lovemaking. He felt at once blessed and humble, grateful and unbearably moved by her generosity. Suddenly alone for a moment, his meandering dance having taken him to the edge of the glow cast by the bright bunched globes of the electric light, he turned back and looked again at the slowly revolving throng, around and around, going nowhere, accompanied by the beautiful music, the chatter of a thousand conversations, the occasional snicker of laughter.

Moving in and out of the crowd, crossing the grassy plots,

crossing the roadway, moving heedlessly, were two little American girls seated astride a barebacked pony, with their blond hair floating loose behind and tied with a big bow of ribbon on one side in the American fashion, their thin bare legs in their velvet slippers dangling side by side on each flank of the pony. The girl in front holding the reins looked happy and exhilarated, her smile wide, her eyes constantly on the move, full of curiosity. But the little girl behind, clutching her sister's dress, looked solemn and fearful, holding tight, her eyes fixed resolutely on the ground. They circled the Luneta twice and then he lost sight of them behind the grouped carriages on the far side. They did not reappear and he felt an overwhelming sense of loss invade his being, a terrible sense of life's impermanency and transience, a sudden understanding of the meaning that this vision held. He crossed the road to the seawall and sat down on it, his legs dangling over the narrow beach, looking out over its wheeled bathing huts and the dark waters of the bay to the last thin slashes of lilac on the horizon. Unobserved, alone, he put his head in his hands and wept.

HIPPOTHEETICAL

*T*HE MERCK AND FRANKL bistoury lay in the middle of Paton Bobby's desk in his office in the Ayuntamiento, its blade end pointing toward Salvador Carriscant.

"So you say there is one missing," Bobby repeated. Needlessly, Carriscant thought.

"According to my inventory."

Bobby frowned and drew his hands from below the level of the desktop and placed his fingertips carefully together, his thumbs resting under his chin. Carriscant noticed that the middle and ring fingers of his right hand were bandaged.

"What happened to your fingers?" he asked.

Bobby looked rueful. "You remember that day when we found the woman's body? And we found the knife? I put it in my pocket and forgot it was there. Ten minutes later I went for my matches and—*ouch*."

"It happens. If you carry a scalpel you need a case, or a little leather scabbard. Like this." Carriscant showed him his own.

"Yeah, well, I don't plan on carrying one around full-time."

"Well, we certainly have one missing, if that's any use."

"It might have been. Except the San Lázaro can't account for three and we got a whole box gone from the First Reserve."

"That's hospitals for you."

Bobby stood up and paced up and down, evidently perplexed. He turned and seemed about to speak and then thought better of it. And then he changed his mind again. Carriscant thought he had rarely seen a man's mental intentions so clearly written on his face—not the best of assets for a policeman, he reckoned. He waited patiently for Bobby to confide in him.

"If that scalpel was from the San Jerónimo," he began, giving a fair impersonation of a man thinking on his feet, "then conceivably—conceivably—it could have been taken by Dr. Quiroga. Yes?"

"Look, Bobby, I've already told you—"

"Merely a supposition. Hypothetical."

He pronounced the word "hippotheetical" and Carriscant had to force himself not to smile.

"The supposition is completely absurd," Carriscant said. "You're implying that Dr. Quiroga has something to do with these murders? Preposterous."

"It's a lead, you've got to admit that. First the General Elpidio connection and now this scalpel. And the surgical precision of the mutilations. 'Competently done'—those were your words, not mine." Bobby paused, pointing an unbandaged finger at Carriscant. "Dr. Quiroga's family come from Batangas in southern Luzon. It was one of the fiercest areas of rebellion. He made three trips there to my knowledge in the last year of the war."

"So what? So have I. My mother lives in San Teodoro."

"And during the war, in February and March of 1902, Colonel Sieverance's regiment was operating there. Too many connections, Carriscant, I can't ignore them."

"You're grasping at straws," Carriscant said. "The flimsiest, most ephemeral of straws . . . Listen, *I* could have taken that scalpel. Any of my staff, any porter. Dr. Cruz, Dr. Wieland. Even Colonel Sieverance, even *you*. You've all been in my operating theater, or have access to it."

Bobby colored and for a second or two looked very uncomfortable. "There's no need for that quality of sarcasm, Carriscant. I have to follow up everything."

Carriscant made an apologetic gesture, bowing his head. "The scalpel does set up all manner of questions, I agree," he said, looking hard at Bobby, who, he thought, seemed particularly uneasy beneath his gaze. "If we hadn't found it I would say that the woman's murder was completely unconnected to the soldiers' . . . She was pregnant, by the way, four months." He paused; he decided to tell Bobby his own hypothesis. "If you want my opinion, that scalpel was deliberately placed there. Not to implicate Dr. Quiroga . . . but to implicate me."

"For God's sake! Now *you're* being absurd. Who would do such a thing?"

"Dr. Cruz or Dr. Wieland. Or both of them."

Bobby laughed, his confidence suddenly returning. "You're saying they murder some peasant woman and then place one of your scalpels by the body? It makes no sense. These are men of genuine standing in the community. No, no."

"I don't say murder. But they're more than capable of, of taking an opportunity to try and disgrace me. Cruz has many contacts with the police. The Tondo police bring many fight victims to the hospital. To Cruz's wards."

"I can't accept that."

"They are completely unscrupulous and sworn enemies of mine."

"This is fantasy. Pure melodrama."

"I have to tell you what I think. They want to discredit me and they don't care how. I don't say they murdered the woman. There's a cholera epidemic in the provinces. Dozens of people die every week. And God knows how many spare bodies Cruz has in his fiendish laboratory. He could have—"

"No, stop. This is completely out of control. My dear Carriscant, these are ravings, nonsense. I'm surprised at you, old fellow, I always had you placed as a cooler, more collected type of person."

"I'm convinced that scalpel was stolen from my operating theater."

"Look, I think we're jumping too far ahead. Damn rain's rotting our minds. Growing mildew."

Carriscant decided to leave it at that. He was satisfied, however: his confession had achieved something unexpected. Bobby's relief at his accusations had been manifest, and too enthusiastically rebuffed. He was convinced now that the theft of the scalpel from his theater was carried out by none other than Chief of Constabulary Paton Bobby.

THE SUTURED HEART

ANNALIESE CARRISCANT SPOONED honey onto another triangle of toast and licked the spoon before returning it to the pot. She's eating too much, Carriscant thought, putting on more weight. There was a small bulge of flesh, an incipient double chin, growing beneath her jaw. With a sour pang of clarity Carriscant saw how unattractive his wife was, all of a sudden—how pinched, despite her new corpulence, how bland. Beside Delphine, she was— He pushed away his plate of chicken and rice. How could she eat toast and honey, slice after slice, all evening?

"I have to go to the hospital," he said.

She looked at him, impassivity shading into contempt, he thought.

"I won't wait up."

CARRISCANT PULLED the dressing back over the wound. The patient was an Englishman, an officer in the coast guard, who had developed a large bronchocele or goitrous cyst on his neck which had grown to the size of an aubergine and which had been removed two days previously. He was still weak, but he appeared to be making progress. He moved on to the next bed but was interrupted by one of the other nurses, Sister Encarnación, who had hurried into the ward.

"Dr. Carriscant, please, ward eleven. An emergency."

Carriscant followed her quickly along the corridor in the direction of the eastern wing of the hospital. Ward 11 was one of Dr. Cruz's wards. As he left his own area of the hospital it was like crossing a frontier, he thought, or traveling backward through time. At the extremities of his sphere of influence were the trestle tables with the enamel basins of disinfectant and carbolic soap, the trays of lime powder on the floor into which everyone entering his wards from Cruz's were obliged to step. Even the quality of the air seemed to change: here were old smells of putrefaction and unchanged linen and unwashed bodies. The corridors were grubby, the floors unswept, the walls printed with finger marks and the greasy shine of human contact. Cruz still believed firmly in the airborne transmission of disease, that infection was caused by foul and noxious currents of air, and as a result all the windows and doors of his wards were tightly sealed. Sister Encarnación pushed open the door of ward 11 and led Carriscant into a long room, fetid and close, divided into cubicles, wooden walls floor to ceiling, with one bed inside each stall. The aim being, Carriscant supposed sardonically, the better to impede the noisome breezes that were killing 60 percent of Cruz's patients. The nurse showed him into a cubicle and Carriscant peered down at a young man, a Filipino, who, he saw at once, had only a few days left to live.

"What's happened here?" he asked.

Sister Encarnación explained that the man had been reroofing his hut, had fallen and had impaled himself on the bamboo fence that surrounded his garden. A sharp sliver of bamboo had entered his body just below the breastbone and had traveled upward to pierce the heart.

A waterproofed canvas bag full of ice was resting on the man's chest. Carriscant lifted it off to reveal the heavy bandaging beneath. To his surprise he saw a rubber tube extending from the bandages leading into a glass bottle which was half full of blood. Drips fell from the tube's end.

"What's this?"

"A drain from the pericardium."

"What?" This made no sense. Carriscant felt the man's pulse, very faint and irregular.

"What operation has Dr. Cruz performed here?"

Sister Encarnación told him, and added that Dr. Cruz had been highly pleased with the result and had wanted the patient closely observed. A messenger had been dispatched to Cruz's house, but the doctor would surely not arrive in time, and seeing that Dr. Carriscant was in the hospital . . .

Carriscant was amazed, more than amazed. Some more questioning elicited the facts that Cruz had opened the man's chest and exposed the sac that contained the heart and that had been pierced by the bamboo sliver. He had sewn up the wound in the pericardium, leaving a trocar pushed into the heart cavity to drain it. Carriscant looked at the man. His face was blanched and pallid, covered in sweat, and he was breathing with difficulty. Cruz may have sewn up the wound in the pericardium, but it was clear that the heart had been pierced also. There must be a tiny wound in the heart still pumping blood into the cavity, too much for any drain. Soon the pressure of the blood filling the heart cavity would stifle and silence the beating, or else the lungs would give out, as the blood had probably flowed into the thoracic cavity too, crowding the lungs. There was nothing he could do. He turned away, frustrated and angry, and paced up the ward looking into the other cubicles, noting the grime on the shuttered windows. Most were empty: in one bed was a dead body, the sheet pulled over the face. Two other cubicles contained patients—a young boy and a young man—both had ice bags on their chests.

"What's this ward for?"

"Only chest wounds. Dr. Cruz has asked that this be kept exclusively for chest wounds." Sister Encarnación looked unhappy. "We get too many criminals, Dr. Carriscant. The police from Tondo bring them here when they are injured in fights. Dr. Cruz has asked only for those with chest wounds. The worst sort of individual . . ." She lowered her voice. "We're not used to this in the San Jerónimo. Not at all."

IT WAS only as he approached the rear of the Sieverance house that Carriscant's thoughts turned to something other than Dr. Isidro Cruz and his daring new operations. He had hired a *carromato* to take him to Uli-Uli, a village just beyond the palace, and had trudged back toward the Calle Lagardo before leaving the road and making his way cross-country toward the cul-de-sac and its sumptuous residences. The sky was largely covered, but from time to time a three-quarter moon appeared between the shreds of cloud to light his way. He reached the rear hedge bordering the Sieverance garden without serious mishap. One slithering fall down the banked dike of a rice paddy had soaked a shoe and muddied a trouser leg, but otherwise he was in good order as he pushed his way through the thick *cogal* and hibiscus bushes and crept across the moon-washed garden toward the house.

And once again he asked himself what exactly he was hoping to achieve, and as always the realization came that it was the effort itself that provided the justification. It was inertia that finished him: to be doing something, however pointless, however foolish, was crucial. So he took up his position behind a dense, humped mass of bougainvillea that had engulfed a wooden pergola, and waited. Perhaps she would venture out onto the *azotea* for some fresh air and he would be able to call discreetly to her. Even to glimpse her would be sufficient reward. He could see that many of the house's rear windows were illuminated and he could hear the chatter of servants and the clanging of pots and utensils from the ground-floor kitchen area. The evening meal over, he guessed. He was sure he knew where her bedroom was, and also the library, but he felt it would be foolhardy to throw a pebble at either of these windows in the hope of attracting her attention. What if a maid was in the room? Or, worse, Nurse Aslinger? He had better wait and pray his luck would hold.

Occasionally, he saw shadows pass in front of the screened windows but they were too vague and diffuse to make identification possible. And then he heard some piano music—that must be her, he thought—a series of arpeggios against a held note, then a haunting snatch of melody, some quickly played scales, up and down, and then silence. More shadows flicked in front of the windows and the fancy entered his mind that she was pacing about the rooms of the house, restless, her mind working, unable to settle, thinking about him just as he was thinking about her. Perhaps his very presence in the garden, his proximity, was provoking this delicious edginess . . . He concentrated hard, sending his thought waves out, willing her to open a door and step out onto the rear terrace. But she did not appear. He heard a door slam, saw the light go out in what he took to be her bedroom, and then nothing more. The wetness in the grass soon soaked through his remaining dry sole and he felt the cooler breezes on his neck carrying with them the earth-reek that warned of approaching rain. It began to drizzle steadily, and in the next-door garden a dog started to bark tetchily, setting off another in the servants' quarters of the Sieverance house. It was time to leave. He felt oddly satisfied as he renegotiated his way through the hedge and regained the road. In anyone else's eyes his damp vigil in the garden would have seemed absurd and a futile waste of time, but to a lover, he said to himself as he tramped into San

Miguel looking for a *carromato*, to a lover such needless discomfort has its own private import, signaling the depth of his devotion. The tune, the melody she had briefly played, remained in his head. He found he was still humming it as he settled down in his divan bed and prepared for sleep.

AN OFFICIAL ENTERTAINMENT

C ARRISCANT WAS TIDYING away his papers into his desk when there was a knock at his door and one of the nursing sisters appeared.

"Excuse me, Dr. Carriscant, Dr. Cruz sends his compliments and would like you to visit him in his theater. It's a matter of some urgency."

Carriscant was very surprised. He and Cruz had barely exchanged a word since the row over Delphine's appendicitis.

"In his theater, you say?"

"Yes. At once, if you please."

Carriscant crossed the courtyard toward Cruz's consulting rooms. He followed the nurse down an ill-lit corridor toward the operating theater. The walls here were painted with ancient yellow distemper which was flaking and peeling, and there was a curious smell in the air, a sweetish fatty cloying reek which lingered in the nose, coating the palate almost as if it were designed to be tasted rather than smelled. It was the smell of old untended food, an exudation of dirty kitchens. Carriscant recognized it at once as the smell of putrefaction.

CRUZ'S OPERATING THEATER was, to Carriscant's eyes, a scene from one of the circles of hell. Old cracked terra-cotta tiles on the floor and smudged plaster walls covered, for some reason, in scribbles of handwriting, ancient wooden trays and tables. Cruz stood tall in his domain, in his famous frock coat with its filthy veneer, its pustulant lichen, the cuffs unbuttoned and the sleeves of his coat and shirt folded back to reveal his powerful forearms with their pelt of dark hair. His hands were smeared with blood as he toweled them off on a scrap of cloth. Three theater nurses stood around the operating table alongside another doctor, Dr. Filomeno, who acted as Cruz's anesthetist. Dr. Filomeno wore a light brown suit, ruined by a splash of blood down the right side. He was dabbing at this with a bundle of swabs and complaining vigorously to one of the nurses.

"Ah, Carriscant," Cruz said, tossing the towel away onto a tray of instruments. "Glad you could make it." The self-satisfaction, the barely suppressed delight in his voice, made him drawl the words out as if he were intoxicated. "I very much wanted you to see this." He waved Carriscant up to the table.

A man lay there, his chest cavity open, retractors holding the wound wide. Peering closer, Carriscant could see that the pericardium had also been cut open, the sides held back by clamp forceps.

"Look," Cruz said. There, amid the coagulated blood and the severed tissue, Carriscant saw the man's beating heart, pulsing irregularly like some sea creature, half vegetable, half shell-less bivalve, something that clung to rocks deep at the bottom of the sea, expanding and contracting weakly, only just alive. Carriscant turned back to Cruz. The man ran his hands through his wiry hair and began to roll down his cuffs.

"I've summoned a photographer," he said proudly. "The world is about to learn about Isidro Cruz. You're not the only surgeon around here that can make an impression."

"What're you talking about?"

"Look," Cruz said, approaching the body. "Just look, Carriscant."

He stared at the twitching heart. Six taut sutures, knotted silk. Cruz's blunt finger entered the chest cavity and touched the pulsing organ.

"Cardiac sutures, Carriscant. In a knife wound."

The nurses fussed over the body, checking the drains from the pericardium and pleura.

"Dr. Filomeno will replace the rib and close the wound. I shall be issuing a statement to the press."

Carriscant could not resist: he reached out a finger and gently touched the surface of the beating heart as it wobbled and bulged, slick in its cavity. The six stitches sealed a neat wound about an inch long in the left ventricle. Carriscant's eye fell on a bag of ice on a nearby trolley. He looked at the man's face.

"May I?" He removed the mask that covered it: the man's skin was practically gray. Carriscant recognized him.

"The left lung collapsed," Dr. Filomeno explained.

Carriscant nodded. This was the man he had seen in Cruz's ward just two days previously. But the nurse had said nothing about a wound in the heart. In the pericardium, she had said. Carriscant's mind began to work: the man could not have had this gash in the heart then or he would have died within the hour. A tiny perforation perhaps, that had been his diagnosis, but not a wound of this size. So where had he received this neat wound that Cruz had sutured? Surely not even Cruz could be so—

"Cardiac sutures," Cruz taunted. "Cardiac sutures, Carriscant."

"This man will die."

"I doubt it. The bleeding has stopped. The lung will reflate."

"Even so. No, it's the filth of this place that will do for him. Look at you. I saw you run your fingers through your hair just before you touched his heart."

"Modern nonsense, Carriscant. Modish dogma."

"You might as well have operated on a cadaver."

"Professional jealousy is the most demeaning of emotions, wouldn't you say, Filomeno?"

"Without any *kapffneu!*"

Filomeno sneezed, his hand going to his nose a second too late. Carriscant turned away and looked around at the fetid, badly lit room full of people in their street clothes, scratching and sniffing, the dried blood and feculence of dozens of operations stiff and crumbling on their coat fronts.

A porter appeared at the doorway. "A gentleman is here from the *Manila Times*, sir," he said.

Carriscant could not resist. Later he'd wish he had let Cruz suffer the full force of public humiliation and ignominy, but this personal victory was too sweet to be resisted.

"I congratulate you on your sutures, Cruz. Neat work, as always. But you're too late. If I were you I would set out straightaway on the road of aseptic surgery. Who knows, you might achieve great things."

"What do you mean, 'too late'?"

"Six years too late, to be precise. The first cardiac sutures performed on a living patient—who survived—took place in 1896. Frankfurt am Main. Dr. Ludwig Rehn was the surgeon." He smiled. "Nice try. Now if you'll excuse me, I have an official entertainment to attend."

THE LAUNCH WAS WAITING for them at the wharf by the Cold Storage buildings. Carriscant helped Annaliese down into the well behind the engine and waited as the other members of their party climbed aboard. The night air was sultry and warm and he found himself wondering why formal receptions in the tropics had to be governed by the same manners and decorum suitable for temperate climates. To be wearing a tailcoat, a stiff collar and white tie to attend a function on an island in the middle of the China Sea seemed to be ludicrously pretentious, not to say sheer folly. All his satisfaction at having put Cruz so unequivocally in his place had evaporated, to be replaced by irritation and bad grace. He dropped down into the launch and it was pushed away from the wharf and began to motor up the Pasig toward the Malacañan Palace. Here at least was some relief, a little coolness, and he stretched his neck above his collar and spread his moist palms to catch the breeze created by their progress. Around him, chattering excitedly, were the members of their party—Annaliese's friends, not his, he corrected himself. The invitation had been extended to the bishop and his staff, hence Annaliese's insistence that they go. He looked back at them: Mr. and Mrs. Freer, middle-aged English, he an oculist; M. and Mme. Champoursin, he a journalist; Señora Pilar Prospero, headmistress of the cathedral school; Father Agoncillo, a plump young priest and a special friend of Annaliese; and Mrs. Kelly, a friend of the Freers, wife of a veterinary surgeon in Iloilo, visiting Manila for a month. What an impoverished crowd, he thought sourly. The men were all in evening dress like him, the women might have been going to a ball in any provincial city in Europe—long dresses, petticoats, demure jewels, silk, lace and taffeta, corsets and hair combs and high-heeled slippers. One or two carried fans, otherwise they might have been in Aberdeen or Bristol, Lyons or Hamburg, Genoa or Seville. He was determined, at all costs, not to enjoy himself.

He soon saw the palace ahead, the gardens down to the river bright with Chinese lanterns and the wide arches on its ground- and first-floor façade picked out with strings of red and yellow electric lights. They disembarked and moved through the surprising number of people to the receiving line. Governor and Mrs. Taft stood on a small dais beneath a flapping sailcloth canopy. To one side the constabulary band was seated in a semicircle energetically playing a gavotte, and just beyond them, laid over some lawn tennis courts, was an open-air ballroom with three banked rows of seats surrounding it. In various positions about the gardens were buffets of food and small tables with punch bowls. The Stars and Stripes were draped everywhere: how the Americans loved their flag, he thought.

He shook Taft's hand. The man looked grotesque in his evening wear, more obese than ever. His bulging face was pink and shiny with sweat, but he greeted everybody with unchanging geniality, shaking their hands vigorously and repeating, "Pleased to meet you, very pleased to meet you," in the American manner. Carriscant waited a little awkwardly as Annaliese chatted with Mrs. Taft. He could not tell if the governor recognized him—his welcome displayed the same booming familiarity to everyone—and he thought this was not the time to remind him of their last encounter. Taft smoothed his mustache and grinned at him like a jolly uncle. Carriscant gave him a little smile in return. He wondered vaguely if Bobby had told him about the murdered woman. The band struck up "Camptown Races" and Taft jovially conducted a few bars.

"My absolute favorite," he said, seemingly directing the remark to Carriscant, though he appeared to be looking into the middle distance.

"What? I'm sorry, I—"

"Such a pretty tune. Always cheers me up."

"Indeed."

To his relief Annaliese had finished her conversation and at last he could shake Mrs. Taft's limp hand, smile at her and move on. He steered Annaliese toward a table where punch was being served by Chinese waiters. Big chunks of ice floated in a suspicious-looking peat-colored liquid. It was hard to tell what its constituents were, but at least it was cold. And powerful. Carriscant drained his first cupful and went back for a refill. Already he could feel the alcohol working on him: perhaps he could survive this evening after all.

He strolled with Annaliese toward the band, stopping to exchange some words with acquaintances. They stood and watched the musicians in their blue uniforms with red epaulettes as they played the official rigadoon to start the dancing and the first couples moved onto the dance floor. Carriscant felt slowed and dulled by the rush of the alcohol, a little addled by the punch, and found his gaze resting on an elegant *mestiza*, her oiled hair hanging in a glossy dark sheet over a hand-painted *camisa* with intricate whorls of embroidery worked on the fan-shaped sleeves. Never seen one quite so delicately done, he thought, and turned to point it out to Annaliese, but she had moved off some paces to talk to Father Agoncillo.

"Good evening, Dr. Carriscant."

His blood stopped and he felt his innards slip and tumble.

She stood a few yards away, in a long slate blue dress with a tightly cinched waist. She carried a slim ebony cane with a silver handle. Her hair was piled high on her head in a style he had not seen before, curled and wild. Her eyes were clear and smiling, and the low frilled front of her dress showed her collarbones and the freckled paleness of her chest.

Annaliese rejoined him.

"My dear, I don't think you've met Mrs. Sieverance." He presented Annaliese. "My wife, Annaliese."

"Mrs. Sieverance, I'm glad to see you looking so well."

"Ah, thanks only to your husband, Mrs. Carriscant."

There was a hellish silence.

"What . . . I mean, no. Ah, no discomfort? No difficulties—"

"Don't worry, Doctor," she said, smiling. "The cane, I must confess, is a bit of a luxury. One hates to abandon such a dashing accessory."

"Yes," he said stupidly, seeing her glance at Annaliese. "Yes."

"Is your husband here?" Annaliese asked.

"He's in Mindanao. They're having trouble, I believe, with the *insurrectos*."

He felt he was about to collapse. "If you'll excuse me, I

think I see Chief Bobby there." He gave a small bow and
marched off, leaving them talking. He had not seen Bobby, but
he made directly for a crowd of people around a buffet table
where he drank two more cupfuls of punch and tried to regain
his composure. He filled a plate with savory biscuits shaped in
stars to take back to Annaliese. He felt . . . He did not know
what he felt. He had never seen anyone so beautiful, he
thought. He had never physically desired someone so much:
the pressure of being beside her and of not being able to touch
her had been intolerable, shocking. After a few moments he
managed to calm himself down, saw that Annaliese was alone
again and crossed the lawn to rejoin her.

"What're these?"

"I thought you might be hungry."

"No, thank you."

He handed the plate to a passing waiter.

"Very much the Gibson Girl," Annaliese said patronizingly.
"Very. What must she think of us poor colonials?"

"Who?"

"Your Mrs. Sieverance. She's certainly 'got right there,' as
they say. Must have six inches of hair pads. At least."

"She's made an excellent recovery."

"I think that all that untidy hair makes them look like
shopgirls."

"To be out and about after an operation of that seriousness
is—"

"Vulgar. So American."

LATER, when Annaliese was sitting around the dance floor
with Mrs. Freer and Mme. Champoursin, Carriscant took his
opportunity to slip away and go in search of her. He saw her
standing under a frangipani tree talking to some Americans—he thought he recognized one from that night on the

Luneta—and he passed close enough to the group so that she would see him. He went to a table draped in the Stars and Stripes and ordered yet another punch—he felt awash with punch, but there was nothing else for it.

"Hello again, Dr. Carriscant."

He turned to face her. He felt tears sting his eyes. Beyond her he noticed the others glancing over.

"Would you like a—? Can I offer you—"

"Doctor's orders? Yes, if you think I should."

She seemed so calm, so controlled. They stood two feet apart. He handed her the punch cup. His hand was trembling and the liquid slopped over the rim.

"You didn't tell me your wife was so attractive. She was very . . . polite, I thought."

"It doesn't matter," he said thickly. "It's not important. There's nothing between us, nothing, I told you."

"I was a bit surprised, I must say."

"I've missed you," he said in a low voice, trying to look like he was engaged in superficial chitchat. "I have to see you again. Can you come to the hospital?"

"No. Come to the house, the day after tomorrow. Three in the afternoon. Return my book."

"I love you," he said. "I adore you."

"I know." She looked at him, that way, then raised her voice. "I'll bear that in mind, Dr. Carriscant. Thank you."

He looked around. Paton Bobby, beaming, was striding across the lawn toward them.

"Evening, Doctor, you look almost distinguished. Almost. Evening, Mrs. Sieverance."

They shook hands. It was clear, much to Carriscant's surprise, that Bobby knew her fairly well. Bobby made an appointment to see him the next day and they chatted awhile about the situation in Mindanao. After a minute Bobby moved on.

"I must go now," she said, her eyes big with secret messages.

"Yes," he said lamely. He felt a thick-tongued dullard. A Cruz semi-mute.

She turned away and sauntered back to her friends. The trembling in Carriscant's legs forced him to move quickly to the low wall that marked the edge of the garden, where he sat down. It was five minutes before he felt able to go and find Annaliese and suggest that it was time they returned home.

THE LIBRARY

S HE LOCKED the door and turned to face him. He could see she was excited also, her chest rising and falling.

"We have ten minutes," she said.

They kissed. He held her fiercely to him, his face in the angle of her neck and shoulder. His lips touched her moist skin, feeding off her salt. He breathed in her smell.

"Jesus Christ," he said. "My God, you don't know how—"

"Don't cry," she said, smiling at him. "You'll set me off."

"Is the nurse—"

"No. But there are servants. I can't risk anything."

They sat down opposite each other, he held both her hands in his and made every banal declaration to her that he could think of. He kissed her knuckles, pressed them to his forehead.

"I have to be with you," he said. "It's killing me. We have to find some way."

"But what?"

"I don't know," he said, real despair in his voice. "I just can't think."

"A hotel?"

"In Manila? There are no secrets in this wretched place. Everyone knows me. Everyone watches everyone else. Impossible." He felt the frustration build in him. "Damn this place. Damn this stinking city." He sank to his knees in front of her, putting his arms around her hips, burying his face in her lap, feeling her hands on his head, his shoulders.

"I could come to the hospital again," she whispered. "Maybe just once more. I can't go unaccompanied too often. I could have another crisis or something. A relapse, maybe."

"Wednesday, the same time. No one will be there."

"Her day off is Friday."

"Friday, then." He kissed her, his tongue in her mouth. Her cool mouth, her slick quick tongue. He squeezed her breasts.

"Salvador, no." She stood up and unlocked the door. She rang a small handbell and sat down, leaving the door ajar. "We have to be careful," she said. "So very careful. Stay and have tea with me, let all the servants see. Nothing could be more natural. When I write to Jepson I'll tell him about your visit. Everything must be above suspicion."

TRIAL RUN

*P*ANTALEON'S HANDS GRIPPED the edge of the
uppermost blade of the propellor. The Aero-Mobile
stood outside its shed; in front of it stretched eighty yards of
new planked roadway. Carriscant stood to one side, his hands
holding the ropes that were attached to large wooden wedges
set against the front wheels of the supporting carriage. Pantaleon jerked down on the propellor and there came a fart of
noise from the engine and a puff of bluish smoke from the exhaust. He pulled again and this time it caught. He leapt back
and the blade began to spin, blurring into a shimmering disk.
Pantaleon walked around the wing, leaned over and pushed a
lever to engage the chain drive of the other propellor, which
began to turn also, slowly at first and then after a second or
two with real speed. The noise of the engine was loud, high
and angry, and the Aero-Mobile shook and quivered, like a
thoroughbred at the start of a race. Pantaleon climbed into the
forward saddle and sat there a moment, head bowed, hands on
his control levers, as if he were at prayer, and then turned to
shout out something to Carriscant—which he could not hear
over the engine—but the sweeping gesture with a hand told
him he wanted the wedges removed. Carriscant hauled them
away, and to his astonishment, for he had never really believed
the Aero-Mobile capable of movement, the machine began to
move slowly forward, thrumming and vibrating like a hovering

dragonfly, as Pantaleon slowly opened the throttle. Carriscant trotted along beside it as it rolled along the roadway, shouting encouragement to Pantaleon, and then began to run as the machine picked up speed, but it soon outstripped him. He stopped, out of breath, and shouted weakly, "Go, Pantaleon, go!" But then Pantaleon cut the engine and the blades abruptly stopped spinning and he saw him reach down to apply the brakes to the front wheels and the Aero-Mobile began to slow, although it started to veer to the right. Carriscant watched as the wheels reached the raised edge of the roadway and the machine, moving at a walking pace now, slowly tipped over onto its nose. There was a distinct crunching sound, as of a bundle of dry twigs being broken.

Carriscant ran up as Pantaleon stepped out of his saddle. He saw that the front elevator was buckled, its doped silk torn and wrinkled. Pantaleon's face was flushed and startled, and his hands were shivering with excitement. Spontaneously he and Carriscant embraced, thumping each other on the back.

"My God, Salvador, you should have felt it. The power. It was straining to leave the ground. I could feel it. And I was only at half throttle. It was longing to fly, I tell you, longing!"

"Congratulations, Panta. You know, I never really believed . . . But I was running, and then it began to outstrip me. Magnificent, magnificent!"

They inspected the damaged elevator at the front and saw that the damage was not too severe. They heaved the machine back onto the roadway with some effort and then pushed it back toward the *nipa* barn.

"One thing is clear: we have to make that rear wheel turnable," Pantaleon said, "to keep it on its true course on the roadway. A simple steering device, a tiller of some kind." His face was alive and mobile, joyful. "Honestly, Salvador, I've never experienced a moment like that. I felt . . ." He paused, he could not think of the exact word. "I don't know. On the verge. Like an explorer, I suppose, discovering a continent, an ocean. Something like that. Everything ahead is blank and I am going to take a step into the void, part a curtain, if you know what I mean."

Carriscant did: he had experienced those sensations himself with the human body. The first time he had opened the stomach cavity. Imagine what it would be like to expose the living brain, the spinal column, the heart. He felt no envy for Pantaleon: they were colleagues, fellow spirits now, both exploring their *terrae incognitae*.

They trundled the Aero-Mobile back into the barn and Pantaleon fussed over the machine, checking its components. One strut had sprung from its mountings and there seemed to be a small leak from the fuel tank. Carriscant stepped back and let Pantaleon tend to his creation.

In one corner of the *nipa* barn, he noticed, a kind of living area had been set up: a low canvas camp bed, a table with a jug and ewer on it and a lantern. He wandered over. On a tin plate was a heel of bread and some fish bones.

"Have you got someone standing guard, Panta?" Carriscant asked, half joking. "Protecting your precious invention?"

"That's for me," Pantaleon said. "I work here through the night more and more often. It made more sense if I set a bed up in here."

Carriscant shook his head in admiration: here was true dedication to a dream. True devotion to a cause. And now that he had seen the Aero-Mobile in motion he was beginning to think that Pantaleon Quiroga's name might well go down in the annals of human endeavor after all.

BRAHMS

*H*ER FACE WAS two inches from his. He ran a finger down her cheek and across her lips. He felt an extraordinary liberation wash through him, an immense gratitude, and he was duly humbled by it. That he could hold her like this in his arms, that her body was pressed against his, that he was free to touch and caress her wherever he wished, seemed to him almost incredible, fantastical. It was a gift surpassing all acts of generosity, and he kept touching her fleetingly—her face, her breasts, her arms, her buttocks—as if to reassure himself that this was still the case.

They had made love on his firm leather examination couch, more orthodoxly this time, but with the same cautious tenderness. Neither of them was naked, as if in mutual acknowledgment that his consulting rooms were not a suitable place for total disrobement, that there was still something snatched and furtive about this moment. She had undressed to a cotton chemise and petticoat; he had removed everything but his shirt and drawers. Then she had lain back on the couch and lifted the hem of the petticoat to her waist. He had climbed between her spread legs and, kneeling there, had fumblingly undone his drawers as she reached to pull them down until they bunched at his knees.

Later, as they lay together, he had lifted her chemise to expose her breasts and had kissed them tenderly, reverentially.

And now he stared into her face, studying its features and contours as if he had to memorize them for an exam.

"I can't believe it," he said. "I can't believe that I have you here, that I can hold and touch you . . ."

She smiled and hunched into his arms, her hands on his ribs, her shoulder fitting snug in his armpit. He moved his leg and felt his foot go over the edge of the examination couch. His elation faded instantly as the brute facts of their circumstances forced themselves in on him once more—the facts of where they were and how short a time they would be together. She seemed to sense his mood change, and touched his face, stretching her neck to kiss his chin.

"What are we going to do?" she said.

"I don't know," he said. He managed a wry smile. "If we were in Paris or London it would be no problem. But in Manila . . ." He raised his eyes to the ceiling. "Why didn't we meet in Europe?"

"Vienna," she said wistfully. "That would be wonderful. Have you been to Vienna?"

"No," he said, saddened. Vienna with this woman: an ache of unlived lives settled itself in his gut. Platoons of alternative existences lined up to mock him.

"I was there in the spring of '97. On the seventh of March I went to a concert and Brahms was there. He was very sick. Almost brown. A thin brown sick old man. But I saw him. They played his Fourth Symphony. Do you know it?"

"No," he said. "No, I'm afraid not." He felt a bitterness in him. "Brahms," he repeated softly, as if the word were a talisman. "Brahms. To be in Vienna with you. To go to a Brahms concert . . ." He thought of a cold European city. A fire in a comfortable room. Maybe snow falling outside. A big white soft bed with Delphine waiting, naked, for him. He groaned. This was agony, it was intolerable, an appalling torture. This was what it did to you, he supposed, this level of infatuation:

sublime delights and fiendish torments. He thought of the Brahms concert again: before he died he would hear the Fourth Symphony. He would pay one of the second-rate touring orchestras that come to Manila to perform it for him, however ineptly. Some other less pleasant visions came to him.

"Was he with you?" If Sieverance had been there he could never possibly hear—

"No. I didn't really know him at that time. We were engaged the following year."

He wanted to ask how someone like her could have married someone so . . . so insipid, so nothing, so unworthy of her. To find out how people became trapped in unions that were so manifestly wrong. Jepson Sieverance with his ephemeral personality, his feeble boy's mustache. His indecisiveness. Pleasant enough manners, he supposed, but where was the man, the true character that had won this fabulous treasure, this *goddess*? He stopped himself, this was madness. He thought sourly of his own marriage, its tired disharmony. As well put the questions to yourself, fool. It happened all too easily.

"He's changed, you know. Jepson."

"Yes?"

"This war did it. He's not the same man. Something's gone from him. A confidence, a generosity. He was never a true soldier, you see. It was like a family trade he had to go into. But now he seems more dedicated to it . . . Soldiery, I mean. He thinks he has a talent for it, he told me. He said he thought his father would be proud of him." She gave a small snort, half disgust, half amusement. "Why is that so important to men? That their father should be proud of them? Why don't they go their own way, be themselves?"

He left the question unanswered for a while: he was not content to be talking about Sieverance. "I never think about my father," he said honestly, bringing that mild, placid stranger to mind for the first time in ages.

"Good," she said, but he could see she was still thinking about her husband.

"I don't hate him," she said with quiet vehemence. "It's more a kind of apathy . . . an apathy of feeling. I feel nothing for him. I don't *quite* despise him, if you know what I mean. Almost-contempt. I can't summon up the energy to hate him."

She paused, her head slightly cocked, as if this were the first time she had articulated such feelings and was surprised to hear the words spoken out loud. Carriscant remained silent.

She went on: "But . . . what fills me with anger is that I didn't see this lying ahead of me. That I made myself blind. Anger at myself, I mean. And then despair."

"Despair?"

She looked at him, her eyes clear with a pure, hard conviction. "I can't spend the rest of my life with him. With a man like that. I can't just waste it away."

He touched her face again, pushed a lock of hair off her forehead.

"Why did you come to me that day?" he asked.

"Because I knew you wanted me to, with all that book nonsense. I knew you wanted me to."

"But did *you* want to?"

She smiled at him teasingly. "I'm here, aren't I?"

"Lots of men would want you, you must know that."

"I was . . . I was intrigued by you. Even that day at the archery, and then on the Luneta. So angry. So cross with me." She grinned, showing her teeth. "And then you saved me. I was lost. Simple as that. Head over heels."

Was she mocking him? This was what thrilled him too, this provocativeness. So new, so American. So different from the European women he knew. A kind of audacity in her, a huge self-confidence. So why had she married that lapdog?

"Why did you marry him?" he asked suddenly. "I'm sorry, it's none of my—"

"No," she said, smiling ruefully. "Good question. I don't know. At the time, he seemed . . . well, not the best, but every-thing someone in my position could reasonably hope for. When he asked me to marry him I couldn't think of any really convincing reasons for saying no." She hunched into him. "It's been a terrible . . . It was a big mistake."

"At least he brought us together."

She stretched her neck and kissed him. "I've had this dream," she said. "A story I heard about an Englishwoman, a true story, who was traveling out to India to rejoin her hus-band. She went ashore at the Suez Canal, at Port Said, with a party of friends and they went to the souk. While she was there she became separated from her group and when they went to look for her they couldn't find her. She had gone, van-ished, never to be seen again."

"So what's your dream about?"

"I have this theory that it was all a plan, and she made her escape, that she's alive and well and living the life she always wanted. Somewhere else. All her friends and family think she's been killed or abducted, but I have this notion of her, living under a false name, in Australia, or Brazil, or Turkey, or Moscow."

"You could escape like that," he said. "Just disappear . . . And then I could come and join you. We could go and live in—"

"Don't say that sort of thing, Salvador. It's not fair. Please."

"No, you could. Then I could—"

She put her finger on his lips to silence him. "Ssssh," she said.

He stayed quiet.

"Did I really nearly hit you with that arrow?" she said.

He held up his hand, forefinger and thumb two inches apart, and she laughed, deep in her throat, causing her breasts to shiver beneath her chemise. He pressed himself against her thigh, very aroused.

"Delphine, we have time, we—"

"No. I must go." She reached down and her fingers trickled across his hardness. "I'm sorry. We have to be careful."

"You're right, you're right." He sat up, all his anger returning. "We have to find some way. We have to."

"Let's go to Paris," she said mock-gaily.

"Vienna."

"Salzburg."

"Samarkand."

"Timbuktu."

"Anywhere but here," he said vehemently.

That silenced them and they dressed quickly, a little morose. Such fantasizing was dangerously double-edged, he realized: it elated and depressed in equal measure.

At the door of the consulting room they kissed.

"I can smell you on me," he said. "It'll drive me mad. What shall we do? When shall I see you?"

"I'll contact you somehow," she said, suddenly troubled. "Perhaps at the house again . . . I'll see."

"I love you, Delphine. I love you."

"Don't say it, please. It upsets me."

"Why?"

"Because . . . Because it makes me think." She took his face between her hands and stared at him. "It makes me think too much and that's bad."

They held each other. Then Carriscant gently broke their grip apart. He unlocked the door and opened it.

Pantaleon stood there, his knuckles raised to knock.

Guilt blazed from them, Carriscant knew, like a fireball. Guilt and shock. Etched on their features like a crude caricature.

That second over, everything resumed a semblance of order. Introductions were needlessly made. Pantaleon inquired in broken English after Mrs. Sieverance's health. Carriscant prattled idiotically, inventing some nonsense about twinges of pain provoking a spontaneous visit, trying to pretend to himself that there was no blush on her cheeks and forehead. Delphine's composure returned enough for her to make an orthodox farewell.

"Take the stairs very slowly, Mrs. Sieverance," Carriscant called heartily after her. "Don't try to run before you can walk." He managed a laugh and turned back into his office where Pantaleon now stood, his back to him, seemingly obsessed with something he could see in the dusk-filled garden.

"Very pleasant woman," Carriscant said. His voice sounded insufferably pompous, he thought, ridiculously formal.

"I'm so sorry, Salvador," Pantaleon said, low-toned, solemn.

"What do you mean?"

"I thought you were gone, then I heard voices. You must believe me, I would never pry, never—" He stopped. "Forgive me."

Carriscant sat down slowly behind his desk, picked up a beveled glass paperweight and turned it in his fingers. Pantaleon was right, of course. It would have been impossible for them to have maintained a pretense of not knowing. He pressed the cool heavy glass to his hot cheek.

"It's useless, Panta," he said, his voice suddenly ripe with the relief of being able to confess. "I'm desperately in love with her. Desperate."

IN THE *NIPA* BARN

CARRISCANT KNEW the routine well by now. He sat in the *nipa* barn and imagined the various stages of her journey to him. Delphine arrives at her front door with her young maid Domenica, carrying her easel, her roll of paper and her box of watercolors. She says goodbye to Nurse Aslinger, reassuring her that her health has never been better. The victoria then takes them down the road to Uli-Uli, where they cross the bridge and wheel left along the Calle de Santa Mesa and proceed along this for half a mile before turning up a narrow vegetation-choked lane called, rather grandly, the Calle Lepanto. They stop at its end: over to the left they can see the squat gray walls of Bilibid Prison; ahead lies open country and small isolated villages. Delphine and Domenica, each carrying their respective bundles, set off along the foot-path toward Sulican. After five minutes they pause. Delphine sets up her easel (the watercolor pretext had been Carriscant's idea) while the maid spreads a grass mat in the shade of a buri palm and sets out a light picnic lunch. Delphine paints for an hour or so, weather permitting, and breaks for lunch. That completed, she picks up her sketchbook and announces she is going to wander around looking for inspiration, reassuring Domenica that she will be back before three-thirty. She sets off across the nearby fields, pausing while in eyeshot to sketch a *carabao* team in a rice paddy, or a clump of bamboo overhanging a meander of an *estero*, before picking up a cart track that leads her over a small wooden bridge to a plumbago hedge. Pushing her way through, she comes upon a wide level meadow, at the far end of which is a recently constructed *nipa* barn . . .

Carriscant was waiting for her. He swung the barn door closed behind her and padlocked it. They embraced and then hurried down to the far end, past the Aero-Mobile to Pantaleon's makeshift living quarters. Carriscant had brought a quilt and some sheets in an attempt to make the bed a little more comfortable. They undressed quickly and with due care settled themselves in the camp bed (surprisingly comfortable and quite sturdy) and then they made love.

It was after he had confessed to Pantaleon that Carriscant had thought about using the *nipa* barn for their assignations. Pantaleon had given him the key ungrudgingly, saying only that he wanted to know nothing more about the affair and adding pointedly that he never worked on the Aero-Mobile in the afternoons. Carriscant began to thank him profusely but he was silenced. "You're my friend," Pantaleon had said, "but that doesn't mean I approve." Carriscant had left it at that: the matter was never mentioned again. As far as Delphine was concerned, Pantaleon knew nothing about the arrangement. Carriscant said merely that he had been given a spare key and that he knew Pantaleon was safely at the hospital on the afternoons they met.

This was the fifth time that he and Delphine had been together in the barn and already little routines and customs had established themselves. He always brought a present—something negligible, something silly—and Delphine would have something left over from her picnic—an apple, a pomegranate, a chicken leg. They made love rapidly and without much ado within the first five minutes of arriving and usually did so again, at a more leisurely pace, toward the end of their allotted time. In between they lay together on the camp bed and talked.

She told him about herself. She had been born in Waterloo, New York, the only child of Dalson and Emma Blythe. They had both died of typhus in the '79 epidemic and she had been adopted by an uncle and aunt, Wallace and Matilda Blythe, he a mathematician and school principal in New Brunswick, New Jersey. She had been well educated and for a while there were older cousins who provided a family life of sorts until they left home. Then her life became increasingly solitary through her teens as she lived on alone with her aging guardians. It had been a school friend and her aunt, an emancipated, intelligent woman, who had sprung her from this moldering domesticity and taken her to Europe on a series of summer trips in the 1890s where, she said, she discovered she had opinions and a personality of her own and at the same time saw how confined and hopeless her life in New Brunswick had been. Her aunt died, her uncle became increasingly infirm. Then one evening at a dinner party in Manhattan she met a young officer called Jepson Sieverance . . .

Carriscant remembered the present he had for her. On this occasion he had brought a box of Turkish cigarettes, oval-shaped with twin bands of gold at one end, and Delphine agreed to try one. Carriscant slipped out of the camp bed, naked, and fetched the matches from his jacket pocket. He crouched down in front of her to light her cigarette and then lit one for himself. He stood up, enjoying being naked in the warm dusty atmosphere of the hut. Thin planks of sunlight squeezed in through gaps in the bamboo walls and illuminated the interior with a soft murky light. He felt the cool packed earth beneath his feet and wandered over to the Aero-Mobile, which was showing distinct signs of being worked upon. The engine had been removed from its mountings and was resting on blocks on the floor, and the chain drives to the propellors were disconnected. He moved around to the front of the machine and climbed into the forward saddle, feeling the leather warm against his buttocks. He turned his head to look back at Delphine, who was sitting upright in the camp bed as she inspected the end of her Turkish cigarette with some disapproval.

"Rather strong for me," she said. He watched her put the cigarette in her mouth, inhale carefully and then blow a plume of bluey smoke up toward the rafters, her throat stretched and pale.

She stubbed the cigarette out on the floor. "What're you doing up there?"

"Panta's having trouble with his machine. He's decided to set the engine sideways, I mean on its side, to minimize the vibrations. He thinks the lateral vibrations—of the pistons, you know—will be better than vertical."

"Makes no sense to me. It'll never work." She threw off the quilt and left the camp bed, sauntering over to him. Her ripe body was ghostly pale in the gloom: he saw the sickle shadows of the underhang of her breasts, the dense golden triangle of her bush dark against her creamy thighs. He felt his desire for her thicken like a clot in his throat.

"It's a mad dream," she said, leaning against his leg, looking up and down the Aero-Mobile, tapping the side with her finger. He saw the tiny dapple of freckles on her bare shoulders. "This thing'll never fly."

"If only we could fly away on it," he said, his voice ragged with feeling.

She leaned forward and kissed his shoulder. "Amen to that," she said. The soft weight of her breast flattened against his arm. He climbed down from the saddle and pulled her to him.

"Maybe we *could* fly away," he said again, carefully.

"Open the doors," she said with a laugh. "Start the engine—lateral or vertical—we'll go as we are!"

He kissed her, laughing too. They made many wistful jokes

about this now, more and more often. It was a way of talking about the subject without facing it foursquare. The jocularities, however, were gaining a poignant weight, a tacit import, that was growing hard to ignore, harder to bear.

"Maybe he'll have an accident in Mindanao," he said audaciously. "Maybe some *insurrecto* will take a potshot at him, solve all our problems."

"Don't say that, Salvador. I don't hate him like that. I don't want him dead. I don't want you to think like that."

"It would make things simpler."

"But I can't even fantasize about that. I can't be a party to thoughts like that."

"But what if *you* were dead?" he said quickly. "What if everyone thought *you* were dead, like that Englishwoman in Port Said?"

"Don't."

"No, I mean it. We wouldn't be harming anyone. What if people thought you'd . . . I don't know—drowned? In a boating accident or something, but in fact you'd swum ashore. Then he would think you were dead. And you would be free."

"Dreams, Salvador, dreams."

They began, almost as a joke, as a kind of exercise, to speculate. A fire. An overturned boat. A trip to the mountains from which one person never returned. She went along with it for a while, but then he saw it was beginning to trouble her with its plausibility, its practical possibilities. But the idea had taken firm root in his mind.

"Come on," he said, and they walked back to the camp bed. He watched her take her little sponge on its string and soak it again in its bottle of clear fluid before, turning away from him and squatting down, she inserted it. He inched over to allow her space as she climbed in beside him.

"I love you," he said. This was another of their new habits.

"Maybe we will fly away," she said softly, as he softly kissed her throat. "One day."

THE RAID

W ITH A COLLECTIVE GROAN of effort the four
constables tipped up the big coffer and a small ava-
lanche of ice granules spilled onto the ground. There was a
soft thud and a bundle rolled free, wrapped in oilcloth. Bobby
pushed it to one side with his boot while the others made sure
there was nothing else in the coffer but ice.

"What is it?" Bobby asked.

Carriscant crouched down and unfolded the material. "It's a
liver," he said. "Human, I think."

"Jesus Christ! Is it Ward's?"

"I can't tell, Bobby. No one can."

The other coffer was dragged out and upended also. They
found three dead dogs and the lower trunk of an unidentified
monkey.

Carriscant said: "I told you this was a bad idea."

The constables rooted around in the compacted ice chips
searching for any other bits and pieces. Half a dozen others
stood in a loose semicircle around Cruz's laboratory, their
Krags held at the ready, keeping the astonished and befuddled
servants at bay. In the bottom corner of the second coffer they
found a canvas bag containing what Carriscant identified as
two hearts, a human hand and a monkey's head with half the
skull cut away.

"Is there any way you can say that hand was Braun's?"
Bobby asked.

"No. The discoloration makes it impossible. Why have you brought me here, Bobby?"

"I need a medical man. I don't know what these lumps of meat are."

"There are lots of American physicians on this island."

"Yeah, but none of them know the case like you." Bobby went into the lab with a lantern and came out a few seconds later.

"Where's everything gone?" he protested. "The last time we came here those two coffers were chockablock."

"I think Dr. Cruz may have given up his experimental work."

"Why should he—"

They were interrupted by an angry shout from the direction of the house and soon they saw Cruz appear, partially dressed, his shirt unbuttoned, exposing his comfortable body with its wobbling belly and its dense fur of gray hair.

Cruz swore and shouted until Bobby showed him the warrant he had, permitting him to search Cruz's premises.

"This is your doing, Carriscant," Cruz yelled at him. "This is a deliberate attempt to destroy my reputation."

"I asked Dr. Carriscant to accompany me on this raid," Bobby explained when Cruz's oaths had been approximately translated. "He was most reluctant to accompany me, but I insisted."

Cruz faced Carriscant over the small scatter of remains, animal and human. The hand lay palm upward, as if begging for alms, the fingers slightly curved.

"You are suspecting me?" Cruz said in English to Bobby.

"I'm just investigating every area I think proper."

Cruz pointed at Carriscant. "This man, this man is man of violence. I have seen him attacking Dr. Wieland. You ask Dr. Wieland. I have heard him threaten to kill Wieland. Wieland will tell you."

"Wieland has been relieved of his duties," Bobby said.

Cruz began to rant on in Spanish again, fulminating against this disgraceful intrusion, his household roused in the middle of the night, his reputation besmirched.

Carriscant looked down and made a little dust pile with the toe of his boot, his eyes roving over the pathetic remains laid out in a row. The liver was beginning to thaw—Ward's liver?—and small oozings of blood and water were forming around it, already receiving the attentions of ants and other crawling insects.

THE LETTER

H E RECOGNIZED the handwriting on the envelope.
"Dr. Salvador Carriscant, San Jerónimo Hospital. Confidential." He smiled: it had only been a week since their last meeting. He ripped open the seal and the familiar deckle edge of her writing paper was revealed. He unfolded the note and frowned. It read: "On the Luneta, this evening," and was unsigned. He looked at his watch, suddenly unsettled: midday. What was she planning?

It rained in the afternoon but by the evening the skies had cleared, so the Luneta was crowded. The carriages circled, the white-clad crowds lingered and chatted around the bandstand as the sky turned tangerine across the bay. Carriscant stepped out of his carriage and walked along the edge of the road by the seawall. There was a gratifyingly stiff breeze coming off the sea this evening and, during certain gusts, he had to place his hand on the crown of his panama hat to hold it in place. He sat on the wall to wait and looked out over the silver water toward Corregidor, swinging his head around until he could see the scattered lights of Cavite down the coast. He concentrated on the view, trying to enjoy the tranquillity and the rare moment of cool and comfort, but a small tremor of foreboding was growing in him and he felt the worry-burn of indigestion flare behind his breastbone. What did she want? And why this method of seeing each other? He forced himself to be optimistic: perhaps she was bringing him good news? Nurse Aslinger was leaving, finally. Or maybe Sieverance had been killed by *insurrectos* in Mindanao. He felt ashamed by that last thought, it was cruel, uncharitable. It was hardly Sieverance's fault that he was married to Delphine; he had not set out to thwart Salvador Carriscant, exactly. However, it was galling to be confronted by Sieverance's luck. Sieverance's luck: which had brought him this woman, which had provided him with a life with Delphine . . . No, he did not wish him dead. As well wish Annaliese dead, he thought. Wish them both dead . . . And then he began to feel disgusted with himself, at the direction his mind was taking. These were desperate thoughts. There must be other ways.

Then he saw her, with another woman, in a landau. She wore navy blue, trimmed with yellow, and a small shoulder cape and her hair high in the Gibson Girl style. He watched them both descend and make for the bandstand. He pushed himself off the wall and followed them, skirting around the bandstand, full of loud crepitations as the band changed sheet music, to emerge—casually, coincidentally—in front of them.

"Mrs. Sieverance, how do you do?"

"Dr. Carriscant. What a pleasure. May I present my friend, Mrs. Oliver. Dr. Carriscant, the most famous surgeon in Manila."

"That sounds suspiciously like faint praise, Mrs. Sieverance. Like being the healthiest man in a leper colony."

Laughter.

"You're teasing me, Doctor," she said. "You know what I mean."

More conversation was indulged in: the strength of the afternoon's rain and the freshness it brought in its wake; the outrageous price of tinned goods in Escolta; the impossibility of providing a decent buffet in the tropics without ice to serve the cold cuts on.

Then Delphine said to Mrs. Oliver, "Oh, Shirley, you see that boy selling sweetmeats? Could you get me the coconut cakes, the little square ones? What about you, Dr. Carriscant?"

"No, thank you, I'm not partial."

Shirley Oliver excused herself and they were alone.

"You look wonderful," Carriscant said.

"There's a problem," she said quickly, her face all of a sudden showing signs of strain. "My menses. I've missed the last two. It's over eight weeks."

"Oh my God . . ." He felt his indigestion replaced by nausea.

"I wouldn't be alarmed, but"—there was a catch in her voice and he could see from her eyes how upset she was—"I'm so regular, normally. You could set your clock—" She could not continue. She turned away to compose herself, she sniffed.

"My God," Carriscant said again. He felt stupid, thick-headed like a peasant. "We must be sure." Mrs. Oliver was approaching with her booty. "The *nipa* barn. Tomorrow afternoon."

"I'll try—Shirley, well done! Sure we can't tempt you, Dr. Carriscant?"

CARRISCANT WAITED in the *nipa* barn from three until six the following afternoon, but she never came. As he sat in the musty gloom of the barn, hearing the rain showers pass overhead, various plans and schemes, some bizarre, some preposterous, skittered across his mind like the kinematograph images he had seen projected in the theater in Quiapo. Imperfect, jerky, histrionic—but telling him something all the same. He supposed it might be a mistake—the only way to be absolutely sure was to hear the beating of the fetal heart, but it was too early for that—however, there was no doubting the conviction in her own voice: she was absolutely certain. He made some quick calculations. If she had missed two . . . It was nearly nine weeks since that first time in his office. His mouth was suddenly dry, tasted rank. He realized that the delicious unreal limbo he and Delphine had been inhabiting for the last two months was now over, forever. This was the watershed, it was the spur to action as well. But what to do? It was clear that something drastic had to occur—some confrontation, some confession—but where would that lead? And as he thought and speculated the one clear purpose that came to dominate his thoughts was that he must not lose her. Whatever they did should ensure that they remained together. That realization relaxed him somewhat, that seemed to narrow the options. No attempt to smooth things over, to reconcile the respective spouses, could be attempted, and any public breach would make life in Manila quite impossible. As he sifted through the alternatives one simple course of action presented itself as the only practical method of both resolving this and allowing them to live together—escape.

Shortly after six he let himself out of the barn and in the fading, yellowing light he saw Pantaleon crossing the meadow with a tool bag, about to begin his night's work. Good old Panta, he thought sentimentally, dear Pantaleon. A true friend.

Pantaleon glanced apprehensively toward the barn door. "I'm so sorry, Salvador, I hope I'm not—"

"No, no. She's not here."

"Are you all right?"

"Yes. No. Well, a bit tired. I've been thinking. Bit of a strain."

"I'm not surprised," Pantaleon said. "I've been noticing how distracted you are. You've got to resolve this. It can't go on."

"You're right. But don't worry, Panta, it'll be resolved."

.   .   .

THE HARBOR MASTER'S OFFICE was behind the customhouse on the Calle Urbistondo. Carriscant stood patiently in front of a counter while a young Chinese clerk laboriously checked list after list of names in a scuffed ledger.

"You say 'Nilson'?"

"No. Axel. Captain Nicanor Axel. His ship is called the *General Blanco*."

"Ah, yes. He leave three day ago. Hong Kong."

"How long does it take to go and come from Hong Kong?"

"That depend how long you stay there."

Jesus Christ. "Captain Axel makes this trip regularly. How long does he normally take? Surely you can check the figures."

Eventually (Carriscant took the ledger from the exasperating boy himself) he calculated that if the *General Blanco* had left Manila three days ago it would very likely be back within the week. That was the information he was after. So, if he could see Axel within the next few days he could set things in motion. He stepped down the stairway from the harbor master's office, his head full of dates and conflicting future plans. He had no real sense of what he wanted to do: once again it was a question of having something in place, a stratagem he could propose to Delphine. He had no doubt that she would come with him, if only he could work it out satisfactorily. No doubt in her at all. He strode out of shadow into eye-dazzling early morning sunlight and progressed around to the front of the customhouse, where there was a rank of *carromatos*. Axel was the right fellow for a job like this. He would find out exactly what the man—

"Carriscant! Dr. Carriscant!"

Carriscant halted and turned, his eyes still watery from the sun's glare. The cry came from the water's edge. A shimmering steam launch at the jetty. He squinted and shaded his eyes. A blob detached itself from the dark blobs around the launch and took on the lineaments of a figure as it came to greet him.

"Fancy finding you here," Sieverance said jovially. "Just set foot on the dockside and there you are. Delighted to see you."

"How are you?" Carriscant managed to say, feeling the skin crawl on his skull. A berserk shriek of despair seemed to echo in his head. "I thought you—I mean the Mindanao posting was for—"

"To hell with Mindanao," Sieverance said, leaning forward confidentially. "I've been promoted. Full colonel. They've given me a desk in the War Department. Just got the news yesterday. I was lucky to catch the steamer."

"The War Department?"

"Yes, thank the good Lord. We're going, Carriscant. Back to the good old US of A."

FROM THE CORNER of his eye Carriscant could see Sieverance supervising the unloading of his trunks. He leaned forward and said to the *carromato* driver: "Calle Lagarda, opposite the palace. As fast as you can, please."

The little cab set off at a fair pace, but they were held up as usual by the mass of traffic on the rise up to the Bridge of Spain. Once over that it was a swift drive down the Calzada de Vidal and on past the low wooden huts of the First Reserve Hospital before recrossing the Pasig via the Avila Bridge and on through San Miguel to the Calle Lagarda.

The maid who opened the door did not recognize him, he was glad to observe, but when he asked if Señora Sieverance was in he was told she was out. He groaned inwardly: he had to reach her before Sieverance did. But at least this absence meant she could not have known her husband was due to return from Mindanao. La Señora, he was told, was playing bridge at the house of Señora Oliver in Ermita. Carriscant ran back down the path to his cab, not leaving his name.

The Olivers' house in Ermita was secluded in large walled

gardens. Carriscant paced around outside the gate desperately trying to pummel his brain into producing a convincing reason why he, Dr. Salvador Carriscant, should be interrupting a ladies' bridge game, midmorning, in Ermita. He could think of nothing. He walked down a narrow grass-choked path beside the garden wall, vaguely thinking that if he could gain the garden he might secretly be able to attract her attention somehow. But, supposing he could achieve this, what could she do then? And in any event, even if he scurried from shrub to shrub like some demented franc-tireur, he would probably be spotted. All the same it was the only solution and he reached up to the top of the wall and pulled himself up to peer over.

The garden was large and well tended, lush from the rains and with a dense close-cut lawn. Just in front of him was an ornamental summerhouse, the walls made of bamboo set in a herringbone pattern and crowned with a thick thatch of woven palm leaves. He hauled himself over the wall and dropped down on the other side. Some way across the garden by a chicken run he could see what he took to be a couple of gardeners. He moistened a finger and held it up to determine the direction of the wind—it would do. He removed his handkerchief from his pocket and, striking a match, held the flame to a corner. When the cotton was well ablaze—he could see the hairs on his left hand beginning to singe, the flames were almost invisible in the sunlight—he tossed it up onto the roof of the summerhouse. He hoped the thatch was dry enough to take and looked up into the milky, hazy sky—no chance of rain. He shimmied up and over the wall and, back on the street, told his cabdriver to go down to the barracks at Malate and tell the guard there that there was a fire at number 14, Calle de la Galería. American ladies were in danger.

From his vantage point on the road he soon saw the smoke from the summerhouse roof and was gratified to note that the breeze did in fact blow it directly toward the house. But then he became a little anxious when the fire took real hold, with six-foot flames shooting from the crackling thatch, with dense drifts of smoke beginning to engulf the house. Still there was no cry of alarm. What were those gardeners doing? Then he heard shouts and a few screams and, right on time, the clanging of the bell on the barracks fire pump. He walked down the road toward the front gates, telling two curious urchins that there was a big fire and that they should run and get help.

The gleaming scarlet fire pump, manned by half a dozen Negro soldiers and pulled by four vigorously trotting ponies, wheeled smartly into the driveway as the house gates were flung open and Carriscant, along with some worried and curious neighbors, augmented by an increasing flow of helpful locals, followed it in to see if they could be of any assistance. Hoses were being run out from the pump and the household seemed to have gathered on the back lawn, at a safe distance, to watch the really rather spectacular blaze. Chinese servants grinned and gaped as a crouching, intrepid gardener threw a useless bucket of water onto the roaring palm thatch. Half a dozen American ladies stood by the rear steps of the house. The bridge party. Carriscant removed his hat as he approached.

"Mrs. Oliver? I'm Dr. Carriscant. I was passing. Can I be of any assistance? Is everything all right? Anyone hurt?"

"Oh, Dr. Carriscant, yes of course. No, no injured. We're just shocked. How could it have happened?"

"Sometimes thick vegetation, the thatch, the heat of the sun, it can combust spontaneously," he invented. "It happens here from time to time."

"Really? But we've had so much rain. Good Lord." She shouted at the gardener, who was returning with a second bucket, "Pu Lin, stop that, please!"

Carriscant turned. Delphine stood on the veranda, staring at him in some amazement.

"Morning, Mrs. Sieverance. I was passing, saw the smoke and flames."

She came down the steps to join him, her eyes now narrow with suspicion. By now hoses were primed and water was being played on the flames. The small crowd began to applaud.

"Salvador, did you have anything to—"

"He's back. I just met him at the docks. Back from Mindanao."

Her face changed: she looked sick, a hand went to her throat. How he loved her for that.

"But how—"

"It's worse," Carriscant said, turning to check that their conversation was attracting no attention. "He has a new posting. Back home. Back in America."

"Oh my God." Despite herself she clutched at his arm, then released it immediately. Just at that moment the summerhouse roof caved in with a damp sigh, sending great billows of white smoke across the lawn, dispersing the coughing onlookers.

Carriscant drew her to one side. "Listen to me," he said urgently. "You must go home. You have to tell him you think you're pregnant."

"Oh, Jesus Lord, I don't think—"

"You must." She was in real distress, he could see, but he pressed on. "When was the last time you and he were . . ."

She put her hands to her temples, massaging. "Ah, about a week, I think, a week before he left. Yes."

"Four months? A bit more?"

"Yes." Her voice was small, frightened. "I think so."

"So don't forget. You're four months pregnant. Four. Send for me and I'll confirm it to him. All right?"

"Salvador, I—"

People were drifting back from inspecting the drenched

ashy remains of the summerhouse. He moved around behind her, his hands on the brim of his hat as if he were taking his leave. "We'll be free soon. I've got an idea. A brilliant plan. Everything is under control. We'll be safe."

He bade a cordial goodbye to Mrs. Oliver and walked out of the garden to his waiting *carromato*.

PRAGMATISM

A NNALIESE WAS TRYING not to cry. Her hands were wringing the napkin, twisting and knotting it, then unknotting it again, spreading it out and smoothing it flat on the table before beginning to twist it up again. All the while she was talking in a low voice, explaining, apologizing, criticizing herself, criticizing Carriscant more mildly, blaming them both for mistakes made.

Carriscant took the napkin from her gently. She was driving him mad with her fidgeting. They were sitting at the dining table, the meal cleared away. Carriscant had been pouring himself a large brandy when Annaliese came through and said she wanted to talk. They had sat down facing each other and she had started to twist the napkin as he listened in some amazement to her apologies. She blamed herself, she said, she had been too unfeeling, too severe. She hated this coldness that existed between them; the lives they were living at the moment were no marriage—worse than no marriage.

"I want us to try again, Salvador, to try and make a go of it, to be man and wife again."

"Annaliese, I don't think—"

"Look, just say we'll *try*. Surely we owe that to each other? I want things to be as they were. Don't you remember, when you first came back from Europe? It was my fault, I know. I turned from you. When Papa and Hannah left, I felt so awful.

And then when Papa died, I felt— And you were at work so much of the time. I drew in on myself, I know. I gave you no affection. I know I made the mistakes. But my nerves, you see . . ."

Carriscant tried to listen but his mind kept returning to the question of whether Delphine would tell Sieverance right away or wait a day or so. Now Annaliese stretched a hand across the tabletop. He took it dutifully, dutifully squeezed it, gently.

"Can we try, Salvador, can we try?"

"Of course, my dear. It's never too late."

"Bless you. I don't deserve you. I'm sorry. Everything will change now for the better, you'll see."

Her tears had exhausted her and she went to bed early. Carriscant stayed up late checking his accounts, running over the plan in his head, making refinements to the organization, trying to establish if anything could go wrong. He retired to his study about midnight and was just drifting into sleep when there was a light tap on the door and it swung open.

"Salvador, it's me."

The room was so dark all he could see of her was the ghostly pale rectangle of her nightdress.

"Annaliese," he said, trying to keep the astonishment out of his voice. "What's wrong?"

"I was waiting for you." The rectangle enlarged as she moved closer to the bed.

"I didn't want to disturb you," he said. "You seemed so tired."

Now the shape of the nightdress was changing again: it shrank to a square, disappeared, reappeared for a brief second, thinner, and then disappeared completely. He heard the whisper of the mosquito netting being raised and the next sensation he was aware of was Annaliese's naked body sliding into the divan bed beside him.

"We must make a new start, my darling," she said.

The absolute darkness of the room and her bed-warm small body squirming beside him was having an effect. He put out a hand and it struck one of her small breasts and he cupped it instinctively. He felt her breath on his cheek and at the same time her hand slid under the hem of his nightgown and traveled up his thigh. He flinched as she grasped him.

"See, Salvador, I knew. I'm so pleased, I—"

"No tears, my love, please."

Her lips were on his face, dabbing, searching for his mouth. In the confusion of tactile messages his body was receiving, some portion of his mind counseled restraint, that this was wrong, that this was some kind of double betrayal. But she was pulling him around on top of her and without thinking he was kissing her breasts. In the darkness she was like a warm writhing anonymous girl, he thought, quite unlike the Annaliese he thought he had come to know and barely tolerate. Why, he thought, as she widened her legs to accommodate him, she might be anybody. And this was the sophistry with which he comforted himself as he lay with her later: a brief physical encounter in the night, and given what was about to ensue with Delphine, it would not have been pragmatic to deny her. It had to be gone through with to allay suspicions. His conscience was clear.

VIENNA, PARIS,
MOSCOW, ROME...

I HAVEN'T TOLD him yet," Delphine said. She looked tired, under strain, her eyes dark. "I just don't think I can face his huge smugness," she went on with some vehemence. "His self-satisfaction."

"Have you had—" Carriscant began unreflectingly. "I'm sorry," he said. "I shouldn't ask." He knew he wanted to ease his own guilt.

"No," she said bluntly. "If you must know. He doesn't... It was part of the problem between us. He..." She squared her shoulders. "He finds it difficult to stay hard." She looked at him unflinchingly. "*Ejaculatio praecox*, I believe, is the correct term."

"Oh." Carriscant tried not to show how pleased he was at this news. "I see what you mean about the smugness, then."

"He'll go mad with joy, ecstatic."

"Don't delay too long, that's all." He reached out and cupped her face. "I've spoken to Axel today. There was no problem, in fact he was positively unperturbed. Everything is ready."

They were sitting, fully clothed, on the camp bed in the *nipa* barn. She reached out for him and pulled him to her and they hugged each other silently for a moment or two.

She was still tense. "You understand now why I said the thing had to be finished once and for all. We can't just run away. You see, once I tell him about the child he'd never let me go. Follow me anywhere, forever." Her face darkened as if she were contemplating this prospect. "Maybe I shouldn't tell him about the child."

"It won't work otherwise. He'd suspect instantly. He'd know everything within hours. This is the only way we can be truly free. For always."

"I know, I know. It's just difficult, I—"

"But look at it this way, now that I know how he feels about being a father it'll work all the better." He could see how she wanted to believe him. "He'll never know. Trust me."

"What about you?"

"I'll say I'm going to the country to see my mother for a week or so. When they come looking for me it'll be too late."

She exhaled and slumped, her shoulders rounding, as she rubbed her face with her hands.

"My God," she said. "Can you believe it? Just think, Salvador. Vienna. We'll be in Vienna in a matter of weeks."

"Or Paris, or Moscow, or Rome, or Athens . . ."

"And nobody will know who we are or where we came from."

He laughed, the joy suddenly effervescent in him. "Nobody'll have heard of the Philippines."

She was sober again. "We're booked for Yokohama on the twenty-fifth."

"That gives us plenty of time. Axel's waiting, ready. I just have to give him a few days' notice. He made absolutely no fuss about the conditions. A routine job for him, probably, all this clandestine stuff."

"All right," she said, making a decision. "I'll tell him tonight."

She rose to her feet and gathered up her pencils and sketch

pad and looked around the barn. She left the grip with a change of clothes that he had asked her to bring.

"I won't see you here again, I suppose," she said a little sadly. "Or this preposterous flying machine. Poor Pantaleon."

"Well, it keeps him busy. And it was a good place for us."

"Yes," she said emphatically. "Yes, it was." Then she kissed him hard, pushing her tongue into his mouth, feeding on him. They broke apart and looked at each other.

"We'll be free," he said. "Don't worry."

"I love you, Salvador," she said.

After she had gone he realized that it was the first time he could remember hearing the words from her lips.

A BOTTLE OF BLOOD

*J*EPSON SIEVERANCE SENT for Dr. Carriscant at nine the next morning. It was raining hard and as Carriscant dashed from the carriage to the front door he saw that it was Sieverance himself who was holding it open.

"It's the most wonderful news," Sieverance kept repeating as he strode beside him down the corridor toward the bedroom. "And I'm sure she's right. Woman has an instinct about these things."

For some reason Carriscant found his use of the general noun offensive. "We'll confirm it soon enough," Carriscant said, managing a thin smile. Delphine was right: the man's preening elation was offensive, rebarbative.

She was in her room, waiting, wearing a plaid robe over her nightgown, sitting in an armchair. She looked calm, he thought, very serene. They greeted each other with their usual cordiality, and then Sieverance obligingly excused himself.

"No Nurse Aslinger?" Carriscant said.

"I was obliged to let her go."

He leaned forward and pressed his lips to her forehead fleetingly. He could hear Sieverance pacing the corridor outside, already a parodical expectant father, he thought. He lowered his voice.

"Everything is organized for the twentieth," he said. "Axel is prepared. I'll have everything ready."

"I know what to do."

He opened his bag and removed a brown medicine bottle, which he gave to her. "Here. You'll need this to make it convincing."

"What is it?"

"Blood." He touched her arm, and her face. She kissed his fingertips as they brushed her mouth.

"You can't bring anything with you, you know. You'll have to tell me what other clothes, powders, rouge, things you need, essentials . . ."

"All right. A complete fresh start," she said, smiling. "Good. I like that."

"I'll make sure they're on the boat." He paused, the reality of what he was asking her to do sinking in. "Won't you miss anything?"

"My books, I suppose. I can always buy more books."

"Axel says he'll get us to Singapore in six or seven days. We can pick up any boat going west to Suez. Then, once we're in the Mediterranean . . ."

"We can get off anywhere we want." Her eyes went distant, as if she were focusing again on those magical cities that had been the context for their fantasies of escape. "What about money?" she said, suddenly practical again.

"I've got plenty. Look, let me take care of the details. You'll have enough to go through."

"I'll be safe, won't I? I mean, nothing could go wrong, could it?"

"Nothing. And remember, we're committing no crime. We're doing nothing wrong."

"Nothing legally wrong." She looked solemn then. "What about you and your . . . I never ask you about her. I feel—"

"It's easy for me," he said bravely. "The whole thing's been a sham for years. A big mistake. I don't think there'll be too much surprise on her part." The words came so easily, he thought. "I'd better go and tell him the good news."

Sieverance was waiting in the living room.

"Congratulations," Carriscant said, feeling oddly formal. "Your wife is expecting a child. She's almost five months pregnant."

Sieverance was overcome, but at least he did not weep, Carriscant thought. He managed to leave the house without having to drink to the baby's health.

THE TOY

NICANOR AXEL ACCEPTED the small jute sack of silver Conant dollars with a look of surprise. Carriscant thought it was the first expression of emotion he had ever seen register on that inscrutable filthy face. The eyes widened and the whites showed unnaturally blanched in their deep swart sockets.

"That's more than generous, Dr. Carriscant."

"Just a down payment. There'll be the same once we make landfall at Singapore. I want you to know how important this is to me and how much I count on your absolute discretion."

"But of course," Axel said, scratching energetically at the volute of a nostril. The nail sickle was quite black against the dull nacreous pink of the nail. Indeed the whole nail was outlined in black as if with a pen or an indelible pencil. But somehow the blond hair always looked clean: how did he manage that?

Axel grew aware he was being studied. "Is there anything wrong?"

"Nothing. And you can guarantee that there will be no other passengers?"

"Completely."

"And that you will not return to Manila for at least two months after you have deposited . . . the two passengers at Singapore."

"Goes without saying." Axel offered his grubby hand and Carriscant shook it. The palm and fingers were astonishingly calloused, as if carved from pumice. Strangely, Carriscant felt he could trust him.

"May I ask who these two passengers are," Axel inquired a little shyly.

"A gentleman and a lady. I think for the moment we should leave it at that."

Axel nodded hastily. "Till the twentieth, then," he said.

Carriscant stowed a suitcase of clothes in the small cabin that had been made available, and walked back on top to the reeking deck. Thin ropes of steam rose from one of the forward holds. It was a hot, fetid night and all the moist warmth of Manila seemed to have congregated around this noisome craft. Across the treacly, smeared waters of the Pasig the lights on Fort Santiago burned, a fuzzy areola of moisture haloing the moth-battered bulbs. Carriscant felt the enormity of what he and Delphine were about to do. Then the awful trepidation passed as he stood there, almost magically, it seemed, giving way to a strange boyish surge of excitement, a vision of horizons receding, of worlds waiting to be explored.

"Goodbye, Doctor," Axel said. "We'll be ready for you." He corrected. "Your passengers."

"Not a word to Udo, mind," Carriscant warned. Axel was no fool. He said goodbye and cautiously made his way across the sagging planks between the moored *cascos* to the quayside, the black waters slapping the wooden hulls. He walked up to Escolta and hailed a *carromato*. Nobody had seen him.

BACK IN his consulting rooms Carriscant, in his new mood of calm, ran through the details of the plan for what seemed the thousandth time. Delphine had told her friends about her pregnancy and was fully involved in the packing up of the house in preparation for the return to America. Everything was as ready as could be. Carriscant had informed the hospital authorities that he was taking two weeks' leave and going south to visit his mother on the twenty-first. Annaliese had protested a little at this news and had offered to accompany him, but as there was scant affection between daughter-in-law and mother-in-law he knew she could be easily dissuaded.

He held his hand out, palm down, fingers spread. Not a tremor. Surgeon's hands. He contemplated his new life ahead with calmness and contained excitement. Somewhere in Europe he and Delphine would settle, raise their child, and he would take up the scalpel again. To be in a center of medical excellence after this backwater: what challenges there would be, what reputations to make! If this was indeed the golden age of surgery, as the great surgeons claimed, then it was only fitting that he . . . He checked himself. He should keep his ambitions more modest: it would not do to become too celebrated. Perhaps his dreams of glory would have to be set aside—a small price to pay, he conceded, a small price to pay.

He poured himself a glass of rum from the bottle he kept in his cabinet, and told himself to relax, everything was in order. He merely had to live out the next few days as normally and as ordinarily as possible. He was going to make a new life in Europe with the only woman he had ever truly loved. He was, he told himself, the luckiest man alive. He grinned. Sieverance's luck had proved to be Carriscant's luck after all, and Carriscant's luck was about to have its day.

He was refilling his glass when Pantaleon rapped on the door and came in. He was carrying a newspaper in his hand and his manner was both agitated and excited.

"There's nothing for it, Salvador. Fate, destiny, demands we go!"

"Steady, steady. What're you talking about?"

Pantaleon spread the newspaper on the desk. It was an edition of *Le Figaro*, about five weeks old. Pantaleon pointed to an announcement on page 7, published by "Le Jury du Prix Amberway-Richault."

"My French isn't good enough. Anyway, this is a bit out-of-date, isn't it?"

"I know. And as a subscriber and competitor I'm meant to be kept fully informed. But who cares about 'some fool in the Philippines.' It's just as well I get these newspapers sent out. Everything could have been lost, ruined."

He calmed himself and began to translate. "Listen: 'A spectacular concurrence, aerial concurrence—aerial challenge—for the Amberway-Richault Prize is scheduled to take place in the Bois de Boulogne on May 30, 1903 . . .' Something about the rules. Ah . . . 'Four flying machines are to participate . . .'—this is the important bit—'with the expected participation of M. Ferdinand Ferber and his Ferber number 6 . . .' Then there's a list of the other flyers: Cody, Karl Jatho, Levavasseur. Unbelievable, isn't it?"

"I don't follow, Panta, what—"

"That's the prize I'm trying to win."

"I know that."

"Well, I've got to do it now, haven't I? Before the thirtieth. I've calculated I have to allow myself time to cable to Paris. Confirmation of witnesses, photographers, et cetera. Any day between now and the twenty-first should be enough." He smiled, seizing Carriscant's arm. "Can you imagine them in Paris, Salvador? 'News had just arrived from the Philippine Islands that, in a fully validated aerial trip, Dr. Pantaleon Quiroga is the winner of the Amberway-Richault Prize.' Can you imagine the effect of that? A bombshell. Cataclysmic!"

"Well, yes, if you can manage, but I don't see—"

The grip on Carriscant's arm grew tighter. "We're going to do it, Salvador. You and me. Some final preparations and the minute we get a pause in the wretched rain we go."

"No, no, no. I told you, Panta. I'm not going up in that thing." He laughed. "Get one of your other friends."

Pantaleon's face had frozen, his mouth slightly open, and Carriscant saw his body visibly tense. "No, Salvador," he said in a quiet voice. "I told you already. I can't trust anyone else. The Aero-Mobile will be ready in a few days. I think we could make the attempt as early as the thirteenth, weather permitting. It'll be perfectly safe."

"No, Panta, I'm not doing it." Carriscant had heard the neurotic edge of madness in Pantaleon's voice. The man's obsession had driven out all reason. He spoke firmly, giving him no option for a misinterpretation. "I won't do it. I'll help all I can. But I won't go up."

Pantaleon looked at him bitterly, miserably, his jaws clenched tight, the fingers of one hand tapping a coat button, one after the other.

"Please don't make me remind you of your obligation to me," Pantaleon said. "I've been determined from the outset that it should be the two of us. All the design calculations have been based on your weight. The precision is vital. And you know exactly what has to be done."

"Panta, you could teach a child of ten what to do in one hour. This insistence of me being the partner is nonsensical."

"Then why did you allow me to believe you would help?"

"I never said I would."

"You never said you wouldn't. You went along with it. Allowed me to believe you would be there."

"Because I like you, that's why. I never thought for one second we'd get to this stage. I didn't want to be harsh. I thought it was just a harmless pastime for you, a toy—"

"A *toy*?" He was furious now, Carriscant saw. He had gone far too far.

"I'm sorry. I never realized it was so important to you."

"What about your obligation to me?"

"What obligation, for heaven's sake?"

"It's thanks to me that you've achieved everything. Without me you're no better than that butcher Cruz. It's my skill that has allowed you to flourish."

Carriscant could not believe what he was hearing. What delusions were these? What fantasies were being aired now? He felt his own anger rise in him at this preposterous claim.

"What are you talking about? Are you mad?"

"You cut and you sew, you cut and you sew, that's all. Nothing more than the skills of a competent tailor. All the magic lies in anesthesia. Without that enchanted sleep you'd still be barbers' assistants, sawbones, killing people."

"Enchanted sleep? Enchanted sleep?" Carriscant felt his spine stiffen with a keening, intense rage. He'd never heard such nonsense: the self-deluding dreams of a disappointed man. "You're out of your mind. You're just a chemist. You mix your potions and drip them on a gauze mask. How dare you spout such disgusting nonsense. For the sake of our friendship I'll forget I heard this. But never, ever, talk to me like this again."

He turned away from him, shocked, deeply offended. The man was lost.

"You don't accept you owe me anything?"

"Nothing more than would exist between colleagues." He turned back to face him, furious. "What do you owe me, come to that? How do you think you paid for your precious flying machine, your barn, your wooden roadway? Thanks to the fees you earn because you work for Salvador Carriscant!" His voice had risen to a shout. His whole body was in spasm, his fists clenched tight. They faced each other, their faces ugly with pride and resentment. It was astonishing how quickly a friendship of years could dissolve within seconds, Carriscant thought, vanish like a chimera. He felt desperately unhappy and profoundly ill at ease. He dragged his fingers down his cheeks. This had to be stopped now, before all ground was irrevocably lost.

"Panta, this is terribly wrong. Let's not ruin—"

"What about your other obligations to me?" His voice was implacable, unmoved.

"What obligations, for pity's sake?"

"That I let you and your concubine fornicate in my bed."

"Oh for God's sake, be a man, Pantaleon!"

"If you don't partner me in the Aero-Mobile I will be obliged to inform Colonel Sieverance of his wife's infidelity. And with whom."

The absurd formality of the expressions made the appalling threat all too real. Carriscant felt an awful, debilitating fear spread through him, weakening him, infecting him with a terrifying uncertainty about everything he had regarded as safe and secure. He walked to the dark window and looked out at the garden, seeing only his own shadowed, blinking, demoralized reflection staring back.

"Under those circumstances, I agree."

"Good, excellent!" Pantaleon's voice was vibrant again, all his old enthusiasm returned at once. Carriscant turned slowly, incredulous. Pantaleon strode across the room to him, beaming, a hand extended. Not thinking, Carriscant meekly accepted it.

"I'm so pleased, Salvador, so pleased. We'll never mention this horrid business again. Everything is perfect now, as it was meant to be." He was still shaking Carriscant's hand. "You'll see, my friend, this prize will make your name live forever."

A FUNERAL

*E*PHRAIM WARD and Maximilian Braun were buried during a steady downpour. The graves in the military cemetery at Paco were half filled with water and the lowered coffins floated for a second before submerging with a syrupy gurgle. Caramel bubbles floated on the surface for a moment before the first shovelfuls of mud and gravel splashed in. Carriscant took the envelope containing the men's death certificates from his pocket and passed it to Paton Bobby.

"Before I forget," he said.

Bobby tucked the envelope away in his jacket. "Thanks," he said. "Uplifting little ceremony."

Apart from the burial party and the army chaplain, Carriscant and Bobby were the only others present. They trudged back through the puddles past the mildewed rows of wooden crosses to Bobby's motorcar, a new acquisition for the constabulary, a neat little Charron 628, and climbed inside, where they sat morosely while the burial party filled the grave and hammered in two fresh and sappy wooden crosses. Bobby waved a goodbye to the chaplain as his carriage pulled out of the cemetery and headed off down the road that would take him back to the barracks at Pasay, a mile or so distant.

Bobby took out a cigar and lit it, a disgruntled expression on his face. Beyond the tattered screen of banana trees that marked the northern boundary of the cemetery was the long thin shape of the Concordia cigar factory. For an idle moment Carriscant wondered if the cigar Bobby was smoking had been made there and wondered further if there was any significance to be drawn from this morbid conjunction of factory, smoker and graveyard. His tired brain could not come up with one, so he let it drop.

"It annoys me," Bobby said slowly, "it annoys me intensely that we couldn't pin these killings on anyone. Those are two murdered American boys lying in their graves in this godforsaken hole and the killers are still out there." He paused. "And that fucking annoys me."

Carriscant shrugged. "You did your best," he said. "It was an impossible case to solve. No one could criticize you."

"Yeah, well . . . Did you bury the woman?"

"Last week. Nobody claimed her."

"That's what really finished me. I mean, where's the connection there? How do you make that fit?"

"You don't. I don't think the woman's death had anything to do with the other two."

"Yeah, well," Bobby said grumpily. He looked uncomfortable again and Carriscant wondered anew why Bobby had placed his scalpel by the body. He looked around at the sound of carriage wheels as a victoria with its canopy up turned into the cemetery and pulled up beside them.

Sieverance leaned out. "I guess I'm too late," he said. "Sorry."

They watched him go to the graveside and bow his head for a minute or two before he rejoined them at the motor. He looked suitably pious.

"Great shame," he said. "Braun was a fine soldier. Real professional. You know, it kind of makes you sick. You survive everything the Plains Indians can throw at you, then you get cut up by some damned gugu." His outrage seemed a little willed, Carriscant thought, a little cooked up. They listened patiently as Sieverance outlined some of Braun's military exploits against the Oglalas and the Hunkpapa Sioux.

"It's a fucking disgrace," Bobby said with feeling. "A damn fucking disgrace."

"I'd better get along," said Sieverance. "By the way, Carriscant, Mrs. Sieverance is feeling fine, in fine fettle."

"I'm so pleased."

They watched him go. Bobby took a long slow draw on his cigar. "It never ceases to amaze me," he said, "how some pissant little cocksucker like that gets to be a full colonel."

"I suppose if your daddy's a general and a friend of Teddy Roosevelt that might have something to do with it."

"You don't say . . ."

"Did you tell him we were burying the men?"

"Sure. I figured he'd need to inform Taft."

"Yes . . ." Carriscant thought further. "Did you ever tell him that the 'Brown' we found was the 'Braun' who used to be in his regiment?"

"No. No, I don't think so," Bobby said with a frown. "I guess he must have made inquiries. Why?"

"Just curious."

WHEN HE RETURNED to Manila Carriscant found a note from Pantaleon on his desk. There had been some further problems with the Flanquin power plant. The attempted flight on the thirteenth was now postponed: the new day set was to be the fifteenth.

THE LOST FLIGHT OF
PANTALEON QUIROGA

*H*E WOKE well before dawn on the morning of May 15, 1903. He had a slight headache and he lay still in the bed for a while, watching the room lighten slowly, telling himself not to think any further ahead than the next hour. If he took the day at that pace, with that absolute concentration on the present moment, he might be able to survive it, he told himself.

Beside him Annaliese slept on, her mouth open, little mumbling snores coming from her. He had rejoined her in the marital bed these last few nights in order not to provoke any suspicions that their reconciliation was not genuine, and the thought came to him as he slid from between the sheets that he would not be sleeping in it for much longer. This brought a mild pang of sadness but it was replaced by a charge of excitement when he considered the future waiting for him. He had no animus against Annaliese, no regret about leaving her, but he did admit that their "reconciliation" made what he was about to do that much harder on her. Still, there was no way he could prevent that.

He dressed and was driven to the hospital without breakfasting. It would have been hard enough counting the hours and days without the added prospect of Pantaleon's assault on the Amberway-Richault Prize complicating matters. He was consoled by the thought that some malfunction was bound to occur and necessitate a further postponement. He might even, he thought, indulge in a spot of covert sabotage himself if the opportunity arose. But whatever happened, he had to go through the motions of participating in order to neutralize Pantaleon's threat. It would occupy some hours of a long day, in any case, keep his mind busy.

At the San Jerónimo he made his final arrangements. He checked the rotas of the night staff for the twentieth, confirmed that his theater nurses had been given the relevant day off and ensured that certain key components in the plan were in their allotted places.

As he set off for the *nipa* barn he felt a strong sense of purposeful calm descend on him, marred only by a feeling of irritation with Pantaleon and his absurd obsession with heavier-than-air powered flight. He had hoped for rain, and indeed a fine drizzle was falling and the day was already overcast and muggy. As Constancio drove him over the Colgante bridge he saw the turning that led to San Miguel and the Calle Lagarda. He wondered how she was bearing up, how the strain of waiting was affecting her . . . But again he felt a quiet confidence return: she was strong too, they both knew exactly what they were doing, together they would come through.

To his surprise the road to the *nipa* barn was busy with pedestrians and some dozens of carriages were parked on the verge of the track where the path led to the meadow. He had expected one or two official witnesses, but this had all the signs of a sizable crowd. As he pushed through the gap in the plumbago hedge he was amazed to see upwards of a hundred people standing or sitting along the western edge of the meadow. On the eastern fringe there was a roped-off area equipped with folding wooden chairs where he imagined the adjudicators and official witnesses would sit. The barn was prettified with palm fronds and bunting, strings of fluttering pennants—crimson, moss green and buttercup yellow. He eased his way through a large group of well-wishers and journalists and found himself confronted by the Aero-Mobile itself, standing in the opening of the barn, the doors thrown wide. Painted on the nose in a cursive cobalt script was *Aero-Móvil número uno. Dr. Pantaleon Quiroga / Dr. Salvador Carriscant.*

Pantaleon was posing for photographs, one hand resting on an elevator strut, wearing an ankle-length leather motoring coat and a flat tweed cap that he had reversed. He looked most peculiar, but something about his outfit suddenly made the prospect of the flight seem terrifyingly real and for the first time Carriscant felt a jolt of fear in his chest. This might—might—just actually happen, he thought, and he felt a squirm of nausea inside him. The Aero-Mobile, caught in a chance gleam of sunlight, all at once looked modern and efficient. The twin pushing propellors were glossy with fresh varnish, the laterally mounted power plant had been regreased and re-painted and looked factory-new, and the five bicycle tires of the supporting carriage had been blacked and the spokes prinked out in white. The machine, he had to admit, appeared horribly plausible; its design, its ungainly functional shape, made it look capable of flight for the first time. It made sense all of a sudden, a fact he thought he would never have con-ceded, and his stomach churned and heaved as saliva squirted into his mouth.

Pantaleon saw him and darted forward to draw him out of the crowd. His brown face was taut with suppressed emotion and his eyes were filled with tears. Pantaleon embraced him, kissing him on both cheeks, as flash powder exploded with dull magnesium *whumph*s around them.

"Aren't you a bit hot?" Carriscant asked.

"Salvador, what are you wearing?" Pantaleon looked him up and down with dismay.

Carriscant contemplated his white linen suit, his black English shoes; his hand went nervously to his polka-dotted bow tie.

"I didn't think," he said. "I dressed for a normal day's work."

"Did you hear that?" Pantaleon called to the assembled journalists. "My dear colleague here has dressed for 'a normal day's work.' What calm confidence! What *élan*, as the French say. This is the spirit that will place the Philippines at the forefront of the great aerial adventure!"

The journalists scribbled all this down in their notebooks, and Pantaleon translated for the English-language papers. Carriscant had never seen him so self-assured, or display such zeal, such evangelical *savoir faire*.

"Everything is in order," Pantaleon said quietly to him. "Tuned to perfection. I ran the engine for ten minutes last night. Like birdsong."

A shower of rain drove them inside the barn, where Carriscant answered journalists' questions as dourly and as dully as possible. No, he had no real enthusiasm for flying; it was a simple favor to a friend that brought him here; no, he did not imagine that being aloft in a flying machine would be injurious to health.

"After all, we've all climbed a tree before," he said, "and Dr. Quiroga assures me we shall not attain an altitude of more than ten feet above the ground. To climb a ten-foot tree can hardly be regarded as life-threatening."

"Unless you fall out," said the man from the *Manila Times*. Everybody found this very amusing.

Pantaleon introduced him to the official adjudicators: there was Henry K. Gallo, president of the Army and Navy Club; Agapita Castaneda of the Philippine Commission; Señor Alejandro Gimson, the deputy editor of *El Renacimiento*; Rafael Martinez Mascardo, curator of the Museo de Ateneo; Mr.

Tiam Lam of the Chinese Chamber of Commerce; and Captain Gaspar Barboza, the Brazilian consul.

Carriscant was mightily impressed with Pantaleon's organizational powers: facets of the man were being revealed today which he would never have believed existed.

"I wanted a complete cross section," Pantaleon explained. "Their signatures on the certificate of attestation will be very impressive, no?" He smiled and looked at his watch. "We're just waiting for the final one—an American—from the governor's office. I thought it was important to have an American."

"Who've you got?" Carriscant asked. His nausea had returned, it was coming and going in waves; he was beginning to wish he had eaten breakfast.

"I don't know. They said they'd send someone along. Are you all right?"

"I'm a bit hungry."

"All I have is some beer. And champagne for afterward."

"Beer will do." Carriscant drank a bottle of gassy San Miguel beer—"*la más sobroisa y sustanciosa*," it said on the label—and spent the next five minutes belching softly to himself. The crowd in the meadow, sheltering beneath umbrellas, had grown to over two hundred. Small boys with stiff-bristled brushes swept any accumulating water off the wooden roadway. Carriscant noticed that the guava trees at the end of the field had been cut down and in the middle of the paddy field beyond was a large square of white canvas stretched between two poles. That marked the target distance, he supposed, and he saw a small group of people huddled not far from it, the better to witness the historic moment. For the first time he asked himself an important, practical question: if indeed they did manage to leave the ground and travel sufficiently far to reach the marker, where and how were they going to come down? He put this point to Pantaleon with some urgency.

"Oh, in the rice fields," he said. "I've paid the farmer in advance. The mud and the water will make a soft landing. Don't worry, I'm not going to attempt anything beyond the demands of the competition."

"Good."

"We can save turning and setting down for another occasion."

"Mmm." Out of the corner of his eye he spotted an American soldier in uniform who looked uncannily like Sieverance.

"Morning, Carriscant," Sieverance called cheerfully, striding over. "I must say this is very intrepid of you." He greeted Pantaleon. "Dr. Quiroga, good to see you. Governor Taft asked me to wish you good luck and sends his best wishes."

"I'm so sorry," Pantaleon said to Carriscant later, when Sieverance had gone. "I had no idea they would send him, believe me, Salvador."

"I suppose he was curious," Carriscant said. The sight of Sieverance had not unsettled him as much as he had expected. "Oh dear, looks like the rain has set in."

But the squall passed and ten minutes later the sun shone brightly, the wooden planks on the roadway steaming visibly as they warmed. The Aero-Mobile was wheeled out of the barn again and set in place at its starting point. Pantaleon climbed on a stepladder and made a short speech.

"We are men of the new century," he said, reading from notes, "and it is thus our signal duty to look forward. The challenge of heavier-than-air powered flight is the greatest objective mankind will face in the coming years. It seems fitting to me that this attempt on the Amberway-Richault Prize should be made by two surgeons, two men who embody the new century's spirit of science walking hand in hand with human endeavor. We who are exploring the innermost recesses of the human body should not neglect this globe's wider frontiers. I want to thank my dear friend, Dr. Salvador Carriscant, for his support and fortitude. I thank you all for being here on this historic day for our country. God bless the Philippine people and our enterprise." Considerable applause greeted this.

The time had come. As if in a dream, Carriscant found himself climbing into the rear saddle in the nose of the Aero-Mobile. The two warping handles jutted up in front of him and without thinking he grasped them firmly, pulling them this way and that and causing the tail to turn in response. A soft salvo of flash powder greeted this impulsive gesture. Behind him Pantaleon began to swing the propellor. Carriscant prayed earnestly for a fuel leak, a faulty connection, a blown gasket, anything, but on the third attempt the pistons fired and the shrill, irate roar of the Flanquin filled his ears. He felt the vibrations travel up his spine and suddenly he wished he were wearing different clothes: he felt a complete fool in his white linen suit and his glossy English brogues. Pantaleon flapped around the wing in his leather coat as the second propellor began to turn. He climbed into the forward saddle and inserted his feet into the stirrup controls. He twisted around to face Carriscant, his eyes bright, two darker spots on his brown face where his blush glowed.

"Thank you, my friend," he said emotionally. "All that bad feeling is behind us now. Please tell me it's so."

"Completely forgotten, Panta." He paused. "Now, you're quite sure this is safe."

"You're more at risk in a *carromato*," he said with serene confidence. "Now remember, only when I reach up for the air-catcher do you take over the warp controls. Otherwise, do nothing."

"Right."

Pantaleon reached up to the twin handles above his shoulder and pushed them, raising the long flap on the leading edge to its full extent. Then he turned up the throttle control to full and the Aero-Mobile began to thrum and judder violently. He gave the signal to the boy to pull away the wooden chocks and released the brake on the bicycle wheels.

With a brutal jerk the Aero-Mobile lurched forward. Carriscant was flung backward, and as the whipcrack effect hurled him forward again his nose smashed heavily into Pantaleon's back between his shoulder blades. His vision dimmed as his eyes flooded with salty tears and he sensed, rather than saw, the hot plumes of blood jet from his nostrils.

He was aware of the tremendous noise of the engine and the hollow drumming sound of the wheels on the roadway planks as the machine began to pick up speed. As he blinked his eyes clear he saw the dark dripping splash of his blood on Pantaleon's coat back and, to his horror, he realized that his entire front was a sopping swathe of red, that pools had gathered in the creases of his lap and that more was still spurting from his nose.

"Stop!" he screamed. "You've got to stop it!"

Pantaleon was sitting hunched forward over his controls, oblivious, like a racing cyclist in a sprint. Carriscant now felt the speed of their passage whip the ribbons of blood and snot away from his nose to sprinkle the rear section behind him, the heavy drops pattering on the stretched fabric. Then there was a sudden decrease in noise and he registered that the drumming of the wheels had ceased. Beyond his left thigh he saw the cruciform shadow of the Aero-Mobile begin to shrink slowly. To his absolute horror he realized that they had taken to the air.

In front of him Pantaleon began to whoop and caw like some maddened, tormented bird. Glancing down, he saw the white disks of the lopped trees at the meadow's end flash beneath them and he noted they were considerably higher than ten feet from the ground. The engine too seemed to be straining unnaturally hard as the sensation of forward motion gave way and was replaced by a kind of dreamlike buoyancy as the Aero-Mobile seemed to rise almost vertically in the air, like a gull gliding in a warm thermal.

"We're too high!" Carriscant yelled.

Pantaleon turned, gaped in shock, and almost fell from his saddle at the sight of his blood-boltered passenger.

"My God! What happened?"

"We're too fucking high!" Carriscant screamed in his face. "Take the controls!"

Panicking, suddenly obedient, Carriscant gripped the two warping levers and felt the animate vibration of the flying machine transfer itself to his body. Pantaleon reached up and took hold of the air-catcher flap handles. And pulled down.

The machine shuddered and the Aero-Mobile slipped nervily sideways.

"Mother of God!" Pantaleon cried in alarm.

Carriscant felt one of the warping levers whip itself forward out of his grasp and the machine began to descend in a quickening sideways glide to the left. Carriscant reached forward and tugged on the handle. It would not move, jammed fast.

"We've passed it!" Pantaleon screeched, pointing.

Carriscant saw the square of white canvas disappear beneath the lower wing. They were higher than the bamboo still, he saw, higher than the palm trees. Jesus. Fifty, sixty feet, he thought. Oh my God. But the left-side wings were still pointing down and there was no doubt that their sideslipping descent was growing speedier by the second.

Suddenly the engine cut out. The straining roar was replaced by a pleasant whistling and creaking noise as the wind sang over the stretched wires and the wooden armature of the flying machine eased and contracted beneath these unfamiliar stresses.

"What's happening?" he yelled in Pantaleon's ear.

"We've done it, my friend! We've done it!" Pantaleon sobbed.

Over to the right Carriscant saw the belvedere of Sampaloc Convent and suddenly thought crazily—"low-flying dove." In front of him, over Pantaleon's heaving shoulders, he saw the thick green mass of the riverine trees that marked the course of the San Roque *estero*.

Lower, lower they went and the pitch of the singing wires grew shriller and less pleasant.

To his absolute shock he saw that Pantaleon was no longer bothering to work the controls. His face was buried in his hands as he sobbed fiercely in his triumph, blubbing and laughing in his moment of ecstasy.

Carriscant tugged at his jammed warping control.

They swooped over a terrified peasant in his *carabao* cart.

The sunlit green wall of trees whooshed up to meet them.

The last sounds he heard were Pantaleon's fervent sobs and the ethereal arctic whistle of the bracing wires.

HE NEVER FELT the impact, but he could not have been unconscious for very long. He came to, winded, on his back, with a horrible silence in his ears. He became aware of a ghastly unfamiliar coolness in his legs from the waist down. His first thought was: I am paralyzed and I shall never live with Delphine. After a second or two's smoldering, bitter despair he raised his head and realized his legs were submerged in water while his torso rested on a crescent of sand formed by a side eddy of the San Roque creek. Then he was jolted anew by the blood-soaked front of his suit, a coruscating red in the hazy sunshine. I must have lost pints, he thought vaguely, a good gallon. He touched his nose gently: tender but unbroken. He rolled onto his front and crawled out of the water. Then he vomited all the beer he had drunk, a lifetime ago, it seemed. He wiped his mouth on his sleeve and stood up with great care.

The Aero-Mobile was twenty yards away, a crumpled, sad-looking mess, its wings sheered off and folded back along its body by the impact of the two trees it had plunged between.

Carriscant approached unsteadily. His entire body was beginning to ache. There was no sign of Pantaleon.

He crouched by the water's edge and washed his face clean of his blood. He told himself that any second now he would hear that daft elated voice saying, "My God, Salvador, what did I tell you! We're the most famous men of our time!" but all that came to his ears was the disturbed twittering of the river birds and the sonorous ringing of the convent bell at Sampaloc, summoning its stunned citizens to come to the aid of the men in the machine that fell from the sky.

He raised his eyes and saw Pantaleon's face through the grasses on the other side of the stream. His eyes were wide, astonished, and his mouth was open. Except it was all wrong: like a face in a spoon, his chin was above his mouth, which was above his nose. His face was upside down, but worse than that, he saw, as he waded across the stream to fetch his friend's broken body, it was in the wrong place, peering out at him in surprise through the twisted crook of his right arm.

ESCAPE

*T*HE MAIDEN FLIGHT of the *Aero-Móvil número uno* lasted approximately seventeen seconds, and observers estimated that at the apex of its climb it had reached a height of eight feet and had traveled a distance of two thousand, eight hundred feet over a pronounced leftward curving course. Unfortunately, Carriscant learned later, according to the rules of the Amberway-Richault Prize, the destruction of the flying machine, or the injury or death of the flyer, rendered any attempt null and void. The senior adjudicator, Mr. Gallo, thought the whole episode a great shame and hoped that Dr. Carriscant would continue with his colleague's pioneering work. He invited him to form the first committee of the Aero-Club of Manila. Carriscant agreed at once, nodding dully. Pantaleon's death and his extraordinary achievement left him feeling both hugely upset and humbled, visited at the same time by an acute sense of loss and awestruck admiration.

After giving his statement to the Sampaloc constabulary and seeing Pantaleon's blanket-shrouded body being carried into the police station, he returned to the *nipa* barn, where he found the place deserted, the crowd quite dispersed. He wondered how many of them were aware that the Aero-Mobilist himself had perished in his attempt to win the Amberway-Richault Prize. Carriscant walked morosely up and down the wooden roadway, trying to come to terms with what had happened, trying to sort and understand those endless seconds of terror and alarm. At least Panta had felt that exhilaration he so craved surge through his body. He remembered his manic shrieks and yelps of triumph as they really flew for the first time, recalled his sobs of helpless gratitude as they hurtled toward the trees on the San Roque *estero*. At least Pantaleon had died happy, full in the knowledge that he had achieved something monumental and triumphant. There were worse ends than that, he reflected, worse ways to die, and he sensed some of his sadness wane, and grew aware that, simultaneously, there was a new emotion blooming inside him, a feeling building of an irrepressible and transforming jubilation. That his own life had been spared now appeared to him the most astonishing miracle and, while he knew that he would still shed a few tears for his lost friend, a voice inside him was whispering delightedly, "You're alive, *alive*, ALIVE!" Whether it was blind chance or divine intervention, he was taking it as a clear sign. Carriscant's luck . . . Carriscant's luck was holding. Salvador Carriscant and Delphine Blythe Sieverance were destined to be together. Everything that was due to happen in the next few days was going to go according to plan. He knew, with a fierce, passionate certainty, that now all was going to be well.

THE NEXT MORNING he woke stiff and bruised, with a large livid weal on his left thigh and a left shoulder that clicked audibly, and ached, whenever he raised his hand above chest level. He endured the next few days in a somnambulist's stupor, doggedly and diligently following the routines of his work and home life, concentrating intensely on the matter in hand, however insignificant and banal. On the morning of the twentieth he rose early and went to the San Jerónimo as usual. He returned home in the afternoon, knowing he would find Annaliese absent, and wrote her a note saying that a long and complicated operation looked like it would necessitate him staying late that night at the hospital and she should not wait up for him. At the end of the afternoon, before leaving, he glanced around his silent house wondering if there was any small object or precious possession he wanted to take with him, but could think of nothing in particular. He remembered Delphine's comments, how nothing was owned, how possessions were merely borrowed from the world's supply for a short period of time, and decided to leave empty-handed. He would stride away from his house with only the clothes he had on. He was going to make as fresh a start as the woman he loved.

The evening routine at the hospital passed in its usual fashion. He tried to keep himself busy, to avoid looking at his watch or any of the clocks positioned at the intersections of passageways. Other members of staff, knowing he was taking two weeks' leave, wished him a pleasant stay in San Teodoro; some even commented he was looking tired and was clearly in need of a rest. News of Pantaleon's death had depressed everyone, and the mood was somber.

At around nine in the evening he was suddenly overcome with fatigue, after the mental and physical stresses of the past few days, and fell asleep in the armchair in his consulting room.

He dreamed about Pantaleon. A Pantaleon impeccably dressed, accepting a soup-plate-sized medal from a tiny potentate; Pantaleon flying like a bird, his arms gracefully flapping as he circled the belvedere at Sampaloc cawing raucously like a rook; Pantaleon making a speech outside the *nipa* barn extolling the beauties of someone who sounded suspiciously like Delphine. Then a jumble of images from the flight itself: the freshly lopped trunks of the guava trees slipping beneath the wing; Sieverance in his uniform shaking hands with the other adjudicators; the stark shock on Pantaleon's face as he registered the blood-soaked clothing of his co-flyer. Then he saw the twisted upside-down stare of Pantaleon dead, his lips moving as he delivered a version of his usual preoperative injunction: "Spring has come, Salvador," he said softly. "It's time to plant rice."

He woke abruptly, immediately awake, and checked his watch. He walked through the dark wards, past the sleeping patients, quietly greeting the nuns at their stations, feeling alert and poised. There was a minimum of staff on duty. In the main reception hall at the front gate a few messengers lounged and snoozed. No other doctors were in the hospital, only a duty sister sat behind her wooden desk, patiently embroidering a muslin *camisa*. The San Jerónimo did not encourage emergencies out of normal working hours.

He returned to his office via his operating theater, just to make sure once again that everything was prepared and ready. As he stood there he felt a shiver of expectation run through him, a thin filament of excitement energizing his body. It would not be long now: he was ready.

In his office he completed his paperwork and tidied his desk. In the desk drawer of Señora Diaz was another sealed letter—with instructions for it to be delivered to Annaliese a week hence—saying that he had left her, forever, and had gone in search of a new life. He wondered now if this was the right note to strike. Or would a simple mysterious disappearance be more effective? If Annaliese thought he had gone to his mother's and heard nothing after two weeks, she would be informed, but there would be no sign. Perhaps he might have been spotted down by the docks? Had he been killed? If not that, why would he run away? There would never be any answers to these questions and perhaps that silence would be kinder to Annaliese. She could then, in her grief and bafflement, construct whatever explanation was the most consoling. He went to Señora Diaz's desk and tore the letter up.

He was impressed and not a little amazed at how coolly he could deliberate about his leaving Annaliese. He felt no guilt: she was well provided for, she would have a large proportion of his money and property. Their marriage had been a sham for many months and he felt no love for her. Surely it was kinder to leave her with a mystery rather than the knowledge of brutal rejection? Surely—

He heard the running feet of the messenger cross the court-yard to his office. It was 1:35 in the morning. It had begun.

He opened the door.

"A man and a woman, Doctor. *Americanos*. She's very sick."

Carriscant ran with the messenger to the reception hall.

He clattered into the hall. Sieverance stood there, half-dressed, his shirt open at the neck. In his arms he held Delphine, pale and moaning, bundled up in a blanket.

"Thank God you're here, Doctor," Sieverance said. "A ghastly accident, ghastly."

Delphine was laid on a wooden gurney and Carriscant went through the motions of peering into her eyes, feeling her brow, checking her pulse. She was pale and feverish from the cordite he had given her to swallow. In a low, faltering voice Sieverance explained how she had risen from her bed in the night and then, minutes later, he had heard her calling for him from the bathroom, where he found her lying on the floor.

"In a pool of blood. Blood everywhere. From inside her."

"Take her to the theater," Carriscant ordered the porters.

The trolley was wheeled away and the two men followed behind as she was propelled rapidly down dim corridors to-ward Carriscant's operating theater.

"She kept saying, 'Get me to Dr. Carriscant. Dr. Car-riscant,' Sieverance said. "But of course neither of us knew where you lived. So I called in here to get your address. I couldn't believe it when the nurse said you were working late."

"I was just about to leave. Did your wife say anything

more?" Carriscant looked grim, as if he suspected the worse. Everything was proceeding very satisfactorily.

"Terrible pain in her stomach, she said. With the child—"

"I'm sure that's— We'll have to see, Colonel. We'll do our best."

They arrived at the theater and Delphine, moaning faintly, moving in discomfort, was lifted out onto the operating table. The two porters stepped back, waiting for instructions. Carriscant gave Delphine an injection of a weak saline solution. Miraculously, it seemed to ease the pain. He told the porters to wait with her and led Sieverance back to his consulting rooms, where he sat the distraught man down and poured him a glass of rum, into which he covertly tipped a few drops of syrup of chloral hydrate. Sieverance gulped it down.

"I'll be back as soon as we know what's wrong," he said.

Sieverance looked at him, terrified, trusting. It's so easy to inspire that trust, Carriscant thought. How they want to trust us! And he knew it was because of that trust that he was going to succeed this night. Carriscant handed him the rum bottle and told him to drink his fill.

Back in the theater Carriscant dismissed the porters.

He waited a few seconds after they had gone before talking. He touched her arm and she opened her eyes.

"Perfect," he said. "Perfect."

CARRISCANT SHOOK Sieverance awake. His eyes were heavy, his lips were slack. He could barely concentrate from the chloral. Carriscant crouched by his chair, his face set, serious. He was wearing his operating gown.

"We cannot save the child," he said. "But we must operate for the sake of the mother."

"Oh God . . ." Sieverance wiped drool from his chin as his dull brain tried to take this in. "I can't, I can't . . ." He shook his head, and tears began to roll from his eyes.

"Stay here," Carriscant said. "Sleep. It's going to be a long night. I'll call you as soon as we know."

HE CLUTCHED Delphine's hand in his, squeezing it, looking into her eyes.

"An hour or two, that's all."

"You will look after me."

"When the sun comes up we'll be putting out to sea."

She smiled at him. "Let's go."

Gently he put the gauze mask over her face and let the chloroform drip from the bottle.

CARRISCANT THREW OPEN the lid of the coffer and scooped a long hollow in the ice. He lifted Delphine's unconscious body off the gurney and laid her down in the shallow depression, then packed the ice chips back over her body until she was almost covered. He pushed up the sleeve of her nightgown and slipped a thermometer into her armpit. This was one area of the whole operation where he had some real concern: he wanted her numbed with cold, literally chilled back to the bone, but not so cold as to damage her bodily systems. He actually had no idea just how far he could safely let her temperature drop, but when it came to shamming death he knew that a body lacking any vestige of human warmth would do the job far more efficiently than one still flushed with heat. He hoped that his instinct would tell him if matters were becoming critical.

He sat patiently beside her as she chilled down, from time to time dripping more chloroform on the gauze mask. He took her pulse regularly. Already pale from the cordite she had eaten, the penetrating cold began to make her look quite bloodless as all color drained from her face and her lips. Her hands felt stiff and lifeless, her flesh seemed to take on the consistency of clay. When her temperature had fallen several degrees below normal and the chill and pallor about her was unignorably worrying, he lifted her out of her ice bed and wheeled her back through to the theater. He laid her on the table and placed a cane blanket cradle over her midriff before draping it with one of the operating cloths in such a way that none of the material touched her chest. There was absolutely no visible movement from her shallow breathing. He dosed her once more with chloroform and then scattered blood-soaked swabs on the floor below the operating table and in receptacles on the instrument trays. He set the steam sterilizers going and switched on the arc lights above the table. He smeared blood from a bottle on his gown and dripped a few strategic drops on his hands and forearms. In the blazing lights she lay completely inert, her face blanched almost to blue. He removed the gauze mask and tilted her head so that her mouth was slackly open. He tucked two chips of ice into her cheeks. Then he covered her face with the end of the operating cloth. Glancing around the theater, he saw it bore all the signs of a hasty emergency operation. Only one further detail was missing. He returned to the morgue and raised the heavy lid on another coffer. Digging into the ice chips, he removed the tiny body of the five-month-old fetus and took it through to the theater. He laid it on a wheeled trolley next to the table and washed it with blood before covering it with a cloth. It was not much bigger than his two cupped hands. Its tiny clenched pug face was frozen in what looked like a rictus of terrible rage. This was his last resort.

IT WAS clear that Sieverance expected the worst even in his fuddled, drugged state. He saw the blood smears on Carriscant's gown and the awful severity of his expression. Carriscant could see the man's gorge rise and how his hand went to his throat as he swallowed desperately.

"I'm so sorry," Carriscant said. "There was nothing we could do."

Sieverance tried to be brave—he was a soldier after all, Carriscant reasoned, accustomed to sudden death—but his eyes were moist with tears and there was a tremolo in his voice as he asked if he could see her. As they walked through to the theater he took great shuddering breaths of air, one hand persistently massaging his face.

Bowed before the shrouded body on the table with its grim detritus—the swabs, the blood, the brilliant knives, the smell—he swayed as if he might fall. Carriscant steadied him and pulled back the corner of the sheet.

He gave a low moan and stumbled. Carriscant caught him and gripped his arm. She does indeed look dead, he thought, a moment's worry overtaking him, so white, so still. Sieverance leaned over her, muttering her name. He kissed her forehead and recoiled as if he had been burned. His fingers touched his lips.

"Jesus God," he said, shocked. "God help me . . ." He looked emptily at Carriscant. "She's so cold . . . already . . ." He turned away. "The baby?"

"A girl."

"Is she here?"

Carriscant showed him the covered fetus in the tray. Sieverance paused before the tiny lump, no bigger than a bread roll beneath a napkin. He lifted the cloth and flinched violently, his whole body bucked. He let the cloth drop and gave a throaty, agonized cry, half moan, half retch. He slowly began to sink to his knees, at which point Carriscant moved forward and caught him by the shoulders, lifting him up, saying, "Here, come now, come away now, don't torment yourself, come with me."

He went quietly, without a backward glance.

As they slowly crossed the courtyard toward the entrance

gate Carriscant—his arm around his shoulders—asked him if there was anyone at his house.

"The servants are there," he said. "The place is all packed up, but they're still there."

"Will you be all right?"

"I . . . Yes, I think so."

"Try and sleep," Carriscant said. "I'll make sure everything is sorted out here."

"Thank you, Doctor, thank you . . . I don't think I'll be capable of anything."

"Leave it to me."

"Will you be here in the morning?"

"Yes," Carriscant lied. "I'll send for you."

He helped Sieverance into his victoria. He sat back, shaking his head with some vigor, whether from the effects of the chloral or the shock he was in Carriscant could not be sure. He was not in the least surprised at the complete success of his subterfuge. It was all a matter of suggestion. Here was a hospital at night, a woman covered in blood, a grave medical crisis. All possible prognoses would be going through Sieverance's mind, especially the worst. Many women die of complications in pregnancy: Carriscant's efforts had merely reproduced the man's darkest fears. If you half expect an event to occur, you rarely question it when it does. And even more, Sieverance trusted him, as a man and as a doctor. He had placed his trust in me absolutely, Carriscant thought, in his hour of need. The fact that his most terrifying fears were realized does not reflect on me at all. With trust all duplicity becomes simple. He looked at Sieverance now and, for a moment, seeing the man in this state, he felt an icy squirm of guilt wriggle through him. There was a price to pay for this elaborate subterfuge and it was Sieverance's awful pain and misery. He watched the man sit there struggling to come to terms with this brutal reckoning life had served him. Carriscant turned away, telling himself to be strong and not to think about it: there was no other way and, he reminded himself without much conviction, time was a great healer.

Sieverance's carriage pulled off and Carriscant walked as fast as he dared back to the theater. Delphine was still unconscious and some warmth was beginning to seep back into her limbs. He lowered the big arc light so the heat of its glare would penetrate better and piled some blankets on top of her. He rubbed her hands and wrapped her feet in hot towels. As he saw her temperature steadily rise he began to clear away the evidence of the operation.

He rang for a porter and told him to bring a coffin from the hospital store. The man showed no curiosity at the news that a patient had died. But then, why should he? Carriscant said to himself. Fetching a coffin or wheeling a cadaver into the morgue was doubtless a task he performed unreflectingly many times a day, especially working from Cruz's wards. So desperate was he to create an illusion of death, he was forgetting just how commonplace and unremarkable it was in a place like this.

The coffin arrived, wheeled on a trolley by two porters. As he opened the door of the theater he allowed them a glimpse of Delphine on the table before dismissing them. Some work had to be done on the body before it went into the coffin, he said. He would call them when everything was ready. Alone again, he locked all doors that communicated with the rest of the hospital and pushed the coffin into his temporary morgue. He lifted the body of the murdered Filipino woman out of its ice chest and laid it in the coffin. He fetched the fetus and placed it alongside its mother. Then he nailed the coffin shut and tied on the necessary label and the envelope containing a copy of the death certificate to the top handle. The coffin was waiting in the corridor outside the theater when the porters returned to collect it. Carriscant told them to take it to the hospital morgue, whence it would be taken for burial the next day.

As the coffin was duly wheeled away the thought came to

Carriscant that Sieverance might not be satisfied with one of the simple, crude coffins that the hospital provided. Indeed, he might not want his wife buried in the Philippines at all and would want to ship her home, in which case the body would have to be embalmed . . . He suddenly felt his heart jolt with alarm. Surely, even if that was what he wanted to do, they would have a day or two's grace? Sieverance was in no state to set about ordering new coffins and searching for a responsible undertaker the next day. The death certificate was signed, the hospital administration would routinely inform the necessary authorities. It would take a man of unusual morbidity—having already been profoundly shocked by the sight of his dead wife and dead child—to order the coffin reopened so he might see them again.

But in any event, Carriscant thought as he hurried back to proceed with the reviving of Delphine, even if he had foreseen that eventuality it would have been one beyond his powers to prevent or forestall. Whatever happened, whatever alarm was raised, he and Delphine would be far out at sea, a day or more's sailing from Manila. The trail vanished, or at any rate was stone-cold.

However—as he watched the color slowly return to Delphine's cheeks, and felt the warmth of her hands spread to her fingertips—the bowel-loosening sense of excited relief he was now beginning to feel was qualified by his small persistent undertone of worry. There was an irredeemable vanity about Sieverance, his every utterance and mannerism testified to it, and it would be very typical of the man to want to order his wife the most splendid casket in Manila, and to organize a funeral of ostentatious grief and circumstance. He was not the sort of man to nurse his sorrow silently or with solitary dignity.

"HOW DO you feel?" he said to Delphine, cupping her sweet face with his hands. "Any better?"

"Very strange . . ." she said. "Sort of distant . . . and groggy."

She sat in a chair in the operating theater dressed in the clothes she had given him days earlier—a simple dark blue dress with a high collar. She had a bonnet on her lap with a deep low brim that would shadow her face.

"Can you manage?"

"Yes." She had not asked him one question about Sieverance and how he had taken the news of her death. "I think so."

She looked up at him, still a little vague. "How was it, I mean . . . Did Jepson—"

"It went perfectly. Not a moment's doubt."

"Good," she said in a small neutral voice. She might have been responding to some news about the weather holding fair for the next twenty-four hours. "Good."

He looked at his watch: it was nearly four. He helped Delphine to her feet and led her down a passage to a rear door that gave onto the hospital garden. There was a moon, enough to provide a faint gray-washed light. The air was warm and moist and the sound of the crickets in the bushes was shrill. They hurried along a path, through the dark shadow-thronged garden, to a back gate that opened onto the Calle Francisco.

Carriscant took the key from his pocket, unlocked the gate—the hinges were stiff and they groaned as the door swung open—and peered out. The carriage he had ordered was waiting by the church fifty yards away. They slipped out the door and walked quickly and silently down the street toward it. The horse nickered and the sleepy driver looked around as they approached. He would have no idea they had come from the hospital, Carriscant was glad to observe. He gave the address of the destination to him.

"Axel will be waiting for you," he said to her in a whisper. "He'll take you to the boat. I'll be there shortly after six."

She gripped his hands. "I can't believe this has actually happened," she said. "He really believes, I mean he has no doubt I'm—"

"Completely. I saw him, comforted him. He saw you dead with his own eyes."

"So we're free—really, truly?"

"Yes, my darling."

He could not hold back, he drew her slightly behind the coach and slipped his arms around her. He kissed her lips and pressed himself against her. Then his lips were on her neck and her hands were on his back and he smelled her smell. Rose water. She must have put on some scent. Carried some scent with her. He felt the warmth of her strong firm body down the length of his. Suddenly, strangely, he wished he were a bigger, taller man, as if a greater physical presence were a better guarantee of the protection he could give her, of the care he could afford. He had an image of her turning to this more imposing, bulkier Salvador Carriscant, snuggling into him, sheltering in the lee of his big frame. He was suddenly light-headed with fatigue and accumulated tension. His longing for her ached like a tumor behind his breastbone, a small hot coin of pain. The thought of their life together beckoned him on like a vision, a white arm of road through a verdant and sunlit country.

He helped her into the carriage. She blew him a kiss and did not take her eyes from his until the carriage turned the corner onto Calle Palacio. He stood there alone for some moments listening to the sound of the horses' hooves die away as they traveled through the dark narrow streets of Intramuros toward the San Domingo gate and the north quays of the Pasig, where Axel was waiting and where their new life would truly begin.

BACK AT HIS HOUSE he could not even think of sleeping. He sat on a cane chair on the *azotea* watching the lemony dawn light slowly expose the dew-drenched trees and shrubs of his garden. At a quarter to six he went through to the bedroom and woke Annaliese. She propped herself on her elbows and stared at him stupidly.

"Are you going already?"

"Yes." He quelled his impatience. It all had to be handled correctly. "I want to make an early start. The roads are always bad in the rains."

She rolled over and hunched into her pillow, closing her eyes.

"Oh, well, if you want to. Say hello to your mother."

"I will. Goodbye."

He closed the main door and walked down the worn stone steps to the *entresuelos*. He walked quietly to the front gate; there was no sign of Constancio or the other servants, the only sound the snort and shifting of the ponies in their stalls. He stepped through the double doors onto the street. Only at this time of the day was there a true coolness in the air, the day's humidity had not had time to build. He felt a slight fresh breeze on his face and neck which made him shiver. He took a deep breath. The rest of his life was about to commence and he savored the sweetness of the moment in the fresh coolness of the morning.

Around the corner, from the Palacio end of the street, strode three men, walking not fast but purposefully all the same, the watery citron sun illuminating the brass buttons on their uniforms, making them wink and flash prettily.

"Salvador Carriscant."

He turned to see Paton Bobby and two other men walking down the street from the other direction. He wondered what was happening and why Bobby referred to him by his full name. He soon had his answer.

Bobby's square, honest face could conceal neither his embarrassment nor his intense sadness.

"Salvador Carriscant—"

"What's happening, Paton? What's going on?"

Bobby could not hold his gaze and looked away as he spoke. "Why did you do it, Salvador?"

"Do what?"

"Kill him."

"Kill? Kill who, for God's sake? I didn't—"

"Sieverance."

"Sieverance? . . ."

"Shot dead while he was sleeping. Two bullets in his brain."

Carriscant could say nothing now.

Bobby turned to face him again and seized his arm.

"Paton, you can't think that I—"

"Salvador Carriscant—" His voice was shaking and he cleared his throat. "Salvador Carriscant, I arrest you for the willful murder of Colonel Jepson George Sieverance."

LISBON,

1936

SUNDAY, MAY 3

*M*Y FIRST VIEW of the city was a solitary one. Carriscant said he was feeling unwell and stayed below as the SS *Herzog* steamed slowly up the Tagus toward the docks. There was a fine rain falling and the sky was full of heavy mouse-gray clouds. The buildings of the city rose up from the dull sheen of the estuary, stacked on their undulating hills, hunched and nondescript in the murky crepuscular light, the stepped façades and rooftops punctuated here and there by a spire or cupola, the baroque dome of a church or the squared teeth of a castellated rampart.

We docked opposite a building that said POSTA DO DESINFECÇÃO and the gangplank was lowered. I saw customs sheds and warehouses, railway lines, and along the north shore a great fritter of ships. Then the vast sweep of water and the blurry green slopes rising to the south. A placid traffic of boats—ferries and tugs, launches and fishing boats—crisscrossed the scene. In the air the periodic curse of gulls and the shouts of the stevedores. A smell of oil, of smoke, and underlying that something fresh and briny, the presence of the great ocean lying beyond these encircling hills.

Carriscant joined me on deck. He did look somewhat pasty-faced, I had to admit, and he had shaved himself badly, leaving a furze of gray bristles under his left ear.

"I'm glad it's raining," he said thoughtfully, after he had stared at the view for a while.

"Why? It's May and we're in Europe."

"It suits my mood. Sun and blue skies would have been wrong, I'd have hated that."

I didn't remonstrate. We leaned on the rail waiting to be summoned for customs, staring out at the damp creams and ochers, the pinks and pale yellows of the terraced buildings, their terra-cotta roofs turned mauve and brown by the rain.

"To think she's out there somewhere," he said, not looking at me.

"I hope you're right. We've come a long way."

"You've got to help me, Kay," he said. "I don't need sarcasm, I need help." He patted my hand on the rail. "Yours."

CARRISCANT, Carriscant. What should I call him, this baffling new presence in my life? My father . . . ? Too uncertain. Or Salvador? Too intimate. The more neutral S.C.? Even after all these days of talk I find my ideas change about him several times an hour. Keep your distance, don't become too involved, watch out for the way he draws you in.

WE CLEARED customs quickly as we had little luggage. I had packed two suitcases, having no idea how long I would be away; Carriscant had only one. As we drove in a taxi to our hotel I found myself wondering, what if she has left Lisbon? We were following a trail that was almost ten years old, what if it led us all over Europe? The notion did not perturb me as much as I thought. The fact that I was here was a tribute to my lack of rationality and absence of common sense; it was a little late to start demanding that logic and prudence be my watchwords now.

· · ·

OUR HOTEL is the Francfort on the Rua de Santa Justa, middle category, "a good commercial house," the guidebook says, with a restaurant, and situated some few streets away from the Rossio. We have adjoining rooms on the third floor, quite large and clean with ample functional furniture. At the end of the corridor is a bathroom. A young man, João, who spoke good English, was at reception and most helpful in undertaking to secure our identity cards and providing us with the address of a photographer. He had the pale waxy skin of those who work indoors under artificial light and his good features were spoiled by a black tooth in his smile. The elevator was tiny, a small cage of elaborately twisted metal that only just managed to contain the three of us. I stood close behind João, his shiny black jacket inches from my eyes. There was a strong smell of camphor coming from him, and in the confined space it set Carriscant off on a sneezing fit that had the small lift rocking.

THE TRIAL of Salvador Carriscant was surprisingly short. Accused of the murder of Sieverance and of conspiracy to murder Ward and Braun, he was acquitted of the first charge and found guilty of the second. He was sentenced to twenty years' imprisonment and was incarcerated in Bilibid Prison. From his cell window he could see in the distance, on a clear day, the fading roof of the *nipa* barn where Pantaleon Quiroga had built his flying machine.

It had been Bobby's idea to introduce the second charge of conspiracy to murder, convinced as he was that the deaths of all three soldiers were connected. In court, under cross-examination, Bobby's theory emerged. He was sure that Pantaleon had been the murderer, aided and abetted by Carriscant. It was the location of the bodies at key sites of the first day of the war that had led him to the unshakable conclusion that the motive was political, or driven by some idea of ideological or nationalist vengeance. The case against Carriscant for the murder of Sieverance was harder to establish as there seemed to be no obvious reason why he should have done the deed. The prosecution tried hard to introduce the implication that owing to the untimely death of his coconspirator, Quiroga, Carriscant was obliged to finish the matter off himself. The key item of evidence was the discovery in the Sieverance house of a gauze face mask from the San Jerónimo Hospital of the sort used for administering anesthesia. It was also held against him that Carriscant had no alibi for his movements between 4:00 and 6:00 a.m., from the time he was seen leaving the hospital to his awakening of Annaliese. His explanation—that he was sitting on his *azotea*, thinking—was regarded as risible. One other piece of evidence counted against him: a torn-up letter was found in his secretary's wastepaper basket which, when fitted together, was found to be to Annaliese, informing her that he was leaving her to start a new life. This was adduced, not very convincingly by the prosecution, to be a tacit admission of guilt, a sign that the cycle of murders was over and that the perpetrator was about to flee. Carriscant admitted his marriage was in difficulties and that he had written the letter in a moment of despair. He attested that, rather than fleeing the country, he was on his way to visit his sick old mother in Batangas. Chief of Constabulary Bobby had arrested him just as he was about to rouse his driver and tell him to make the carriage ready for the journey. The idea that, having fought vainly all night to save the life of Mrs. Sieverance, he then should follow her husband home to murder him was simply incomprehensible, and unless the prosecution could establish any reason why Salvador Carriscant should have committed such a bizarre act, the defense argued, then the charge was simply not worthy of consideration and should be thrown out.

Carriscant remembered the courtroom with the newly installed electric roof fans that kept breaking down. One minute
a veritable breeze would be rustling the weighted papers on
the lawyers' desks, the next there would be a sharp crack and
a smell of burning and handkerchiefs would be applied to
moist brows and slick, collar-chafed necks. A pause would be
called while a nervous workman mounted a stepladder to investigate the recalcitrant machinery. Eventually, after seven in-
terruptions in one day, the judge called for the fans to be
switched off, the windows were thrown open as wide as possible and matters continued in the usual sweltering fug.

He remembered Bobby perjuring himself shamelessly
in the witness box, telling, with phenomenal recall of detail,
how he had found the scalpel by the body of the murdered
woman—"a scalpel identified by the defendant himself as coming from his own stores at the San Jerónimo Hospital." He remembered too the daily mutter of speculation and fascinated
curiosity that would arise as he entered the courtroom each
morning. Carried in, he felt, on a foaming susurrus of gossip,
the public benches and the gallery packed with the craning,
ogling faces of Manila's expatriate bourgeoisie. The celebrated
surgeon, Dr. Carriscant, turned conspirator, assassin and clandestine *insurrecto*. . . . Once, on the journey back to his cell at
Bilibid, the police carriage had been obliged to make a detour
through the back streets of Santa Cruz, where the local *indios*,
when they realized who was held inside, cheered him heartily
on his way, children running after the carriage yelling
"Carriscant! Carriscant!" until the prison doors swung closed
behind it.

Carriscant's lawyer, a young *ilustrado* called Felix de la
Rama, was a young man of slight build and unimpressive demeanor with a long neck and prominent Adam's apple. Luck-
ily, his voice was unusually deep—some special reverberating
capacity in that laryngeal prominence, Carriscant fantasized.

His voice emerged from his mouth as a fruity, sagacious baritone giving everything he said a considered, experienced air. Every observation, however inconsequential, seemed to have been brewed in gravitas and authority. It probably made the vital difference, Carriscant reflected. Upon such trifles hang our fates.

De la Rama doggedly hammered away at the implausibilities in the murder charge but in so doing rather neglected to expose the deficiencies in the second alleged offense. As the trial progressed, all manner of speculation was introduced as to why Pantaleon Quiroga wanted to kill American enlisted men and the prosecution managed to build a semi-convincing picture of these two eminent surgeons, infected by disappointed *insurrecto* zeal, trying either to instill terror among the occupying colonial forces or to exact some revenge for the insurgents' defeat. In the end reason and fantasy both emerged triumphant. The jury (eight Americans, a Chinese and three *mestizos*) threw out the murder charge and then, almost by default, found Carriscant guilty of the lesser crime. The judge (Judge Charles K. Weller) took the opportunity of handing down an exemplary sentence.

De la Rama had been particularly effective when it came to diminishing the damage done by the discovery of the gauze mask. He did not deny that it might well have been brought to the Sieverance house by Carriscant himself—more than likely, in fact, as the defendant had been a regular visitor during Mrs. Sieverance's convalescence. Furthermore, it had to be taken into account that Nurse Aslinger had been living in the same abode for several weeks; the piece of gauze was a very common medical item, and no one could say with any accuracy when it might have been introduced into the household.

Carriscant sat impassively through the farcical proceedings, simply counting the days off as they went by. He could not believe his luck that in the huge fuss and scandal of his arrest and trial, Delphine Sieverance's "death" had been virtually forgotten. What had happened was this: with Jepson Sieverance dead, no one thought to claim or make arrangements for the coffined body lying in the San Jerónimo morgue. It was not until four days after Carriscant's arrest that Delphine's friend Mrs. Oliver suddenly remembered and decided that someone should arrange a funeral. This was done discreetly and with great speed as the warm and humid weather had significantly accelerated the decomposition of the body. The funeral took place the next day and the body was buried at the Paco cemetery in a small ceremony attended by a few friends and, as a mark of respect, Mrs. William Taft. Sieverance's body was embalmed and shipped home to his family, where he was buried with full military honors.

Carriscant's explanation of this oversight was that it was due to Bobby's obsession. He was so convinced that Pantaleon Quiroga was the murderer of Ward and Braun that the only explanation of Sieverance's killing was that it had to have been carried out by an accomplice, and Salvador Carriscant regrettably fitted that bill. The last person seen with Sieverance had been Carriscant—talking outside the San Jerónimo. To Bobby's mind, the gauze mask, the absence of an alibi and recollections of the testimony of the old man who claimed to have seen Carriscant out and about on the night of the Braun murder were sufficient to justify the arrest. Any other route of investigation—such as the last murder not being connected to the first two—was never followed up. The death in premature childbirth of Delphine Sieverance and the murder of her husband by rebels was seen by polite Manila society as a ghastly double tragedy, a potent illustration of the white man's burden, and no one sought to establish any connection that might have existed between the two. So Carriscant sat in court silent and unforthcoming, knowing exactly who was responsible for the death of Colonel Jepson Sieverance (although baffled as to the motive) and knowing too that any attempt to protest or establish his own innocence would have terrible consequences. As innuendo and circumstance, blustering argument and gimcrack reasoning slowly wound a skein of guilt about him, so, as each day and week passed by, was the guilty party's freedom more assured. And that freedom became absolute the day he was sentenced and the case was effectively closed.

Carriscant spent eight years behind the gray walls of Bilibid Prison before he was transferred to the island of Guam, to a prison camp for former unrepentant *insurrectos* (battles were still being waged in the hills of Mindanao as late as 1913) run by the U.S. military. In 1919, after serving sixteen years of his sentence, he was paroled and went to live in Capiz, on Panay Island, where he opened a small restaurant in the main square of that pretty provincial town. He was still obliged to report to the authorities in Iloilo once a month until the full term of his sentence was up. He never returned to Manila and lived quietly and forgotten in Capiz, where his restaurant, La Esperanza, earned him a decent living. It was only in 1935, when he bought the house of a former Portuguese manager of the sugar refinery there and came across a stack of old illustrated magazines through which he idly leafed, that he ever thought about moving.

I ASKED Carriscant how he had survived his sixteen years of incarceration. "It was hard," he said simply. "Very hard. You see, every waking moment I thought of Delphine, I thought of her out there and wondered what she was doing . . . And then after a while, after a year or so, I began to wonder less. It hurt just the same, but I couldn't imagine anymore, couldn't imagine what her life would be like." He screwed up his face for a moment. "I think in fact I was unconsciously shutting down my imagination, trying to keep my thoughts as simple as possible . . . I think that's how I survived—maybe that's how anyone survives. I kept my mind concentrated on a few very vital things and refused to allow my imagination to roam free." He smiled. "It makes you a little strange. It's not natural. In prison the only free life you have is the life of the mind, you see, and when you rein that in . . ." He did not finish.

"What few things did you concentrate on?"

"Two things, really," he said, "though I have to tell you conditions were not so tough, especially on Guam. It was more like a farm there, and I ended up running the camp's kitchens." The first was the ever-sustaining knowledge that Delphine at least was free, that she had escaped, and somewhere was leading a new life that they had both planned. "I was the only person in the world who knew she was not buried in the Paco cemetery. A big secret, that, a secret worth keeping. I was consoled by it. As long as I kept the secret she was safe. It helped to know that."

"What was the second thing?"

"You."

L O V E I S not a feeling. It does not belong to that category of bodily experience which would include, for instance, pain. Love and pain are not the same at all. Love is put to the test—pain is not. You do not say of pain, as you do of love, "That was not true pain, or it would not have disappeared so quickly."

I T W A S Udo Leys who told Carriscant about Annaliese's pregnancy. Udo died in 1905 and in the years up to his death he was Carriscant's only visitor in Bilibid. It was a month after the verdict that he broke the news that Annaliese was leaving the Philippines.

"She's going back to Germany," Udo told him morosely. "I tell her no but she says she can't live here. The shame, the scandal. Everyone knows her as the woman married to the murderer."

"But I wasn't found guilty of murder."

"Salvador, I have to tell you, everyone talks as if you did it."

"Jesus Christ . . . Anyway, I'm sorry about Annaliese, I knew it would be hard on her." He thought for a while. "I'd like to see her before she goes."

"Ah, Salvador, she'll never see you. Never again, she says. She's even given up her job with the bishop. She stays indoors, she can't face anyone."

"Did you give her my last letter?"

"She tear it up, before my eyes. She won't see you."

"Poor Annaliese . . . I should've thought how difficult it would be for her to stay here."

"Listen, it's not so easy for me," Udo protested equably. "Everybody talks about it, everybody wonders how and why, why were those men selected as victims . . . A *cause célèbre*, Salvador. They'll be talking about it for years."

"I didn't do it, Udo. I didn't do anything. I'm an innocent man."

"Of course you are. *I* know that. But you'll never stop people talking." He smiled apologetically. "Anyway, it'll be better for the child to grow up away from this atmosphere."

"What child?"

Udo frowned. "Didn't Annaliese write to you? She's pregnant."

WE DINED in the hotel: a mutton stew which I disliked but which Carriscant declared was among the finest he had ever tasted.

"Mutton is a coarse, fibrous meat with a strong taste. This

dish is not pretending to be anything else. Garlic, potatoes, carrots and cabbage, what more could you ask for?" Back on dry land his appetite had returned. The dessert was a dense flat triangle of cake, a kind of heavy sponge, served with syrup from a green and gold can. The clientele were all smartly dressed, the dining tables covered with clean linen, the silverware much used but well shined.

"I like this hotel," Carriscant said, spooning more syrup. "I could live here."

A D U L T H O O D . When the prospect of physical or sensual excess is no longer enticing. Is this why I feel an adult? Is this why I feel so old beside Salvador Carriscant?

MONDAY, MAY 4

I SIT at the pine table in my room and stare out at the street at the trams going by with a clatter and fizz. Their approach is announced by a singing of the electric wires, a kind of ghostly monotone whistle. A weak sun is shining today and new fragile green leaves flutter bravely in the cool breeze that blows off the estuary.

SO:S.C.'S VERSION goes like this. During the false period of reconciliation with Annaliese they made love. He only specified one occasion, when she came into his study, but he did say he "reoccupied the marital bed." It is not unreasonable to suppose that the event reoccurred. Annaliese became pregnant but probably only became aware of her condition after the arrest and trial. She never saw him again after he was arrested. She refused to attend the trial or visit him in prison after she was aware of the unsent farewell letter. Then she left Manila sometime toward the end of 1903 for German New Guinea. So let us say the child was conceived in early May 1903 . . . It would have been born in January 1904. My date of birth is January 9, 1904.

My head fills with clamoring questions when I try to come to terms with these facts. How did she end up in German New Guinea? Carriscant said Udo Leys told him she was returning to Germany . . . How did she meet Hugh Paget? Was she married to him by the time I was born, or did he marry her afterward and adopt the baby girl as his own? . . . The thought comes to me that Hugh Paget might be merely a convenient fiction. An old photograph of a man of the cloth, found somewhere. A handy sad story to relate to a kind fellow like Rudolf Fischer; a neat explanation for the presence of a baby daughter. My mother is no fool. Widow's weeds hide a great deal . . .

QUESTION: How did Carriscant know my name? How did he know to come looking for me in Los Angeles?

WE WENT out to buy Carriscant a new suit—his idea. We found a tailor's on the Rua Conceição and Carriscant bought a three-piece suit off the peg. It was a dark navy blue with a thin red and white chalk-stripe, a double-breasted coat and a vest with small lapels. With it we purchased a cream soft-collared shirt and a maroon tie. The trousers had to be taken up an inch or so, which they did on the premises while we waited. He looked well in it: a fit, boxy, broad-shouldered older man, and the cream shirt set off the olive tones of his skin. And all of a sudden I see the young surgeon in Manila—confident, gifted and so very sure of himself. Carriscant celebrates by having a haircut and a professional shave. I stand outside the barber's and watch the thick suds applied to his face, see the poised careful scraping as the swathes of smooth skin are exposed. And the thought comes to me, as that face is revealed, how well I understand it now. It is no longer simply an act of recognition: it is a man I *know* who heaves himself out of the chair—my father. Carriscant studies himself in the mirror, his fingers on his chin, pulling and pushing, testing the grain. He is dressing for someone—not me—and intends to look his best.

IN THE AFTERNOON we went to an annex of the U.S. legation, a new building of tawny stone, on the Rua do Alecrim, where we had an appointment with Mr. Shelburne Dillingham, the second secretary. The envoy himself, a Mr. James Marion Minnigarde, was visiting the consulate at Oporto. Also he was a recent appointment: we needed to talk to someone who had been in Lisbon for some years, who would at least be familiar with the legation's business in the 1920s.

Mr. Dillingham was a serious young man with a pronounced overbite which he tried to disguise by pushing his bottom lip out and up to cover his protruding top teeth, a trick which had the effect of making him look oddly pugnacious. But whenever he talked or smiled, the old overbite reestablished itself until he remembered his trick again. I became so fascinated with this labial maneuver that I found I was paying scant attention to his words. I concentrated once again.

". . . I'm pretty sure that the Ailshie Cup lapsed in '30 or '31," he was saying. He smiled at me toothily. "I've only been here three years."

Carriscant pushed his photograph across the desk. "This is the woman we are interested in. She was the wife of an embassy official here, I'm sure."

Dillingham looked at the picture. "Very elegant lady," he said. "What age would she be there?"

"Early fifties."

"Let me see." He went to his bookshelf and drew out a slim navy blue book from a row of identically bound volumes. On the cover was a gold seal and lettering that read: DEPARTMENT OF STATE, FOREIGN SERVICE LIST, 1927. He flicked through the pages.

"The envoy in '27 was Warrick Ailshie and we know that the lady in question is not Mrs. Ailshie . . . The only other diplomats of an age to have a wife in her fifties are . . ." He consulted the list. "Hmm. Mr. Parker Gade, vice consul in Funchal, and Commander Mason Shoemaker, the naval attaché for air." He made an impressed noise. "That was forward-looking for us in '27. Now"—he reached for the 1930 service list— "let's see where they are today."

"Naval commander?" Carriscant said, drawing the photo back. "Could that be him in the picture?"

"I couldn't tell you, sir," Dillingham said as he checked the index. "No reference. Both of these gentlemen appear to have retired from the service. Or they're deceased." He made an unhappy face. "I could cable the State Department, but I'm fairly sure they wouldn't give out any personal information."

Carriscant suddenly looked glum and unhappy, shifting uncertainly in his seat, his fingers tugging at the collar of his new shirt, and I felt sorry for him, his hopes raised and dashed so swiftly.

"Isn't there anyone here in the legation who was here in '27?" I asked. "There must be some member of staff who goes back that far."

"Good point," Dillingham said, throwing me an admiring glance. "Please excuse me one moment."

Carriscant stood up and went to the window to look down on the little courtyard outside. I joined him. Some small scruffy pigeons pecked around the base of a lime tree, pecking in a dilatory and routine manner at the sparse blades of grass, as if the search for nourishment itself was sufficient to satisfy their hunger.

"If she did marry this naval commander she could be anywhere," I said gently.

"No," Carriscant said with complete confidence. "She's here, I'm certain of it."

I turned away, exasperated. He had all the doggedness of a flat-earther. These people had to find out the hard way.

Dillingham returned with an elderly Portuguese man in a black suit. He had gray hair combed brutally back from his forehead and held in place with some fiercesomely adhesive grease or potion. He wore small round tortoiseshell glasses and a neatly trimmed toothbrush mustache dyed a disconcerting shade of coppery brown.

"Senhor Liceu," Dillingham said, presenting him. "Our esteemed chancery clerk. Been here forever."

Senhor Liceu shook hands with us, inclining his trunk forward at a slight angle each time. Carriscant showed him the photograph and asked if he could identify Commander Shoemaker.

He did so at once. "That's Commander Shoemaker," he said. "A good likeness." His English was excellent.

Carriscant pointed to Delphine. "And is that Mrs. Shoemaker?"

Liceu tried not to smile at some memory. "No sir, there was no Mrs. Shoemaker. The commander was a confirmed bachelor."

"Do you recognize that lady?"

"No, I'm afraid not. I was there that day, I remember it well. I was a great admirer of Senhorita Barrera." He gave a sad smile. "I think I only had eyes for her. This lady was probably Commander Shoemaker's guest. Or Mr. Ailshie's."

Despair was creeping back into Carriscant's face.

"Could this lady have been French?" Liceu said, frowning. "I have some recollection of a very elegant French lady at one of the receptions."

"I don't think so." Carriscant shrugged. "Unless she married a Frenchman."

"I'll ask some of the other staff," Liceu volunteered. "Perhaps someone will remember. It was a great day for the legation. Most memorable. There may be others with better recall than I."

We thanked them both and left the place somewhat cast down. We walked down the front steps slowly. Evening was coming on and the streetlamps were lit. In the sky above were a few pink-touched clouds. A taxi pulled up and a young man with bad acne descended and spent some time searching his pockets for change while the taxi ticked patiently at the curb. I felt Carriscant's depression settle around my shoulders like a shawl. I had to say something.

"How does it go? 'At the violet hour, something something, like a taxi throbbing at the door' . . . No, 'the human engine waits, like a taxi throbbing waiting.' "

"What on earth are you talking about?" Carriscant rather snapped at me.

"Just a line of poetry. Came to mind. 'At the violet hour, et cetera.' " I pointed up at the rose-flushed evening sky. "It's nothing important. Just the conjunction of the light effect and that taxi. Ignore it."

He was staring at me, a slow smile widening his face. "At the violet hour," he said. "Don't you see?"

"What? No, I don't."

"Violets."

W E SPENT the morning walking around the Baixa going from sweetshop to sweetshop looking for one that
sold crystallized violets. Out of six *confeiteiros* we found only
one with a stock of the sweets. We returned with João from
the hotel to help us translate.

"They sell many types of sweets," João said needlessly as we
looked around the small shop. It was narrow and dark and
looked more like an apothecary's with its crammed shelves of
ornate glass bottles, some of them tinted green and blue. "But
they have no regular order for the violets. They do not dis-
patch them to special clients."

"What about regular customers?"

João conferred with the bemused couple who ran the shop.
Yes, they did have some regular customers. They peered curiously at Carriscant's picture. No, they didn't recognize the
woman.

Undeterred, Carriscant secured the name of the wholesaler
who supplied them with the sweets; from him he would obtain
a list of other stockists in the city, he explained.

I was beginning to look a little worried. If ever there was an
example of clutching at straws . . . But Carriscant persisted, ex-
tracting a promise from them that they would ask anyone who
bought the sweets to provide their name and address. They
would try, they said, obviously affected by the earnestness of

Carriscant's demand, but they warned that not everyone would be prepared to divulge that information.

We found a small café nearby, the Café Adamastor, and stopped there for refreshment. It was little more than a smoke-darkened room with a long zinc-topped bar running the length of the rear wall with a shelf above ranged with small dumpy barrels, with spigots attached, labeled MOSCATEL, CLARETE, GINEBRA. Affixed to the ceiling was a small fan mounted vertically on the end of a hanging pole so that it resembled a pro-pellor shaft on an outboard motor. This revolved slowly around and around, ensuring that the cigarette smoke reached every corner of the room.

We sat at a round marble-topped table. I ordered a *vinho verde*, Carriscant a brandy. I sipped eagerly at my cold wine, it tasted fresh and young, like crushed grass. I took out my cigarettes.

"I don't think you should do that, Kay."

"Do what?"

"Smoke."

"Everyone else is, why not me, for heaven's sake?"

"None of the women are ... I have a feeling it's not the done thing."

"Well, I shall blaze a trail," I said, defiantly setting fire to my Picayune. Carriscant's instincts were correct, however; I became the object of fascinated stares and whispered conversa-tions for a minute or two.

"We've made a real start," Carriscant said with genuine en-thusiasm, "a real start. I'll look into that shop daily. I'll find out others in the city. We should begin to build up a list of names."

I felt indescribably weary at the prospect of seeking out ev-ery crystallized violets lover in Lisbon.

"Dr. Carriscant, you really can't—"

"How many times have I told you, Kay? I wish you'd call me Father."

"It's hard for me, you know that."

"I don't see why. At least 'Salvador,' then. We're friends, Kay, good chums, you and I. I don't want to feel that I'm here on sufferance. I'll have another brandy, I think. What about you?"

WEDNESDAY, MAY 6

W E F O U N D two more sweetshops which stocked crystallized violets, one a tobacconist on the Praça do Comércio, the other in Bairro Alto. Unable to make our complicated requests understood, we resolved to return later with João.

I prevailed upon Carriscant to attempt another method of finding Delphine. I suggested we obtain an enlargement of the photograph and place an advertisement in a newspaper, asking anyone who recognized Delphine to contact us at the Comércio. We could even offer a reward, I suggested. He thought this was a fine idea, so we ended our day with a visit to the photographer's studio where we had had our photographs taken for our identity cards and where the enlargement was duly made.

When we returned to the hotel there was a note from the U.S. legation, from Senhor Liceu, beautifully written in exquisite copperplate. A colleague in the office thought the woman who had been with the guests of honor on the day of the inaugural Ailshie cup was not French but Portuguese. He had spoken to her and recalled her name as Senhora Lopes do Livio. "A melodious appellation," Liceu had added, "which is why it stayed in his head." This fact was confirmed when they found the official visitors' book for the day. But there was no address by the signature.

"Portuguese?" Carriscant said. "There must be some mistake."

According to João there were three Lopes do Livios in the Lisbon telephone directory. One was a beautician's, one was at an address in the Alfama—"I don't think a lady of distinction would live there," João averred—the third was in a respectable part of town near the Jardim Botânico. We decided to investigate in the morning.

WE SAUNTERED OUT arm in arm for a *digestif* after our meal that evening, heading for the Café Martinho, situated between the station and the National Theater on the Rossio. We walked through the dimly lit streets into the enormous square, still loud with trams and taxis, the shouts of lottery-ticket vendors and the calls of shoeshine boys, with groups of people strolling about the fountains and the monument, the café windows under their faded awnings glowing orange, and beyond the classic bulk of the theater rose the city on one of its higher hills, a loose heap of spangling lights in the luminous dark. For the first time I experienced the authentic thrill of travel, that strangeness of displacement, as we strolled, anonymous foreigners in this hospitable, scruffy city, among its idling denizens, their laughter and their chatter falling on our uncomprehending ears. I was in Europe, I remembered, albeit on its very western edge, and I should draw some sustenance from this trip I was paying for—and, my God, did I need it—and stop behaving like the tolerant chaperone of a testy and eccentric old man. But the testy and eccentric old man, I could see, was enjoying himself too as he strode briskly across the square, proud in his new suit, toward the blurry warmth of the Martinho, from whose open doors a smell of roasting coffee wafted.

The Martinho was a grandly capacious place. A large room

with solid pillars, encrusted cornices and tall gilt mirrors. It was filled with neat ranks of simple wooden tables with marble tops, laid out with a schoolroom precision in immaculate rows. Drooping lights with frosted glass shades sprouted like wilting tulips from the central pillars, sending out a diffuse yellow light. All the waiters were stout middle-aged men with long white aprons and generous mustaches. The place was crowded, full of men who did not remove their hats and who sat, most oddly, I thought, with one hand resting on their walking sticks and canes as they drank and chatted, as if at any moment they were about to spring to their feet and stride off into the night.

We found a table for two at one side of the room, beneath a baroquely carved mirror whose sides were formed by two golden caryatids, bare-breasted pubescent beauties emerging from a tangle of lianas and tropical fruits. We ordered coffee, with a brandy for Carriscant, and sat back to survey the scene.

"This is the life," Carriscant said, upending his brandy into his coffee cup. He looked at me slyly: "You won't find anything like this in Los Angeles."

"Which is why one travels," I said a little frostily, irritated by his patronizing manner. "How boring it would be if every new place merely reproduced your hometown. Someone from Lisbon doesn't go to Los Angeles looking for a Café Martinho."

"He'd be pleased to find one, however," Carriscant said in a self-satisfied way.

A silence fell as I decided not to prolong this discussion.

"How did you know," I said abruptly, irritated with him for souring the excitement and pleasure I had experienced crossing the Rossio, "that I lived in Los Angeles? How did you know Mother had gone to live there?"

My tone took him aback and he looked startled. "Udo told me," he said. "Annaliese used to write to him once a month until he died." He paused, remembering. "The bishop annulled our marriage very promptly. Then Udo told me she had married an American called Fischer, a coir importer, from Los Angeles. When I got there it wasn't hard to track him down. Or you."

"What about Hugh Paget?"

"I know nothing about any Hugh Paget."

I felt the weight of my dissatisfaction descend on me, a sensation of living a personal history concocted of half-truths and opportune fictions. Now other uncertainties and key ambiguities of Carriscant's story rose up to nag at me, making me fretful and ill at ease. In many ways Carriscant had been as honest and as unsparing as anyone I could imagine. He seemed to have held nothing back, providing me with details and intimacies I would never have asked for myself. But in the end it was *his* story and he was free to emphasize and ignore what he wished, to select and choose, shape and redirect . . .

I sipped my coffee, looking at him over the rim of the cup as his quick eyes scanned the busy room. He turned to meet my gaze and smiled at me, raising his cup in salute. He was in a good mood.

'Thanks for everything, Kay. I think tomorrow we—"

"Who killed Ward and Braun?"

The question blurted from me, unplanned, spontaneous, as my mind sifted through the tale he'd told me. Carriscant didn't flinch: he thought about it, tugged at an earlobe and set his cup down in its saucer without a rattle. He shrugged.

"Your guess is as good as mine . . . Who do *you* think? I told you everything I know."

"So you say. But that can't be true. There must be things you forgot, or didn't think were relevant."

"Of course." To my vague surprise I seemed to sense a pleasure in him now, as he settled back in his chair, a kind of mischievous delight at the line my questioning was taking. "Look, I told you the story you asked me to tell—about me and

Delphine—why we were making this trip. But who knows?" He paused, a tolerant smile on his lips. "You may find the answer to other questions. Everything's there if you know where to find it."

This intrigued me. "What? You mean like clues?"

"Yes and no. It applies to both of us. I'm sure that in telling you what happened there are connections I haven't spotted. Got to be. Maybe we can force them out. Two heads are better than one, and all that."

This seemed to me to be an oblique challenge. I wished I had my notes with me, but as I began to reflect, certain hints, certain omissions began to reveal themselves.

"Think, Kay, think hard. What've I forgotten? Now that you know the whole story and can look back, what seems significant?"

I thought for a while before I came across something. A completely innocuous remark early on, the sort of casual parenthesis that at the time seems quite unremarkable.

I looked at him closely. "You said at one stage that you had seen Sieverance before. Before you met him that day in the Ayuntamiento."

He frowned and looked up at the ceiling. "No I didn't. I said I wondered if we had met before. He reminded me of someone."

"Who?"

"It's a long story. It happened a good while before I met Delphine. I don't know if it has any bearing on all this."

"Tell me about it, anyway."

"All right." He looked at me shrewdly, and then signaled to the waiter to renew our coffees. I ordered a glass of port for myself. When in Rome . . .

"You remember when I visited my mother in San Teodoro . . . I hadn't seen her for some time, not since my last visit, which had been, I think, in February 1902. I went to her because I was worried about what was happening in the southern provinces, in south Luzon. The war was still going on. After Balangiga the fighting—"

"What's Balangiga?"

"It's a place. Forty-eight American soldiers were massacred there, on the island of Sarmar, by *insurrectors*. General Smith issued an order that all Filipinos capable of carrying arms who did not surrender were to be shot." Carriscant gave a tired smile. "General Smith worked on the assumption that any male over the age of ten was capable of carrying arms." He spread his hands. "It all got out of control. People assumed once Aguinaldo had been captured the war was virtually over. Not at all. The early months of 1902 were a bad time, the worst in some ways. Not for us in Manila, of course, but in south Luzon—in Cavite, Batangas, Tayabas—there was a lot of fighting. There was a fine *insurrecto* general there, Esteban Elpidio—"

"Pantaleon's uncle."

"Yes. There was a punitive expedition sent out, led by a young general, Franklin Bell. People were concentrated in military zones, all food outside these zones was destroyed. Whenever an American soldier was killed a Filipino prisoner was chosen by lot and executed. When they finally caught Elpidio in April the war was effectively over, but in February there were still many problems . . ."

So Carriscant told me about the trip he had made south to visit his mother. He had gone in his carriage with supplies of food, driven by Constancio. The journey down to Los Baños on Laguna de Bay was quiet. When they turned inland to San Teodoro they entered one of the areas under military control where the curfew was enforced. They reached the village before nightfall and Carriscant was safely in his mother's house by the time the curfew fell at eight.

The next morning, however, none of the household servants

arrived and his mother, alarmed, asked him to return to the village to investigate. She was particularly concerned because her majordomo, Flaviano, was infallible. And if he had been ill, his son, Ortega, would have come to the house with the news.

San Teodoro was completely deserted when Carriscant arrived there with Constancio. Cooking fires had been lit for breakfast and two of three market stalls had been set out beneath the old acacia tree in the square, but apart from hens and nosing pye-dogs, there was no sign of the inhabitants.

Then they found an old lady hiding behind the wooden church. She told them that the *americanos* had come at first light and had herded together everyone in the village—men, women and children—and had taken them up the track toward the river, the road to Santa Rosa.

Carriscant left Constancio with her and set off up the track. He knew that it crossed a small creek that flowed into the Laguna. He had been walking for ten minutes when he heard the final shot. Then two more. Then there was a pause of a few seconds before there was another shot. He left the track and circled through the undergrowth toward the direction of the noise. On the way he counted another five reports, nine in all.

He came to a break in the trees, at the edge of the clearing where the track crossed the wooden bridge over the small river. Here, huddled together, were thirteen men and young boys guarded by several dozen American soldiers, big men, bearded, in their stained blue shirts and their dented wide-brimmed hats. Some way off, on the bridge, were three other American soldiers. Below the bridge the river widened into a dammed pool and around this were gathered the female members of the village, a few very old men and the children below the age of ten. In the pool nine bodies floated at the lip of the dam.

From his vantage point in the trees above the clearing Carriscant watched as one by one the men and boys were led out onto the bridge. The officer leveled his pistol at the prisoner's head and called in a clear voice, "Remember Balangiga!" and shot him. The body was then heaved over the parapet by the other two men and was carried gently down the stream to join the others bobbing at the edge of the dam, budged together by the sluggish current, like soft logs.

The atmosphere was strangely calm. The sun shone in a milky, hazy sky and the calls of the birds were silenced by the noise of the guns. There was a faint moaning from the group gathered by the pool and some of the littlest children were crying. But the men and boys waited silently to be selected, their heads bowed, saying nothing. While the officer reloaded his pistol, the other two men took over. And always there was the same cry, "Remember Balangiga!" before the sound of the gun going off. This went on until all the men and boys had been shot, then the Americans shouldered their rifles and packs and marched off down the road to Santa Rosa. Both Flaviano and Ortega had been among the victims. Carriscant learned later that the column had been shot at the previous night while it was bivouacking about a mile from San Teodoro and two men had been killed and four wounded. The assault on the villagers was their act of reprisal. Twenty-two men and boys had been killed.

Carriscant related all this to me in an even, unemotional voice. We sat there in silence after he had finished as I tried to take in the implications of all this.

"Do you think," I asked him, "that the officer was Sieverance?"

"I don't know. Certainly Sieverance reminded me of him. That officer was bearded, but fair like Sieverance. Something about his posture too. I couldn't be sure. I asked Delphine if Sieverance had ever served in Batangas, but she said she had no idea." He shrugged. "There was a likeness, but I was quite far away, forty, fifty yards."

"Was it Sieverance's unit? Do you know the name of the unit?"

"No."

"Did you report it?"

Carriscant screwed up his face. "You've got to remember that fifty-four thousand people died in Batangas in those months. Killed, or died from disease, starvation, cholera. My mother wrote to protest to General Bell but received no reply. Such incidents were commonplace." He paused, then said carefully, "The only person I told was Pantaleon."

"Why?"

"I had to tell someone."

"Some American officers were tried for atrocities."

"And General Smith was even cashiered. Unfortunately I had no names, no information. And the San Teodoro massacre was small beer. In Batangas one group of thirteen hundred prisoners was systematically killed over six days after digging their own graves. It was a nasty little war." He sighed. "In some ways it's as well that the world has forgotten it."

We looked at each other. His face gave nothing away: his features were set, his eyes tired, as if the telling of his story had exhausted him.

"Any the wiser?" he asked.

"No. But you haven't answered my question. Who killed Ward and Braun?"

"I thought it was obvious. It must have been Cruz."

"Cruz? Are you serious?"

"The man was mad. He hated Americans. He was obsessed with his heart operation. Remember he had deliberately made an incision in that man's heart in order to make some cardiac sutures. I think Cruz was slowly going mad, anyway. The war, the loss of the colony. Even my presence at the hospital meant his reputation was in decline also. So he became obsessed with making his name in some way. And in those days the heart was the organ that most frustrated us. That's the only explanation for the mutilations. I remember once he told me he needed European hearts, I don't know why, some mad prejudice, I suppose. I don't think he killed the woman, though. That was random. A Tondo stabbing that confused the picture."

I sighed, uncertain, troubled by this shocking story. One sunny morning in San Teodoro . . .

Carriscant leaned forward, his chin on the knuckles of his clasped hands, staring at me.

"I hope you don't mind me saying this, Kay. You're an attractive woman, but you don't want to get any stouter. Shall we go?"

I SIT in my room, bathed, ready for bed, and write the names of the dead down. Ward, Braun, the unnamed woman, Sieverance. Then I make another list.

PANTALEON QUIROGA
DR. ISIDRO CRUZ
JEPSON SIEVERANCE

I am not sure why I am doing this, or what I hope it will achieve, but I suppose I have to accept that ever since the first day I saw Salvador Carriscant, he has had some kind of strange hold on me, and now I know more about him, perhaps, than any daughter should about her father. And still the revelations come, more doors open, and yet the complexities multiply, the shadows gather . . . My brain is sluggish after all this new information, but I need to write things down as they occur to me, almost as an exercise, simply to set some process of deduction rolling, to see if the name on the page, in stark black and white, will tell me something. I consider the options.

Pantaleon—Paton Bobby's suspect. He knew about the massacre, he knew about Carriscant's suspicion about Sieverance. Were Ward and Braun the other two soldiers on the bridge? Perhaps Pantaleon's connection with General Elpidio provided him with that sort of information. But I found it hard to figure Pantaleon as an *insurrecto* fifth columnist.

Carriscant's suspect was Cruz. Seeking strong American hearts for his experiments. But why dump the bodies at key sites of the first day of the war? Or was that just coincidence? Almost everywhere around Manila had some significance, considered in the light of the fourth of February 1899. Cruz did seem somewhat deranged, but I found it hard to believe that he would go so far in his need to make a name for himself. But Bobby clearly suspected him as well, why else raid his laboratory? . . .

Jepson Sieverance was my idea. A notion I had. Carriscant told me that an official commission—the Lodge Commission—investigating the post-Balangiga atrocities was sitting throughout 1902. Sieverance, an ambitious young officer, might just have thought it worth removing his two accomplices. Or perhaps Braun and Ward were blackmailing him in some way? Assuming, of course, that the man Carriscant saw had been Sieverance in the first place, and Carriscant had never been fully convinced of this . . . On the other hand, Sieverance certainly didn't commit suicide. But then we knew who killed him. Or did we?

I SEEM to be achieving nothing. I write down one more name.

SALVADOR CARRISCANT

Tomorrow we go to pay a visit to Senhora Lopes do Livio. Let us see what revelations the new day brings.

THURSDAY, MAY 7

WE BREAKFASTED in the dining room on small hard rolls and honey, washed down with a reasonable pot of coffee. Carriscant didn't seem at all nervous and ate three of the rolls with a gourmandizing enthusiasm, asking the waiter to confirm if the honey was clover, or from bees feeding on some other species of flower.

"I can taste it, can't you? The clover," he said to me. "A fragrance, a stratum below the surface. But if not clover, then lavender, or broom, perhaps."

The waiter was unable to help him, and to me the honey tasted of honey. Besides, I was not hungry: I left half my roll, drank a cup of coffee and smoked a cigarette rather earlier in the day than normal. I asked Carriscant if we should telephone ahead or send a note to explain who we were, but he preferred to go unannounced.

"Suppose it's not her," he explained. "We don't want to waste their time. We'll just turn up, much the best way. Bound to be in on a Sunday." I let him do as he wished. His mood was calm, almost buoyant, whereas I felt a curious sense of foreboding, as if I were about to visit a doctor or specialist, on the point of learning facts about which I would rather remain ignorant.

At about midday we met at the hotel entrance and hailed a taxi. The day was fresh and sunny, and above our heads the strip of sky between the buildings was a perfect washed-out blue. João hurried out from the reception with an umbrella, which he insisted on our taking. "There will be rain in the afternoon," he said with adamantine certainty. "Better to be prepared."

We asked the taxi to drop us outside the gates to the botanical garden and we walked the short distance to Senhora Lopes do Livio's address. She lived on the second floor of a large apartment block with ornately wrought balconies. A high arched doorway led through to a narrow cobbled courtyard; to the left was the entrance foyer, where a stooped old porter stood on a strip of red carpet leading to the elevator. The walls were lined with a small collection of pots containing dusty undernourished ferns struggling to grow in the perpetual gloom. We decided to walk up the stairs to the second floor— Carriscant's suggestion. I think he was beginning to feel the enormous pressures of this encounter for the first time, and the chance of delaying matters even for a few seconds was suddenly very desirable.

I reached to press the bell—set beneath a worn and polished brass plate reading LOPES DO LIVIO—but Carriscant's touch on my elbow made me hesitate.

"How do I look?" he said. He stood stiffly in his new suit, awkward suddenly, almost to attention, his hands half clenched by his side. I could see one of his jaw muscles working. His hair was neatly brushed and shone damply with a pomade he had applied.

"Very good," I said. "Very handsome and distinguished." He smiled broadly at me, his pleasure manifest, and my heart went out to him. I leaned forward and kissed him on the cheek. He was most surprised and his hand went instantly to the spot where my lips had touched him, as if I'd daubed him with paint or pricked him with a pin.

"Bless you, Kay," he said, moved. "I don't know what I'd have done without you."

"Don't give it a thought," I said. "Look, it may not even be her. We may be tramping around the sweetshops of Europe for a while yet."

I rang the bell and after some moments we heard footsteps and the door was opened by a young man, about my age. He was tall with unruly curly hair forced severely into an immaculate middle parting, and full, rather pouting lips. There was a guarded, suspicious quality about him; he seemed to hold his body angled back slightly, as if preemptively fearful of some act of aggression.

He said a few words to us in Portuguese.

"Do you speak English?" I asked.

"Yes, I do," he said with a slight accent. "Are you English?"

"We're American. We would like to see Senhora Lopes do Livio, if that were possible."

"I regret. My mother is not well. She does not receive visitors."

I could sense Carriscant stiffen beside me.

"I'm a very old friend," Carriscant said. "I've come all the way from the United States to meet her again."

The man frowned. "She said nothing of this to me."

"She didn't know I was coming. It took me some time to find her."

"I am not knowing if my mother had some friends in America . . ." His suspicion was acute; suddenly we were importunate salesmen, hawkers who had not used the trademen's entrance.

"If you tell her that Dr. Salvador Carriscant has come to see her I'm sure she'll grant me a moment of her time."

The tone of confidence and marginal hostility in Carriscant's voice was sufficient to have us admitted even though the young man's reluctance was palpable. He showed us into a large pale green sitting room, dimly lit, the shutters drawn half to. The style of the furnishings was old and the swagged green velvet drapes at the three long windows were threadbare. But the proportions of the room were elegant and the furniture of good quality, well chosen. Dark overvarnished portraits of whiskered and waxed military types hung on the walls. I wondered if these were the Lopes do Livio forebears. We took our seats on a gilded bergère, sitting primly, our hands on our knees, like candidates waiting for an interview.

"Nervous?" Carriscant asked.

"No . . . Yes, actually, very."

"I'm terrified," he said with a grin. "Blood turned to ice water."

We waited for a good ten minutes before the young man returned. His manner had not altered.

"My mother will see you," he said, clearly annoyed at this decision. "But I'd ask you to be staying for a short time. She becomes most tired. Please follow me."

"Do you want me to come with you?" I asked Carriscant.

He stood rigid for a moment and said nothing, not hearing me. Then he followed the young man out of the room. I rose to my feet, hesitated the briefest moment, then strode after them.

I stayed behind Carriscant as we were led down a surprisingly long corridor—the apartment was huge—loose parquet tiles clicking dully under our feet like dice shaken in a leather cup. The stern young man rapped lightly on a door and held it open for us. And now I felt the fear flow through me, a fear for Carriscant rather than myself. Every facet, every aspect of his life had been conditioned for over thirty years by the possibility of this moment one day occurring, and here we now were. The prospect of it somehow disappointing him, of letting him down—or, worse, of destroying him—was almost insupportable. He bowed his head a moment, then stepped into the room. I followed.

This is what I saw. An old lady sat in an armchair before a tall muslin-draped window that gave onto a distant prospect of the botanical garden. The screened light that fell on her face was soft and pearly. She was thin and her face had sharpened with age, her skin stretched and seamed, but still strong-looking, the nose prominent, the eyes dark and watchful. Her gray hair was pulled loosely behind her head in a bun. She was still beautiful, I thought, in a severe way, in that semihidden manner you encounter with certain old women, that still allows you to see the young woman that once was. She seemed far older than Carriscant. Her hands rested in her lap, or, rather, rested in the air above her lap, shaking quite noticeably, unnaturally. The thumb and forefinger of her right hand made continuous small movements, as if rolling a pill between them.

Carriscant moved forward toward her while I stepped to one side.

"Salvador?" she said, her voice soft, her American accent barely pronounced.

"Yes, Delphine."

"Don't lurk in the shadows like that. I can't see you."

"Here I am."

She looked at him. "You've got a belly on you."

"Big appetite, you know me."

He knelt beside her chair and took her shaking hands in his, their heads moving together. They kissed each other, long and slow, full of a decent and selfless ardor, a real and gentle carnality. I thought of the last kiss they had shared in the darkness of the Calle Francisco, in Intramuros, in Manila, in 1903 . . . A whole generation had intervened, half a lifetime vanished. They broke apart. She touched Carriscant's face with her trembling fingers. He pressed her palm to his mouth.

"Mother, please, this is intolerable!" the young man said. I could see the shock on his face, disturbed to see such passion in old people.

"Oh, shut up, Nando," she said, her eyes never leaving Carriscant. "Don't be such a prig."

Carriscant touched her jaw with his knuckles, touched her

neck. "Beautiful Delphine," he said dreamily. "How beautiful you look."

"Who's this?" she said, her gaze turning to me.

"My daughter Kay. She helped me find you."

I stepped forward to grasp her moving hand—so light—and stared into her face. It was the most curious sensation, encountering for the first time someone I felt I knew so intimately, like meeting a character from a work of fiction, or some long-dead historical figure, in the flesh.

"You have a look of him, you know," she said. "Quite distinct."

I muttered some words of greeting, how pleased I was to meet her finally.

Carriscant rose to his feet. "Now I want you to go," he said. "Delphine and I have much to talk about."

"Mother, I don't think—"

"Please leave us, Nando," she said firmly. Which he did at once, with histrionic huffiness.

Carriscant walked me to the door.

"Thank you," he whispered, a smile on his face. "I'm fine now. Everything will be fine now."

THE WAITER OPENED the bottle and poured the wine into two glasses. It was yellow and cold and in the warm sun the glasses frosted at once, beads of condensation forming quickly. We each reached for our glasses and raised them, chiming the edges briefly, and Carriscant said to me, "Here's to us, Kay. Here's to us."

He and Delphine were alone together for just over an hour while I sat in the green sitting room, waiting. When he eventually rejoined me he was openingly thumbing tears from his eyes, but he was smiling too, and as we left the apartment his face was serene and confident.

"The delightful Nando is not my son," he said almost at

once, as we descended the stairs to the gloomy foyer, "I'm very happy to tell you."

We found a taxi on the Rua do Pedro V. and Carriscant told the driver to "take us to a café with a view of the river." We were driven up into Bairro Alto and were dropped at a nondescript place called the Café Pacifico but which turned out to have a pretty terrace with a fine view of the wide estuary and the hills beyond Almada. We sat down and ordered our bottle of wine—"the most expensive and the coldest"—and, while we waited for it, munched at a plate of small green olives which had been brought to our table as we sat down.

"She sent you the photograph from the magazine, didn't she?" I asked, my voice kind but serious. Certain matters had to be cleared up now.

"Of course." He looked at me, almost disappointed it had taken so long for me to figure it out. "She sent it to the San Jerónimo. My one remaining ally on the hospital board made sure it reached me, eventually. It took about three months."

"Why didn't you tell me?"

"Well..." He gave me an apologetic smile. "I thought it seemed more dramatic, more of a challenge the way I told it. Would enthuse you more." He shrugged. "Maybe I should have told you."

"It was obviously some sort of cryptic cry for help."

"Yes. Or a test. Wanting to make sure. Just to see if I was still there, if I remembered." His face saddened. "I'm sure it was the onset of her illness that provoked it. Time running out, and all that."

"Or guilt?"

"No, Kay. No."

"So you dropped everything..."

"More or less." He paused. "I'll never forget that day. My youngest son came running in waving this envelope, saying could he have the pretty stamp. I couldn't believe..."

"A son?"

That shrewd look again. How he eked out his revelations! "I have two," he said. "And a young daughter. I've been married for fourteen years. My wife—Mayang—is looking after the restaurant."

I felt a baffled amused anger rise in me like a bubble. It burst harmlessly. "And you'll be going back to them?"

"Naturally," he said, almost offended. "I hope you'll come and visit us soon."

I said I would. Why not? Anything seemed possible now. Carriscant would have me peeling vegetables in his kitchen, more than likely.

"She waited for me in Singapore, for six weeks," Carriscant said, his eyes focusing on something in the distance. "Then she heard of the trial and knew I wasn't coming. She miscarried the child there too. A boy."

"A boy?"

"Yes. And Axel came with her to Europe, all the way, saw her safely there, she said." Carriscant smiled. "He was probably in love with her, poor grimy Nicanor . . ." He sipped some wine. "She went to Vienna, as I knew she would, we had planned that, and she lived there for some years. It was a bad time for her, of course. Alone, with the thought of the dead child, with the thought always of the life we might have led . . . A dark time for her." He paused, thinking. "She couldn't be alone forever, though, she had to be with someone, start her life again . . ." He squared his shoulders. "She married an Austrian—I didn't ask his name—but he was killed in the war. She met Lopes do Livio in Spain in 1920, in Santander. He was a widower, the boy, Fernando, was his. Do Livio died six years ago. Nando has cared for her ever since: they are very close, she says, he's devoted to her. She's lived in Lisbon since 1923. She has Austrian citizenship. No one knows her background, not even her husbands did, neither of them."

We drank some more wine, it was tangy and sharp, and Carriscant topped up the glasses. Inland, continents of dark plum-gray clouds were building, threatening the rain that João had promised, while out west, over the Atlantic, the afternoon sun shone with that silvery flinty brilliance you find over big oceans, light reflecting back from the huge expanse of shifting waters. We sat in silence for a while and watched the track of a small white steamer trail its saltspill across the flat windless stretch of the Mar de Palha, the Sea of Straw, as it headed lethargically for the docks at Alfama.

I felt full of sadness for Salvador Carriscant. He was in the rare and terrible position of having experienced for an hour or so glimpses of the life he might have led. He had contemplated a parallel existence for himself and had had to face full square the what-might-have-been. This is something we can all do, in moments of idle despair; these possibilities exist for us, but only as reveries or as wistful hindsight. For Carriscant, however, the notional had been made flesh, embodied in the frail shaking old lady he had talked with that afternoon. If only, if only, if only . . .

"She killed Sieverance," he said. "She told me. After she left me she went back to their house for her play, she said, for her play . . ." He shook his head incredulously. "It was an accident. She was creeping out when he surprised her. He had his gun drawn, thinking she was an intruder. She tried to run out, there was a struggle as he tried to prevent her, the gun went off."

I thought about this: you hear a noise in your house in the small hours of the morning, you arm yourself with a revolver, but the burglar turns out to be your dead wife, whom you saw lying cold and pale beside the body of your stillborn child hours previously . . . You don't *struggle* with her, it seemed to me. You might scream, you might collapse in shock. But would you fight?

"I thought," I said gently, "that Sieverance was found shot in his bed."

Carriscant looked at me shrewdly. "Then she must have dragged him back."

"Does she know what happened to you?"

"She knew about the trial. That was when she decided to leave Singapore. She just assumed . . ." he trailed off. "She knew then we could never be together."

The clouds build to the east, a great purple range, a massive presence in the panorama, while we sit on, warm in the sun shining upon us from over the ocean.

I thought carefully before I spoke. "I don't believe her, Salvador," I said in a measured, quiet voice. "I just don't. She went back to kill Sieverance. To make absolutely sure. It was the most appalling risk. I understand why she wanted to do it, but if she hadn't, if she had gone straight to the docks, straight to Axel . . . Don't you see? Then everything would have gone according to plan. That's the only explanation that—"

"Oh, no, no, no. It was a mistake, a terrible accident." He said this with simple conviction, looking hard at me. "I believe her."

"I don't."

"What do you believe then?"

There was a silence before I decided to speak.

"That you killed Sieverance. To set her free. To make sure."

He laughed. "Kay, Kay," he said fondly, "I love you for that, it makes me sound so very noble." He reached out and patted my hand. "She just confessed to me. She told me everything. Let's go back there and ask her, if you want."

He knew I wouldn't; it was not a convincing gesture and I remained unconvinced. I let it go. What good would my deductions do, my reasoned detections? Carriscant's faith was sure and constant. His belief in Delphine Sieverance and what she had done that night was no more absurd than any of the other notions we use to prop up our shaky lives. And he was happy, too, that was important. He had achieved what he had set out to—no mean accomplishment—and he had seen the woman he had loved for all these years once more.

"Will you see her again?" I asked.

"No. She asked me not to and I agreed. Besides, I don't want to, don't need to." He exhaled, and I felt the sadness skewer through him. "She's going to die soon," he said. "She has shaking palsy, paralysis agitans, she can hardly walk. She's looking forward to it, can't wait to die, she said. But she's glad she saw me, glad we were together again. I think it helped her enormously."

His eyes filled with tears, I saw them shimmer and bulge at the eyelid as he thought about her and her approaching extinction. And that provoked my tears too, and I felt the salt sting. I was full of doubts, full of conflicting versions and explanations of this strange and complex story I had been told. But at least I knew now there had been a man called Salvador Carriscant and he had been in love with a woman named Delphine Sieverance. That much at least I could confirm, having witnessed it with my own eyes, and perhaps that was what was most significant. As for the rest, I had my theories, my dark thoughts, my suspicions, my version of events as they had unfolded all those years ago in Manila. But what did it matter? I sat here on this sunny terrace looking out at the Sea of Straw, at the steamer's track, the glass of yellow wine in my hand, and I found that I envied Salvador Carriscant, my father. Carriscant's luck. He has loved. That face was implicit in everything he had done since he had met her and since she had left him. It was a real presence in his messy, crazy life, there but invisible, hidden below the surface, like softly stirring green fields of kelp under a stormy, thrashing sea. And I was also witness to the fact that he still loved that old lady with her dark eyes and her shaking hands. And his life was therefore good. And therefore I envy him. I loved too, once: my blue baby, Coleman. But Coleman died. And Delphine is going to die. Aren't we all.

"Look at this," Carriscant said, gesturing at the scene before us. "It's very rare, this trick of the light. Quite wonderful."

The purple livid mass of the thunderclouds seemed to dominate the overarching sky, but still the sun shone on our faces as the charged light thickened and changed color around us. My finger traced a track through the cold beaded moisture on the sweating bottle; the little steamer had almost reached the quay at Alfama; the sound of traffic and voices rose faintly from the busy streets below us, and I smelled the musky bouquet of the wine as I brought the glass to my lips and drank deep.

So what makes the difference—here and now—on this terrace on this eloquent blue afternoon, as we sit caught between perpetuities of sun and rain, held in this particular moment? I look over at Salvador Carriscant, who is smiling at me, his old broad face radiant with his tremendous good fortune, and I know the answer.

A NOTE ON THE TYPE

This book was set in Janson, a typeface long thought to have been made by the Dutchman Anton Janson, who was a practicing type founder in Leipzig during the years 1668–1687. However, it has been conclusively demonstrated that these types are actually the work of Nicholas Kis (1650–1702), a Hungarian, who most probably learned his trade from the master Dutch type founder Dirk Voskens. The type is an excellent example of the influential and sturdy Dutch types that prevailed in England up to the time William Caslon (1692–1766) developed his own incomparable designs from them.

Composed by Creative Graphics,
Allentown, Pennsylvania

Printed and bound by Arcata Graphics/Martinsburg,
Martinsburg, West Virginia

Designed by Cassandra J. Pappas